P9-DOB-927

Praise for Mario Puzo's

THE FOURTH

K

"A mesmerizing political thriller suffused with profundity as well as suspense."
—*Boston Sunday Herald*

"Keeps your mind racing."
—*The Denver Post*

"Fiercely moral, magisterial melodrama that shows Puzo a Balzac at the top of his form. This is Puzo's most strongly knit novel. Lean, mean, no fat. A rocket through the roof."
—*Kirkus Reviews*

"Astute characterizations, vivid drama and Puzo's shrewd analyses of the paradoxes of evil detonate a top-notch thriller. . . . A surefire success."
—*Publishers Weekly*

By Mario Puzo

Published by The Random House Publishing Group

Books published by The Random House Publishing Group
are available at quantity discounts on bulk purchases for
premium, educational, fund-raising, and special sales use.
For details, please call 1-800-733-3000.

THE FOURTH
K

A Novel

Mario Puzo

BALLANTINE BOOKS • NEW YORK

Sale of this book without a front cover may be unauthorized. If this book is coverless, it may have been reported to the publisher as "unsold or destroyed" and neither the author nor the publisher may have received payment for it.

The Fourth K is a work of fiction. Names, characters, places, and incidents are the products of the author's imagination or are used fictitiously. Any resemblance to actual events, locales, or persons, living or dead, is entirely coincidental.

A Ballantine Book
Published by The Random House Publishing Group

Copyright © 1990 by Mario Puzo

All rights reserved.

Published in the United States by Ballantine Books, an imprint of The Random House Publishing Group, a division of Random House, Inc., New York, and simultaneously in Canada by Random House of Canada Limited, Toronto. Originally published by Random House, an imprint of The Random House Publishing Group, a division of Random House, Inc., in 1990.

BALLANTINE and colophon are registered trademarks of Random House, Inc.

ISBN 978-0-345-47673-9

Printed in the United States of America

www.ballantinebooks.com

First Edition: December 1990
First Bantam Books Mass Market Edition: November 1991
First Ballantine Books Mass Market Edition: December 2004

FOR MY CHILDREN

Anthony
Dorothy
Eugene
Virginia
Joseph

THE FOURTH
K

THE FOURTH

K

BOOK

I

GOOD FRIDAY– EASTER SUNDAY

CHAPTER
1

OLIVER OLIPHANT WAS one hundred years old and his mind was as clear as a bell. Unfortunately for him.

It was a mind so clear, yet so subtle, that while breaking a great many moral laws, it had washed his conscience clean. A mind so cunning that Oliver Oliphant had never fallen into the almost inevitable traps of everyday life: he had never married, never run for political office and never had a friend he trusted absolutely.

On a huge heavily guarded secluded estate only ten miles from the White House, Oliver Oliphant, the richest man in America and possibly the most powerful private citizen, awaited the arrival of his godson, the Attorney General of the United States, Christian Klee.

Oliphant's charm equaled his brilliance; his power rested on both. Even at the advanced age of one hundred his advice was still sought by great men who relied on his analytic powers to such an extent that he had been nicknamed the "Oracle."

As adviser to presidents the Oracle had predicted economic crises, Wall Street crashes, the fall of the dollar, the flight of foreign capital, the fantasies of oil prices. He had predicted the political moves of the Soviet Union, the unexpected embraces of rivals in the Democratic and Republican parties. But above all he had amassed ten billion dollars. It was natural that advice from such a rich man be valued, even when wrong. But the Oracle was nearly always right.

Now on this Good Friday, the Oracle was worried about one thing: the birthday party to celebrate his one hundred years on this earth. A party to be held on Easter Sunday in the Rose Garden of the White House, the host none other than the President of the United States, Francis Xavier Kennedy.

It was a permissible vanity for the Oracle to take great pleasure in this spectacular affair. The world would again remember him for one brief moment. It would be, he thought sadly, his last appearance on stage.

In Rome, on Good Friday, seven terrorists made their final preparations to assassinate the Pope of the Roman Catholic Church. This band of four men and three women believed they were liberators of mankind. They called themselves the Christs of Violence.

The leader of this particular band was an Italian youth well seasoned in the technique of terrorism. For this particular operation he had assumed the code name Romeo; it pleased his youthful sense of irony, and its sentimentality sweetened his intellectual love of mankind.

On the late afternoon of Good Friday, Romeo rested in a safe house provided by the International One Hundred.

Lying on rumpled bed sheets stained with cigarette ash and days of night sweat, he read a paperback edition of *The Brothers Karamazov.* His leg muscles cramped with tension, perhaps fear, it didn't matter. It would pass as it always did. But this mission was so different, so complex, involved so much danger to the body and the spirit. On this mission he would be truly a Christ of Violence, that name so Jesuitical it always moved him to laughter.

Romeo had been born Armando Giangi, to rich high-society parents, who subjected him to a languid, luxurious, religious upbringing, a combination that so offended his ascetic nature that at the age of sixteen he renounced worldly goods and the Catholic Church. So now, at twenty-three, what greater rebellion could there be for him than the killing of the Pope? And yet there was still, for Romeo, a superstitious dread. As a child he had received holy confirmation from a red-hatted cardinal. Romeo remembered always that ominous red hat painted in the very color of the fires of hell.

So confirmed by God in every ritual, Romeo prepared himself to commit a crime so terrible that hundreds of millions would curse his name, for his true name would become known. He would be captured. That was part of the plan. But in time he, Romeo, would be acclaimed as a hero who helped change the existing cruel social order. What was infamous in one century would be seen as saintly in the next. And vice versa, he thought with a smile. The very first Pope to take the name of Innocent, centuries ago, had issued a papal bull authorizing torture, and had been hailed for propagating the true faith and rescuing heretic souls.

It also appealed to Romeo's youthful sense of irony that the Church would canonize the Pope he was planning to kill. He would create a new saint. And how he hated them, all these popes. This Pope Innocent IV, Pope Pius, Pope Benedict, oh they sanctified too much, these amassers of wealth, these suppressors of the true faith of human freedom, these pompous wizards who smothered the wretched of the earth with their magic of ignorance, their hot insults to credulity.

He, Romeo, one of the First Hundred of the Christs of Violence, would help erase that crude magic. Vulgarly called terrorists, the First Hundred were spread over Japan, Germany, Italy, Spain and even the tulipy Dutch. It was worth noting that there were none of the First Hundred in America. That democracy, that birthplace of freedom, had only intellectual revolutionaries who fainted at the sight of blood. Who exploded their bombs in empty buildings after warning people to leave; who thought public fornication on the steps of houses of state an act of idealistic rebellion. How contemptible they were. It was not surprising that America had never given one man to the Revolutionary Hundred.

Romeo put a halt to his daydreaming. What the hell, he didn't know if there were a hundred. There might be fifty or sixty, it was just a symbolic number. But such symbols rallied the masses and seduced the media. The only fact he really knew was that he, Romeo, was one of the First Hundred, and so was his friend and fellow conspirator Yabril.

One of the many churches of Rome chimed its bells. It was nearly six in the evening of this Good Friday. In another hour Yabril would arrive to review all the mechanics of the complicated operation. The killing of the Pope would be the opening move of a brilliantly conceived chess game, a series of daring acts that delighted Romeo's romantic soul.

Yabril was the only man who had ever awed Romeo, physically and mentally. Yabril knew the treacheries of governments, the hypocrisies of legal authority, the dangerous optimism of idealists, the surprising lapses in loyalty of even the most dedicated terrorists. But most of all Yabril was a genius of revolutionary warfare. He was contemptuous of the small mercies and infantile pity that affect most men. Yabril had but one aim, to free the future.

And Yabril was more merciless than Romeo could ever be. Romeo had murdered innocent people, betrayed his parents and his friends, assassinated a judge who had once protected him. Romeo understood that political killing might be a kind of insanity—he was willing to pay that price. But when Yabril said to him, "If you cannot throw a bomb into a kindergarten, then you are not a true revolutionary," Romeo told him, "That I could never do."

But he could kill a Pope.

Yet in the last dark Roman nights, horrible little monsters, only the fetuses of dreams, covered Romeo's body with sweat distilled from ice.

Romeo sighed, rolled off his filthy bed to shower and shave before Yabril arrived. He knew that Yabril would judge his cleanliness a good sign, that morale was high for the coming mission. Yabril, like many sensualists, believed in a certain amount of spit and polish. Romeo, a true ascetic, could live in shit.

On the Roman streets, on his walk to visit Romeo, Yabril took the usual precautions. But in fact everything really depended on internal security, the loyalty of the fighting cadres, the integrity of the First Hundred. But not they, not even Romeo, knew the full extent of the mission.

Yabril was an Arab who easily passed for a Sicilian, as indeed many Arabs could. He had the thin dark face, but the lower part, the chin and jaw, was surprisingly heavier, coarser, as if it had an extra layer of bone. In his leisure time he grew a silky fur of a beard to hide the coarseness. But when he was part of an operation, he shaved himself clean.

As the Angel of Death he showed his true face to the enemy.

Yabril's eyes were a pale tan, his hair had only isolated strands of gray, and the heaviness of the jaw was repeated in the thickness of his chest and shoulders. His legs were long for the shortness of his body and masked the physical power he could generate. But nothing could hide the alert intelligence of his eyes.

Yabril detested the whole idea of the First Hundred. He thought it a fashionable public relations gimmick, despised its formal renunciation of the material world. These university-trained revolutionaries like Romeo were too romantic in their idealism, too contemptuous of compromise. Yabril understood that a little corruption in the rising bread of revolution was necessary.

Yabril had long ago given up all moral vanity. He had the clear conscience of those who believe and know that they are devoted with all their souls to the betterment of mankind. And he never reproached himself for his acts of self-interest. There had been his personal contracts with oil sheiks to kill political rivals. Odd jobs of murder for those new African heads of state, who, educated at Oxford, had learned to delegate. Then the random acts of terror for sundry respectable political chiefs—all those men in the world who control everything except the power of life and death.

These acts were never known to the First Hundred, and certainly never confided to Romeo. Yabril received funds from the Dutch, English and American oil companies, money from Russian and Japanese intelligence, and even, long ago in his career, payment from the American CIA for a very special secret execution. But all that was in the early days.

Now he lived well, he was not ascetic—after all, he had been poor, though not born so. He was fond of good wine and gourmet food, preferred luxury hotels, enjoyed gambling, and often succumbed to the ecstasy of union with a woman's flesh. Always paying for that ecstasy with money, gifts and his personal charm. He had a dread of romantic love.

Despite these "revolutionary weaknesses," Yabril was famous in his circles for the power of his will. He had absolutely no fear of death, which was not so extraordinary, but more uniquely he had no fear of pain. And it was perhaps because of this that he could be so ruthless.

Yabril had proved himself over the years. He was totally unbreakable under any kind of physical or psychological persuasion. He had survived imprisonment in Greece, France, Russia and two months of interrogation by Israeli security, whose expertness inspired his admiration. He had defeated them, perhaps because his body had the trick of losing feeling under duress. At last everyone understood. Yabril was granite under pain.

When he was the captor, he often charmed his victims. That he recognized a certain insanity in himself was part of his charm and part of the fear he inspired. Or perhaps it was the lack of malice in his cruelties. Yet all in all he savored life, he was a lighthearted terrorist. Even now he thoroughly enjoyed the fragrant streets of Rome and the twilight of Good Friday filled with the chimes of countless holy bells, though he was preparing the most dangerous operation of his life.

Everything was in place. Romeo's cadre was in place. Yabril's own group would arrive in Rome the next day. The two cadres would be in separate safe houses, their only link the two leaders. Yabril knew that this was a great moment. This coming Easter Sunday and the days after would be a brilliant creation.

He, Yabril, would direct nations down roads they abhorred treading. He would throw off all his shadowy masters, they would be his pawns, and he would sacrifice them all, even poor Romeo. Only death or failure of nerve could defeat his plans. Or, to be truthful, one of a hundred possible errors in timing. But the operation was so complicated, so ingenious, it gave him pleasure. Yabril stopped in the street to enjoy the beauty of the cathedral spires, the happy faces of the citizens of Rome, his melodramatic speculation about the future.

But like all men who think they can change the course of history by their own will, their own intelligence, their own strength, Yabril did not give due weight to the accidents and coincidences of history, nor to the possibility that there could be men more terrible than himself. Men bred within the strict structure of society, wearing the mask of benign lawgivers, could be far more ruthless and cruel.

Watching the devout and joyful pilgrims in the streets of Rome, believers in an omnipotent God, he was filled with a sense of his own invincibility. Proudly he would go beyond their God's forgiveness, for at the uttermost reaches of evil, good must necessarily begin.

Yabril was now in one of the poorer districts of Rome, where people could more easily be intimidated and bribed. He came to Romeo's safe house as darkness fell. The ancient four-story apartment building had a large courtyard half encircled by a stone wall; all the apartments were controlled by the underground revolutionary movement. Yabril was admitted by one of the three females in Romeo's cadre. She was a thin woman in jeans and a blue denim shirt that was unbuttoned almost down to her waist. She wore no bra, there was no roundness of breasts visible. She had been on one of Yabril's operations before. He did not like her, but he admired her ferocity. They had quarreled once, and she had not backed down.

The woman's name was Annee. She wore her jet-black hair in a Prince Valiant cut that did not flatter her strong blunt face, but drew notice to her blazing eyes that measured everyone, even Romeo and Yabril, with a sort of fury. She had not yet been fully briefed on the mission, but the appearance of Yabril told her it was of the utmost importance. She smiled briefly, without speaking, then closed the door after Yabril stepped inside.

Yabril noted with disgust how filthy the interior of the house had become. There were dirty dishes and glasses and remnants of food scattered in the living room, the floor littered with newspapers. Romeo's cadre was composed of four men and three women, all Italian. The women refused to clean up; it was contrary to their revolutionary belief to do domestic chores on an operation unless the men did their share. The men, all university students, still young, had the same belief in the rights of women, but they were the conditioned darlings of Italian mothers, and also knew that a backup cadre would clean the house of all incriminating marks after they left. The unspoken compromise was that the squalor would be ignored. A compromise that irritated only Yabril.

He said to Annee, "What pigs you are."

Annee measured him with a cool contempt. "I'm not a housekeeper," she said.

And Yabril recognized her quality immediately. She was not afraid of him or any man or woman. She was a true believer. She was quite willing to burn at the stake.

Romeo came racing down the stairs from the apartment above—so handsome, so vital that Annee lowered her eyes—and embraced Yabril with real affection, then led him out into the courtyard, where they sat on a small stone bench. The night air was filled with the scent of spring flowers, and there was a faint hum, the sound of countless thousands of pilgrims shouting and talking in the streets of Lenten Rome. Above it all, the ascending and descending tolls of hundreds of church bells acclaimed the approaching Easter Sunday.

Romeo lit a cigarette and said, "Our time has finally come, Yabril. No matter what happens, our names will be known forever."

Yabril laughed at the stilted romanticism, felt a little contempt for this desire for personal glory. "Infamous," he said. "We compete with a long history of terror." Yabril was thinking of their embrace. An embrace of professional love on his part, but shot through with remembered terror as if they were parricides standing over a father they had murdered together.

There were dim electric lights along the courtyard walls, but their faces were in darkness. Romeo said, "They will know everything in time. But will they give us credit for our motives? Or will they paint us as lunatics? What the hell, the poets of the future will understand us."

Yabril said, "We can't worry about that now." It embarrassed him when Romeo became theatrical; it made him question the man's efficiency though it had been proved many times. Romeo, despite delicate good looks and fuzziness of concept, was a truly dangerous man. But there was a fundamental difference between them: Romeo was too fearless, Yabril perhaps too cunning.

Just a year before, they had walked the streets of Beirut together. In their path was a brown paper sack, seemingly empty, greased with the food it had contained. Yabril walked around it. Romeo kicked and sailed the sack into the gutter.

Different instincts. Yabril believed that everything on this earth was dangerous. Romeo had a certain innocent trust.

There were other differences. Yabril was ugly with his small marbled tan eyes, Romeo was almost beautiful. Yabril was proud of his ugliness, Romeo was ashamed of his beauty. Yabril had always understood that when an innocent man commits absolutely to political revolution, it must lead to murder. Romeo had come to that belief late, and reluctantly. His conversion had been an intellectual one.

Romeo had won sexual victories with the accident of physical beauty, and his family money had protected him from economic humiliations. Romeo was intelligent enough to know that his good fortune was not morally correct, and so the very goodness of his life disgusted him. He drowned himself in literature and his studies, which confirmed his belief. It was inevitable that he would be convinced by his radical professors that he should help make the world a better place.

He did not want to be like his father, an Italian who spent more time in barbershops than courtesans at their hairdresser's. He did not want to spend his life in the pursuit of beautiful women. Above all, he would never spend money reeking with the sweat of the poor. The poor must be made free and happy, and then he too could taste happiness. And so he reached out, for a second Communion, to the books of Karl Marx.

Yabril's conversion was more visceral. As a child in Palestine he had lived in a Garden of Eden. He had been a happy boy, extremely intelligent, devotedly obedient to his parents—especially to his father, who spent an hour each day reading to him from the Koran.

The family lived in a large villa with many servants, on extensive grounds that were magically green in that desert land. But one day, when Yabril was five years old, he was cast out of this paradise. His beloved parents vanished, the villa and gardens dissolved into a cloud of purple smoke. And suddenly he was living in a small dirty village at the bottom of a mountain, an orphan living on the charity of kin. His only treasure was his father's Koran printed on vellum, with illuminated figures of gold and calligraphy of a rich blue. And he always remembered his father's reading it aloud, exactly from the text, according to Muslim custom. Those orders of God given to the Prophet Mohammed, words that could never be discussed or argued. As a grown man, Yabril had remarked to a Jewish friend, "The Koran is not a Torah," and they had both laughed.

The truth of exile from the Garden of Eden had been revealed to him almost at once, but he did not fully understand it until a few years later. His father had been a secret supporter of Palestine liberation from the state of Israel, a leader of the underground. His father had been betrayed, gunned down in a police raid, and his mother had committed suicide when the villa and grounds were blown up by the Israelis.

It was most natural for Yabril to become a terrorist. His kin and his teachers in the local school taught him to hate all Jews but did not fully succeed. He did hate his God for banishing him from his childhood paradise. When he was eighteen he sold his father's Koran for an enormous sum of money and enrolled at the university in Beirut. There he spent most of his fortune on women, and finally, after two years, became a member of the Palestinian underground. And over the years he became a deadly weapon in that cause.

But his people's freedom was not his final aim. In some way his work was a search for inner peace.

Now together in the courtyard of the safe house, Romeo and Yabril took a little over two hours to go over every detail of their mission. Romeo smoked cigarettes constantly. He was nervous about one thing. "Are you sure they will give me up?" he asked.

Yabril said softly, "How can they not with the hostage I will be holding? Believe me, you will be safer in their hands than I will be in Sherhaben."

They gave each other a final embrace in the darkness. After Easter Sunday they would never see each other again.

On this same Good Friday, President Francis Xavier Kennedy met with his senior staff of top advisers and his Vice President to give them news that he knew would make them unhappy.

He met with them in the Yellow Oval Room of the White House, his favorite room, larger and more comfortable than the more famous Oval Office. The Yellow Room was more a living room, and they could be comfortable while being served an English tea.

They were all waiting for him and they rose when his Secret Service bodyguards ushered him into the room. Kennedy motioned his staff to sit down while telling the bodyguards to wait outside the room. Two things irritated him about this little scene. The first was that according to protocol he had to personally order the Secret Service men out of the room, and the second was that the Vice President had to stand out of respect for the presidency. What annoyed him about this was that the Vice President was a woman, and political courtesy overruled social courtesy. This was compounded by the fact that Vice President Helen Du Pray was ten years older than he, was still quite a beautiful woman, and had extraordinary political and social intelligence. Which was, of course, why he had picked her as his running mate despite the opposition of the heavyweights in the Democratic party.

"Damn it, Helen," Francis Kennedy said. "Stop standing up when I come into a room. Now I'll have to pour tea for everybody to show my humility."

"I wanted to express my gratitude," Helen DuPray said. "I figured you summoned the Vice President to your staff meeting because somebody has to do the dishes." They both laughed. The staff did not.

Romeo smoked a final cigarette in the darkness of the courtyard. Beyond the stone walls he could see the domes of the great churches of Rome. Then he went inside. It was time to brief his cadre.

The woman Annee served as the cadre's armorer and she unlocked a huge trunk to distribute the weapons and ammunition. One of the men spread on the living-room floor a dirty bed sheet, on which Annee put gun oil and rags. They would clean and oil their weapons as they listened to the briefing. For hours they listened and asked questions, and rehearsed their movements. Annee handed out the operational clothing and they made jokes about that. Finally they all sat down together to a meal that Romeo and the men had prepared. They toasted the success of their mission with new spring wine, and then some of them played cards for an hour before retiring to their rooms. There was no need for a guard; they had locked themselves in securely, and they had their weapons beside their beds. Still, they all had trouble falling asleep.

It was after midnight when Annee knocked on Romeo's door. Romeo was reading. He let her in and she quickly threw his copy of *The Brothers Karamazov* on the floor. She said almost contemptuously, "You're reading that shit again?" Romeo shrugged and smiled and said, "He amuses me, his characters strike me as Italians trying hard to be serious."

They undressed quickly and lay down on the soiled sheets, both on their backs. Their bodies were tense not with the excitement of sex but with a mysterious terror. Romeo stared straight up at the ceiling and the woman Annee closed her eyes. She was on his left and used her right hand to slowly and gently masturbate him. Their shoulders barely touched, the rest of their bodies was apart. When she felt Romeo become erect, she continued the strokes with her right hand and at the same time masturbated herself with her left hand. It was a continuous slow rhythm during which Romeo once reached out tentatively to touch her small breast, but she made a grimace like a child, her eyes tightly shut. Now her pulling became tighter and stronger, the stroking frantic and unrhythmical, and Romeo came to orgasm. As the semen flowed over Annee's hand she too came to orgasm, her eyes flew open and her slight body seemed to hurl itself into the air, lifting and turning to Romeo as if to kiss him, but she ducked her head and buried her face in his chest for a moment until her body shuddered to a stop. Then very matter-of-factly she sat up and wiped her hand on the soiled sheet of the bed. She then took Romeo's cigarettes and lighter from the marble night table and started to smoke.

Romeo went into the bathroom and wet a towel. He came back and washed her hands and then wiped himself. Then he gave her the towel and she rubbed it between her legs. They had done this on another mission, and Romeo understood that this was the only kind of affection she could permit. She was so fierce in her independence, for whatever reason, that she could not bear that a man she did not love should penetrate her. And as for fellatio and cunnilingus, which he had suggested, they were also another form of surrender. What she had done was the only way she could satisfy her need without betraying her ideals of independence.

Romeo watched her face. It was not so stern now, the eyes not so fierce. She was so young, he thought, how did she become so deadly in so short a time? "Do you want to sleep with me tonight, just for company?" he said.

Annee stubbed out the cigarette. "Oh no," she said. "Why would I want to do that? We've both got what we needed." She started to dress.

Romeo said jokingly, "At least you could say something tender before you leave."

She stood in the doorway briefly and then turned. For a moment he thought she would return to the bed. She was smiling, and for the first time he saw her as a young girl he could love. But then she seemed to stand on tiptoe and said, "Romeo, Romeo, wherefore art thou, Romeo?" She thumbed her nose at him and disappeared.

At Brigham Young University in Provo, Utah, two students, David Jatney and Cryder Cole, prepared their kits for the traditional once-a-term assassination hunt. This game had again come back into favor with the election of Francis Xavier Kennedy to the presidency of the United States. By the rules of the game a student team had twenty-four hours to commit the assassination—that is, fire their toy pistols at a cardboard effigy of the President of the United States from no more than five paces away. To prevent this, there was a law-and-order fraternity defense team of more than a hundred students. The "money prize bet" was used to pay for the victory banquet at the conclusion of the hunt.

The college faculty and administration, influenced by the Mormon Church, disapproved of these games, but they had become popular on campuses all over the United States—an example of the vexing excesses of a free society. Poor taste, an appetite for the gross in life, was part of the very high spirits of the young. And such a game was an outlet for the resentment of authority, a form of protest by those who had not yet achieved anything against those who had already become successful. It was a symbolic protest, and certainly preferable to political demonstrations, random violence and sit-ins. The hunting game was a safety valve for rioting hormones.

The two hunters David Jatney and Cryder Cole strolled the campus arm in arm. Jatney was the planner and Cole the actor, so it was Cole who did the talking and Jatney nodded as they made their way toward the fraternity brothers guarding the effigy of the President. The cardboard figure of Francis Kennedy was a recognizable likeness but was extravagantly colored to show him wearing a blue suit, a green tie, red socks and no shoes. Where the shoes should have been was the Roman numeral IV.

The law-and-order gang threatened Jatney and Cole with their toy pistols and the two hunters veered off. Cole shouted a cheerful insult, but Jatney was grim-faced. He took his mission very seriously. Jatney was reviewing his master plan and already feeling a savage satisfaction over its certain success. This walk in view of the enemy was to establish that they were wearing ski gear, to establish a visual identity and so prepare for a later surprise. Also to plant the idea that they were leaving the campus for the weekend.

Part of the hunting game required that the itinerary of the presidential effigy be published. The effigy would be at the victory banquet that was scheduled for that evening before midnight. Jatney and Cole planned to make their strike before the midnight deadline.

Everything worked out as planned. Jatney and Cole re-united at 6:00 P.M. in the designated restaurant. The proprietor had no knowledge of their plans. They were just two young students who had been working for him for the past two weeks. They were very good waiters, especially Cole, and the proprietor was delighted with them.

At nine that evening when the law-and-order guards, a hundred strong, entered with their presidential effigy, guards were posted at all the entries to the restaurant. The effigy was placed in the center of the circle of tables. The proprietor was rubbing his hands at this influx of business, and it was only when he went into the kitchen and saw his two young waiters hiding their toy pistols in the soup tureens that he caught on. "Oh, for Christ's sake," he said. "That means you two guys are quitting tonight." Cole grinned at him, but David Jatney gave him a menacing scowl as they marched into the dining room, soup tureens lifted high to shield their faces.

The guards were already drinking victory toasts when Jatney and Cole placed the tureens on the center table, whipped off the covers and took out the toy pistols. They held their weapons against the garishly colored effigy and fired the little pops of the mechanism. Cole fired one shot and burst out laughing. Jatney fired three shots very deliberately, then threw his pistol on the floor. He did not move, he did not smile until the guards mobbed him with congratulatory curses and all of them sat down to dinner. Jatney gave the effigy a kick so that it slid down to the floor where it could not be seen.

This had been one of the more simple hunts. In other colleges across the country the game was more serious. Elaborate security structures were set up, effigies squirted synthetic blood.

In Washington, D.C., the Attorney General of the United States, Christian Klee, had his own file on all these playful assassins. And it was the photographs and memos on Jatney and Cole that caught his interest. He made a note to assign a case team to the lives of David Jatney and Cryder Cole.

On the Friday before Easter, two serious-minded young men drove from the Massachusetts Institute of Technology to New York, and deposited a small suitcase in a baggage locker of the Port Authority Building. They picked their way fastidiously through the cluster of drunken homeless bums, the sharp-eyed pimps, the whores who thronged the halls of the building. The two were prodigies, at age twenty assistant professors of physics and members of an advanced program at the university. The suitcase held a tiny atom bomb they had constructed using stolen lab materials and the necessary plutonium. It had taken them two years to steal these materials from their programs, bit by bit, falsifying their reports and experiments so that the theft would not be noticed.

Adam Gresse and Henry Tibbot had been classified as geniuses since they were twelve. Their parents had brought them up to be aware of their responsibilities to humankind. They had no vices except knowledge. Their particular brilliance made them disdain those appetites that were lice on the hide of humanity, such as alcohol, gambling, women, gluttony and drugs.

What they succumbed to was the powerful drug of clear thinking. They had a social conscience and saw the evil in the world. They knew that the making of atomic weapons was wrong, that the fate of humanity hung in the balance, and they decided to do what they could to avert an infernal disaster. So after a year of boyish talk they decided to scare the government. They would show how easy it was for a crazed individual to inflict grave punishment on mankind. They built the tiny atom bomb, only half a kiloton in power, so that they could plant it and then warn the authorities of its existence. They thought of themselves and their contemplated deed as unique, as godlike. They did not know that this precise situation had been predicted by the psychological reports of a prestigious think tank funded by the government as one of the possible hazards of the atomic age of mankind.

While they were still in New York, Adam Gresse and Henry Tibbot mailed their warning letter to *The New York Times* explaining their motives and asking that the letter be published before being sent to the authorities. The composing of the letter had been a long process, not only because it had to be worded precisely to show no malicious intent but because they used scissored printed words and letters lifted out of old newspapers that they pasted onto blank sheets of paper.

The bomb would not go off till the following Thursday. By that time the letter would be in the hands of the authorities and the bomb surely found. It would be a warning to the rulers of the world.

And in Rome on that Good Friday, Theresa Catherine Kennedy, daughter of the President of the United States, prepared to end her self-imposed European exile and return to live with her father in the White House.

Her Secret Service security detail had already made all the travel arrangements. Obeying her instructions, they had booked passage on the Easter Sunday flight from Rome to New York.

Theresa Kennedy was twenty-three years old and had been studying philosophy in Europe, first at the Sorbonne in Paris and then at the university in Rome, where she had just ended a serious affair with a radical Italian student, to their mutual relief.

She loved her father but hated his being President because she was too loyal to publicly voice her own differing views. She had been a believer in socialism; now she was an advocate of the brotherhood of man, the sisterhood of women. She was a feminist in the American style; economic independence was the foundation of freedom, and so she had no guilt about the trust funds that guaranteed her freedom.

With a curious yet very human morality she had rejected the idea of any privilege and rarely visited her father in the White House. And perhaps she unconsciously blamed her father for her mother's death because he had struggled for political power while his wife was dying. Later she had wanted to lose herself in Europe, but by law she had to be protected by the Secret Service as a member of the immediate presidential family. She had tried to sign off on that security protection, but her father had begged her not to. Francis Kennedy told her he could not bear it if something were to happen to her.

A detail of twenty men, spread over three shifts a day, guarded Theresa Kennedy. When she went to a restaurant, if she went to a movie with her boyfriend, they were there. They rented apartments in the same building, used a command van in the street. She was never alone. And she had to give her schedule to the chief of the security detail every single day.

Her guards were two-headed monsters: half servant, half

master. With advanced electronic equipment they could hear the lovemaking when she brought a male friend back to her apartment. And they were frightening—they moved like wolves, gliding silently, their heads tilted alertly as if to catch a scent on the wind, but actually they were straining to listen to their earplug radios.

Theresa had refused a "net security," that is, security of the closest kind. She drove her own car, refused to let the security team take an adjoining apartment, refused to walk with guards alongside her. She had insisted that the security be a "perimeter security," that they erect a wall around her as if she were a large garden. In this way she could lead a personal life. This arrangement led to some embarrassing moments. One day she went shopping and needed change for a telephone call. She thought she had seen one of her security detail pretending to shop nearby. She had gone up to the man and said, "Could you give me a quarter?" He had looked at her with shocked bewilderment, and she realized that she had made a mistake, that he was not her security guard. She had burst out laughing and apologized. The man was amused and delighted as he gave her the quarter. "Anything for a Kennedy," he said jokingly.

Like so many of the young, Theresa Kennedy believed, on no particular evidence, that people were "good," as she believed herself to be good. She marched for freedom, spoke out for the right and against the wrong. She tried to never commit petty mean acts in everyday life. As a child she gave the contents of her piggy bank to the American Indians.

In her position as daughter of the President of the United States it was awkward for her when she spoke out for pro-choice abortion activists, and lent her name to radical and left-wing organizations. She endured the abuse of the media and the insults of political opponents.

Innocently, she was scrupulously fair in her love affairs; she believed in absolute frankness, she abhorred deceit.

In her years abroad there were incidents from which she should have learned some valuable lessons. In Paris a group of tramps living under one of the bridges tried to rape her when she roamed the city in search of local color. In Rome two beggars tried to snatch her purse as she was giving them money, and in both cases she had been rescued by her vigilant Secret Service detail. But this made no impression on her general faith that man was good. Every human being had the immortal seed of goodness in his soul, no one was beyond redemption. As a feminist she had, of course, learned of the tyranny of men over women, but did not really comprehend the brutal force men used when dealing with their own world. She had no sense of how one human being could betray another human being in the most false and cruel ways.

The chief of her security detail, a man too old to guard the more important people in government, was appalled by her innocence and tried to educate her. He told her horror stories about men in general, stories taken from his long experience in the service; he was more frank than he would ordinarily have been, since this job was his last assignment before retiring.

"You're too young to understand this world," he said. "And in your position you have to be very careful. You think because you do good for someone they will do good for you." Just the day before, she had picked up a male hitchhiker, who assumed that this was a sexual invitation. The security chief had acted immediately; the two security cars forced Theresa's car to the edge of the road just as the hitchhiker put his hand in Theresa's lap.

"Let me tell you a story," the chief said. "I once worked

for the smartest and nicest man in the government service. In clandestine operations. Just once he got outsmarted, caught in a trap, and this bad guy had him at his mercy. Could just blow him away. And this guy was a real bad guy. But for some reason he let my boss off the hook and said, 'Remember, you owe me one.' Well, we spent six months tracking this guy down and we nailed him. And my boss blew him away, never gave him a chance to surrender or turn 'double.' And you know why? He told me himself. This bad guy once had the power of God and therefore was too dangerous to be allowed to live. And my boss didn't have a feeling of gratitude, he said the guy's mercy was just a whim and you can't count on whims the next time around." The chief did not tell Theresa his boss had been a man named Christian Klee.

The election of Francis Xavier Kennedy as President was a miracle of American politics. He had been elected on the magic of his name and his extraordinary physical and intellectual gifts, despite the fact that he had served only one term in the Senate before being elected to the presidency.

He was called the "nephew" of John F. Kennedy, the President who had been assassinated in 1963, but was outside the organized Kennedy clan still active in American politics. In reality, he was a cousin, and the only one of the far-flung family who had inherited the charisma of his two famous uncles John and Robert Kennedy.

Francis Kennedy had been a boy genius in the law, a professor at Harvard at the age of twenty-eight. Later he had organized his own law firm, which crusaded for broad liberal reforms in the government and the private business sector. His law firm did not make a great deal of money, which was not important to him, since he had inherited considerable wealth, but it did bring him a great deal of national fame. He crusaded for the rights of minorities and the welfare of the economically disabled, he defended the helpless.

Kennedy had swept the country along with him in his campaign for the presidency. He had proclaimed he would write a new social contract for the American people. What makes a civilization endure? he asked them. It is the contract between the governors and the governed. The government must promise public safety from crime, from economic hardship; it must promise to every citizen the right and the means to pursue the individual dream of enjoying personal happiness in this life. And then, only then, would the governed be obligated to obey the common laws that ensure civilization. And Kennedy proposed that as part of that sacred social contract all major questions in American society be settled by referendums rather than by decisions made by the Congress, by the Supreme Court or by the President.

He promised that he would wipe out crime. He promised that he would wipe out poverty, which was a root of crime and a crime in and of itself. He promised a national health insurance program financed by the state and a Social Security System that would truly enable workingmen to have a comfortable retirement.

To affirm his dedication to these ideals and to remove the armor of his own personal wealth, he proclaimed on television that he would give his personal fortune of forty million dollars to the Treasury of the United States. This was done in a highly public legal ceremony that was shown by every television-station news program in the country. The image of Francis Kennedy's grand gesture had a huge impact on every voting citizen.

He flew to every major city in the country, and his automobile cavalcade covered the small towns. His wife and daughter by his side, their beauty flanking his, he overwhelmed the public consciousness. His three debates with the Republican presidential incumbent were triumphs. The combination of his wit, his intelligence and his youthful exuberance completely destroyed his opponent. No President had ever entered his first term of office more beloved by the populace. He had conquered everything except fate. His wife had died of cancer before his inauguration.

Despite his crushing sorrow, Francis Xavier Kennedy managed to enact the first step of the program. During the election process he had made the daring political move of naming his personal staff in advance so that the electorate could approve them. He had named Oddblood Gray, a black activist, as his liaison with Congress on domestic affairs. He had selected a woman to be his running mate and made the political decision that she would also function as a member of his staff. The other nominations were more conventional. And it was this staff that helped push through his first victory, the revision of the Social Security laws so that every workingman could be sure of enough money to live on when he retired. The tax to finance this revision was paid by the profits of the giant corporations of America, and these immediately became his deadly enemies.

But after this initial victory, Kennedy seemed to lose momentum. His bill to give the people a referendum vote on major issues was defeated by Congress, as was his call for a national health insurance plan. And Kennedy himself was losing energy in confronting the stone wall Congress put up before him. Though Kennedy and his White House staff fought with an almost desperate ferocity, more and more of their plans were defeated.

The knowledge that in the last year of his presidency the battle was being lost filled him with a despairing anger. He knew that his cause was just, that he was on the side of what was right, that he held the moral high ground, that his course of action was the most intelligent for the survival of America. But it seemed to him now that intelligence and morality had no weight in the political process.

President Kennedy waited until everyone on his senior staff had been served tea.

"I may not run for a second term," he said evenly. Looking over to the Vice President, he added, "Helen, I want you to prepare to make your run for the presidency."

They were all struck dumb, but Helen Du Pray smiled at him. The fact that this smile was one of her great political weapons was not lost on these men. She said, "Francis, I think a decision not to run requires a full-length review by your staff without my presence. Before I leave, let me say this. At this particular point in time I know how discouraged you are. But I won't be able to do any better, assuming I could be elected. I think you should be more patient. Your second term could be more effective."

President Kennedy said impatiently, "Helen, you know as well as I do that a President of the United States has more clout in his first term than in his second."

"True in most cases," Helen Du Pray said. "But maybe we could get a different House of Representatives for your second term. And let me speak of my own self-interest. As Vice President for only one term I am in a weaker position than if I served for two terms. Also your support would be more valuable as a two-term President and not a President who's been chased out of office by his own Democratic Congress."

As she picked up her memorandum file and prepared to leave, Francis Kennedy said, "You don't have to leave."

Du Pray gave everybody the same sweet smile. "I'm sure your staff can speak more freely if I'm not present," she said, and she left the Yellow Oval Room.

The four men around Kennedy were silent. They were his closest aides. Kennedy had appointed them personally and they were responsible solely to him. The President was like a strange kind of Cyclops with one brain and four arms. The senior staff was his four arms. They were also his best friends, and, since the death of his wife, his only personal family.

Du Pray closed the door behind her, and there was a small flurry of movement as the men straightened their folders of memorandum sheets and reached for tea and sandwiches. The President's chief of staff, Eugene Dazzy, said casually, "Helen may be the smartest person in this administration."

Kennedy smiled at Dazzy, who was known to have a weakness for beautiful women. "And what do you think, Euge?" he said. "Do you think I should be more patient and run again?"

Eugene Dazzy had been the head of a huge computer firm ten years before, when Francis Kennedy first entered politics. He had been a cruncher, a man who could eat up rival companies, but he had come from a poor family, and he retained his belief in justice more out of a practical sense than a romantic idealism. He had come to believe that concentrated money held too much power in America and that in the long run this would destroy true democracy. And so when Francis Kennedy entered politics under the banner of a true social democracy, Dazzy organized the financial support that helped Kennedy ascend to the presidency.

He was a large affable man whose great art was the avoidance of making enemies of people whose important wishes and special requests the President denied. Dazzy bowed his balding head over his notes, his tubby upper body straining the back of his well-tailored jacket. He spoke in a casual voice. "Why not run?" he said. "You'll have a nice goof-off job. Congress will tell you what to do and refuse to do what you want done. Everything will stay the same. Except in foreign policy. There you can have some fun. Maybe even do some good.

"Look at it this way. Our army is fifty percent under quota, we've educated our kids so well they are too smart to be patriotic. We have technology but no one wants to buy our goods. Our balance of payments is hopeless. You can only go up. So go get reelected and relax and have a good time for four years. What the hell, it's not a bad job and you can use the money." Dazzy smiled and waved a hand to show that he was at least half kidding.

The four men of the staff watched Kennedy closely, despite seemingly casual attitudes. None of them felt Dazzy was being disrespectful; the playfulness of his remarks was an attitude that Kennedy had encouraged in the past three years.

Arthur Wix, the national security adviser, a burly man with a big-city face—that is, ethnic, born of a Jewish father and an Italian mother—could be savagely witty, but also a little in awe of the presidential office and Kennedy.

Wix had met Kennedy ten years before, when he had first run for the Senate. He was an Eastern seaboard liberal, a professor of ethics and political science at Columbia University. He was also a very rich man who had contempt for money. Their relationship had grown into a friendship based on their intellectual gifts. Kennedy thought Arthur Wix the most intelligent man he had ever met. Wix thought Kennedy the most moral man in politics. This was not—could not be—the basis of a warm friendship, but it did form the foundation for a relationship of trust.

As national security adviser, Wix felt that his responsibilities obliged him to be more serious in tone than the others. He spoke in a quiet persuasive voice that still had a New York buzz. "Euge," he said, motioning to Dazzy, "may think he's kidding, but you can make a valuable contribution to our country's foreign policy. We have far more leverage than Europe or Asia believes. I think it's imperative you run for another term. After all, in foreign policy, the President of the United States has the power of a king."

Kennedy turned to the man on his left. Oddblood "Otto" Gray was the youngest man on Kennedy's staff, only ten years out of college. He had come out of the black left-wing movement, via Harvard and a Rhodes Scholarship. A tall, imposing man, he had been a brilliant scholar and a first-rate orator in his college days. Kennedy had spotted under the firebrand a man with a natural courtesy and sense of diplomacy, a man who could persuade without threats. And then in a potentially violent situation in New York, Kennedy had won Gray's admiration and trust. Kennedy had used his extraordinary legal skills, his intelligence and charm, and his clear lack of racial bias to defuse the situation, thus winning the admiration of both sides.

After that, Oddblood Gray had supported Kennedy in his political career, and urged him to run for the presidency. Kennedy appointed him to his staff as liaison with the Congress, as head man to get the President's bills pushed through. Gray's youthful idealism warred with his instinctive genius for politics. And to some extent, naturally, idealism suffered defeats, because he really knew how government worked, where leverage could be applied, when to use the brute force of patronage, when to skip in place, when to surrender gracefully.

"Otto," Kennedy said. "Give us the word."

"Quit," Gray said. "While you're only just losing." Kennedy smiled and the other men laughed. Gray went on. "You want it straight? I'm with Dazzy. Congress shits on you, the press kicks your ass. The lobbyists and big business have strangled your programs. And the working class and the intellectuals feel you betrayed them. You're driving this big fucking Cadillac of a country and there ain't even power steering. And you want to give every damn maniac in this country another four years to knock you off, to boot? I say let's all get us the fuck out of here."

Kennedy seemed delighted, the handsome Irish planes of his face breaking into a smile and his satiny blue eyes sparkling. "Very funny," he said. "But let's get serious." He knew they were trying to goad him into running again by appealing to his pride. None of them wanted to leave this center of power, this Washington, this White House. It was better to be a clawless lion than not to be a lion at all.

"You want me to run again," Kennedy said. "But to do what?"

Otto Gray said, "Damn right I want you to run. I joined this administration because you begged me to help my people. I believed in you and believe in you still. We did help, and we can help more. There's a hell of a lot more to do. The rich get richer, the poor get poorer, and only you can change that. Don't quit that fight now."

Kennedy said, "But how the hell can I win? The Congress is virtually controlled by the Socrates Club."

Gray looked at his boss with the kind of passion and forcefulness found only in the young. "We can't think like that. Look what we've won against terrible odds. We can win again. And even if we don't, what could be more important than trying?"

The room was quiet for a moment, as everyone seemed to become aware of the silence of one man, the most powerful influence on Francis Kennedy. Christian Klee. All eyes focused on him now.

Klee held Kennedy in some sort of reverence, though they were dear friends. This always surprised Kennedy, because Klee valued physical bravery and knew Kennedy had a fear of assassination. It was Christian who had begged Francis to run for the presidency and guaranteed his personal safety if he was appointed Attorney General and head of the FBI and Secret Service. So now he essentially controlled the whole internal security system of the United States, but Kennedy had paid a heavy political price for this. He had traded Congress the appointment of two justices of the Supreme Court and the ambassadorship to Britain.

Now Kennedy stared at Christian Klee, and finally Klee spoke. "You know what worries people most in this country? They don't really give a shit about foreign relations. They don't give a shit about economics. They don't care if the earth dries up into a raisin. They worry in the big and little cities that they can't walk the streets at night without getting mugged. That they can't sleep safely in their beds at night without worrying about burglars and murderers.

"We live in a state of anarchy. The government does not fulfill its part of the social contract to protect each and every individual citizen. Women go in fear of rape, men go in fear of murder. We are descending into some sort of morass of animal behavior. The rich eat up the people economically and the criminals massacre the poor and middle class. And you, Francis, are the only one who can lead us to the higher ground. I believe that, I believe you can save this country.

That's why I came to work for you. And now you want to desert us." Klee paused. "You have to try again, Francis. Just another four years."

President Kennedy was touched. He could see that these four men still truly believed in him. And in one part of his mind he knew that he had maneuvered them into saying these things, had made them reaffirm their faith in him, had made them equally responsible with him. He smiled at them with genuine delight.

"I'll think it over," he said.

They took this as a dismissal and left, except for Christian Klee.

Christian said casually, "Will Theresa be home for the holidays?"

Kennedy shrugged. "She's in Rome with a new boyfriend. She'll be flying in on Easter Sunday. As usual, she makes a point of ignoring religious holidays."

Christian said, "I'm glad she's getting the hell out. I really can't protect her in Europe. And she thinks she can shoot off her mouth there and it won't be reported here." He paused a moment. "If you do run again, you'll have to keep your daughter out of sight or disown her."

"I can't. If I do run again, I'll need the radical feminist vote."

Christian laughed. "OK," he said. "Now, about the birthday party for the Oracle. He is really looking forward to it."

"Don't worry," Kennedy said. "I'll give him the full treatment. My God, a hundred years old and he still looks forward to his birthday party."

"He was and is a great man," Christian said.

Kennedy gave him a sharp look. "You were always fonder of him than I ever was. He had his faults, he made his mistakes."

"Sure," Christian said. "But I never saw a man control his life better. He changed my life with his advice, his guidance." Christian paused for a moment. "I'm having dinner with him tonight, so I'll just tell him the party is definitely on."

Kennedy smiled dryly. "You can safely tell him that," he said.

At the end of the day Kennedy signed some papers in the Oval Office, then sat at his desk and gazed out the window. He could see the tops of the gates that surrounded the White House grounds, black iron tipped with white electrified thorns. As always, he felt uneasy about his proximity to the streets and to the public, though he knew that the seeming vulnerability to attack was an illusion. He was extraordinarily well protected. There were seven perimeters guarding the White House. For two miles away every building had a security team on the roofs and in apartments. All the streets leading to the White House had command posts with concealed rapid-fire and heavy weapons. The tourists who came mornings to visit the ground floor of the White House in their many hundreds were heavily infiltrated with Secret Service agents, who circulated constantly and took part in the small talk, their eyes alert. Every inch of the White House that these tourists were permitted to visit behind the ropes was covered by TV monitors and special audio equipment that could pick up secret whispers. Armed guards manned special computer desks that could serve as barricades at every turn in the corridors. And during these visits by the public Kennedy would always be up on the new specially built fourth floor that served as his living quarters. Living quarters guarded by specially reinforced floors, walls and ceilings.

Now in the famous Oval Office, which he rarely used

except for signing official documents in special ceremonies, Francis Kennedy relaxed to enjoy one of the few minutes he was completely alone. He took a long thin Cuban cigar from the humidor on his desk, felt the oiliness of the leafy wrapper on his fingers. He cut the end, lit it carefully, took the first rich puff and looked out through the bulletproof windows.

He could see himself as a child walking across the vast green lawn, from the faraway guard post painted white, then running to greet his uncle Jack and uncle Robert. How he had loved them. Uncle Jack so full of charm, so childlike, and yet so powerful, to give hope that a child could wield power over the world. And Uncle Robert, so serious and earnest and yet so gentle and playful. And here Francis Kennedy thought, no, we called him Uncle Bobby, not Robert, or did we sometimes? He could not remember.

But he did remember one day more than forty years ago when he had run to meet both his uncles on that very same lawn and how they had each taken one of his arms and swung him so that his feet never touched the ground as they went toward the White House.

And now he stood in their place. The power that had awed him as a child was now his. It was a pity that memory could evoke so much pain and so much beauty, and so much disappointment. What they had died for he was thinking of giving up.

On this Good Friday Francis Xavier Kennedy did not know that all this would be changed by two insignificant revolutionaries in Rome.

CHAPTER
2

ON EASTER SUNDAY morning, Romeo and his cadre of four men and three women in full operational gear disembarked from their van. In the Roman streets outside St. Peter's Square they mingled with the crowds attired in Easter finery—the women glorious in the pastel colors of spring and operatic in churchgoing hats, the men handsome in silk cream-colored suits with yellow palm crosses stitched into their lapels. The children were even more dazzling: little girls wearing gloves and frilly frocks, the boys in navy blue confirmation suits with red ties on snowy shirts. Scattered throughout were priests smiling benedictions on the faithful.

Romeo was a more sober pilgrim, a serious witness to the Resurrection that this Easter morning celebrated. He was dressed in a dead-black suit, a white shirt heavily starched, and a pure white tie almost invisible against it. His shoes were black but rubber-soled. And now he buttoned the camel-hair coat to conceal the rifle that hung in its special sling. He had practiced with this rifle for the past three months until his accuracy was deadly.

The four men in his cadre were dressed as monks of the Capuchin order, in long flowing robes of dingy brown, girdled by fat cloth belts. Their tonsured heads were covered with skullcaps. Concealed inside the loose robes were grenades and handguns.

The three women—one of them Annee—were dressed as nuns in black and white and they too had weapons beneath their loose-fitting clothing. Annee and the other two nuns walked ahead as people made way for them, and Romeo followed easily in their wake. After Romeo came the four monks of the cadre, observing everything, ready to intercede if Romeo was stopped by papal police.

And so Romeo's band made their way to St. Peter's Square, invisible in the huge crowd that was assembling. And finally like dark corks bobbing in an ocean of many colors, Romeo and his cadre came to rest on the far side of the square, their backs protected by marble columns and stone walls. Romeo stood a little apart. He was watching for a signal from the other side of the square, where Yabril and his cadre were busy attaching holy figurines to the walls.

Yabril and his cadre of three men and three women were in casual attire with loose-fitting jackets. The men carried concealed handguns, while the women were working with the religious figurines, small statues of Christ, that were loaded with explosives designed to go off by radio signal. The backs had adhesive glue so strong that they could not be detached from the walls by any of the curious in the crowd. Also, the figurines were beautifully designed and made of expensive-looking terra-cotta painted white and formed around a wired skeleton. They gave the appearance of being part of the Easter decorations and as such were inviolate.

When this operation was completed, Yabril led his cadre through the crowd and out of St. Peter's Square to his own waiting van. He sent one of his men to Romeo to give him the radio signal device for the detonating of the figurines. Then Yabril and his cadre got into their van and started the drive to the Rome airport. Pope Innocent would not appear on the balcony until three hours later. They were on schedule.

In the van, closed off from the Easter world of Rome, Yabril thought about how this whole exercise had begun. . . .

On a mission together a few years before, Romeo had mentioned that the Pope had the heaviest security guard of any ruler in Europe. Yabril had laughed and said, "Who would want to kill a Pope? Like killing a snake that has no poison. A useless old figurehead and with a dozen useless old men ready to replace him. Bridegrooms of Christ, a set of a dozen red-capped dummies. What would change in the world with the death of a Pope? I can see kidnaping him, he's the richest man in the world. But killing him would be like killing a lizard sleeping in the sun."

Romeo had argued his case and intrigued Yabril. The Pope was revered by hundreds of millions of Catholics all over the world. And certainly the Pope was a symbol of capitalism; the bourgeois Western Christian states propped him up. The Pope was one of the great buttresses of authority in the edifice of that society. And so it followed that if the Pope was assassinated it would be a shocking psychological blow to the enemy world because he was considered the representative of God on earth. The royalty of Russia and

France had been murdered because they too thought they had the divine right to rule, and those murders had advanced humanity. God was the fraud of the rich, the swindler of the poor, the Pope an earthly wielder of that evil power. But still it was only half an idea. Yabril expanded the concept. Now the operation had a grandeur that awed Romeo and filled Yabril with self-admiration.

Romeo for all his talk and sacrifices was not what Yabril considered a true revolutionary. Yabril had studied the history of Italian terrorists. They were very good at assassinating heads of state; they had studied at the feet of the Russians, who had finally killed their Czar after many attempts—indeed the Italians had borrowed from the Russians the name that Yabril detested: the Christs of Violence.

Yabril had met Romeo's parents once. The father, a useless man, a parasite on humanity. Complete with chauffeur, valet and a great big lamblike dog that he used as bait to snare women on the boulevards. But a man with beautiful manners. It was impossible not to like him if you were not his son.

And the mother, another beauty of the capitalistic system, voracious for money and jewels, a devout Catholic. Beautifully dressed, maids in tow, she walked to mass every morning. That penance accomplished, she devoted the rest of her day to pleasure. Like her husband, she was self-indulgent, unfaithful, and devoted to their only son, Romeo.

So now this happy family would finally be punished. The father a Knight of Malta, the mother a daily communicant with Christ, and their son the murderer of the Pope. What a betrayal, Yabril thought. Poor Romeo, you will spend a bad week when I betray you.

Except for the final twist that Yabril had added, Romeo knew the whole plan. "Just like chess," Romeo said. "Check to the king, check to the king, and the checkmate. Beautiful."

Yabril looked at his watch, it would be another fifteen minutes. The van was going at moderate speed along the highway to the airport.

It was time to begin. He collected all the weapons and grenades from his cadre and put them in a suitcase. When the van stopped in front of the airport terminal, Yabril got out first. The van went on to discharge the rest of the cadre at another entrance. Yabril walked through the terminal slowly, carrying the suitcase, his eyes searching for undercover security police. Just short of the checkpoint, he walked into a gift and flower shop. A CLOSED sign in bright red and green letters hung on a peg inside the door. This was a signal that it was safe to enter and also that the shop would be kept clear of customers.

The woman in the shop was a dyed blonde with heavy makeup and quite ordinary looks, but with a warm inviting voice and a lush body shown to advantage in a plain woolen dress belted severely at the waist.

"I'm sorry," she said to Yabril. "But you can see by the sign that we are closed. It is Easter Sunday, after all." But her voice was friendly, not rejecting. She smiled warmly.

Yabril gave her the code sentence, designed merely for recognition. "Christ is risen but I must still travel on business." She reached out and took the suitcase from his hand.

"Is the plane on time?" Yabril asked.

"Yes," the woman said. "You have an hour. Are there any changes?"

"No," Yabril said. "But remember, everything depends on you." Then he went out. He had never seen the woman before and would never see her again and she knew only about this phase of the operation. He checked the schedules on the departure board. Yes, the plane would leave on time.

The woman was one of the few female members of the First Hundred. She had been planted in the shop three years ago as owner, and during that time she had carefully and seductively built up relationships with airline terminal personnel and security guards. Her practice of bypassing the scanners at the checkpoints to deliver parcels to people on planes was cleverly established. She had done it not too often but just often enough. In the third year she began an affair with one of the armed guards, who could wave her through the unscanned entry. Her lover was on guard duty this day; she had promised him lunch and a siesta in the back room of her shop. And so he had volunteered for the Easter Sunday duty.

The lunch was already laid out on the table in the back room when she emptied the suitcase to pack the weapons in gaily colored Gucci gift boxes. She put the boxes into mauve paper shopping bags and waited until twenty minutes before departure time. Then, cradling the bag in her arms because it was so heavy and she was afraid the paper might break, she ran awkwardly toward the unscanned entry corridor. Her lover on guard duty waved her through gallantly. She gave him a brilliantly affectionate smile. As she boarded the plane the stewardess recognized her and said with a laugh, "Again, Livia." The woman walked through the tourist section until she saw Yabril seated with the three men and three women of his cadre beside him. One of the women raised her arms to accept the heavy package.

The woman known as Livia dropped the bag into those waiting arms and then turned and ran out of the plane. She went back to the shop and finished preparing lunch in the back room.

The security guard, Faenzi, was one of those magnificent specimens of Italian manhood who seemed deliberately created to delight womanhood. That he was handsome was the least of his virtues. More important, he was one of those sweet-tempered men who are totally satisfied with the range of their talents and the scope of their ambition. Faenzi wore his airport uniform as grandly as a Napoleonic field marshal; his mustache was as neat and pretty as the tilted nose of a soubrette. You could see that he believed he had a significant job, an important duty to the state. He viewed passing women fondly and benevolently, because they were under his protection. The woman Livia had spotted him almost immediately on his first day of duty as a security guard in the airport, and marked him as her own. At first he had treated her with an exquisitely filial courtliness, but she had soon put an end to that with a torrent of flirtatious flattery, a few charming gifts that hinted at hidden wealth, and then evening snacks in her boutique at night. Now he loved her or was at least as devoted to her as a dog is to an indulgent master—she was a source of treats.

And Livia enjoyed him. He was a wonderful and cheerful lover without a serious thought in his head. She much preferred him in bed to those gloomy young revolutionaries consumed with guilt, belabored by conscience.

He became her pet and she fondly called him Zonzi. When he entered the shop and locked the door, she went to him with the utmost affection and desire, but she had a bad conscience. Poor Zonzi, the Italian antiterrorist branch would track everything down, and note her disappearance from the scene. Zonzi had undoubtedly boasted of his conquest—after all, she was an older and experienced woman, her honor need not be protected. Their connection would be uncovered. Poor Zonzi, this lunch would be his last hour of happiness.

Quickly and expertly on her part, enthusiastically and joyfully on his, they made love. Livia pondered the irony that here was an act that she thoroughly enjoyed and yet served her purposes as a revolutionary woman. Zonzi would be punished for his pride and his presumption, his condescending love for an older woman; she would achieve a tactical and strategic victory. And yet poor Zonzi. How beautiful he was naked, the olive skin, the large doelike eyes and jet-black hair, the pretty mustache, the penis and balls firm as bronze. "Ah, Zonzi, Zonzi," she whispered into his thighs, "always remember that I love you."

She fed him a marvelous meal, they drank a superior bottle of wine and then they made love again. Zonzi dressed, kissed her good-bye, and glowed with the belief that he truly deserved such good fortune. After he left she took a long look around the shop. She gathered all her belongings together with some extra clothes and used Yabril's suitcase to carry them. That had been part of the instructions. There should be no trace of Yabril. Her last task was to erase all the obvious fingerprints she might have left in the shop, but that was just a token task. She would probably not get all of them. Then carrying the suitcase, she went out, locked up the shop, and walked out of the terminal. Outside in the brilliant Easter sunshine, a woman of her own cadre was waiting with a car. She got into it, gave the driver a brief kiss of greeting and said almost regretfully, "Thank God, that's the end of that." The other woman said, "It wasn't so bad. We made money on the shop."

Yabril and his cadre were in the tourist section because Theresa Kennedy, daughter of the President of the United

States, was traveling first class with her six-man Secret Service security detail. Yabril did not want the delivery of the gift-wrapped weapons to be seen by them. He also knew that Theresa Kennedy would not get on the plane until just before takeoff, that the security guards would not be on the plane beforehand because they never knew when Theresa Kennedy would change her mind and, Yabril thought, because they had become lazy and careless.

The plane, a jumbo jet, was far from fully occupied. Not many people in Italy choose to travel on Easter Sunday, and Yabril wondered why the President's daughter was doing so. After all, she was a Roman Catholic, though lapsed into the new religion of the liberal left, that most despicable political division. But the sparsity of passengers suited his plans—a hundred hostages, easier to control.

An hour later, with the plane in the air, Yabril slumped down in his seat as the women began tearing the Gucci paper off the packages. The three men of the cadre used their bodies as shields, leaning over the seats and talking to the women. As there were no passengers seated near them, they had a small circle of privacy. The women handed Yabril the grenades wrapped in gift paper and he adorned his body with them quickly. The three men accepted the small handguns and hid them inside their jackets. Yabril also took a small handgun, and the three women armed themselves.

When all was ready, Yabril intercepted a stewardess going down the aisle. She saw the grenades and the gun even before Yabril whispered his commands and took her by the hand. The look of amazement, then shock, then fear was familiar to him. He held her clammy hand and smiled. Two of his men positioned themselves to command the tourist section. Yabril still held the stewardess by the hand as they entered first class. The Secret Service bodyguards saw him immedi-

ately, took note of the grenades and saw the guns. Yabril
smiled at them. "Remain seated, gentlemen," he said. The
President's daughter slowly turned her head and gazed into
Yabril's eyes. Her face became taut but not frightened. She
is brave, Yabril thought, and handsome. It was really a pity.
He waited until the three women of the cadre had taken their
positions in the first-class cabin and then had the stewardess
open the door leading to the pilots' cockpit. Yabril felt he
was entering the brain of a huge whale and making the rest
of the body helpless.

When Theresa Kennedy first saw Yabril, her body suddenly
shook with the nausea of unconscious recognition. He was
the demon she had been warned against. There was a ferocity
in his narrow dark face; its brutal, massive lower jaw gave
it the quality of a face in a nightmare. The grenades strung
over his jacket and in his hand looked like squat green toads.
Then she saw the three women dressed in dark trousers and
white jackets with the large steel guns in their hands. After
that first shock, Theresa Kennedy's second reaction was that
of a guilty child. Shit, she had gotten her father into trouble;
she would never ever be able to get rid of her Secret Service
security detail. She watched Yabril go to the door of the
pilots' cabin holding the stewardess by the hand. She turned
her head to exchange a look with the chief of her security
detail, but he was watching the armed women very intently.

At that moment one of Yabril's men came into the first-
class cabin holding a grenade in his hand. One of the women
made another stewardess pick up the intercom. The voice
came over the phone. It quavered only slightly. "All passengers, fasten your seat belts. The plane has been comman-
deered by a revolutionary group. Please remain calm and
await further instructions. Do not stand up. Do not touch

your hand luggage. Do not leave your seats for any reason. Please remain calm. Remain calm."

In the cockpit the pilot saw the stewardess enter and said to her excitedly, "Hey, the radio just said somebody shot at the Pope." Then he saw Yabril enter behind the stewardess and his mouth opened into a silent "O" of surprise, words frozen there just as in a cartoon, Yabril thought, as he raised his hand that held the grenade. But the pilot had said, " . . . shot at the Pope." Did that mean Romeo had missed? Had the mission already failed? In any case Yabril had no alternative. He gave his orders to the pilot to change course and head for the Arab state of Sherhaben.

In the sea of humanity in St. Peter's Square, Romeo and his cadre floated to a corner backed by a stone wall, and formed their own island. Annee in her nun's habit stood directly in front of Romeo, gun ready beneath her habit. She had the responsibility to protect him, give him time for his shot. The other members of the cadre, in their religious disguises, formed a circle, a perimeter to give him space. They had three hours to wait before the Pope appeared.

Romeo leaned back against the stone wall, shuttered his eyes against the Easter-morning sun and quickly his mind ran over the rehearsed moves of the operation. When the Pope appeared, Romeo would tap the shoulder of the man on his left, who would then set off the radio signal device that would detonate the holy figurines on the opposite wall of the square. In that moment of the explosions he would take out his rifle and fire—the timing had to be exact so that his shot would seem to be a reverberation of the other explosions. Then he would drop the rifle, his monks and nuns would form a circle around him and they would flee with the others. The figurines were also smoke bombs, and St. Peter's Square would be enveloped by dense clouds. There would be enormous confusion and there would be panic. With all this he should be able to make his escape. Those spectators near him in the crowd might be dangerous, for they would be aware of his actions, but the movement of the multitude in flight would soon separate them. Those who were foolhardy enough to persist in pursuing him would be gunned down.

Romeo could feel the cold sweat on his chest. The vast crowd waving flowers aloft became a sea of white and purple, pink and red. He wondered at their joy, their belief in the Resurrection, their ecstasy of hope against death. He wiped his hands against the outside of his coat and felt the weight of his rifle in its sling. He could feel his legs begin to ache and go numb. He sent his mind outside his body to pass the long hours he would have to wait for the Pope to appear on his balcony.

Lost scenes from his childhood formed again. Tutored for confirmation by a romantic priest, he knew that a red-hatted senior cardinal always certified the death of a Pope by tapping him on the forehead with a silver mallet. Was that still really done? It would be a very bloody mallet this time. But how big would such a mallet be? Toy-sized? Heavy and big enough to drive a nail? But of course it would be a precious relic from the Renaissance, encrusted with jewels, a work of art. No matter, there would be very little of the Pope's head left to tap; the rifle under his coat held explosive bullets. And Romeo was sure he would not miss. He believed in his left-handedness, to be *mancino* was to be successful, in sports, in love and, certainly by every superstition, in murder.

As he waited, Romeo wondered that he had no sense of sacrilege—after all, he had been brought up a strict Catholic in a city whose every street and building reminded one of the beginnings of Christianity. Even now he could see the domed roofs on holy buildings like marble disks against the sky, hear the deep consoling yet intimidating bells of churches. In this great hallowed square he could see the statues of martyrs, smell the very air choked with the countless spring flowers offered by true believers in Christ.

The overpowering fragrance of the multitudinous flowers washed over him and he was reminded of his mother and father and the heavy scents they always wore to mask the odor of their plush and pampered Mediterranean flesh.

And then the vast crowd in their Easter finery began shouting *"Papa, Papa, Papa!"* Standing in the lemon light of early spring, stone angels above their heads, the people chanted incessantly for the blessing of their Pope. Finally two red-robed cardinals appeared and stretched out their arms in benediction. Then Pope Innocent was on the balcony.

He was a very old man dressed in a chasuble of glittering white; on it was a cross of gold, the woolly pallium, embroidered with crosses. On his head was a white skullcap and on his feet the traditional low, open red shoes, gold crosses embroidered on their fronts. On one of the hands raised to greet the crowd was the pontifical fisherman's ring of Saint Peter.

The multitude sent their flowers up into the sky, the voices roared in ecstasy, the balcony shimmered in the sun as if to fall with the descending flowers.

At that moment Romeo felt the dread these symbols had always inspired in his youth, recalling the red-hatted cardinal of his confirmation, who was pockmarked like the Devil, and then he felt an elation that lifted his whole being into bliss, ultimate joy. Romeo tapped the shoulder of the man on his left to send the radio signal.

The Pope raised his white-sleeved arms to answer the cries of "*Papa, Papa!*" to bless them all, to praise the Eastertide, the Resurrection of Christ, to salute the stone angels that rode around the walls. Romeo slid his rifle out from beneath his coat; two monks of his cadre in front of him knelt to give him a clear view. Annee placed herself so that he could lay his rifle across her shoulder. The man on his left flashed the radio signal that would set off the mined figurines on the other side of the square.

The explosions rocked the foundations of the square, a cloud of pink floated in the air, the fragrance of the flowers turned rotten with the stench of burnt flesh. And at that moment Romeo, rifle sighted, pulled the trigger. The explosions on the other side of the square changed the welcoming roar of the crowd to what sounded like the shrieking of countless gulls.

On the balcony the body of the Pope seemed to rise up off the ground, the white skullcap flew into the air, swirled in the violent winds of compressed air and then drifted down into the crowd, a bloody rag. A wail of horror, of terror and animal rage, filled the square as the body of the Pope slumped over the balcony rail. His cross of gold dangled free, the pallium drenched red.

Clouds of stone dust rolled over the square. Marble fragments of shattered angels and saints fell. There was a terrible silence, the crowd frozen by the sight of the murdered Pope. They could see his head blown apart. Then the panic began. The people fled from the square, trampling the Swiss Guards who were trying to seal off the exits. The gaudy Renaissance uniforms were buried by the mass of terror-stricken worshipers.

Romeo let his rifle drop to the ground. Surrounded by his cadre of armed monks and nuns, he let himself be swept out of the square into the streets of Rome. He seemed to have lost his vision and staggered blindly; Annee grasped him by the arm and thrust him into the waiting van. Romeo held his hands over his ears to shut out the screams; he was shaking with shock, and then with a sense of exaltation followed by a sense of wonder, as if the murder had been a dream.

On the jumbo jet scheduled from Rome to New York, Yabril and his cadre were in full control, the first-class section cleared of all passengers except Theresa Kennedy.

Theresa was now more interested than frightened. She was fascinated that the hijackers had so easily cowed her Secret Service detail by simply showing detonation devices all over their bodies, which meant that any bullet fired would send the plane flying into bits through the skies. She noted that the three men and three women were very slender with faces screwed up in the tension shown by great athletes in moments of intense competition. A male hijacker gave one of her Secret Service agents a violent push out of the first-class cabin and kept pushing him down the open aisle of the tourist section. One of the female hijackers kept her distance, her gun at the ready. When a Secret Service agent showed some reluctance to leave Theresa's side, the woman raised her gun and pressed the barrel to his head. And her squinting eyes showed plainly she was about to shoot; her lips were parted slightly to relieve pressure from the clenching of the muscles around her mouth. At that moment Theresa pushed her guard away and put her own body in front of the woman hijacker, who smiled with relief and waved her into the seat.

Theresa watched Yabril supervise the operation. He seemed almost distant, as if he were a director watching his actors perform, not seeming to give orders but providing only hints, suggestions. With a slight reassuring smile he motioned that she should keep to her seat. It was the action of a man looking after someone who had been put in his special care. Then he went into the pilots' cabin. One of the male hijackers guarded the entry into first class from the tourist cabin. Two women hijackers stood back to back in the section with Theresa, guns at the ready. There was a stewardess manning the intercom phone that relayed messages to the passengers under the direction of the male hijacker. They all looked too small to cause such terror.

In the cockpit Yabril gave the pilot permission to radio that his plane had been hijacked and relay the new flight plan to Sherhaben. The American authorities would think their only problem was negotiating the usual Arab terrorist demands. Yabril stayed in the cabin to listen to the radio traffic.

As the plane flew on there was nothing to do but wait. Yabril dreamed of Palestine, as it had been when he was a child, his home a green oasis in the desert, his father and mother angels of light, the beautiful Koran as it rested on his father's desk always ready to renew faith. And how it had all finished in dead gray rolls of smoke, fire and the brimstone of bombs falling from the air. And the Israelis had come, and it seemed as if his whole childhood was spent in some great prison camp of ramshackle huts, a vast settlement united in only one thing, their hatred of the Jews. Those very same Jews that the Koran praised.

He remembered how even at the university some of the teachers spoke of a botched job as "Arab work." Yabril himself had used the phrase to a gunmaker who had given him defective weapons. Ah, but they would not call this day's business "Arab work."

He had always hated the Jews—no, not the Jews, the Israelis. He remembered when he was a child of four, maybe five, not older, the soldiers of Israel had raided the settlement camp in which he went to school. They had received false information, "Arab work," that the settlement was hiding terrorists. All the inhabitants had been ordered out of their houses and into the streets, with their hands up. Including the children in the long yellow-painted tin hut that was the school and lay just a little outside the settlement. Yabril with other small boys and girls his age had clustered together wailing, their little arms and hands high in the air, screaming their surrender, screaming in terror. And Yabril always remembered one of the young Israeli soldiers, the new breed of Jew, blond as a Nazi, looking at the children with a sort of horror, and then the fair skin of that alien Semite's face was streaming with tears. The Israeli lowered his gun and shouted at the children to stop, to put down their hands. They had nothing to fear, he said, little children had nothing to fear. The Israeli soldier spoke almost perfect Arabic, and when the children still stood with their arms held high, the soldier strode among them trying to pull down their arms, weeping all the while. Yabril never forgot the soldier, and resolved, later in life, never to be like him, never to let pity destroy him.

Now, looking below, he could see the deserts of Arabia. Soon the flight would come to an end and he would be in the Sultanate of Sherhaben.

Sherhaben was one of the smallest countries in the world but had such an abundance of oil that its camel-riding Sultan's hundreds of children and grandchildren all drove Mercedeses and were educated at the finest universities abroad. The original Sultan had owned huge industrial companies in Germany and the United States and had died the single most wealthy person in the world. Only one of his grandchildren had survived the murderous intrigues of half brothers and become the present Sultan—Maurobi.

The Sultan Maurobi was a militant and fanatically devout Muslim, and the citizens of Sherhaben, now rich, were equally devout. No woman could go without a veil; no money could be loaned for interest; there was not a drop of liquor in that thirsty desert land except at the foreign embassies.

Long ago Yabril had helped the Sultan establish and consolidate power by assassinating four of the Sultan's more dangerous half brothers. Because of these debts of gratitude, and because of his own hatred of the great powers, the Sultan had agreed to help Yabril in this operation.

The plane carrying Yabril and his hostages landed and rolled slowly toward the small glass-encircled terminal, pale yellow in the desert sun. Beyond the airfield was an endless stretch of sand studded with oil rigs. When the plane came to a stop, Yabril could see that the airfield was surrounded by at least a thousand of Sultan Maurobi's troops.

Now the most intricate and satisfying part of the operation, and the most dangerous, would begin. He would have to be careful until Romeo was finally in place. And he would be gambling on the Sultan's reaction to his secret and final checkmate. No, this was not Arab's work.

Because of the European time difference Francis Kennedy received the first report of the shooting of the Pope at 6:00 A.M. Easter Sunday. It was given to him by Press Secretary Matthew Gladyce, who had the White House watch for the holiday. Eugene Dazzy and Christian Klee had already been informed and were in the White House.

Francis Kennedy came down the stairs from his living quarters and entered the Oval Office to find Dazzy and Christian waiting for him. They both looked grim. Far away on the streets of Washington there were long screams of sirens. Kennedy sat down behind his desk. He looked at Eugene Dazzy, who as chief of staff would do the briefing.

"Francis, the Pope is dead. He was assassinated during the Easter service."

Kennedy was shocked. "Who did it? And why?"

Klee said, "We don't know. There's even worse news."

Kennedy tried to read the faces of the men who stood before him, feeling a deep sense of dread. "What could be worse?"

"The plane Theresa is on has been hijacked and is now on its way to Sherhaben," Klee said.

Francis Kennedy felt a wave of nausea hit him. Then he heard Eugene Dazzy say, "The hijackers have everything under control, there are no incidents on the plane. As soon as it lands we'll negotiate, we'll call in all our favors, it will come out OK. I don't think they even knew Theresa was on the plane."

Christian said, "Arthur Wix and Otto Gray are on their way in. So are CIA, Defense, and the Vice President. They will all be waiting for you in the Cabinet Room within the half hour."

"OK," Kennedy said. He forced himself to be calm. "Is there any connection?" he said.

He saw that Christian was not surprised but that Dazzy didn't get it. "Between the Pope and the hijacking," Kennedy said. When neither of them answered, he said, "Wait for me in the Cabinet Room. I want a few moments by myself." They left.

Kennedy himself was almost invulnerable to assassins, but he had always known he could never fully protect his daughter. She was too independent, she would not permit him to restrict her life. And it had not seemed a serious danger. He could not recall that the daughter of the head of a nation had ever been attacked. It was a bad political and public relations move for any terrorist or revolutionary organization.

After her father's inauguration Theresa had gone her own way, lending her name to radical and feminist political groups, while stating her own position in life as distinct from her father's. He had never tried to persuade her to act differently, to present to the public an image false to herself. It was enough that he loved her. And when she visited the White House for a brief stay, they always had a good time together arguing politics, dissecting the uses of power.

The conservative Republican press and the disreputable tabloids had taken their shots, hoping to damage the presidency. Theresa was photographed marching with feminists, demonstrating against nuclear weapons and once even marching for a homeland for Palestinians. Which would now inspire ironic columns in the papers.

Oddly enough, the American public responded to Theresa Kennedy with affection, even when it became known she was living with an Italian radical in Rome. There were pictures of them strolling the ancient streets of stone, kissing and holding hands; pictures of the balcony of the flat they shared. The young Italian lover was handsome; Theresa was pretty in her blondness with her pale milky Irish skin and the Kennedy satiny blue eyes. And her almost lanky Kennedy frame draped in casual Italian clothes made her so appealing that the caption beneath the photographs was drained of poison.

A news photo of her shielding her young Italian lover from Italian police clubs brought back long-buried feelings in older Americans, memories of that long-ago terrible day in Dallas.

She was a witty heroine. During the campaign she had been cornered by TV reporters and asked, "So you agree with your father politically?" If she answered "yes" she would appear a hypocrite or a child manipulated by a power-hungry father. If she answered "no," the headlines would indicate that she did not support her father in his race for the presidency. But she showed the Kennedy political genius. "Sure, he's my dad," she said, hugging her father. "And I know he's a good guy. But if he does something I don't like I'll yell at him just as you reporters do." It came off great on the tube. Her father loved her for it. And now she was in mortal danger.

If only she had remained close to him, if only she had been more of a loving daughter and lived with him at the White House, if only she had been less radical, none of this would be happening. And why did she have to have a foreign lover, a student radical who perhaps had given the hijacker crucial information? And then he laughed at himself. He was feeling the exasperation of a parent who wanted his child to be as little trouble as possible. He loved her, and he would save her. At least this was something he could fight against, not like the terrible long and painful death of his wife.

Now Eugene Dazzy appeared and told him it was time. They were waiting for him in the Cabinet Room.

When Kennedy entered, everyone stood up. He quickly motioned for them to be seated, but they surged around him to offer their sympathy. Kennedy made his way to the head of the long oval table and sat in the chair near the fireplace.

Two pure-white-light chandeliers bleached the rich brown of the table, glistened the black of the leather chairs, six to each side of the table, and more chairs along the back of the far wall. And there were other sconces of white light that shone from the walls. Next to the two windows that opened to the Rose Garden were two flags, the striped flag of the

United States and the flag of the President, a field of deep blue filled with pale stars.

Kennedy's staff took the seats nearest him, resting their information logs and memorandum sheets on the oval table. Farther down were the Cabinet members and the head of the CIA, and at the other end of the table, the chairman of the Joint Chiefs of Staff, an Army general in full uniform, a gaudy color cutout in the somberly dressed group. Vice President Du Pray sat at the far side of the table, away from Kennedy, the only woman in the room. She wore a fashionable dark blue suit with a white silk blouse. Her handsome face was stern. The fragrance of the Rose Garden filled the room, seeping through the heavy curtains and drapes that covered glass-paneled doors. Below the drapes the aquamarine rug reflected green light into the room.

It was the CIA chief, Theodore Tappey, who gave the briefing. Tappey, who had once been head of the FBI, was not flamboyant or politically ambitious. And had never exceeded the CIA charter with risky, illegal or empire-building schemes. He had a great deal of credit with Kennedy's personal staff, especially Christian Klee.

"In the few hours we had, we've come up with some hard information," Tappey said. "The killing of the Pope was carried out by an all-Italian cadre. The hijacking of Theresa's plane was done by a mixed team led by an Arab who goes by the name Yabril. The fact that both incidents happened on the same day and originated in the same city seems to be coincidence. Which, of course, we must always mistrust."

Kennedy said softly, "At this moment the killing of the Pope is not primary. Our main concern is the hijacking. Have they made any demands yet?"

Tappey said quickly and firmly, "No. That's an odd circumstance in itself."

Kennedy said, "Get your contacts on negotiation and report to me personally at every step." He turned to the Secretary of State and asked, "What countries will help us?"

The Secretary said, "Everyone—the other Arab states are horrified, they despise the idea of your daughter being held hostage. It offends their sense of honor and also they think of their own custom of the blood feud. They believe they cannot derive any good from this. France has a good relationship with the Sultan. They offered to send in observers for us. Britain and Israel can't help—they are not trusted. But until the hijackers make their demands we're sort of in limbo."

Kennedy turned to Christian. "Chris, how do you figure it, they're not making demands?"

Christian said, "It may be too early. Or they have another card to play."

The Cabinet Room was eerie in silence; in the blackness of the many high heavy chairs the white sconces of light on the walls turned the skin of the people in the room into a very light gray. Kennedy waited for them to speak, all of them, and he closed down his mind when they spoke of options, the threat of sanctions, the threat of a naval blockade, the freezing of Sherhaben assets in the United States—the expectation that the hijackers would extend the negotiation interminably to milk the TV time and news reports all over the world.

After a time Kennedy turned to Oddblood Gray and said abruptly, "Schedule a meeting with the congressional leaders, the relevant committee chairmen, for me and my staff." Then he turned to Arthur Wix. "Get your national security staff working on plans if this thing turns into something wider." Then Kennedy stood up to leave. He addressed them all. "Gentlemen," he said, "I must tell you I don't believe in coincidence. I don't believe the Pope of the Roman Catholic Church can be murdered on the same day in the same city that the daughter of the President of the United States is kidnaped."

Adam Gresse and Henry Tibbot had put aside Easter Sunday as a day of work. Not on their scientific projects but on cleaning up all traces of their crime. In their apartment, they bundled up all their old newspapers from which they had cut letters to compose their message. They vacuumed to remove the tiny fragments of scissored papers. They even got rid of the scissors and glue. They washed down the walls. Then they went to their university workshop to get rid of all the tools and equipment they had used to construct their bomb. It did not occur to them to turn on the television until their task was completed. When they heard the news of the killing of the Pope and the kidnaping of the President's daughter, they looked at each other and smiled. Adam Gresse said, "Henry, I think our time has come."

It was a long Easter Sunday. The White House was filling up with staff personnel of the different action committees set up by the CIA, the Army and the Navy, and the State Department. They all agreed that the most baffling fact was that the terrorists had not yet made their demands for the release of the hostages.

Outside, the streets were congested with traffic. Newspaper and TV reporters were flocking into Washington. Government staff workers had been called to their desks despite its being Easter. And Christian Klee had ordered a thousand extra men from the Secret Service and the FBI to provide additional protection for the White House.

The telephone traffic in the White House increased in

volume. There was bedlam, people rushing to and fro from the White House to the Executive Office Building. Eugene Dazzy tried to bring everything under control.

The rest of that Sunday in the White House consisted of Kennedy's receiving reports from the Situation Room, long solemn conferences on what options were open, telephone conversations between heads of foreign countries and the Cabinet members of the United States.

Late Sunday night the President's staff had dinner with him and prepared for the next day. They monitored the TV news reports, which were continuous.

Finally, Kennedy decided to go to bed. He was confident that his staff would keep vigil throughout the night and wake him when necessary. A Secret Service man led the way as Kennedy went up the small stairway that led to the living quarters on the fourth floor of the White House. Another Secret Service man trailed behind. They both knew that the President hated to take the elevators in the White House.

The top of the stairs opened into a lounge, which held a communications desk and two more Secret Service men. When he passed through that lounge, Kennedy was in his own living quarters, with only his personal servants: a maid, a butler and a valet, whose duty it was to keep track of the extensive presidential wardrobe.

What Kennedy did not know was that even these personal servants were members of the Secret Service. Christian Klee had invented this setup. It was part of his overall plan to keep the President free from all harm, part of the intricate shield Christian had woven around Francis Kennedy.

When Christian had put this wrinkle into the security system he had briefed the special platoon of Secret Service men and women. "You're going to be the best goddamn personal servants in the world, and you can go straight from here and get a job in Buckingham Palace. You already know your first duty is to take any bullets thrown at the President. But it will be as much your duty to make the private life of the President comfortable."

The chief of the special platoon was the manservant on duty this night. Ostensibly he was a black naval steward named Jefferson with the rank of chief petty officer. Actually he had top rank in the Secret Service and was exceptionally well trained in hand-to-hand combat. He was a natural athlete and had been a college all-American in football. And his IQ was 160. He also had a sense of humor, which made him take a special delight in becoming the perfect servant.

Now Jefferson helped Kennedy take off his jacket and hung it up carefully. He handed Kennedy a silk dressing gown, as he had learned that the President did not like to be helped putting it on. When Kennedy went to the small bar in the living room of the suite, Jefferson was there before him, mixing a vodka with tonic and ice. Then Jefferson said, "Mr. President, your bath is drawn."

Kennedy looked at him with a little smile on his face. Jefferson was a little too good to be true. Kennedy said, "Please turn off all the phones. You can wake me personally if I'm needed."

He soaked in the hot bath for nearly a half hour. The tub's jets pounded his back and thighs and soothed the weariness out of his muscles. The bathwater had a pleasant masculine scent and the ledge around the tub was filled with an assortment of soaps, liniments and magazines. There was even a plastic basket that held a pile of memos.

When Kennedy came out of the bath, he put on a white terry-cloth robe that had a monogram in red, white and blue lettering that said THE BOSS. This was a gift from Jefferson himself, who thought it part of the character he was playing to give such a present. Francis Kennedy rubbed his white, almost hairless body with the robe to get himself dry. He had always been dissatisfied with the paleness of his skin and his lack of body hair.

In the bedroom, Jefferson had pulled the curtains closed and switched on the reading light. He had also turned down the bedcovers. There was a small marble-topped table with specially attached wheels near the bed and a comfortable armchair nearby. The table was covered with a beautifully embroidered pale rose cloth, and on it was a dark blue pitcher containing hot chocolate. Chocolate had already been poured into a cup of lighter cerulean blue. There was an intricately painted dish holding six varieties of biscuits. Comfortingly, there was a pure white crock of pale unsalted butter and four crocks of different colors for different jams: green for apple, blue spotted white for raspberry, yellow for marmalade and red for strawberry.

Kennedy said, "That looks great," and Jefferson left the room. For some reason these little attentions comforted Kennedy more than they should, he felt. He sat in the armchair and drank the chocolate, tried to finish a biscuit and could not. He rolled the table away and got into bed. He tried to read from a pile of memos, but he was too tired. He turned off the light and tried to sleep.

But through the muffling of the drapes he could very faintly hear a little of the immense noise that was building up outside the White House as the media of the whole world assembled to keep a twenty-four-hour-a-day watch. There would be dozens of communications vehicles for the TV cameras and crews. And a marine battalion was being set up as extra security.

Francis Kennedy felt that deep sense of foreboding that had come to him only once before in his life. He let himself think directly about his daughter, Theresa. She was sleeping on that plane, surrounded by murderous men. And it was not bad luck. Fate had given him many omens. His two uncles had been killed when he was a boy. And then just over three years ago his wife, Catherine, had died of cancer.

The first great defeat in Francis Kennedy's life was Catherine Kennedy's discovery of a lump in her breast six months before her husband won the nomination for President. After the diagnosis of cancer, Kennedy offered to withdraw from the political process, but she forbade him, saying she wanted to live in the White House. She would get well, she said, and her husband never doubted her. At first they worried about her losing her breast and Kennedy consulted cancer experts all over the world about a lumpectomy that could remove only the cancerous growth. One of the greatest cancer specialists in the United States looked at Catherine's medical file and encouraged removal of the breast. He said, and Francis Kennedy forever remembered the words, "It is a very aggressive strain of cancer."

She was on chemotherapy when he won the Democratic nomination for the presidency in July, and her doctors sent her home. She was in remission. She put on weight, her skeleton hid again behind a wall of flesh.

She rested a great deal, she could not leave the house, but she was always on her feet to greet him when he came home. Theresa went back to school, Kennedy went on the campaign trail. But he arranged his schedule so that he could fly home every few days to be with her. Each time he returned she seemed to be stronger, and those days were sweet, they had never loved each other more. He brought her gifts; she knitted him mufflers and gloves.

One time she gave the day off to the nurses and servants

so that she and her husband could be alone in the house, to enjoy the simple supper she had prepared. She was getting well. It was the happiest moment in his life, nothing could be measured against it. Kennedy wept tears of pure joy, relieved of anguish, of dread. The next morning they went for a walk in the green hills around their house, her arm around his waist. She had always been vain about her appearance, anxious about how she fitted into her new dresses, her bathing suits, the extra fold of flesh beneath her chin. But now she tried to put on weight. He felt each bone in her body when they walked with their arms entwined. When they returned he cooked her breakfast and she ate heartily, more than he ever remembered her eating.

Her remission gave Kennedy the energy to rise to the peak of his powers as he continued his campaign for the presidency. He swept everything before him; everything was malleable, to be shaped to his lucky destiny. His body generated enormous energy, his mind worked with a precision that was extraordinary.

And then on one of his trips home he was plunged into hell. Catherine was ill again, she was not there to greet him. And all his gifts and strength were meaningless.

Catherine had been the perfect wife for him. Not that she had been an extraordinary woman, but she had been one of those women who seem to be almost genetically gifted in the art of love. She had what seemed to be a natural sweetness of disposition that was remarkable. He had never heard her say a mean word about anyone; she forgave other people's faults, never felt herself slighted or done an injury. She never harbored resentments.

She was in all ways pleasing. She had a willowy body and her face had a tranquil beauty that inspired affection in nearly everyone. She had a weakness, of course: she loved beautiful clothes and was a little vain. But she could be teased about that. She was witty without being insulting or mordant and she was never depressed. She was well educated and had made her living as a journalist before she married, and she had other skills. She was a superb amateur pianist; she painted as a hobby. She had brought up her daughter well and they loved each other; she was understanding of her husband and never jealous of his achievements. She was one of those rare accidents, a contented and happy human being.

The day came when the doctor met Francis Kennedy in the corridor of the hospital and quite brutally and frankly told him that his wife must die. The doctor explained. There were holes in the bones of Catherine Kennedy's body, her skeleton would collapse. There were tumors in her brain, tiny now but inevitably they would expand. And her blood ruthlessly manufactured poisons to put her to death.

Francis Kennedy could not tell his wife this. He could not tell her because he could not believe it. He mustered all his resources, contacted all his powerful friends, even consulted the Oracle. There was one hope. At medical centers all around the United States there were research programs testing new and dangerous drugs, experimental programs available only to those who had been pronounced doomed. Since these new drugs were dangerously toxic, they were used only on volunteers. And there were so many doomed people that there were a hundred volunteers for each spot in the programs.

So Francis Kennedy committed what he would have ordinarily thought an immoral act. He used all his power to get his wife into these research programs; he pulled every string so that his wife could receive these lethal but possibly life-preserving poisons into her body. And he succeeded. He felt a new confidence. A few of the people had been cured in these research centers. Why not his wife? Why could he not save her? He had triumphed all his life, he would triumph now.

And then began a reign of darkness. At first it was a research program in Houston. He put her in a hospital there, and stayed with her for the treatment that so weakened her that she was helplessly bedridden. She made him leave her there so that he could continue campaigning for the presidency. He flew from Houston to Los Angeles to make his campaign speeches, confident, witty, cheerful. Then late at night he flew to Houston to spend a few hours with his wife. Then he flew to his next campaign stop to play the part of lawgiver.

The treatment in Houston failed. In Boston they cut the tumor from her brain and the operation was a success, though the tumor tested malignant. Malignant, too, were the new tumors in her lungs. The holes in her bones on X ray were larger. In another Boston hospital new drugs and protocols worked a miracle. The new tumor in her brain stopped growing, the tumors in her remaining breast shriveled. Every night Francis Kennedy flew from his campaign cities to spend a few hours with her, to read to her, to joke with her. Sometimes Theresa flew from her school in Los Angeles to visit her mother. Father and daughter dined together and then visited the patient in her hospital room to sit in the darkness with her. Theresa told funny stories of her adventures in school; Francis related his adventures on the campaign trail to the presidency. Catherine would laugh.

Of course Kennedy again offered to drop out of the campaign to be with his wife. Of course Theresa wanted to leave school to be with her mother constantly. But Catherine told them she would not, could not, bear their doing so. She might be ill for a long time. They must continue their lives. Only that could give her hope, only that could give her the strength to bear her torture. On this she could not be moved. She threatened to check out of the hospital and return home if they did not continue as if things were normal.

Francis, on the long trips through the night to her bedside, could only marvel at her tenacity. Catherine, her body filled with chemical poison fighting the poisons of her own body, clung fiercely to her belief that she would be well and that the two people she loved most in the world would not be dragged down with her.

Finally the nightmare seemed to end. Again she was in remission. Francis could take her home. They had been all over the United States; she had been in seven different hospitals with their protocols of experimental treatments, and the great flood of chemicals seemed to have worked, and Francis felt an exultation that he had succeeded once again. He took his wife home to Los Angeles, and then one night he, Catherine and Theresa went out to dinner before he resumed the campaign trail. It was a lovely summer night, the balmy California air caressing them. There was one strange moment. A waiter had spilled just a tiny drop of sauce from a dish on the sleeve of Catherine's new dress. She burst into tears, and when the waiter left she asked weeping, "Why did he have to do that to me?" This was so uncharacteristic of her—in former times she would have laughed such an incident away—that Francis Kennedy felt a strange foreboding. She had gone through the torture of all those operations, the removal of her breast, the excision from her brain, the pain of those growing tumors, and had never wept or complained. And now obviously this stain on her sleeve seemed to sink into her heart. She was inconsolable.

The next day Kennedy had to fly to New York to campaign. In the morning Catherine made him his breakfast. She was radiant, and her beauty seemed greater than ever. All the newspapers had polls that showed Kennedy was in the lead, that he would win the presidency. Catherine read them aloud. "Oh, Francis," she said, "we'll live in the White House and I'll have my own staff. And Theresa can bring her friends to stay for weekends and vacations. Think how happy we'll be. And I won't get sick again. I promise. You'll do great things, Francis, I know you will." She put her arms around him and wept with happiness and love. "I'll help," Catherine said. "We'll walk through all those lovely rooms together and I'll help you make your plans. You'll be the greatest President. I'm going to be all right, darling, and I'll have so much to do. We'll be so happy. We'll be so good. We're so lucky. Aren't we lucky?"

She died in autumn, October light became her shroud. Francis Kennedy stood among fading green hills and wept. Silver trees veiled the horizon, and in dumb agony he closed his eyes with his own hands to shut out the world. And in that moment without light, he felt the core of his mind break.

And some priceless cell of energy fled. It was the first time in his life that his extraordinary intelligence was worth nothing. His wealth meant nothing. His political power, his position in the world meant nothing. He could not save his wife from death. And therefore it all became nothing.

He took his hands away from his eyes and with a supreme effort of will fought against the nothingness. He reassembled what was left of his world, summoned power to fight against grief. There was less than a month to go before the election and he made the final effort.

He entered the White House without his wife, with only his daughter, Theresa. Theresa, who had tried to be happy but who had wept all that first night because her mother could not be with them.

And now, three years after his wife's death, Francis Kennedy, President of the United States, one of the most powerful men on earth, was alone in his bed, fearful for his daughter's life, and unable to command sleep.

Sleep forbidden, he tried to stave off the terror that kept him from sleep. He told himself the hijackers would not dare harm Theresa, that his daughter would come safely home. In this he was not powerless—he did not have to rely on the weak, fallible gods of medicine, he did not have to fight invincible cancerous cells. No. He could save his daughter's life. He could bend the power of his country, spend its authority. It all rested in his hands and thank God he had no political scruples. His daughter was the only thing he had left on this earth that he really loved. He would save her.

But then anxiety, a wave of such fear it seemed to stop his heart, made him put on the light above his head. He rose and sat in the armchair. He pulled the marble table close and sipped the residue of cold chocolate from his cup.

He believed that the plane had been hijacked because his daughter was on it. The hijacking was possible because of the vulnerability of established authority to a few determined, ruthless and possibly high-minded terrorists. And it had been inspired by the fact that he, Francis Kennedy, President of the United States, was the prominent symbol of that established authority. So by his desire to be President of the United States, he, Francis Kennedy, was responsible for placing his daughter in danger.

Again he heard the doctor's words: "It is an extremely aggressive strain of cancer," but now he understood their full implication. Everything was more dangerous than it appeared. This was a night when he must plan, to defend; he had the power to turn fate aside. Sleep would never come to the chambers of his brain so sown with mines.

What had been his wish? To arrive at a successful destiny of the Kennedy name? But he had been only a cousin. He remembered his great-uncle Joseph Kennedy, legendary womanizer, one who amassed gold, a mind so sharp for the instant but so blind to the future. He remembered Old Joe fondly, though he would have been Francis Kennedy's opposite politically if he were alive today. Old Joe had given Francis gold pieces for his early birthdays and set up a trust fund for him. What a selfish life the man had led, screwing Hollywood stars, lifting his sons high. Never mind that he had been a political dinosaur. And what a tragic end. A lucky life until the last chapter: the murder of his two sons, so young, so highly placed. The old man defeated, a final stroke exploding his brain.

Making your son President—could a father have greater joy? And had the old kingmaker sacrificed his sons for nothing? Had the gods punished him not so much for his pride but for his pleasure? Or was it all accident? His sons Jack and Robert, so rich, so handsome, so gifted, killed by those powerless nobodies who wrote themselves into history with the murder of their betters. No, there could be no purpose, it was all accident. So many little things could turn fate aside, tiny precautions reverse the course of tragedy.

And yet—and yet there was the odd feeling of doom. Why the linking of the Pope's killer and the kidnaping of the President's daughter? Why the delay before stating their demands? What other strings in the labyrinth were there to be played out? And all this from a man he had never heard of, a mysterious Arab named Yabril, and an Italian youth named, in scornful irony, Romeo.

In the darkness he was terrified at how it all might end.

He felt the familiar always-suppressed rage, the dread. He remembered the agonizing day when he had heard the first whisper that his uncle Jack was dead, and his mother's long terrible scream.

Then, mercifully, the chambers of his brain unlocked, his memories fled. He fell asleep in his armchair.

CHAPTER
3

THE MEMBER OF the President's staff with the most influence on Kennedy was the Attorney General. Christian Klee had been born into a wealthy family stretching back into the first days of the republic. His trust funds were now worth over a hundred million dollars, thanks to the guidance and advice of his godfather, the Oracle, Oliver Oliphant. He had never wanted for anything, and there had come a time when he wanted nothing. He had too much intelligence, too much energy to become another of the idle rich who invest in movies, chase women, abuse drugs and booze or descend into a religious viciousness. Two men, the Oracle and Francis Xavier Kennedy, led him finally into politics.

Christian first met Kennedy at Harvard, not as fellow undergraduates but as teacher and student. Kennedy had been the youngest professor to teach law at Harvard. In his twenties, he had been a prodigy. Christian still remembered that opening lecture. Kennedy had begun with the words: "Everybody knows or has heard of the majesty of the law. It is the power of the state to control the existing political organization that permits civilization to exist. That is true. Without the rule of law, we are all lost. But remember this, the law is also full of shit."

Then he had smiled at his student audience. "I can get around any law you may write. The law can be twisted out of shape to serve a wicked civilization. The rich can escape the law and sometimes even the poor get lucky. Some lawyers treat the law the way pimps treat their women. Judges sell the law, courts betray it. All true. But remember this, we have nothing better that works. There is no other way we can make a social contract with our fellow human beings."

When Christian Klee graduated from Harvard Law School he had not the faintest idea of what to do with his life. Nothing interested him. He was worth millions, but he had no interest in money, nor did he have a real interest in the law. He had the usual romanticism of a young man.

Women liked him. He had a smudged handsomeness— that is, classic features just slightly askew. A Dr. Jekyll beginning to turn into Mr. Hyde, but you would notice that only when he was angry. He had the exquisite courtesy attained by the patrician rich in their early schooling. Despite all this he commanded an instinctual respect from other men, because of his extraordinary gifts. He was the iron fist in Kennedy's velvet glove, but had the intelligence and courtesy to keep it hidden from public view. He liked women, had brief affairs but could not summon up that feeling of true belief in love that leads to a passionate attachment. He was desperately looking for something to commit his life to. He was interested in the arts, but had no creative drive, no talent for painting, music, writing. He was paralyzed by his security in society. He was not so much unhappy as bewildered.

He had, of course, tried drugs for a brief period; they were, after all, as integral a part of American culture as they had once been of the Chinese empire. And for the first time he discovered a startling thing about himself. He could not bear the loss of control that drugs caused. He did not mind being unhappy as long as he had control of his mind and body. Loss of that control was the ultimate in despair. And the drugs did not even make him feel the ecstasy that other people felt. So at the age of twenty-two with everything in the world at his feet, he could not feel that anything was worth doing. He did not even feel what many young men felt, a desire to improve the world he lived in.

He consulted his godfather, the Oracle, then a "young" man of seventy-five, who still had an inordinate appetite for life, who kept three mistresses busy, who had a finger in every business pie and who conferred with the President of the United States at least once a week. The Oracle had the secret of life.

The Oracle said, "Pick out the most useless thing for you to do and do it for the next few years. Something that you would never consider doing, that you have no desire to do. But something that will improve you at least physically and mentally. Learn a part of the world that you think you will never make part of your life. Don't squander your time. Learn. That's how I got into politics originally. And this would surprise my friends, I really had no interest in money. Do something you hate. In three or four years more things will be possible and what is possible becomes more attractive."

The next day Christian applied for an appointment to West Point and spent the next four years becoming an officer in the United States Army. The Oracle was astounded, then delighted. "The very thing," he said. "You will never be a soldier. And you will develop a taste for denial."

Christian, after four years at West Point, remained another four years in the Army training in special assault brigades and becoming proficient in armed and unarmed combat. The feeling that his body could perform any task he demanded of it gave him a sense of immortality.

At the age of thirty he resigned his commission and took a post in the operations division of the CIA. He became an officer in clandestine operations and spent the next four years in the European theater. From there he went to the Middle East for six years and rose high in the operational division of the Agency until a bomb took off his foot. This was another challenge. He learned to use and manage a prosthetic device, an artificial foot, so that he did not even limp. But that ended his career in the field and he returned home to enter a prestigious law firm.

Then for the first time he fell in love, and married a girl he thought was the answer to all his youthful dreams. She was intelligent, she was witty, she was very good-looking and very passionate. For the next five years he was happy in marriage, happy as the father of two young children, and found satisfaction in the political maze through which the Oracle was guiding him. He was, finally, he thought, a man who had found his place in life. Then misfortune. His wife fell in love with another man and sued for divorce.

Christian was dumbstruck, then furious. He was happy; how could his wife not be? And what had changed her? He had been loving and attentive to her every wish. Of course he had been busy in his work, to build a career. But he was rich and she lacked for nothing. In his rage he was determined to resist her every demand, to fight for custody of the children, deny her the house she wanted so badly, restrict all monetary rewards that come to a divorced woman. Above all, he was astounded that she planned to live in their house with her new husband. True, it was a palatial mansion, but what about the sacred memories of the life they had shared in that house? And he had been a faithful husband.

He had gone again to the Oracle and poured out his grief and pain. To his surprise the Oracle was completely unsympathetic. "You were faithful, so that makes you think your wife should be faithful? How does that follow, if you no longer interest her? Of course it is more natural for a male to be unfaithful. Infidelity is the precaution of a prudent man who knows that his wife can unilaterally deprive him of his house and children without a moral cause. You accepted that deal when you married; now you must abide by it." Then the Oracle had laughed in his face. "Your wife was quite right to leave you," he said. "She saw through you, though I must say you gave quite a performance. She knew you were never truly happy. But believe me, it's the best thing. You are now a man ready to assume his real station in life. You've got everything out of the way—a wife and children would only be a hindrance. You are essentially a man who has to live alone to do great things. I know because I was that way. Wives can be dangerous to men with real ambition, children are the very breeding grounds of tragedy. Use your common sense, use your training as a lawyer. Give her everything she wants, it will make only a small dent in your fortune. Your children are very young, they will forget you. Think of it this way. Now you are free. Your life will be directed by yourself."

And so it had been.

So late on Easter Sunday night Attorney General Christian Klee left the White House to visit Oliver Oliphant, to ask his advice and also to inform him that his one-hundredth birth-day party had been postponed by President Kennedy.

The Oracle lived on a fenced estate that was expensively guarded; its security system had bagged five enterprising burglars in the last year. His large staff of servants, well paid and well pensioned, included a barber, a valet, a cook and maids, for there were still many important men who came to the Oracle for advice and sometimes had to be fed elabo-rate dinners or provided with lodging.

Christian looked forward to his visit with the Oracle. He enjoyed the old man's company, the stories he told of terrible wars on the battlefields of money, the strategies of men dealing with fathers, mothers, wives and lovers. He talked of how to defend against the government, its strength so prodi-gious, its justice so blind, its laws so treacherous, its free elections so corrupting. Not that the Oracle was a profes-sional cynic, he was merely clear-sighted. And he insisted that one could lead a happy successful life while observing the ethical values on which true civilization endures. The Oracle could be dazzling.

The Oracle received Christian in his second-story suite of rooms, which consisted of a narrow bedroom, an enormous bathroom tiled blue that held a Jacuzzi and a shower with a marble bench and handholds sculpted into its walls. There was also a den with an impressive fireplace, a library and a cozy sitting room with a brightly colored sofa and armchairs.

The Oracle was in the sitting room resting in a specially built motorized wheelchair. Beside him was a table, and facing him were an armchair and a table set for an English tea.

Christian took his place in the armchair opposite the Ora-cle and helped himself to tea and one of the little sandwiches. As always, Christian was delighted by the appearance of the

Oracle, the intensity of the man's gaze so remarkable in one who had lived for a hundred years. And it seemed logical to Christian that the Oracle had evolved from a homely sixty-five-year-old to a striking ancientness. The skin was shell-like, as was his bald pate, which showed liver spots dark as nicotine. Leopard-skin hands protruded from his exquisitely cut suit—extreme age had not vanquished his sartorial vanity. The neck, encircled loosely by a silk tie, was scaly and ridged; the back broad, curved like glass. The front of the body fell away to a tiny chest; you could encircle his waist with your fingers, and his legs were hardly more than two strands in a spider's web. But the facial features were not yet ravaged by approaching death.

Christian poured the Oracle his cup, and for the first few minutes they smiled at each other, drinking tea.

The Oracle spoke first. "You've come to cancel my birthday party, I assume. I've been watching the TV with my secretaries. I told them the party would be postponed." His voice had the low growl of a worn larynx.

"Yes," Christian said. "But only for a month. Think you can hold out that long?" He was smiling.

"I sure do," the Oracle said. "That shit is on every TV station. Take my advice, my boy, buy stock in the TV companies. They will make a fortune out of this tragedy and all the forthcoming tragedies. They are the crocodiles of our society." He paused for a moment and said more softly, "How is your beloved President taking all this?"

"I admire that man more than ever," Christian said. "I have never seen someone in his position more composed over a dreadful tragedy. He is much stronger now than after his wife died."

The Oracle said dryly, "When the worst that can happen to you actually happens, and you bear it, then you are the strongest of men in the world. Which, actually, may not be a very good thing."

He paused for a moment to sip his tea, his colorless lips closed into a pale white line like a scratch on the seamed nicotine-spotted skin of his face. Then he said, "If you feel it's not breaking your oath of office or your loyalty to the President, why don't you tell me what action is being taken."

Christian knew that this was what the old man lived for. To be inside the skin of power. "Francis is very concerned that the hijackers have not yet made any demands. It's been ten hours," Christian said. "He thinks that's sinister."

"So it is," the Oracle said.

They were both silent for a long time. The Oracle's eyes had lost their vibrancy, and seemed extinguished by the pouches of dying skin beneath them.

Christian said, "I'm really worried about Francis. He can't take much more. If something happens to her . . ."

The Oracle said, "There will be a very dangerous confrontation. You know, I remember Francis Kennedy as a little boy. Even then I was struck by how he dominated his cousins. He was a natural hero, even as a young boy. He defended the smaller ones, he made peace. And sometimes he did more damage than any of the bullies would have done. Black eyes darkened in the name of virtue."

The Oracle paused and Christian poured him some hot tea though the cup was still more than half full. He knew the old man could not taste anything unless it was very hot or very cold.

Christian said, "Whatever the President tells me to do, I'll do it."

The Oracle's eyes were suddenly very bright and visible. He said musingly, "You've become a very dangerous man in these past years, Christian. But not terribly original. All through history there have been men, some considered 'great,' who have had to choose between God and country. And some very religious men have chosen country over God, believing they would go to everlasting hell, thinking it noble. But, Christian, we have come to a time when we must decide whether to give our lives to our country or to help mankind continue to exist. We live in a nuclear age. That is the new and interesting question, a question never before posed to individual men. Think in those terms. If you side with your President, do you endanger mankind? It's not so simple as rejecting God."

"It doesn't matter," Christian said. "I know Francis is better than Congress, the Socrates Club and the terrorists."

The Oracle said, "I've always wondered about your overwhelming loyalty to Francis Kennedy. There are some vulgar gossips who say it's a very faggy business. On your part. Not his. Which is odd, since you have women and he does not, not since the death of his wife three years ago. But why do the people around Kennedy hold him in such veneration, when he's recognized as a political dunderhead? All those reformist and regulatory laws he tried to shove down that dinosaur Congress's throat. I thought that you were smarter than that, but I presume you were overruled. Still, your inordinate affection for Kennedy is a mystery to me."

"He's the man I always wished I could be," Christian said. "It's as simple as that."

"Then you and I would not have been such longtime friends," the Oracle said. "I never cared for Francis Kennedy."

"He's just better than anybody else," Christian said. "I've known him for over twenty years, and he's the only politician who has been honest with the public, he doesn't lie to them."

The Oracle said dryly, "The man you described could never be elected President of the United States." He seemed to puff out his insect body, his shiny-skinned hands tapped the controls of his wheelchair. The Oracle leaned back. Above the dark suit, the ivory shirt and simple blue streak of his tie, the glazed face looked like a piece of mahogany. He said, "His charm escapes me, but we never got on. Now I must warn you. Every man in his lifetime makes many mistakes. That is human, and unavoidable. The trick is never to make the mistake that destroys you. Beware of your friend Kennedy, who is so virtuous, remember that evil can spring from the desire to do good. Be careful."

"Character doesn't change," Christian said confidently.

The Oracle fluttered his arms like bird wings. "Yes, it does," he said. "Pain changes character. Sorrow changes character. Love and money, certainly. And time erodes character. Let me tell you a little story. When I was a man of fifty, I had a mistress thirty years younger than myself. She had a brother who was ten years older than she, about thirty. I was her mentor, as I was with all my young women. I had their interests at heart. Her brother was a Wall Street hotshot and a careless man, which later got him into big trouble. Now, I was never jealous—she went out with young men. But on her twenty-first birthday, her brother gave a party and as a joke hired a male stripper to perform before her and her friends. It was all above board, they made no secret of it. But I was always conscious of my homeliness, my lack of physical appeal to women. And so I was affronted, and that was unworthy of me. We all remained friends and she went on to marriage and a career. I went on to younger mistresses. Ten years later her brother gets into financial trouble, as many of those Wall Street types do. Inside tips, finagling with money entrusted to him. Very serious trouble that landed him a couple of years in prison and of course the end of his career.

"By this time I was sixty years old, still friends with both of them. They never asked for my help, they really didn't know the extent of what I could do. I could have saved him but I never lifted a finger. I let him go down the drain. And ten years later it came to me that I didn't help him because of that foolish little trick of his, letting his sister see the body of a man so much younger than myself. And it wasn't sexual jealousy, it was the affront to my power, or the power I thought I had. I've thought of that often. It is one of the few things in my life that shame me. I would never have been guilty of such an act at thirty or at seventy. Why at sixty? Character does change. That is man's triumph and his tragedy."

Christian switched to the brandy that the Oracle had provided. It was delicious and very expensive. The Oracle always served the very best. Christian enjoyed it, though he would never buy it; born rich, he never felt he deserved to treat himself so well. He said, "I've known you all my life, over forty-five years, and you haven't changed. You are going to be a hundred next week. And you're still the great man I always thought you were."

The Oracle shook his head. "You know me only in my old age, from sixty to a hundred. That means nothing. The venom is gone then and the strength to enforce it. It's no trick to be virtuous in old age, as that humbug Tolstoy knew." He paused and sighed. "Now, how about this great birthday party of mine? Your friend Kennedy never really liked me and I know you pushed the idea of the White House Rose Garden and a big media event. Is he using this crisis situation to get out of it?"

Christian said, "No, no, he values your life's work, he

wants to do it. Oliver, you were and are a great man. Just hang on. Hell, what's a few months after a hundred years?" He paused. "But if you prefer, since you don't like Francis, we can forget about his big plans for your birthday party, mass coverage by the media, your name and picture in all the papers and on TV. I can always throw you a little private party right away and get the whole thing over with." He smiled at the Oracle to show that he was joking. Sometimes the old man took him too literally.

"Thank you, but no," the Oracle said. "I want to have something to live for. Namely, a birthday party given by the President of the United States. But let me tell you, your Kennedy is shrewd. He knows my name still means something. The publicity will enhance his image. Your Francis Xavier Kennedy is as crafty as was his uncle Jack. Now, Bobby would have shown me the back of his hand."

Christian said, "None of your contemporaries are left, but your protégés are some of the great men and women in the country, and they look forward to doing you this honor. Including the President. He doesn't forget that you helped him on his way. He's even inviting your buddies in the Socrates Club and he hates them. It will be your best birthday party."

"And my last," the Oracle said. "I'm hanging on by my fucking fingernails."

Christian laughed. The Oracle had never used bad language until he was ninety, so now he used it as innocently as a child.

"That's settled," the Oracle said. "Now let me tell you something about great men, Kennedy and myself included. They finally consume themselves and the people around them. Not that I concede your Kennedy is a great man. So he's become President of the United States. But that is an illusionist's trick. Do you know, by the way, that in show business the magician is considered to be completely without artistic talent?" Here the Oracle cocked his head; he astonishingly resembled an owl.

"I will concede that Kennedy is not your typical politician," the Oracle said. "He is an idealist, he is far more intelligent and he has morals, though I wonder whether sexual rigidity is healthy. But all these virtues are a handicap to political greatness. A man without a vice? A sailing ship without a sail!"

Christian asked, "You disapprove of his actions. What course would you take?"

"That is not relevant," the Oracle said. "His whole three years, he's got his dick half in, half out, and that's always trouble." Now the Oracle's eyes became cloudy. "I hope it doesn't interfere with my birthday party too long. What a life I had, eh? Who had a better life than I? Poor at birth, so that I could appreciate the wealth I earned later. A homely man who learned to captivate and enjoy beautiful women. A good brain, a learned compassion so much better than the genetic kind. Enormous energy, enough to power me past old age. A good constitution, I've never been really sick in my life. A great life, and long! And that's the trouble, maybe a little too long. I can't bear to look at myself in the mirror now, but as I said, I was never handsome." He paused for a time and then said abruptly to Christian, "Leave government service. Dissociate yourself from everything that is happening now."

"I can't do that," Christian said. "It's too late." He studied the old man's freckled head and marveled at the brain that was still so alive. Christian stared into those aged eyes shrouded like a never-ending misty sea. Would he ever be so old, with his body shriveling like some dead insect?

And the Oracle watching him thought, How transparent they all are, as guileless as little children. It was obvious to the Oracle that his advice had been given too late, that Christian would commit a treachery to himself.

Christian finished his brandy and rose to leave. He tucked the blankets around the old man and rang for the nurses to come into the room. Then he whispered into the glazed skin of the Oracle's ear. "Tell me the truth about Helen Du Pray, she was one of your protégées before she got married. I know you arranged for her first entry into politics. Did you ever screw her, or were you too old?"

The Oracle shook his head. "I was never too old until after ninety. And let me tell you that when your cock leaves you, that is real loneliness. But to answer your question. She didn't fancy me, I was no beauty. I must say I was disappointed, she was very beautiful and very intelligent, my favorite combination. I could never love intelligent homely women—they were too much like myself. I could love beautiful dumb women, but when they were intelligent, then I was in heaven. Helen Du Pray—ah, I knew she would go far, she was very strong, a strong will. Yes I tried but never succeeded, a rare failure I must say. But we always remained good friends. That was a talent she had, to refuse a man sexually and yet be an intimate friend. Very rare. That was when I knew she was a seriously ambitious woman."

Christian touched his hand, it felt like a scar. "I'll phone or drop in to see you every day," he said. "I'll keep you up to date."

The Oracle was very busy after Christian left. He had to pass on the information Klee had given him to the Socrates Club, whose members were important figures in the structure of

America. He did not consider this a betrayal of Christian, whom he dearly loved. Love was always secondary.

He had to take action, his country was sailing in dangerous waters. It was his duty to help guide it to safety. And what else could a man his age do to make life worth living? And to tell the truth he had always despised the Kennedy legend. Here was a chance to destroy it forever.

Finally the Oracle let the nurse fuss over him and prepare his bed. He remembered Helen Du Pray with affection, and now without disappointment. She had been very young, in her early twenties, her beauty enhanced by a tremendous vitality. He had often lectured her on power, its acquisition and uses, and, more important, on abstaining from its use. And she had listened with the patience that is necessary to acquire power.

He told her that one of the great mysteries of mankind was how people acted against their own self-interest. Points of pride ruined their lives. Envy and self-delusion took them down paths that led to nothingness. Why was it so important for people to maintain a self-image? There were those who would never truckle, never flatter, never lie, never back down, never betray or never deceive. There were those who lived in envy and jealousy of the happier fate of others.

It had all been a special sort of pleading and she had seen through it. She rejected him and went on, without his help, to achieve her own dream of power.

One of the problems of having a mind as clear as a bell when you are a hundred years old is that you can see the hatching of unconscious villainy in yourself, and ferret it out in past history. He had been mortified when Helen Du Pray had refused to make love with him. He knew she had other lovers, she was not prissy. But at seventy he, amazingly, had still been vain.

He had gone to the rejuvenation center in Switzerland, submitted to surgical erasing of wrinkles, the sanding of his skin, the injection of animal fetus pulp into his own veins. But nothing could be done for the shrinking of his skeleton, the freezing of his joints, the very turning of his blood into water.

Though it no longer did him any good, the Oracle believed he understood men and women in love. Even when he was past his sixtieth year young mistresses adored him. The whole secret was never to impose any rules on their behavior, never to be jealous, never to hurt their feelings. They took young men as their true loves and treated the Oracle with careless cruelty. It didn't matter. He showered them with expensive gifts, paintings, jewelry in the best of taste. He let them call on his power to get unearned favors from society and the use of his money in generous but not lavish amounts. He was a prudent man and would always have three or four mistresses at one time. For they had their own lives to lead. They would fall in love and neglect him, they would take trips, they would be working hard at their careers. He could not make too many demands on their time. But when he needed female company (not only for sex but for the sweet music of their voices, the innocent deviousness of their wiles), one of the four would be available. And of course to be seen at important functions in his company gave them entree into circles it would be more difficult for them to penetrate on their own. Social cachet was one of his assets.

He made no secrets, they all knew about one another. He believed that in their hearts women disliked monogamous men.

How cruel that he remembered bad things he had done more often than the good. His money had built medical centers, churches, rest homes for the elderly; he had done many good things. But his memories of himself were not good. Fortunately he thought about love often. In an interesting and peculiar way, it had been the most commercial thing in his life. And he had owned Wall Street firms, banks, airlines.

Anointed with the power of money, he had been invited to share in world-shaking events, been adviser to the powerful. He had helped shape the very world people lived in. A fascinating, important, valuable life. And yet the managing of his countless mistresses was far more vivid in his hundred-year-old brain. Ah, those intelligent headstrong beauties, how delightful they had been, and how they had vindicated his judgment, most of them. Now they were judges, heads of magazines, powers in Wall Street, TV news queens. How cunning they had been in their love affairs with him and how he had outwitted them. But without cheating them of their due. He had no guilt, only regrets. If one of them had truly loved him, he would have raised her to the skies. But then his mind reminded him that he had not deserved to be so loved. They had recognized his love, it was a hollow drum that made his body thump.

It was at the age of eighty that his skeleton began to contract inside its envelope of flesh. Physical desire receded and a vast ocean of youthful and lost images drowned his brain. And it was at this time he found it necessary to employ young women to lie innocently in his bed just so that he could look at them. Oh, that perversity so scorned in literature, so mocked by the young who must grow old. And yet what peace it gave his crumbling body to see the beauty he could no longer devour. How pure it was. The rolling mound of breast, satiny white skin crowned with its tiny red rose. The mysterious thighs, their rounded flesh giving off a golden glow, the surprising triangle of hair—a choice of colors—and then on the other side the heartbreak of buttocks divided into two exquisite haunches. So much beauty, to his bodily senses dead and lost, but sparking the flickering billions of cells in his brain. And their faces, the mysterious shells of ears spiraling into some inner sea, the hollowed eyes with their banked fires of blue and gray and brown and green looking out from their private eternal cells, the planes of their faces descending into unshielded lips, so open to pleasure and to wounds. He would look upon them before he went to sleep. He would reach out and touch the warm flesh; the satin of thigh and buttocks, touch the burning lips, and oh so rarely smooth the crinkled pubic hair to feel the throbbing pulse beneath. There was so much comfort there that he would fall asleep and the pulse would soften the terror of his dreams. In his dreams he hated the very young and would devour them. He dreamed of the bodies of young men piled high in trenches, sailors by the thousands floating fathoms deep beneath the sea, vast skies clouded by the space-suited bodies of celestial explorers spinning endlessly into the black holes of the universe.

Awake he dreamed. But awake he recognized his dreams as a form of senile madness, his disgut of his own body. He hated his skin, which gleamed like scar tissue, the brown spots on his hands and bald pate, those deadly freckles of death, his failing sight, the feebleness of his limbs, the spinning heart, the evilness tumoring his brain clear as a bell.

Oh, what a pity that fairy godmothers came to the cradle of newborn infants to bestow their three magical wishes! Those infants had no need; old men like himself should receive such gifts. Especially those with minds as clear as a bell.

BOOK
II

EASTER
WEEK

CHAPTER
4

ROMEO'S ESCAPE FROM Italy had been meticulously planned. From St. Peter's Square the van took his cadre to a safe house, where he changed clothes, was furnished with an almost foolproof passport, picked up an already packed suitcase and was taken by underground routes over the border into southern France. There in the city of Nice he boarded the flight to Paris that continued on to New York. Though he had gone without sleep for the past thirty hours, Romeo remained alert. This was all tricky detail, the easy portion of an operation that sometimes went wrong because of some crazy fluke or hitch in planning.

The dinner and wine on Air France planes were always good, and Romeo gradually relaxed. He gazed down at endless pale green water and horizons of white and blue sky. He took two strong sleeping pills. But still some nerve of fear in his body kept him awake. He thought of passing through

United States customs—would something go wrong there? But even if he was caught at that time and place, it would not make any difference to Yabril's scheme. A treacherous survival instinct kept him awake. Romeo had no illusions about the suffering he would have to endure. He had agreed to commit a self-sacrificing act to atone for the sins of his family, his class and his country, but now that mysterious nerve of fear tautened his body.

Finally the pills worked and he fell asleep. In his dreams he fired the shot and ran out of St. Peter's Square, and now still running, he came awake. The plane was landing at Kennedy Airport in New York. The stewardess handed him his jacket, and he reached for his carry-on case from the overhead bin. When he passed through customs, he acted his part perfectly, and carried his bag outside to the central plaza of the airport terminal.

He spotted his contacts immediately. The girl wore a green ski cap with white stripes. The young man pulled out a red billed cap and put it on his head so that the blue stencil reading "Yankees" was visible. Romeo himself wore no signal markers; he had wanted to keep his options open. He bent down and fiddled with his bags, opening one and rummaging through it as he studied the two contacts. He could observe nothing that was suspicious. Not that it really mattered.

The girl was skinny and blond and too angular for Romeo's taste, but her face had a feminine sternness that some serious-minded girls have and he liked that in a woman. He wondered how she would be in bed and hoped he would remain free long enough to seduce her. It shouldn't be too difficult. He had always been attractive to women. In that way he was a better man than Yabril. She would guess that he was connected to the killing of the Pope, and to a serious-minded revolutionary girl, sharing his bed might be the fulfillment of a romantic dream. He noticed that she did not lean toward or touch the man who was with her.

That young man had such a warm, open face, he radiated such American kindliness, that Romeo immediately disliked him. Americans were such worthless shits, they had too comfortable a life. Imagine, in over two hundred years they had never come close to having a revolutionary party. And this in a country that had come into existence through revolution. The young man sent to greet him was typical of such softness. Romeo picked up his bags and walked directly to them.

"Excuse me," Romeo said, smiling, his English heavily accented. "Could you tell me where the bus leaves for Long Island?"

The girl turned her face toward him. She was much prettier up close. He saw a tiny scar on her chin and that aroused his desire. She said, "Do you want the North Shore or the South Shore?"

"East Hampton," Romeo said.

The young girl smiled, it was a warm smile, even a smile of admiration. The young man took one of Romeo's bags and said, "Follow us."

They led the way out of the terminal. Romeo followed. The noise of traffic, the density of people, almost stunned him. A car was waiting with a driver, who wore another red billed baseball cap. The two young men sat in the front, the girl got into the backseat with Romeo. As the car rolled into traffic the girl extended her hand and said, "My name is Dorothea. Please don't worry." The two young men up front also murmured their names. Then the girl said, "You will be very comfortable and very safe." And in that moment Romeo felt the agony of a Judas.

That night the young American couple took great pains to cook Romeo a good dinner. He had a comfortable room overlooking the ocean, though the bed was lumpy, which made little difference because Romeo knew he would sleep in it only one night, if he slept at all. The house was expensively furnished, but with no real taste; it was modern, beach America. The three of them spent a quiet evening talking in a mixture of Italian and English.

The girl, Dorothea, was a surprise. She was extremely intelligent as well as pretty. She also turned out not to be flirtatious, which destroyed Romeo's hopes of spending his last night of freedom playing sexual fun games. The young man, Richard, was also quite serious. It was evident that they had guessed he was involved in the murder of the Pope, but they did not ask specific questions. They simply treated him with the frightening respect that people show to someone slowly dying of a terminal illness. Romeo was impressed by them. They had such lithe bodies when they moved. They talked intelligently, they had compassion for the unfortunate and they radiated confidence in their beliefs and their abilities.

Spending that quiet evening with the two young people, so sincere in their beliefs, so innocent in the necessities of true revolution, Romeo felt a little sick of his whole life. Was it necessary that these two be betrayed along with himself? He would be released eventually, he believed in Yabril's plan—he thought it so simple, so elegant. And he had volunteered to place himself in the noose. But the young man and woman were also true believers, people on their side. And they would be in handcuffs, they would know the sufferings of revolutionaries. For a moment he thought of warning them. But it was necessary that the world know that there were Americans involved in the plot; these two were the sacrificial lambs. And then he was angry with himself, he was too softhearted. True, he could never throw a bomb into a kindergarten, as Yabril could, but surely he could sacrifice a few adults. He had killed a Pope, after all.

And what real harm would come to them? They would serve a few years in prison. America was so soft from top to bottom that they might even go free. America was a land of lawyers who were as fearsome as the Knights of the Round Table. They could get anybody off.

And so he tried to go to sleep. But all the terrors of the past few days came over the ocean air blowing through the open window. Again he raised his rifle, again he saw the Pope fall, again he was rushing through the square, and heard the celebrating pilgrims screaming in horror.

Early the next morning, Monday morning, twenty-four hours after he had killed the Pope, Romeo decided he would walk along the American ocean shore and get his last whiff of freedom. The house was silent as he came down the stairs, but he found Dorothea and Richard sleeping on the two couches in the living room, as if they had been standing guard. The poison of his treachery drove him out the door into the salt breeze of the beach. On sight, he hated this foreign beach, the barbaric gray shrubs, the tall wild yellow weeds, the sunlight flashing off silver-red soda cans. Even the sunshine was watery, and the early spring colder in this strange land. But he was glad to be out in the open while treachery was being done. A helicopter sailed overhead and then out of sight; there were two boats motionless in the water with not a sign of life aboard. The sun rose the color of a blood orange, then yellowed into gold as it rose higher in the sky. He walked for a long time, rounded a corner of the bay, and lost sight of the house. For some reason this panicked him, or perhaps it was the sight of a veritable forest of thin high mottled gray weeds that came almost to the water's edge. He turned back.

It was then that he heard the sirens of police cars. Far down the beach he saw the flashing lights and he walked rapidly toward them. He felt no fear, no doubt in Yabril, though he could still flee. He felt contempt for this American society that could not even organize his capture properly, how stupid they were. But then the helicopter reappeared in the sky, the two ships that had seemed so still and deserted were racing toward shore. He felt fear and panic. Now that there was no chance of escape he wanted to run and run and run. But he steeled himself and walked toward the house surrounded by men and guns. The helicopter hovered over its roof. There were more men coming up the beach and down the beach. Romeo prepared his charade of guilt and fright; he started to run out into the ocean but men rose out of the water in masks. Romeo turned and ran back toward the house, and then he saw Richard and Dorothea.

They were chained, in handcuffs, ropes of iron rooted their bodies to the earth. And they were weeping. Romeo knew how they felt—so he had stood once long ago. They were weeping in shame, in humiliation, stripped of their sense of power. And filled with the unutterably nightmarish terror of being completely helpless, their fate no longer determined by whimsical, perhaps merciful, gods but by their implacable fellowmen.

Romeo gave them both a smile of helpless pity. He knew he would be free in a matter of days, he knew he had betrayed these true believers in his own faith, but after all, it had been a tactical decision, not an evil or malicious one. Then armed men swarmed over him and linked him with steel and heavy iron.

• • •

Far across the world, that world whose roof of sky was riddled with spying satellites, its ozone patrolled by voodoo radar, across the seas filled with American warships sweeping toward Sherhaben, across continents spaced with missile silos and stationary armies rooted to the earth to act as lightning rods for death, Yabril had breakfast in the palace with the Sultan of Sherhaben.

The Sultan of Sherhaben was a believer in Arab freedom, of the Palestinian right to a homeland. He regarded the United States as the bulwark of Israel—Israel could not stand without American support. Therefore America was the ultimate enemy. And Yabril's plot to destabilize America's authority had appealed to his subtle mind. The humiliation of a great power by Sherhaben, militarily so helpless, delighted him.

The Sultan had absolute power in Sherhaben. He had vast wealth; every pleasure in life was his for the asking, but all this had become stale and unsatisfying. The Sultan had no vices to add spice to his life. He observed Muslim law, he lived a virtuous life. The standard of living in Sherhaben, with its vast revenues of oil, was one of the highest in the world; the Sultan had built new schools and new hospitals. Indeed his dream was to make Sherhaben the Switzerland of the Arab world. His only eccentricity was his mania for cleanliness, of his person and in his state.

The Sultan had taken part in this conspiracy because he relished the sense of adventure, the gambling for high stakes, the striving for high ideals. And there was little personal risk to himself and to his country, since he had a magic shield, billions of barrels of oil safely locked beneath his desert land.

Another strong motive was his love for and gratitude to Yabril. When the Sultan was only a minor prince, there had been a fierce struggle for power in Sherhaben, especially after the oil fields proved to be so vast. The American oil companies had supported the Sultan's opponents, who naturally favored the American cause. The Sultan, who had been educated abroad, understood the true value of the oil fields, and fought to retain the fields for Sherhaben. Civil war broke out. It had been the then very young Yabril who helped the Sultan achieve power by killing off the Sultan's opponents. For the Sultan, though a man of personal virtue, recognized that political struggle had its own rules.

After his assumption of power, the Sultan gave Yabril sanctuary when needed. Indeed in the last ten years Yabril had spent more time in Sherhaben than in any other place. He established a separate identity with a home and servants and a wife and children. He was also, in that identity, employed as a special government official in a minor capacity. This identity was never penetrated by any foreign intelligence service. During those ten years he and the Sultan became close. They were both students of the Koran, educated by foreign teachers, and they were united in their hatred of Israel. And here they made a special distinction: they did not hate the Jews as Jews; they hated the official state of the Jews.

The Sultan of Sherhaben had a secret dream, one so bizarre he did not dare to share it with anyone, not even Yabril. That one day Israel would be destroyed and the Jews dispersed again all over the world. And then he, the Sultan, would lure Jewish scientists and scholars to Sherhaben. He would establish a great university that would collect Jewish brains. For had not history proved that this race owned the genes to greatness of the mind? Einstein and other Jewish scientists had given the world the atom bomb. What other mysteries of God and nature could they not solve? And were they not fellow Semites? Time erodes hatred; Jew and Arab could live in peace together and make Sherhaben great. Oh, he would lure them with riches and sweet civility; he would respect all their stubborn whims of culture. Who knew what would happen? Sherhaben could become another Athens. The thought made the Sultan smile at his own foolishness, but still, where was the harm in a dream?

But now Yabril's plot was perhaps a nightmare. The Sultan had summoned Yabril to the palace, spirited him from the plane, to make sure that his ferocity would be controlled. Yabril had a history of adding his own little twists to his operations.

The Sultan insisted that Yabril be bathed and shaved and enjoy a beautiful dancing girl of the palace. Then, with Yabril refreshed, and in the Sultan's minor debt, they sat on the glassed-in air-conditioned terrace.

The Sultan felt he could speak frankly. "I must congratulate you," he said to Yabril. "Your timing has been perfect, and I must say lucky. Allah watches over you, without a doubt." Here he smiled affectionately at Yabril. Then he went on. "I have received advance notice that the United States will meet any demands you make. Be content. You have humiliated the greatest country in the world. You have killed the world's greatest religious leader. You will achieve the release of your killer of the Pope and that will be like pissing in their faces. But go no further. Give thought to what happens afterwards. You will be the most hunted man in the history of this century."

Yabril knew what was coming, the probing for more information on how he would handle the negotiations. For a moment he wondered if the Sultan would try to take over the operation. "I will be safe here in Sherhaben," Yabril said. "As always."

The Sultan shook his head. "You know as well as I do that they will concentrate on Sherhaben after this is over. You will have to find another refuge."

Yabril laughed. "I will be a beggar in Jerusalem. But you should worry about yourself. They will know you have been a part of it."

"Not probable," the Sultan said. "And I sit on the greatest and cheapest ocean of oil in the world. Also, the Americans have fifty billion dollars invested here, the cost of the oil city of Dak and even more. No, I think I will be forgiven much more quickly than you and your Romeo. Now, Yabril, my friend, I know you well, you have gone far enough this time, really a magnificent performance. Please, do not ruin everything with one of your little flourishes at the end of the game." He paused for a moment. "When do I present your demands?"

Yabril said softly, "Romeo is in place. Give the ultimatum this afternoon. They must agree by eleven Tuesday morning, Washington time. I will not negotiate."

The Sultan said, "Be very careful, Yabril. Give them more time."

They embraced before Yabril was taken back to the plane, which was now held by the three men of his cadre and four other men who had come aboard in Sherhaben. The hostages were all in the tourist section of the plane, including the crew. The plane was sitting isolated in midfield, the crowds of spectators, along with the TV people from all over the world, with their camera equipment and vehicles, pushed back five hundred yards from the aircraft where the Sultan's army had established a cordon.

Yabril was smuggled back onto the plane as a member of

the crew of a provisioning truck that was bringing food supplies and water for the hostages.

In Washington, D.C., it was very early Monday morning. The last thing that Yabril had said to the Sultan of Sherhaben was "Now we will see what this Kennedy is made of."

IT IS OFTEN dangerous to all concerned when a man rejects the pleasures of this world and devotes his life to helping his fellowman. The President of the United States, Francis Xavier Kennedy, was such a man.

Before he entered politics Kennedy had achieved spectacular success and wealth before he was thirty years of age. He then addressed the problem of what it is worthwhile to do in life. Because he was religious, because he had a strict moral sense, because of the tragedy of losing his uncles when he was a child, he believed he could do nothing better than to improve the world he lived in. In essence to better Fate itself.

When he was elected to the presidency, he said that his administration would declare war on all human misery. He would represent the millions of people who could not afford lobbyists and other pressure groups.

All this in ordinary circumstances would have been far too radical for the voting populace of America had it not been for Kennedy's magical presence on the TV screen. He was handsomer than his two famous "uncles" and a far better actor. He also had a better brain than his two uncles and was far superior in education, a true scholar. He could back up his rhetoric with an array of statistics. He could present the skeleton of plans that had been prepared by eminent men in different fields with dazzling eloquence. And a somewhat caustic wit.

"With a good education," Francis Kennedy said, "any burglar, stickup man, any mugger, will know enough to steal without hurting anyone. They'll know how to steal like the people on Wall Street, learn how to evade their taxes like respectable people in our society. We may create more white-collar crime, but at least nobody will get hurt."

But there was another side to Kennedy. "I'm a reactionary to the left and a terror to the right," Kennedy had said to Klee on the day he gave him a new FBI charter with wide discretionary powers. "When a man commits what is called a criminal act, I feel it is a sin. Law enforcement is my theology. A man who commits a criminal act exercises the power of God over another human being. Then it becomes the decision of the victim whether to accept this other god in his life. When the victim and society accept the criminal act in any way, we destroy our society's will to survive. Society and even the individual have no right to forgive or to dilute punishment. Why impose the tyranny of the criminal over a law-abiding populace that adheres to the social contract? In terrible cases of murder and armed robbery and rapes, the criminal proclaims his godhead."

Christian said, smiling, "Put them all in jail?"

Kennedy said grimly, "We haven't got enough jails."

Christian had given him the latest computerized statistical report on crime in America. Kennedy studied it for a few minutes. And he began to rage.

"If only people knew the statistics on crime," he said. "If only people knew the crimes that never get into statistics. Burglars, even those with prior records, rarely go to prison. That home which the government shall not invade, that precious freedom, that sacred social contract, that sacred home, is invaded routinely by armed fellow citizens intent on theft, murder and rape."

Kennedy recited that beloved bit of English common law: "The rain may enter, the wind may enter, but the king may not enter," and said, "What a piece of bullshit that is." He went on: "California alone had six times as many murders as the whole of England in a year. In America murderers do less than five years in prison. Provided that by some miracle you can convict them."

"The people of America are terrorized by a few million lunatics," Kennedy said. "They are afraid to walk the streets at night. They guard their homes with private security that costs thirty billion dollars a year."

Kennedy especially hated one aspect. He said, "Do you know that ninety-eight percent of the crimes go unpunished? Nietzsche called it a long time ago: 'A society when it becomes soft and tender takes sides with those who harm it.' The religious outfits with all their mercy shit forgive criminals. They have no right to forgive criminals, those bastards. The worst thing I ever saw was this mother on TV whose daughter was raped and killed in an awful way, saying 'I forgive them.' What fucking right did she have to forgive them?"

And then to Christian's slightly snobbish surprise,

Kennedy attacked literature. "Orwell had it all wrong in
1984," he said. "The individual is the beast, and Huxley, in
Brave New World, he made it out as a bad thing. But I
wouldn't mind living in a *Brave New World*, it's better than
this. It's the individual who is the tyrant, not the government."

Christian said earnestly and a little ingenuously, "I am
really astonished by the figures in the statistical report I
showed you. The population of this country is being terrorized."

"Congress must pass the legislation we need. The newspapers and other media scream bloody murder about the Bill
of Rights, the sacred Constitution." Kennedy paused to
weigh his friend's reaction. Klee looked somewhat shocked.
Kennedy smiled and went on.

"Let me give you a little insight, buy it or not. The amazing thing is that I've discussed this situation with the really
powerful men in this country, the ones with all the money.
I gave a speech to the Socrates Club. I thought that they
would be concerned. But what a surprise. They had the clout
to move Congress, they wouldn't do it. And you could never
in a million years guess the reason. I couldn't." He paused
as if he expected Christian to guess.

His face grimaced in what could have been a smile or an
expression of contempt. "The rich and powerful in this country can protect themselves. They don't rely on the police or
government agencies. They surround themselves with expensive security systems. They have private bodyguards. They
are sealed off from the criminal community. And the prudent
ones don't get mixed up with the wild drug elements. They
can sleep peacefully at night behind their electric walls."

Christian moved restlessly and took a sip of brandy. Then
Kennedy went on.

"OK," he said. "The point is this. Let's say we pass laws to crush crime, we are then punishing the black criminals more than anyone else. And where are those ungifted, uneducated, unpowered people going to go? What other resource do they have against our society? If they have no outlet in crime they will turn to political action. They will become active radicals. And they will shift the political balance of this country. We may cease to be a capitalist democracy."

Christian said, "Do you really believe that?"

Kennedy sighed. "Jesus, who knows? But the people who run this country believe it. They figure, let the jackals feast on the helpless. What can they steal, a few billion dollars? A small price to pay. Thousands get raped, burglarized, murdered, mugged, it doesn't matter, it happens to unimportant people. Better that minor damage than a real political upheaval."

Christian said, "You're going too far."

"That may be," Kennedy said.

"And when it goes too far," Christian said, "you'll have all kinds of vigilante groups, fascism in an American form."

"But that's the kind of political action that can be controlled," Kennedy said. "That will actually help the people who run our society."

Then he smiled at Christian and picked up the computer report. "I'd like to keep this," he said. "Just to frame it and put up on the wall of my den as a relic of the days before Christian Klee became Attorney General and head of the FBI."

Now on the Monday after Easter, at seven in the morning, the members of President Francis Kennedy's staff, his Cabinet and Vice President Helen Du Pray assembled in the

Cabinet Room of the White House. And on this Monday morning they were fearful of what action he would take.

In the Cabinet Room, the CIA chief, Theodore Tappey, waited for a signal from Kennedy and then opened the session. "Let me say first that Theresa is OK," he said. "No one has been injured. As yet no specific demands have been made. But demands will be made by evening, and we have been warned that they must be met immediately, without negotiation. But that's standard. The hijacker leader, Yabril, is a name famous in terrorist circles and indeed known in our files. He is a maverick and usually does his own operations with help from some of the organized terror groups, like the mythical One Hundred."

Klee cut in, "Why mythical, Theo?"

Tappey said, "It's not like Ali Baba and the forty thieves. Just liaison actions between terrorists of different countries."

Kennedy said curtly, "Go on."

Tappey consulted his notes. "There is no doubt that the Sultan of Sherhaben is cooperating with Yabril. His army is protecting the airfield to prevent any rescue attempt. Meanwhile the Sultan pretends to be our friend and volunteers his services as a negotiator. What his purpose is in this no one can guess, but it is to our interest. The Sultan is reasonable and vulnerable to pressure. Yabril is a wild card."

The CIA chief hesitated; then, at a nod from Kennedy, he went on reluctantly. "Yabril is trying to brainwash your daughter, Mr. President. They have had several long conversations. He seems to think she's a potential revolutionary and that it would be a great coup if she gave out some sort of sympathetic statement. She doesn't seem afraid of him."

The others in the room remained silent. They knew better than to ask Tappey how he had gotten such information.

The hall outside the Cabinet Room hummed with voices, they could hear the excited shouts of the TV camera crews waiting on the White House lawn. Then one of Eugene Dazzy's assistants was let into the room and handed Dazzy a handwritten memo. Kennedy's chief of staff read it in a glance.

"This has all been confirmed?" he asked the aide.

"Yes, sir," the aide said.

Dazzy stared directly at Francis Kennedy. "Mr. President," he said, "I have the most extraordinary news. The assassin of the Pope has been captured here in the United States. The prisoner confirms that he is the assassin, that his code name is Romeo. He refuses to give his real name. It has been checked with the Italian security people and the prisoner gives details that confirm his guilt."

Arthur Wix exploded, as if an uninvited guest had arrived at some intimate party, "What the hell is he doing here? I don't believe it."

Dazzy patiently explained the verifications. Italian security had already captured some of Romeo's cadre and they had confessed and identified Romeo as their leader. The chief of Italian security, Franco Sebbediccio, was famous for his ability to extract confessions. But he could not learn why Romeo had fled to America and how he had been so easily captured.

Francis Kennedy went to the French doors overlooking the Rose Garden. He watched the military detachments patrolling the White House grounds and adjoining streets. Again he felt a familiar sense of dread. Nothing in his life was an accident, life was a deadly conspiracy, not only between fellow humans but between faith and death.

Francis Kennedy turned back from the window and returned to the conference table. He surveyed the room filled with the highest-ranking people in the country, the cleverest, the most intelligent, the schemers, the planners. He said almost jokingly, "What do you guys want to bet that today we get a set of demands from the hijacker? And one of the demands will be that we release this killer of the Pope."

The others stared at Kennedy in amazement. Otto Gray said, "Mr. President, that's an awful big stretch. That is an outrageous demand, it would be nonnegotiable."

Tappey said carefully, "Intelligence shows no connection between the two acts. Indeed it would be inconceivable for any terrorist group to launch two such important operations in the same city on the same day." He paused for a moment and turned to Christian Klee. "Mr. Attorney General," he asked, "just how did you capture this man?" and then added with distaste, "Romeo."

Klee said, "Through an informer we've been using for years. We thought it impossible, but my deputy, Peter Cloot, followed through with a full-scale operation, which seems to have succeeded. I must say I'm surprised. It just doesn't make any sense."

Francis Kennedy said quietly, "Let's adjourn this meeting until the hijackers make their demands."

In one instant of paranoid divination he had comprehended the whole plan that Yabril had created with such pride and cunning. Now for the first time he truly feared for his daughter's safety.

Yabril's demands came through the White House Communications Center late Monday afternoon, relayed through the seemingly helpful Sultan of Sherhaben. The first demand was a ransom of fifty million dollars for the aircraft; the second, the freeing of six hundred Arab prisoners in Israeli jails. The third was for the release of Romeo, the newly captured assassin of the Pope, and his transport to Sherhaben. Also, that if the demands were not met in twenty-four hours, one hostage would be shot.

Francis Kennedy and his personal staff met in the large northwest dining room on the second floor of the White House to discuss the demands of Yabril. The antique table was set for Helen Du Pray, Otto Gray, Arthur Wix, Eugene Dazzy and Christian Klee. Kennedy's place was at one end of the table and set so that he had more space than the others.

Francis Kennedy put himself in the minds of the terrorists—he had always had this gift of empathy. Their primary aim was to humiliate the United States, to destroy its mantle of power in the eyes of the world, even in the eyes of friendly nations. And Kennedy thought it a master psychological stroke. Who would ever take America seriously again if its nose was rubbed in the dirt by a few armed men and a small oil Sultanate? Must he allow this to happen to bring his daughter safely home? Yet in his empathy he divined that the scenario was not complete, that there were more surprises to come. But he did not speak. He let the others in the dining room begin their briefings.

Eugene Dazzy, as chief of staff, opened the discussion. His voice was heavy with fatigue; he had not slept for thirty-six hours. "Mr. President," he said, "it is our judgment that we comply with the terrorist demands to a limited extent. That we release Romeo, not to Yabril but to the Italian government, which is just and legally correct. We don't agree we have to pay the money, and we cannot make Israel release its prisoners. In this way we won't look too weak but we won't provoke them. When Theresa is back, then we can handle the terrorists."

Klee said, "I promise that problem will be solved within a year."

Francis Kennedy remained silent for a long time, then said, "I don't think this will work."

Arthur Wix said, "But this is our public response. Behind the scenes we can promise them that Romeo will go free completely, that we will pay the ransom and that we will lean on Israel. I do think this will work. At least it will give them pause and we can negotiate further."

"It won't do any harm," Dazzy said. "In these situations ultimatums are just part of the negotiation process. That's understood. The twenty-four-hour deadline means nothing."

Kennedy pondered their advice. "I don't think this will work," he said again.

Oddblood Gray said, "We do. And, Francis, you have to be very careful. Congressman Jintz and Senator Lambertino have told me that Congress may ask you to remove yourself completely from this crisis because of your personal interest. That is a very dangerous development."

Kennedy said, "That will never happen."

"Let me deal with Congress," Vice President Du Pray said. "Let me be the lightning rod. I'll be the voice that proposes any surrenders on our part."

It was Dizzy who summed it up. "Francis, in this situation, you must trust the collective judgment of your staff. You know we will protect you and do what is best for you."

Kennedy sighed and paused for a long time, then finally said, "Then go ahead."

Peter Cloot had proved to be a superbly efficient deputy in running the FBI. Cloot was very spare, his body a flat slate of muscles. He had a tiny mustache, which did nothing to soften his bony face. Despite his virtues Cloot had his faults. He was too unbending in discharging his responsibilities, too fierce in discharging his duties, and believed too much in internal security. Tonight, grim-faced, he greeted Christian with a handful of memos and a three-page letter that he handed Christian separately.

It was a letter composed with type cut from newspapers. Christian read it. It was another of those crazy warnings that a homemade atom bomb would explode in New York City. Christian said, "For this you pull me out of the President's office?"

Cloot said, "I waited until we went through all the checking procedures. It qualifies as a possible."

"Oh, Christ," Christian said. "Not now." He read the letter again but much more carefully. The different types of print disoriented him. The letter looked like a bizarre avant-garde painting. He sat down at his desk and read it slowly word for word. The letter was addressed to *The New York Times*. First he read the paragraphs that were isolated by heavy green Magic Marker to identify the hard information.

The marked parts of the letter read:

"We have planted a nuclear weapon with the minimum potential of one half kiloton and maximum of 2 kilotons, in the New York City area. This letter is written to your newspaper so that you may print it and warn the inhabitants of the City to vacate and escape harm. The device is set to trigger off seven days from the date above. So you know how necessary it is to publish this letter immediately." Klee looked at the date. The explosion would be Thursday. He read on: "We have taken this action to prove to the people of the United States that the government must unite with the rest of the world on an equal partnership basis to control nuclear energy, or our planet can be lost.

"There is no way we can be bought off by money or any other condition. By publishing this letter and forcing the evacuation of New York City you will save thousands of lives.

"To prove that this is not a crackpot letter, have the envelope and paper examined by government laboratories. They will find residues of plutonium oxide.

"Print this letter immediately."

The rest of the letter was a lecture on political morality and an impassioned demand that the United States cease making nuclear weapons.

Christian said to Peter Cloot, "Have you had it examined?"

"Yes," Peter Cloot said. "It does have residue. The individual letters are cut from newspapers and magazines to form the message but they give a clue. The writer or writers were smart enough to use papers from all over the country. But there is just a slight edge over the normal for Boston newspapers. I sent an extra fifty men to help the bureau chief up there."

Christian sighed. "We have a long night ahead of us. Let's keep this very low-key. And seal it off from the media. Command post will be my office and all papers to come to me. The President has enough headaches—let's just make this thing disappear. It's a piece of bullshit like all those other crank letters."

"OK," Peter Cloot said. "But you know, someday one of them *will* be real."

It was a long night. The reports kept flowing in. The Nuclear Energy and Research Agency chief was informed so that his agency search teams could be alerted. These teams were specially recruited personnel with sophisticated detecting equipment that could search out hidden nuclear bombs.

Christian had supper brought in for him and Cloot and read the reports. *The New York Times* of course had not published the letter; they had routinely turned it over to the FBI. Christian called the publisher of the *Times* and asked him to black out the item until the investigation was completed. This was also a matter of routine. Newspapers had received thousands of similar letters over the years. But because of this very casualness the letter had gotten to them Monday instead of Saturday.

Sometime before midnight Peter Cloot returned to his own office to manage his staff, which was receiving hundreds of calls from the agents in the field, most of them from Boston. Christian kept reading the reports as they were brought in. More than anything else he didn't want this to add to the President's burdens. For a few moments he thought about the possibility that this might be another twist to the hijacker's plot, but even they would not dare to play for such high stakes. This had to be some aberration that society had thrown up. There had been atom bomb scares before, crazies who had claimed they had planted homemade atom bombs and demanded ransoms of ten to a hundred million dollars. One letter had even asked for a portfolio of Wall Street stocks, shares of IBM, General Motors, Sears, Texaco and some of the gene technology companies. When the letter had been submitted to the Energy Department for a psycho profile the report had come back that the letter posed no bomb threat but that the terrorist was very savvy about the stock market. Which had led to the arrest of a minor Wall Street broker who had embezzled his clients' funds and was looking for a way out.

This had to be another of those crackpot things, Christian thought, but meanwhile it was causing trouble. Hundreds of millions of dollars would be spent. Luckily on this issue the media would suppress the letter. There were some things that those coldhearted bastards didn't dare fuck around with. They knew that there were classified items in the atom bomb control laws that could be invoked, that could even make a hole in the sacred freedom of the Bill of Rights erected around them. He spent the next hours praying that this would all go away. That he would not have to go to the President in the morning and lay this load of crap on him.

CHAPTER
6

IN THE SULTANATE OF SHERHABEN, Yabril stood in the doorway of the hijacked aircraft preparing for the next act he would have to perform. Then his absolute concentration relaxed and he let himself check the surrounding desert. The Sultan had arranged for missiles to be in place, and radar had been set up. An armored division of troops had established a perimeter so that the TV vans could come no nearer to the plane than a hundred yards, and beyond them there was a huge crowd. And Yabril thought that tomorrow he would have to give the order that the TV vans and the crowds would be allowed to come closer, much closer. There would be no danger of assault; the aircraft was lavishly booby-trapped, and Yabril knew he could blow everything into fragments of metal and flesh so completely that the bones would have to be sifted out of the desert sands.

Finally he turned from the aircraft doorway and sat down

next to Theresa Kennedy. They were alone in the first-class cabin. Terrorist guards kept the passenger hostages in the tourist section, and there were also guards in the cockpit with the crew.

Yabril did his best to put Theresa at ease. He told her that the passengers, her fellow hostages, were being well looked after. Naturally, they were not all that comfortable; neither was she or, for that matter, he himself. He said with a wry face, "You know it is in my own best interests that no harm comes to you."

Theresa believed him. Despite everything, she found that dark, intense face sympathetic, and though she knew he was dangerous she could not really dislike him. In her innocence she believed her high station made her invulnerable.

Yabril said almost pleadingly, "You can help us, you can help your fellow hostages. Our cause is just, you once said so yourself a few years ago. But the American Jewish establishment was too strong. They shut you up."

Theresa shook her head. "I'm sure you have your justifications, everybody always has. But the innocent people on this plane have never done you or your cause any harm. They should not suffer for the sins of your enemies."

It gave Yabril a peculiar pleasure that she was courageous and intelligent. Her face, so pleasant and pretty in the American fashion, also pleased him, as if she were some kind of American doll.

Again he was struck by the fact that she was not afraid of him, was not fearful of what would happen to her. The blindness of the highborn to fate, the hubris of the rich and powerful. And of course it was in her family history.

"Miss Kennedy," he said in a courteous voice that cajoled her to listen, "it is well known to us that you are not the usual spoiled American woman, that your sympathies go out to the poor and oppressed of the world. You have doubts even about Israel's right to expel people from their own land to found a warring state of their own. Perhaps you would make a videotape saying this and be heard all over the world."

Theresa Kennedy studied Yabril's face. His tan eyes were liquid and warm, the smile made his dark thin face almost boyish. She had been brought up to trust the world, to trust other human beings and to trust her intelligence and her own beliefs. She could see that this man sincerely believed in what he was doing. In a curious way he inspired respect.

She was polite in her refusal. "What you say may be true. But I would never do anything to hurt my father." She paused for a moment, then said, "And I don't think your methods are intelligent. I don't think murder and terror change anything."

With this remark Yabril felt a powerful surge of contempt. But he replied gently, "Israel was established by terror and American money. Did they teach you that in your American college? We learned from Israel but without your hypocrisy. Our Arab oil sheiks were never as generous with money to us as your Jewish philanthropists were to Israel."

Theresa said, "I believe in the state of Israel, I also believe the Palestinian people should have a homeland. I don't have any influence with my father, we argue all the time. But nothing justifies what you're doing now."

Yabril became impatient. "You must realize that you are my treasure," he said. "I have made my demands. A hostage will be shot every hour after my deadline. And you will be the first."

To Yabril's surprise, there was still no fear on her face. Was she stupid? Could such an obviously sheltered woman be so courageous? He was interested in finding out. So far she had been well treated. She had been isolated in the first-class cabin and treated with the utmost respect by her guards. She looked very angry, but calmed herself by sipping the tea he had served her.

Now she looked up at him. He noticed how severely her pale blond hair framed her delicate features. Her eyelids were bruised with fatigue, her lips, without makeup, a pale pink.

Theresa said in a flat even voice, "Two of my great-uncles were killed by people like you. My family grew up with death. And my father worried about me when he became President. He warned me that the world had men like you, but I refused to believe him. Now I'm curious. Why do you act like such a villain? Do you think you can frighten the whole world by killing a young girl?"

Yabril thought, Maybe not, but I killed a Pope. She didn't know that, not yet. For a moment he was tempted to tell her. The whole grand design. The undermining of authority that all men fear, the power of great nations and great churches. And how man's fear of power could be eroded by solitary acts of terror.

But he reached out a hand to touch her reassuringly. "You will come to no harm from me," he said. "They will negotiate. Life is negotiation. You and I as we speak, we negotiate. Every terrible act, every word of insult, every word of praise is negotiation. Don't take what I've said too seriously."

She laughed.

He was pleased she found him witty. She reminded him of Romeo; she had the same instinctive enthusiasm for the little pleasures of life, even just a play on words. Once Yabril had said to Romeo, "God is the ultimate terrorist," and Romeo had clapped his hands in delight.

And now Yabril's heart sickened, he felt a wave of dizziness. He was ashamed of wanting to charm Theresa Kennedy. He had believed he had come to a time in his life when he was beyond such weakness. If only he could persuade her to make the videotape, he would not have to kill her.

CHAPTER
7

ON THE TUESDAY morning after the Easter Sunday hijacking and the murder of the Pope, President Francis Kennedy entered the White House screening room to watch a CIA film smuggled from Sherhaben.

The White House screening room was a disgraceful affair, with dingy green armchairs for the favored few and metal folding chairs for anyone under Cabinet level. The audience was composed of CIA personnel, the Secretary of State, the Secretary of Defense, their respective staffs, and the members of the White House senior staff.

All rose when the President entered. Kennedy took a green armchair; the CIA director, Theodore Tappey, stood alongside the screen to provide commentary.

The film started. It showed a truck pulling up to the back of the hijacked plane. The workers unloading supplies wore brimmed hats against the sun; they were clad in brown twill trousers and short-sleeved brown cotton shirts. The film showed the workers leaving the plane and then froze on one of them. Under the floppy hat the features of Yabril could be seen, the dark angled face with brilliant eyes, the slight smile on his lips. Yabril got into the supply truck with the other workers.

The film stopped and Tappey spoke. "That truck went to the compound of the Sultan of Sherhaben. Our information is that they had an elaborate banquet complete with dancing girls. Afterward Yabril returned to the plane in the same fashion. Certainly the Sultan of Sherhaben is a fellow conspirator in these acts of terrorism."

The voice of the Secretary of State boomed in the darkness. "Certain only to us. Secret intelligence is always suspect. And even if we could prove it, we couldn't make it public. It would upset all political balances in the Persian Gulf. We would be forced to take retaliatory action, and that would be against our best interest."

Otto Gray muttered, "Jesus Christ."

Christian Klee laughed outright.

Eugene Dazzy, who could write in the dark—a sure mark of administrative genius, he always told everyone—made notes on a pad.

The CIA chief continued, "Our information boils down to this. You'll get the memos in detail later. This seems to be an operation cadre financed by the international terrorist group called the First Hundred, or sometimes the Christs of Violence. It seems to be a liaison between Marxist-oriented revolutionary groups from elite universities in different countries, supplying safe houses and material. And it is limited mostly to Germany, Italy, France and Japan, and exists very vaguely in Ireland and England. But according to our information even the Hundred never really knew what was going on here. They thought the operation ended with the killing of the Pope. So what we come down to is that only this man, Yabril, with the Sultan of Sherhaben, controls this conspiracy."

The film started to roll again. It showed the airplane isolated on the tarmac and the ring of soldiers and antiaircraft guns that protected the approaches to the plane. It showed the crowds that were kept over a hundred yards away.

The CIA director's voice sounded over the film. "This film and other sources indicate there can be no rescue mission. Unless we decide to simply overpower the whole state of Sherhaben. And of course Russia will never allow that, nor perhaps will the other Arab states. Also, over fifty billion dollars of American money has gone to build up their city of Dak, which is another sort of hostage they hold. We are not going to blow away fifty billion dollars of our citizen-invested money. Plus the fact that the missile sites are manned mostly by American mercenaries, but at this point we come to something much more curious."

On the screen appeared a wobbly shot of the hijacked plane's interior. The camera was obviously hand-held and moved down the aisle of the tourist section to show the mass of frightened passengers strapped into their seats. Then the camera moved back up into the first-class cabin and held on a passenger sitting there. Then Yabril moved into the picture. He wore cotton slacks of a light brown and a tan short-sleeved shirt the color of the desert outside the plane. The film cut to Yabril sitting next to that lone passenger, revealed now as Theresa Kennedy. Yabril and Theresa seemed to be talking in an animated and friendly way.

Theresa Kennedy had a small, amused smile on her face, and this made her father, watching the screen, almost turn his head away. It was a smile he remembered from his own childhood, the smile of people entrenched in the central halls of power, who never dream they can be touched by the malicious evil of their fellowmen. Francis Kennedy had seen that smile often on the faces of his uncles.

Kennedy asked the CIA director, "How recent is that film and how did you get it?"

Tappey replied, "It's twelve hours old. We bought it at great cost, obviously from someone close to the terrorists. I can give you the details in private after this meeting, Mr. President."

Kennedy made a dismissive motion. He was not interested in details.

Tappey went on: "Further information. None of the passengers have been mistreated. Also, curiously enough, the female members of the hijacking cadre have been replaced, certainly with the connivance of the Sultan. I regard this development as a little sinister."

"In what way?" Kennedy asked sharply.

Tappey said, "The terrorists on the plane are male. There are more of them, at least ten. They are heavily armed. It may be they are determined to kill their hostages if an attack is made. They may think that female guards would not be able to carry through such a slaughter. Our latest intelligence evaluation forbids a rescue operation by force."

Klee said sharply, "They may be using different personnel simply because this is a different phase of the operation. Or Yabril might just feel more comfortable with men—he's an Arab, after all."

Tappey smiled at him. He said, "Chris, you know as well as I do that this replacement is an aberration. I think it's happened only once before. From your own experience in clandestine operations you know damn well this rules out a direct attack to rescue the hostages."

Kennedy remained silent.

They watched the little bit of film remaining. Yabril and Theresa talking animatedly, seeming to grow more and more friendly. Then finally Yabril was actually patting her shoulder. It was obvious that he was reassuring her, giving her some good news, because Theresa laughed delightedly. Then Yabril made her an almost courtly bow, a gesture that she was under his protection and that she would come to no harm.

Klee said, "I'm afraid of that guy. Let's get Theresa out of there."

Eugene Dazzy sat in his office going over all his options to help President Kennedy. First he called his mistress to tell her he would not be able to see her until the crisis was over. Then he called his wife to check their social schedule and cancel everything. After much thought he called Bert Audick, who over the last three years had been one of the most bitter enemies of the Kennedy administration.

"You've got to help us, Bert," he said. "I'll owe you a big one."

Audick said, "Listen, Eugene, in this we are all Americans together."

Bert Audick had already swallowed two of the giant American oil companies, gulping them like a frog swallowing flies, so his enemies said. Actually, he did look like a frog, the wide mouth in a great jowly face, eyes slightly popping. And yet he was an impressive man, tall and bulky, with a massive head and a jaw as boxy as his oil rigs. He had always been an oil man. Conceived in oil, raised in oil, matured in oil. Born wealthy, he had increased that wealth a hundredfold. His privately held company was worth twenty billion dollars and he owned 51 percent of it. Now at seventy he knew more about oil than any man in America. Said he knew every spot on the globe where it was buried beneath the earth.

In his Houston corporate headquarters, computer screens made a huge map of the world that showed every one of the countless tankers at sea, its port of origin and destinations. Who owned it, what price it had been bought for, how many tons it carried. He could slip any country a billion barrels of oil as easily as a man-about-town slips a fifty-dollar bill to a maître d'.

He had made part of his great fortune in the oil scare of the 1970s, when the OPEC cartel seemed to have the world by the throat. But it was Bert Audick who applied the squeeze. He had made billions of dollars out of a shortage he knew was just a sham.

But he had not done so out of pure greed. He loved oil and was outraged that this life-giving force could be bought so cheaply. He helped rig the price of oil with the romantic ardor of a youth rioting against the injustices of society. And then he had given a great part of his booty away to worthy charities.

He had built nonprofit hospitals, free nursing homes for the elderly, art museums. He had established thousands of college scholarships for the underprivileged without regard to race or creed. He had, of course, taken care of his relatives and friends, made distant cousins rich. He loved his country and his fellow Americans, and never contributed money for anything outside the United States. Except, of course, for the necessary bribes to foreign officials.

He did not love the political rulers of his country or its crushing machinery of government. They were too often his enemies with their regulatory laws, their antitrust suits, their interference in his private affairs. Bert Audick was fiercely loyal to his country, but it was his business, his democratic right, to squeeze his fellow citizens, make them pay for the oil he worshiped.

Audick believed in holding his oil in the ground as long as possible. He often thought lovingly of those billions and billions of dollars that lay in great puddles beneath the desert sands of Sherhaben and other places on earth, safe as they could be. He would keep that vast golden lake as long as possible. He would buy other people's oil, buy other oil companies. He would drill the oceans, buy into England's North Sea, get a piece of Venezuela. And then there was Alaska. Only he knew the size of the great fortune that lay beneath the ice.

He was as nimble as a ballet dancer in his business dealings. He had a sophisticated intelligence apparatus that gave him a far more accurate estimate of the oil reserves of the Soviet Union than the CIA. Such information he did not share with the United States Government, as why should he, since he paid an enormous amount of cash to get it, and its value to him was its exclusivity.

And he truly believed, as did many Americans—indeed he proclaimed it a linchpin of a democratic society—that a free citizen in a free country has the right to put his personal interests ahead of the aims of elected government officials. For if every citizen promoted his own welfare, how could the country not prosper?

On Dazzy's recommendation, Kennedy agreed to see this man. To the public, Audick was a shadowy figure presented in the newspapers and *Fortune* magazine as a cartoonish Czar of Oil. But he had enormous influence with the elected representatives in the Congress and the House. He also had many friends and associates among the few thousand men who controlled the most important industries of the United

States and belonged to the Socrates Club. The men in this
club controlled the print media and the TV media, ran companies that controlled the buying and shipping of grain; they
were the Wall Street giants, the colossi of electronics and
automobiles, the Templars of Money who ran the banks.
And most important, Audick was a personal friend of the
Sultan of Sherhaben.

Bert Audick was escorted into the Cabinet Room, where
Francis Kennedy was meeting with his staff and the appropriate Cabinet members. Everybody understood that he had
come not only to help the President but to caution him. It
was Audick's oil company that had fifty billion dollars invested in the oil fields of Sherhaben and the principal city of
Dak. He had a magical voice, friendly, persuasive and so
sure of what it was saying that it seemed as if a cathedral bell
tolled at the end of every sentence. He could have been a
superb politician had it not been for the fact that in all his
life he had never been able to lie to the people of his country
on political issues, and his beliefs were so far right that he
could not be elected in the most conservative districts of the
country.

He started off by expressing his deepest sympathy for
Kennedy with such sincerity that there could be no doubt
that the rescuing of Theresa Kennedy was the main reason
he had offered his services.

"Mr. President," he said to Kennedy, "I have been in
touch with all the people I know in the Arab countries. They
disavow this terrible affair, and they will help us in any way
they can. I am a personal friend of the Sultan of Sherhaben
and I will bring all my influence to bear on him. I've been
informed that there is certain evidence that the Sultan is part
of the hijacking conspiracy and the murder of the Pope. I

assure you that no matter what the evidence, the Sultan is on our side."

This alerted Francis Kennedy. How did Audick know about the evidence against the Sultan? Only the Cabinet members and his own staff held this information, and it had been given the highest security classification. Could it be that Audick was the Sultan's free ticket to absolution after this affair was over? That there would be a scenario where the Sultan and Audick would be the saviors of his daughter?

Then Audick went on. "Mr. President, I recommend that you meet the hijacker's demands. True, it will be a blow to American prestige, its authority. But that can be repaired later. But let me give you my word on the matter that I know is closest to your heart. No harm will come to your daughter." The cathedral bell in his voice tolled with assurance.

It was the certainty of this speech that made Kennedy doubt him. For Kennedy knew from his own experience in political warfare that complete confidence is the most suspect quality in any kind of leader.

"Do you think we should give them the man who killed the Pope?" Kennedy asked.

Audick misread the question. "Mr. President, I know you are a Catholic. But remember that this is a mostly Protestant country. Simply as a foreign policy matter we need not make the killing of a Catholic Pope the most important of our concerns. It is necessary for the future of our country that we preserve our lifelines of oil. We need Sherhaben. We must act carefully, with intelligence, not passion. Again here is my personal assurance. Your daughter is safe."

He was beyond a doubt sincere, and impressive. Kennedy thanked him and walked him to the door. When he was gone Kennedy turned to Dazzy and asked, "What the hell did he really say?"

"He just wants to make points with you," Dazzy said. "And maybe he doesn't want you to get any ideas of using that fifty-billion-dollar oil city of Dak as a bargaining chip." He paused for a moment and then said, "I think he can help."

Christian leaned closer to Kennedy's ear. "Francis, I have to see you alone."

Kennedy excused himself from the meeting and took Christian to the Oval Office. Though Kennedy hated using the small room, the other rooms of the White House were filled with advisers and staff planners awaiting final instructions.

Christian liked the Oval Office. The light coming from the three long bulletproof windows, the two flags—the cheerful red, white and blue national flag on the right of the small desk and on the left the presidential flag, which was more somber and a darker blue.

Kennedy waved to Christian to sit down. Christian wondered how the man could look so composed. Though they had been such close friends for so many years, he could detect no sign of emotion.

"We have more trouble," Christian said. "Right here at home. I hate to bother you, but it's necessary."

He briefed Kennedy on the atom bomb letter. "It's probably all bullshit," Christian said. "There's one chance in a million there is such a bomb. But if there is, it could destroy ten city blocks and kill thousands of people. Plus radioactive fallout would make the area uninhabitable for who knows how long. So we have to treat that one chance in a million seriously."

Francis Kennedy snapped, "I hope to hell you're not going to tell me this is tied up with the hijacker."

"Who knows," Christian said.

"Then keep this contained, clean it up without a fuss," Kennedy said. "Slap the Atomic Secrecy classification on it." Kennedy flipped on the speaker to Eugene Dazzy's office. "Euge," he said. "Get me copies of the classified Atomic Secrecy Act. Also get me all the medical files on brain research. And set up a meeting with Dr. Annaccone."

Kennedy switched off the intercom. He stood up and glanced through the windows of the Oval Office. He absently ran his hand over the furled cloth of the American flag standing by his desk. For a long time he stood there thinking.

Christian wondered at the man's ability to separate this from everything else that was happening. He said, "I think this is a domestic problem, some kind of psychological fallout that has been predicted in think tank studies for years. We're closing in on some suspects."

Again Kennedy stood by the window deep in thought. Then he spoke softly. "Chris, seal this off from every other compartment of government. This is just between you and me. Not even Dazzy or other members of my personal staff should know. It's just too much to add on to everything else."

The city of Washington overflowed with the influx of media people and their equipment from all over the world. There was a hum in the air as in a crowded stadium, and the streets were filled with people who gathered in vast crowds in front of the White House as if to share the suffering of the President. The skies were filled with transport aircraft, specially chartered overseas airliners. Government advisers and their staff were flying to foreign countries to confer about the crisis. Special envoys were flying in. An extra division of Army troops was brought into the area to patrol the city and guard the White House approaches. The huge crowds seemed to be prepared to maintain an all-night vigil as if to reassure the President that he was not alone in his trouble. The noise of that crowd enveloped the White House and its grounds.

On television all the stations had preempted regular programming to broadcast the mourning for the Pope's death. Memorial services in all the great cathedrals of the world, with the huge throngs weeping and millions in funeral black, saturated the airwaves. In all that grief there was an implicit howl for vengeance, though the sermons were full of charity. In these services there were also prayers for the safe deliverance of Theresa Kennedy.

Rumors leaked out that the President was willing to free the killer of the Pope to obtain the release of the hostages and his daughter. The political experts recruited by the TV networks were divided about the wisdom of such a move, but felt that the initial demands were certainly open to negotiation, as in the many other hostage crises over the past years. They more or less agreed that the President had panicked because of the danger to his daughter.

And while all of this was going on, the crowds outside the White House grew larger and larger through the night. The streets of Washington were clogged with vehicles and pedestrians, all converging on the symbolic heart of their country. Many of them brought food and drink for the long vigil. They would wait through the night with their President, Francis Xavier Kennedy.

When Kennedy retired to his bedroom Tuesday night, he prayed that the hostages would be released the next day. With the stage set, Yabril would win. For the moment. On Kennedy's night table were stacked the papers prepared by the CIA, the National Security Council, the Secretary of

State, the Secretary of Defense and the covering memos from his own staff. His butler, Jefferson, brought him hot chocolate and biscuits, and he settled down to read these reports.

He read between the lines. He brought together the seemingly divergent viewpoints of the different agencies. He tried to put himself in the role of a rival world power reading these reports. It would see that America was a country on its last decadent legs, an obese, arthritic giant getting its nose tweaked by malevolent urchins. Within the country itself there was an internal hemorrhaging of the giant. The rich were getting much richer, the poor were sinking into the ground. The middle class was struggling desperately for its share of the good life.

Kennedy recognized that this latest crisis, the killing of the Pope, the hijacking of the plane, the kidnaping of his daughter and the humiliating demands were a deliberately planned blow aimed at the moral authority of the United States.

But then there was also the internal attack, the threat of the atom bomb. The cancer from within. The psychological profiles had predicted that such a thing could happen and precautions had been taken. But not enough. And it had to be internal, it was too dangerous a ploy for terrorists, too rough a tickling of the obese giant. It was a wild card that the terrorists, no matter how bold, would never dare to play. It could open a Pandora's box of repression, for they knew that if governments, especially that of the United States, suspended the laws protecting civil liberties, any terrorist organization could easily be destroyed.

Kennedy studied the reports that summarized information on known terrorist groups and the nations that lent them support. He was surprised to see that China gave the Arab terrorist groups financial support. There were specific organizations that at this moment did not seem to be linked with Yabril's operation; it was too bizarre and without a definite advantage for the cost involved, the negative aspect. The Russians had never advocated free enterprise in terrorism. But there were the splinter Arab groups, the Arab Front, the Saiqua, the PLFP-G and the host of others designated just with initials. Then there were the Red Brigades, the Japanese Red Brigade, the Italian Red Brigade, the German Red Brigade, which had swallowed up all the German splinter groups in murderous internecine warfare.

Finally it was all too much for Kennedy. In the morning, on Wednesday, the negotiations would be completed, the hostages would be safe. Now there was nothing he could do but wait. All this went beyond the twenty-four-hour deadline, but it was all agreed. His staff had assured him that the terrorists would surely be patient.

Before he fell asleep he thought of his daughter and her bright confident smile as she spoke to Yabril, the reincarnated smile of his own dead uncles. Then he fell into tortured dreams and, groaning, called for help. When Jefferson came running to the bedroom, he stared at the agonized face of the sleeping President, waited a moment, then woke him out of his nightmare. He brought in another cup of hot chocolate and gave Kennedy the sleeping pill the doctor had ordered.

Wednesday Morning
Sherhaben

AS FRANCIS KENNEDY slept, Yabril rose. Yabril loved the early morning hours of the desert, the coolness fleeing the sun's internal fire, the sky turning to incandescent red. In these moments he always thought of the Mohammedan Lucifer, called Azazel.

The angel Azazel, standing before God, refused to acknowledge the creation of man, and God hurled Azazel from Paradise to ignite these desert sands into hellfire. Oh, to be Azazel, Yabril thought. When he was young and romantic, he had used Azazel as his first operational name.

This morning the sun flaming with heat made him dizzy. Though he stood in the shaded door of the air-conditioned aircraft, a terrible surf of scalding air sent his body reeling backward. He felt nausea and wondered if it was because of what he had to do. Now he would commit the final irrevocable act, the one last move in his chess game of terror that he had not revealed to Romeo or the Sultan of Sherhaben, nor to the supporting cadres of the Red Brigades. A final sacrilege.

Far away by the air terminal he saw the perimeter guarded by the Sultan's troops who kept the thousands of newspaper, magazine and TV reporters at bay. He had the attention of the entire world; he held the daughter of the President of the United States. He had a bigger audience than any ruler, any Pope, any prophet. Yabril turned away from the open door to face the plane's interior.

Four men of his new cadre were eating breakfast in the first-class cabin. Twenty-four hours had passed since he gave the ultimatum. Time was up. He made them hurry, then sent them on their errands. One went with Yabril's handwritten order to the chief of security on the perimeter, ordering that TV crews be allowed close to the plane. Another of the cadre was given the stack of printed leaflets proclaiming that since Yabril's demands had not been met within the twenty-four-hour deadline, one of the hostages would be executed.

Two men of the cadre were ordered to bring the President's daughter back from the isolated front row of the tourist cabin into the first-class cabin and Yabril's presence.

When Theresa Kennedy came into the first-class cabin and saw Yabril waiting, her face relaxed into a relieved smile. Yabril wondered how she could look so lovely after spending these days on the plane. It was the skin, he thought—she had no oil in her skin to collect dirt. He smiled back at her and said in a kindly half-joking way, "You look beautiful but a little untidy. Freshen yourself, put on some makeup, comb your hair. The TV cameras are waiting for us. The whole world will be watching and I don't want them to think I've been treating you badly."

He let her into the aircraft toilet and waited. She took almost twenty minutes. He could hear flushing and he imagined her sitting there like a little girl and he felt a needlelike pain lance his heart and he prayed, Azazel, Azazel be with me now. And then he heard the great thunderous roar of the crowd standing in the blazing desert sun; they had read the leaflets. He heard the TV mobile units coming closer.

Theresa appeared. Yabril saw a look of sadness in her face. Also stubbornness. She had decided she would not speak, would not let him force her to make his videotape. She was well scrubbed, pretty, with faith in her strength. But she had lost some of her heart's innocence. Now she smiled at Yabril and said, "I won't speak."

Yabril took her by the hand. "I just want them to see you," he said. He led her to the open door of the aircraft; they stood on the ledge. The red air of the desert sun fired their bodies. Six mobile TV tractors seemed to guard the plane like prehistoric monsters, almost blocking the huge crowd beyond the perimeter. "Just smile at them," Yabril said, "I want your father to see you are safe."

At that moment he smoothed the back of her head, feeling the silky hair, pulling it to leave the nape of her neck clear, the ivory skin so frighteningly pale, the only blemish a small black mole on her shoulder.

She flinched at his touch and turned to see what he was doing. His grip tightened and he forced her head to turn front so that the TV cameras could see the beauty of her face. The desert sun framed her in gold, his body was her shadow.

One hand raised and pressed against the roof door to give him balance, he pressed the front of his body into her back so that they teetered on the very edge, a tender touching. He drew the pistol with his right hand and held it to the exposed skin of her neck. And then before she could understand the touch of metal, he pulled the trigger and let her body fall from his.

She seemed to float upward into the air, into the sun, into the halo of her own blood. Then her body tumbled so that her legs pointed to the sky and then turned again before she hit the cement runway, lying there, smashed beyond any mortality, with her ruined head cratered by the burning sun. At first the only sound was the whirring of TV cameras and mobile trucks, the grinding of sand, then rolling over the desert came the wail of thousands of people, an endless scream of terror.

The primal sound without the expected jubilance surprised Yabril. He stepped back from the door to the interior of the aircraft. He saw his cadre looking at him with horror, with loathing, with almost animal terror. He said to them, "Allah be praised," but they did not answer him. He waited for a long moment, then told them curtly, "Now the world will know how serious we are. Now they will give us what we ask." But his mind noted that the roar of the crowd had not had the ecstasy he had expected. The reaction of his own men seemed ominous. The execution of the daughter of the President of the United States, that extinction of some exempt symbol of authority, violated a taboo he had not taken into account. But so be it.

He thought for one moment of Theresa Kennedy, her sweet face, the violet smell of her white neck, he thought of her body caught in the red halo of dust. And he thought, Let her be with Azazel, flung from the golden frame of heaven down into the desert sands forever and ever. His mind held one last picture of her body, her loose-fitting white slacks bunched around her calves, showing her sandaled feet. Fire from the sun rolled through the aircraft and he was drenched in sweat. And he thought, I am Azazel.

Washington

BEFORE DAWN ON Wednesday morning, deep in a nightmare filled with the anguished roar of a huge crowd, President Kennedy found himself being shaken by Jefferson. And oddly, though he was now awake, he could still hear the massive roll of thunderous voices that penetrated the walls of the White House.

There was something different about Jefferson—he did not look like a maker of hot chocolate, a brusher of clothes, the deferential servant. He looked more like a man who had tensed his body and face to receive a dreadful blow. He was saying over and over, "Mr. President, wake up, wake up."

But Kennedy was awake and he said, "What the hell is that noise?"

The whole bedroom was awash with light from the chandelier, and a group of men stood behind Jefferson. He recognized the naval officer who was the White House physician, the warrant officer entrusted with the nuclear "football," and there were Eugene Dazzy, Arthur Wix and Christian Klee. He felt Jefferson almost lifting him out of the bed to stand him on his feet, then in a quick motion slipping him into a bathrobe. For some reason his knees sagged and Jefferson held him up.

All the men seemed stricken, the features of their faces ghostly white, eyes rigidly wide open. Kennedy stood facing them with astonishment and then with an overwhelming dread. For a moment he lost all sense of vision, all sense of hearing, as the dread poisoned his very being. The naval officer opened his black bag and took out a needle already prepared and Kennedy said, "No." He looked at the other men one by one, but they did not speak. He said tentatively, "It's OK, Chris, I knew he would do it. He killed Theresa, didn't he?" And then waited for Christian to say no, that it was something else, that it was some natural catastrophe, the blowing up of a nuclear installation, the death of a great head of state, the sinking of a battleship in the Persian Gulf, a devastating earthquake, flood, fire, pestilence. Anything else. But Christian, his face so pale, said, "Yes."

And it seemed to Kennedy that some long illness, some lurking fever, crested over. He felt his body bow and then was aware that Christian was beside him, as if to shield him from the rest of the people in the room because his face was streaming with tears and he was gasping for breath. Then all the people in the room seemed to come close, the doctor plunged the needle into his arm, and Jefferson and Christian were lowering his body onto the bed.

They waited for Francis Kennedy to recover from shock. Finally, when he had regained some control over himself, he gave them instructions. To commence all the necessary staff sections, to set up liaisons with congressional leaders and to clear the crowds from the streets of the city and from around the White House. And to bar all media. He said he would meet with them at 7:00 A.M.

Just before daybreak, Kennedy made everyone leave. Then Jefferson brought in the customary tray of hot chocolate and biscuits. "I'll be right outside the door," Jefferson said. "I'll check with you every half hour if that is OK, Mr. President." Kennedy nodded and Jefferson left.

Kennedy extinguished all the lights. The room was gray with approaching daybreak. He forced himself to think clearly. His grief was the result of a calculated attack by an enemy and he tried to repulse that grief. He looked at the long oval windows, remembering as he always did that they were special glass, he could look out but nobody could see in, and they were bulletproof. Also the vista he faced, the White House grounds, the buildings beyond, were occupied by Secret Service personnel, with the park equipped with special beams and dog patrols. He himself was always safe; Christian had kept his promise. But there had been no way to keep Theresa safe.

It was over, she was dead. And now after the initial wave of grief he wondered at his calmness. Was it because she had insisted on living her own life after her mother died? Refused to share his life in the White House because she was far to the left of both parties and therefore was his political opponent? Was it a lack of love for his daughter?

He absolved himself. He loved Theresa and she was dead. But the impact had been lessened because he had been preparing himself for that death in the last days. His unconscious and cunning paranoia, rooted in the Kennedy history, had sent him warning signals.

There was the coordination of the killing of the Pope and the hijacking of the plane that held the daughter of the leader of the most powerful nation on earth. There was the delay in the demands until the assassin had been in place and captured in the United States. Then the deliberate arrogance of the demand for the release of the assassin of the Pope.

By a supreme effort of will Francis Kennedy banished all personal feeling from his mind. He tried to follow a logical line. It was really all so simple: a Pope and a young girl had lost their lives. Objectively viewed, this fact was essentially not terribly important on a world scale. Religious leaders can be canonized, young girls mourned with sweet regret. But there was something else. People the world over would have a contempt for the United States and its leaders. Other attacks would be launched in ways not foreseen. Authority spat upon cannot keep order. Authority taunted and defeated cannot presume to hold together the fabric of its particular civilization. How could he defend it?

The door of the bedroom opened and light flooded in from

the hall. But the bedroom now aglow with the rising sun blotted it out. Jefferson, in fresh shirt and jacket, wheeled the breakfast table through and prepared it for Kennedy. He gave Kennedy a searching look, as if inquiring whether to stay, then finally went out.

Kennedy felt tears on his face and knew suddenly that they were the tears of impotence. Again he realized that his grief was gone and wondered. Then he felt consciously overwhelming his brain the waves of blood carrying terrible rage, even a rage at his staff, who had failed him, a rage he had never known and which all his life he had disdained in others. He tried to resist it.

He thought now of how his staff had tried to comfort him. Christian had shown his personal affection shared over long years, Christian had embraced him, helped him to his bed. Oddblood Gray, usually so cool and impersonal, had gripped him by the shoulders and just whispered, "I'm sorry, I'm goddamn sorry." Arthur Wix and Eugene Dazzy had been more reserved. They had touched him briefly and murmured something he could not hear. And Kennedy had noted the fact that Dazzy as his chief of staff had been one of the first to leave the bedroom to get things organized in the rest of the White House. Wix had left with Dazzy. As head of the National Security Council he had urgent work, and perhaps he was afraid of hearing some wild order of retaliation from a man overwrought by a father's grief.

In the short time before Jefferson came back with the breakfast, Francis Kennedy knew his life would be completely different, perhaps out of his control. He tried to exclude anger from his reasoning process.

He remembered strategy sessions in which such events were discussed. He remembered Iran, remembered Iraq.

His mind went back almost forty years. He was a seven-

year-old boy playing on the sandy shores of Hyannisport
with the children of Uncle Jack and Uncle Bobby. And the
two uncles, so tall and slim and fair, had played with them
a few minutes before ascending into their waiting helicopter
like gods. As a child he had always liked his uncle Jack best
because he had known all his secrets. He had once seen him
kiss a woman, then lead her into his bedroom. And he had
seen them come out an hour later. He had never forgotten
the look on Uncle Jack's face, such a happy look as if he had
received some unforgettable gift. They had never noticed the
little boy hidden behind one of the tables in the hallway. At
that time of innocence the Secret Service was not so close to
the President.

And there were other scenes out of his childhood, vivid
tableaux of power. His two uncles being treated like royalty
by men and women much older than themselves. The music
starting when Uncle Jack stepped out on the lawn, all faces
turning toward him, the cessation of speech until he spoke.
His two uncles sharing their power and their grace in wearing it. How confidently they waited for the helicopters to
drop out of the sky, how safe they seemed surrounded by
strong men who shielded them from hurt, how they were
whisked up to the heavens, how grandly they descended
from the heights. . . .

Their smiles gave light, their godhead flashed knowledge
and command from their eyes, the magnetism radiated from
their bodies. And with all this they took the time to play with
the little boys and girls who were their sons and daughters,
their nieces and nephews, playing with the utmost serious-
ness, gods who visited tiny mortals in their keeping. And
then. And then . . .

He had watched on television, with his weeping mother,
the funeral of Uncle Jack, the gun carriage, the riderless

horse, the millions of grief-stricken people, and had seen his little playmate as one of the actors on the world stage. And his uncle Bobby and his aunt Jackie. His mother at some point took him into her arms and said, "Don't look, don't look," and he was blinded by her long hair and sticky tears.

Now, the shaft of yellow light from the open door cut through his memories and he saw that Jefferson had wheeled in a fresh table. Kennedy said quietly, "Take that away and give me an hour. Don't interrupt me before then." He had rarely spoken so abruptly or sternly and Jefferson gave him an appraising look. Then he said, "Yes, Mr. President," and wheeled the table back out and closed the door.

The sun was strong enough to light the bedroom yet not strong enough to give it heat. But the throb of Washington entered the room. The television trucks were filling the streets outside the gates and countless car motors hummed like a giant swarm of insects. Planes flew constantly overhead, all military—airspace had been closed to civilian traffic.

He tried to fight the overwhelming rage, the bitter bile in his mouth. What was supposed to be the greatest triumph of his life had proved to be his greatest misfortune. He had been elected to the presidency and his wife had died before he assumed the office. His great programs for a utopian America had been eroded by Congress. And now his daughter had paid the price for his ambition and his dreams. Nauseating saliva made him gag as it ran over his tongue and lips. His body seemed to fill with a poison that weakened him in every limb and the feeling that only rage could make him well, and at that moment something happened in his brain, an electric charge fighting the sickness of his bodily cells. So much energy flowed through his body that he flung his arms outward, fists clenched to the now sun-filled windows.

He had power, he would use that power. He could make his enemies tremble, he could make their saliva bitter in *their* mouths. He could sweep away all the small insignificant men with their cheap tubes of iron, all those who had brought such tragedy into his life and to his family.

He felt now like a man who, long enfeebled, is finally cured of a serious illness and wakes one morning to find he has regained his strength. He felt an exhilaration, almost a peace he had not felt since his wife died. He sat on the bed and tried to control his feelings, to restore caution and a rational train of thought. More calmly he reviewed all his options and all their dangers and then finally he knew what he must do and what dangers he must forestall. He felt one last thrust of pain that his daughter no longer existed.

BOOK
III

BOOK

III

CHAPTER
8

AT 11:00 A.M., Wednesday morning, the most politically significant people in the government gathered in the Cabinet Room to decide what course of action the country should pursue. There was Vice President Helen Du Pray, there were the members of the Cabinet, the head of the CIA, the chief of the Joint Chiefs of Staff, not usually present at such meetings but instructed to attend by Eugene Dazzy following the President's request. When Kennedy entered the room they all rose.

Kennedy motioned to them to sit down. Only the Secretary of State remained standing. He said, "Mr. President, all of us here wish to express our heartbreak at your loss. We offer our personal condolences, our love. We assure you of our utmost loyalty and devotion in your personal crisis and this crisis in our nation. We are here to give you more than our professional counsel. We are here to give you our individual devotion." There were tears in the eyes of the Secretary of State. And he was a man noted for his coolness and reserve.

Kennedy bowed his head for a moment. He was the only man in the room who seemed to show no emotion except for the pallor of his face. He looked at them all for a long moment, as if acknowledging every person in the room, their feelings of affection and his gratefulness. Knowing that he was about to shatter this good feeling. He said, "I want to thank all of you, I am grateful and I am counting on you. But now I beg all of you to put my personal misfortune out of the context of this meeting. We are here to decide what is best for our country. This is our duty and sacred obligation. The decisions I have made are strictly nonpersonal." He paused for a moment to let the shock and recognition sink in that he alone would control.

Helen Du Pray thought, Oh Christ, he's going to do it.

Kennedy went on. "This meeting will deal with our options. I doubt that any of your options will be taken but I must give you your opportunity to argue them. But first let me present my scenario. Let me say that I have the support of my personal staff." He paused again to project all his personal magnetism. He stood up and said, "One: The analysis. All the recent tragic events have been the dynamic of one boldly conceived and ruthlessly executed master plan. The murder of the Pope on Easter Sunday, the hijacking of the plane on the same day, the deliberate logistical impossibility of the demands for the release of the hostages, and though I agreed to meet all those demands, finally the unnecessary murder of my daughter early this morning. And even the capture of the assassin of the Pope here in our country, an event far beyond the realm of any chance of destiny, that too was part of the overall plan so that they could demand the release of the assassin. The evidence supporting this analysis is overwhelming."

He could see the looks of disbelief on their faces. He paused and then went on: "But what could be the purpose of such a terrifying and complicated scenario? There is in the world today a contempt for authority, the authority of the state, but specifically a contempt for the moral authority of the United States. It goes far beyond the usual historical contempt for authority exhibited by the young, which is often a good thing. The purpose of this terrorist plan is to discredit the United States as an authority figure. Not only in the lives of billions of common people but in the eyes of the governments of the world. We must at some time answer these challenges and that time is now.

"For the record. The Arab states have no part in this plot. Except for Sherhaben. Certainly the worldwide terrorist underground known as the First Hundred gave logistical and personnel support. But the evidence points to only one man in control. And it seems that he does not accept being controlled except perhaps by the Sultan of Sherhaben."

Again he paused.

"We now know for certain that the Sultan is an accomplice. His troops are stationed to guard the aircraft from outside attacks, not to help us with the hostages. The Sultan claims to act in our interest, but in reality is involved in these acts. However, to give him his due, there is evidence that he did not know that Yabril would murder my daughter."

He glanced around the table to again impress them with his calmness. Then he said, "Second: The prognosis. This is not the usual hostage situation. This is a clever plot to humiliate the United States to the utmost. To make the United States beg for the return of the hostages after suffering a series of humiliations that make us seem impotent. It is a situation that will be wrung dry for weeks with media coverage all over the world. And with no guarantee that all the remaining hostages will be returned safely. Under those circumstances I cannot imagine anything but chaos afterwards. Our own people will lose faith in us and our country."

Again Kennedy paused, he saw that he was making an impression now, that the people in this room understood that he had a point. He went on: "Remedies: I've studied the memo on options we have. I think they are the usual lame recourses of the past. Economic sanctions, armed rescue missions, political arm-twisting, concessions given in secret while maintaining that we never negotiate with terrorists. The concern that the Soviet Union will refuse to permit us to make a large-scale military assault in the Persian Gulf. All these imply that we must submit and accept our profound humiliation in the eyes of the world. And in my opinion more of the hostages may well be lost."

The Secretary of State interrupted. "My department has just received a definite promise from the Sultan of Sherhaben to release all the hostages when the terrorists' demands have been met. He is outraged by Yabril's action and claims he is ready to launch an assault on the plane. He has secured Yabril's promise to release fifty of the hostages now to show good faith."

Kennedy stared at him for a moment. The cerulean-blue eyes seemed veined with tiny black dots. Then in a voice cold with taut courtesy, and so controlled that the words rang metallically, he said, "Mr. Secretary, when I am done, everyone here will be given time to speak. Until that time, please do not interrupt. Their offer will be suppressed, it will not be made known to the media."

The Secretary of State was obviously surprised. The President had never spoken so coolly to him before, had never so blatantly shown his power. The Secretary of State bowed his head to study his copy of the memo; only his cheeks reddened slightly. Kennedy went on: "Solution: I hereby instruct the chief of staff to direct and plan an air strike on the oil fields of Sherhaben and their industrial oil city of Dak. The mission of the air strike will be the destruction of all oil equipment, drilling rigs, pipelines, etc. The city will be destroyed. Four hours before the bombing, leaflets will be dropped on the city warning the inhabitants to evacuate. The air strike will take place exactly thirty-six hours from now. That is, on Thursday, eleven P.M., Washington time."

There was dead silence in the room that held more than thirty people who wielded all the arms of power in America. Kennedy went on: "The Secretary of State will contact the necessary countries for overflight approval. He will make it plain to them that any refusal will bring about a cessation of all economic and military accommodations with this country. That the results of a refusal will be dire."

The Secretary of State seemed to levitate from his seat to protest, then restrained himself. There was a murmur through the room of surprise or shock.

Kennedy held up his hands, the gesture almost angry, but he was smiling at them, a smile that seemed to be one of reassurance. He seemed to become less commanding, almost casual, smiling at the Secretary of State and speaking directly to him. "The Secretary of State will send to me, at once, the ambassador from the Sultanate of Sherhaben. I will tell the ambassador this: The Sultan must deliver up the hostages by tomorrow afternoon. He will deliver up the terrorist Yabril in a way that he will not be able to take his own life. If the Sultan refuses, the entire country of Sherhaben itself will cease to exist." Kennedy paused for a moment; the room was absolutely still. "This meeting has the highest security classification. There will be no leaks. If there are, the most extreme action under the law will be taken. Now you can all speak."

He could see the audience was stunned by his words, that the staff looked down, refusing to meet the eyes of the others in the room.

Kennedy sat down, sprawling in his black leather chair, his legs out from under the table and visible to the side. He stared out into the Rose Garden as the meeting continued.

He heard the Secretary of State say, "Mr. President, again I must argue your decision. This will be a disaster for the United States. We will become a pariah among nations by using our force to crush a small nation." And the voice went on and on, but he could not hear the words.

Then he heard the voice of the Secretary of the Interior, a voice almost flat and yet commanding attention. "Mr. President, when we destroy Dak, we destroy fifty billion American dollars, that's American oil company money, money the middle class of America spent to buy stock in the oil companies. Also, we curtail our sources of oil. The price of gasoline will double for the consumers of this country."

There was the confused babble of other arguments. Why did the city of Dak have to be destroyed before any satisfaction was given? There were many avenues still to be explored. The great danger was in acting too hastily. Kennedy looked at his watch. This had been going on for over an hour. He stood up.

"I thank each of you for your advice," he said. "Certainly the Sultan of Sherhaben could save the city of Dak by meeting my demands immediately. But he won't. The city of Dak must be destroyed or our threats will be ignored. The alternative is for us to govern a country that any man with courage and small weapons can humiliate. Then we might as

well scrap our Navy and Army and save the money. I see our
course very clearly and I will follow it.

"Now, as to the fifty-billion-dollar loss to American stockholders. Bert Audick heads the consortium that owns that
property. He has already made his fifty billion dollars and
more. We will do our best to help him, of course. I will
permit Mr. Audick an opportunity to save his investment in
another way. I am sending a plane to Sherhaben to pick up
the hostages and a military plane to transport the terrorists
to this country to stand trial. The Secretary of State will
invite Mr. Audick to go to Sherhaben on one of those planes.
His job will be to help persuade the Sultan to accept my
terms. To persuade him that the only way to save the city
of Dak, the country of Sherhaben and the American oil in
that country is to accede to my demands. That's the deal."

The Secretary of Defense said, "If the Sultan does not
agree, that means we lose two more planes, Audick, and the
hostages."

Kennedy said, "Most likely. Let's see if Audick has the
balls. But he's smart. He will know, as I do, that the Sultan
must agree. I'm so sure that I am also sending the national
security adviser, Mr. Wix."

The CIA chief said, "Mr. President, you must know that
the antiaircraft guns around Dak are manned by Americans
on civilian contract to the Sherhaben government and the
American oil companies. Specially trained Americans who
man missile sites. They may put up a fight."

Kennedy smiled. "Audick will order them to evacuate. Of
course, as Americans, if they fight us they will be traitors,
and the Americans who pay them will also be prosecuted as
traitors."

He paused to let that sink in. Audick would be prosecuted.

He turned to Christian. "Chris, you can start working on the legal end."

Among those present were two members of the legislative branch. The Senate majority leader, Thomas Lambertino, and the Speaker of the House, Alfred Jintz. It was the senator who spoke first. He said, "I think this too drastic a course of action to be taken without a full discussion in both houses of the Congress."

Kennedy said to him courteously, "With all due respect, there is no time. And it is within my power as the chief executive to take this action. Without question the legislative branch can review it later and take action as they see fit. But I sincerely hope that Congress will support me and this nation in its extremity."

Senator Lambertino said almost sorrowfully, "This is dire, the consequences severe. I implore you, Mr. President, not to act so quickly."

For the first time Francis Kennedy became less than courteous. "Congress has always opposed me," he said. "We can argue all the complicated options until the hostages are dead and the United States is ridiculed in every nation and every little village in the world. I hold by my analysis and my solution; my decision is within my power as chief executive. When the crisis is over, I will go before the people and give them a full report. Until then, I remind you all again, this discussion is of the highest classification. Now, I know you all have work to do. Report your progress to my chief of staff."

It was Alfred Jintz who answered. "Mr. President," he said, "I had hoped not to have to say this. But Congress now insists that you remove yourself from these negotiations. Therefore, I must give notice that this very day the Congress and the Senate will do everything to prevent your course of action on the grounds that your personal tragedy makes you incompetent."

Kennedy stood over them. His face with its beautiful planes and lines were frozen into a mask, his blue eyes as blind as a statue's. "You do so at your peril," he said, "and America's." He left the room.

In the Cabinet Room, there was a flurry of movement, a babble of voices. Oddblood Gray huddled with Senator Lambertino and Congressman Jintz. But their faces were grim, their voices cold. The congressman said, "We can't allow this to happen. I think the President's staff has been delinquent in not dissuading him from this course of action."

Oddblood Gray said, "He convinced me he was not acting out of personal anger. That it was the most effective solution to the problem. It is dire, of course, but so are the times. We can't let the situation be drawn out. That could be catastrophic."

Senator Lambertino said, "This is the first time that I have ever known Francis Kennedy to act in so high-handed a fashion. He was always a courteous President to the legislative branch. He could at least have pretended that we were party to the decision process."

"He's under a great deal of stress," Oddblood Gray said. "It would be helpful if the Congress did not add to that stress." Fat chance, he thought as he said it.

Congressman Jintz said worriedly, "Stress may be the issue here." Oddblood Gray thought, Oh shit, hastily said a cordial farewell and ran back to his office to make the hundreds of calls to members of the Congress. Though he was privately dismayed at Kennedy's rashness, he was determined to sell Kennedy's policy on the Hill.

The national security adviser, Arthur Wix, was trying to

sound out the Secretary of Defense. And making sure that there would be an immediate meeting with the Joint Chiefs of Staff. But the Secretary of Defense seemed to be stunned by events and mumbled his answers, agreeing but not volunteering anything.

Eugene Dazzy had noted Oddblood Gray's difficulties with the legislators. There was going to be big trouble.

Dazzy turned to Helen Du Pray. "What do you think?" he asked her.

She looked at him coolly. She was a very beautiful woman, Dazzy thought. He must invite her to dinner. Then she said, "I think you and the rest of the President's staff have let him down. His response to this crisis is far too drastic. And where the hell is Christian Klee to deal with this right now?" Klee had vanished, which surprised Du Pray, it was not like him to disappear at a crucial moment like this.

Dazzy was angry. "His position has logic, and even if we disagree we have to support him."

Helen Du Pray said, "It's how Francis presented it. Obviously, Congress will try to take the negotiations out of his hands. They will try to suspend him from office."

"Over the graves of his staff," Dazzy said.

Helen Du Pray said to him quietly, "Please be careful. Our country is in great danger."

CHAPTER
9

ON THIS WEDNESDAY afternoon Peter Cloot was certainly the only official in Washington who paid almost no attention to the news that the President's daughter had been murdered. His energies were focused on the nuclear bomb threat.

As deputy chief of the FBI, he had almost full responsibility for that agency. Christian Klee was the titular head but only to hold the reins of power, to bring it more firmly under the direction of the Attorney General's office, which Klee also held. That combination of offices had always bothered Peter Cloot. It also bothered him that the Secret Service had also been placed under Klee. That was too much concentration of power for Cloot's taste. He also knew that there was a separate elite branch ostensibly in the FBI table of organization that Klee administered directly, and that this special security branch was composed of Christian Klee's former colleagues in the CIA. That affronted him.

But this nuclear threat was Peter Cloot's baby. He would run this show. And luckily there were specific directives to guide him, and he had attended the think-tank seminars that directly addressed the problem of internal nuclear threats. If anyone was an expert on this particular situation, it was Cloot. And there was no shortage of manpower. During Klee's tenure the number of FBI personnel had increased threefold.

When he had first seen the threatening letter with its accompanying diagrams Cloot had taken the immediate action as outlined in the standing directives. He had also felt a thrill of fear. Up to this time there had been hundreds of such threats, only a few of them plausible, but none so convincing as this. All these threats had been kept secret, again according to directives.

Immediately, Cloot forwarded the letter to the Department of Energy command post in Maryland, using the special communications facilities for this purpose only. He also alerted the Department of Energy search teams based in Las Vegas called NEST. NEST was already flying their pod containing tools and detection equipment to New York. Other planes would be flying specially trained personnel into the city, where they would use disguised vans loaded with sophisticated equipment to explore the streets of New York. Helicopters would be used; men on foot carrying Geiger counter briefcases would cover the city. But all this was not Cloot's headache. All he would have to do was supply armed FBI guards to protect the NEST searchers. Cloot's job was to find the villains.

The Maryland Department of Energy people had studied the letter and sent him a psychological profile of the writer. Those guys were really amazing, Cloot thought—he didn't know how they did it. Of course, one of the obvious clues was that the letter did not ask for money. Also it did define a definite political position. As soon as he got the profile Cloot sent a thousand men checking.

The profile had said that the letter writer was probably very young and highly educated. That he was probably a student of physics in a highly rated university. And on this information alone Cloot in a matter of hours had two very good suspects and after that it was amazingly easy. He had worked all through the night, directing his field office teams. When he was informed of the murder of Theresa Kennedy, he had resolutely put it out of his mind except for the flash that all this stuff might be linked together in some way. But his job tonight was to find the author of the nuclear bomb threat. Thank God, the bastard was an idealist. It made him easier to track down. There were a million greedy sons of bitches who would do something like this for money and it would have been tough to find them.

While he waited for the information to come in, he put the files of all previous nuclear threats through his computer. There had never been a nuclear weapon found, and those blackmailers who had been caught while trying to collect their bribe money had confessed that there had never been one. Some of them had been men with a smattering of science. Others had picked up convincing information from a left-wing magazine that had printed an article describing how to make a nuclear weapon. The magazine had been leaned on not to publish that article, but it had gone to the Supreme Court, which had ruled that suppression would be a violation of free speech. Even thinking of that now made Peter Cloot tremble with rage. The fucking country was going to destroy itself. One thing he noted with interest: none of the over two hundred cases had involved a woman or a black or even a foreign terrorist. They were all fucking true-blue greedy American men.

When he finished with the computer files he thought a minute about his boss, Christian Klee. He really didn't like the way Klee was running things. Klee thought the whole job of the FBI was to guard the President of the United States. Klee used not only the Secret Service Division but had special squads in every FBI office in the country whose main job was to sniff out possible dangers to the office of the President. Klee diverted a great deal of manpower from other operations of the FBI to do this.

Cloot was leery of Klee's power, his special division of ex-CIA men. What the hell did they do? Peter Cloot didn't know and he had every right to know. That division reported directly to Klee, and that was a very bad thing in a government agency so sensitive to public opinion as the FBI. So far nothing had happened. Cloot spent a great deal of time covering his ass, making sure that he could not be caught in the fireworks when that special division pulled some shit that would bring the Congress down on their heads with their special investigation committees.

At 1:00 A.M. Cloot's assistant deputy came in to report that two suspects were under surveillance. Proof was in hand that confirmed the psychological profile, and there was other circumstantial evidence. Only the order to make the arrest was needed.

Cloot said to his deputy, "I have to brief Klee first. Stay here while I call him."

Cloot knew that Klee would be in the President's chief of staff's office or that the omnipotent White House telephone operators would track him down if he was not. He got Klee on his first try.

"We have that special case all wrapped up," Cloot told him. "But I think I should brief you before we bring them in—can you come over?"

Klee's voice was strained. "No, I cannot. I have to be with the President now, surely you understand that."

"Shall I just go ahead and fill you in later?" Cloot asked.

There was a long pause at the other end. Then Klee said, "I think we have time for you to come over here. If I'm not available, just wait. But you have to rush."

"I'm on my way," Cloot said.

It had not been necessary for either of them to suggest doing the briefing over the phone. That was out of the question. Anybody could pick messages out of the infinite trailways of airspace.

Cloot got to the White House and was escorted into a small briefing room. Klee was waiting for him; his prosthesis was off and he was massaging his stump through his stocking.

"I only have a few minutes," Klee said. "Big meeting with the President."

"Jesus, I'm sorry about that," Cloot said. "How is he taking it?"

Klee shook his head. "You can't ever tell with Francis. He seems OK." He shook his head in a sort of bewilderment, then said briskly, "OK, let's have it." He looked at Cloot with a sort of distaste. The man's physical exterior always irritated him. Cloot never looked tired, and he was one of those men whose shirt and suit never got wrinkled. He always wore ties of knitted wool with square knots, usually of a light gray color and sometimes a sort of bloody black.

"We spotted them," Cloot said. "Two young kids, twenty years old, in MIT nuclear labs. Geniuses, IQ's in the 160s, come from wealthy families, left-wing, marched with the nuclear protesters. These kids have access to classified memorandums. They fit the think-tank profile. They are sitting in their lab up in Boston, working on some government and university project. A couple of months ago they came to New York and a buddy got them laid and they loved it. He was sure it was their first time. A deadly combination, idealism and the raging hormones of youth. Right now I have them sealed off."

"Do you have any firm evidence?" Christian asked. "Anything concrete?"

"We're not trying them or even indicting them," Cloot said. "This is preventive arrest as authorized under the atom bomb laws. Once we have them, they'll confess and tell us where the damn thing is if there is one. I don't think there is. I think that part is bullshit. But they certainly wrote the letter. They fit the profile. Also the date of the letter—it's the day they registered at the Hilton in New York. That's the clincher."

Christian had often marveled at the resources of all the government agencies with their computers and high-grade electronic gear. It was amazing that they could eavesdrop on anyone anywhere no matter what precautions were taken. That computers could scan hotel registers all over the city in less than an hour. And other complicated serious things. At ghastly expense, of course.

"OK, we'll grab them," Christian said. "But I'm not sure you can make them confess. They're smart kids."

Cloot stared into Christian's eyes. "OK, Chris, they don't confess, we're a civilized country. We just let the bomb explode and kill thousands of people." He smiled for a moment almost maliciously. "Or you go to the President and make him sign a medical interrogation order. Section IX of the Atomic Weapons Control Act."

Which was what Cloot had been coming to all the time.

Christian had been avoiding the same thought all night. He had always been shocked that a country like the United States could have such a secret law. The press could easily have uncovered it, but again there was that covenant between the owners of the media and the governors of the country. So the law was not really known to the public, as was true of many laws governing nuclear science.

Christian knew Section IX very well. As a lawyer he had marveled at it. It was that savagery in the law that had always repelled him.

Section IX essentially gave the President the right to order a chemical brain scan that had been developed to make anyone tell the truth, a lie detector right in the brain. The law had been especially designed to extract information about the planting of a nuclear device. It fitted this case perfectly. There would be no torture, the victim would suffer no physical pain. Simply, the chemical changes in the brain would be measured to verify that he invariably told the truth when asked questions. It would be humane, the only catch being that nobody really knew what happened to the brain after the operation. Experiments indicated that in rare cases there would be some loss of memory, some slight loss of functioning. He would not be retarded—that would be unconscionable—but as the old joke had it, there go the music lessons. The only catch was that there was a 10 percent chance that there would be complete memory loss. Complete long-term amnesia. The subject's entire past could be erased.

Christian said, "Just a long shot, but could this be linking up with the hijacking and the Pope? Even that guy being captured on Long Island looks like a trick. Could this all be a part of it, a smoke screen, a booby trap?"

Cloot studied him for a long time as if debating his answer.

"Could be," Cloot said. "But I suspect this is one of those famous coincidences of history."

"That always lead to tragedy," Christian said wryly.

Cloot went on. "These two kids are just crazy in their own genius style. They are political. They are obsessed by the nuclear danger to the whole world. They are not interested in current political quarrels. They don't give a shit about the Arabs and Israel or the poor and rich in America. Or the Democrats and Republicans. They just want the globe to rotate faster on its axis. You know." He smiled contemptuously. "They all think they're God. Nothing can touch them."

But Christian's mind was at rest on one thing. There was political shrapnel flying all around with these two problems. Don't move too fast, he thought. Francis was in terrible danger now. Kennedy would have to be protected. Maybe they could play one off against the other.

He said to Cloot, "Listen, Peter, I want this to be the most secret of operations. Seal it off from everybody else. I want those two kids grabbed and put into the hospital detention facility we have here in Washington. Just you and me and the agents we use from the special division. Shove the agents' noses into the Atomic Weapons Control Act, absolute secrecy. Nobody sees them, nobody talks to them except me. I'll do the interrogation personally."

Cloot gave him a funny look. He didn't like the operation being turned over to Klee's special division. "The medical team will want to see a presidential order before they shoot chemicals into those kids' brains."

Christian said, "I'll ask the President."

Peter Cloot said casually, "Time is crucial on this thing, and you said nobody interrogates except you. Does that include me? What if you're tied up with the President?"

Christian Klee smiled and said, "Don't worry, I'll be there. Nobody but me, Peter. Now give me the details." He had other things on his mind. Shortly he would meet with the chiefs of his FBI special division and order them to mount an electronic and computer surveillance on the most important members of the Congress and the Socrates Club.

Adam Gresse and Henry Tibbot had planted their tiny atom bomb, a bomb they had constructed with much labor and ingenuity. They were perhaps so proud of their labors that they could not resist using it for such a high cause.

They kept watching the newspapers, but their letter did not appear on the front page of *The New York Times*. There were no news items on the subject. They had not been given the opportunity to lead the authorities to the bomb after their demand was met. They were being ignored. This frightened them and yet angered them too. Now the bomb would explode and cause thousands of deaths. But possibly that would be for the best. How else could the world be alerted to the dangers of the use of atomic power? How else could the necessary actions be taken for the men in authority to install the proper safeguards? They had calculated that the bomb would destroy at least four to six square blocks of New York City. Their consciences were clear; they had ensured in the construction of the bomb that there would be a minimum of radioactive fallout. They regretted that, it would cost a certain number of human lives. But it would be a small price for mankind to pay to see the error of its ways. Impregnable safeguards must be established; the making of nuclear bombs must be banned by all the nations of the world.

On Wednesday Gresse and Tibbot worked in the laboratory until everyone in the institute had gone home, and then they argued whether they should make a phone call to alert the authorities. At the beginning it had never been their intention to actually let the bomb go off. They had wanted to see their letter of warning published in *The New York Times* and then they had planned to go back to New York to disarm the bomb. But now it seemed a war of wills. Were they to be treated as children, sneered at, when they could accomplish so much for humanity? Or would they be listened to? In all conscience they could not go on with their scientific work if it was to be misused by the political establishment.

They had chosen New York City to be punished because on their visits there they had been so horrified by the feeling of evil that seemed to them to pervade the streets. The threatening beggars, the insolent drivers of wheeled vehicles, the rudeness of clerks in stores, the countless burglaries, street muggings and murders. They had been particularly revolted by Times Square, that area so crowded with people that it seemed to them like a huge sink of cockroaches. In Times Square the pimps, the dope pushers and the whores seemed so menacing that Gresse and Tibbot had retreated with fright to their hotel room uptown. And so with fully justifiable anger they had decided to plant the bomb in Times Square itself.

Adam and Henry were as shocked as the rest of the nation when the television screen showed the murder of Theresa Kennedy. But they were also a little annoyed that this diverted attention from their own operation, which, ultimately, was more important to the fate of humanity.

But they had become nervous. Adam had heard peculiar clickings on his telephone and had noticed that his car seemed to be followed; he had felt an electric disturbance when certain men passed him in the street. He told Tibbot about these things.

Henry Tibbot was very tall and very lean, and seemed to be made of wires joined together with scraps of flesh and transparent skin. He had a better scientific mind than Adam and stronger nerves. "You're reacting the way all criminals act," he told Adam. "It's normal. Every time there's a knock on the door I think it's the Feds."

"And if it is one time?" Adam Gresse asked.

"Keep your mouth shut until the lawyer comes," Henry Tibbot said. "That is the most important thing. We would get twenty-five years just for writing the letter. So if the bomb explodes, it will just be a few more years."

"Do you think they can trace us?" Adam asked.

"Not a chance," Henry said. "We've gotten rid of anything that could be evidence. Christ, are we smarter than them or not?"

This reassured Adam, but he wavered a bit. "Maybe we should make a call and tell them where it is," he said.

"No," Henry said. "They are on the alert now. They will be ready to zero in on our call. That will be the only way to catch us. Just remember, if things go wrong, just keep your mouth shut. Now, let's go to work."

Adam and Henry were working late in the lab this night really because they wanted to be together. They wanted to talk about what they had done, what recourse they had. They were young men of intense will, they had been brought up to have the courage of their convictions, to detest an authority that refused to be swayed with a reasonable argument. Though they conjured up mathematical formulas that might change the destiny of mankind, they had no idea of the complicated relationships of civilization. Glorious achievers, they had not yet grown into humanity.

As they were preparing to leave, the phone rang. It was

Henry's father. He said to Henry, "Son, listen carefully. You are about to be arrested by the FBI. Say nothing to them until they let you see your lawyer. Say nothing. I know —"

At that moment the door of the room opened and men with guns swarmed in.

CHAPTER
10

THE RICH IN America, without a doubt, are more socially conscious than the rich in any other country of the world. This is true, of course, especially of the extremely rich, those who own and run huge corporations, exercise their economic strength in politics and propagandize in all areas of culture. And this applied especially to members of the Socratic Country Golf and Tennis Club of Southern California, which had been founded nearly seventy years before by real estate, media, cinematic and agricultural tycoons as a politically liberal organization devoted to recreation. It was an exclusive organization; you had to be very rich to join. Technically, you could be black or white, Jewish or Catholic, man or woman, artist or magnate. In reality there were very few blacks and no women.

The Socrates Club, as it was commonly known, finally evolved into a club for the very enlightened, very responsible rich. Prudently, it had an ex–deputy director of CIA operations as head of security systems, and its electronic fences were the highest in America.

Four times a year, the club was used as a retreat for fifty to a hundred men who in effect owned nearly everything in America. They came for a week, and in that week, service was reduced to a minimum. They made their own beds, served their own drinks and sometimes even cooked their own food in the evening on outside barbecues. There were, of course, some waiters, cooks and maids, and there were the inevitable aides to those important men; after all, the world of American business and politics could not come to a stop while they recharged their spiritual batteries.

During this weeklong stay these men would gather into small groups and spend their time in private discussions. They would participate in seminars conducted by distinguished professors from the most famous universities, on questions of ethics, philosophy, the responsibility of the fortunate elite to the less fortunate in society. They would be given lectures by famous scientists on the benefits and dangers of nuclear weapons, brain research, the exploration of space, economics.

They also played tennis, swam in the pool, had backgammon and bridge tournaments and held discussions far into the night on virtue and villainy, on women and love, on marriage and adventure. And these were responsible men, the most responsible men in American society. But they were trying to do two things: they were trying to become better human beings while recovering their adolescence, and they were trying to unite in bringing about a better society as they perceived a better society to be.

After a week together they returned to their normal lives, refreshed with new hope, a desire to help mankind, and a sharper perception of how all their activities could be meshed to preserve the structure of their society, and perhaps with closer personal relationships that could help them do business.

This present week had started on the Monday after Easter Sunday. Because of the crisis in national affairs with the killing of the Pope and the hijacking of the plane carrying the President's daughter and her murderer, the attendance had dropped to less than twenty.

George Greenwell was the oldest of these men. At eighty, he could still play tennis doubles, but out of a carefully bred courtesy did not inflict himself on the younger men who would be forced to play in a forgiving style. Yet, he was still a tiger in long sessions of backgammon.

Greenwell considered the national crisis none of his business unless it involved grain in some way, for his company was privately owned and controlled most of the wheat in America. His shining hour had been thirty years ago when the United States had embargoed grain to Russia as a political ploy to muscle Russia in the cold war.

George Greenwell was a patriot but not a fool. He knew that Russia could not yield to such pressure. He also knew that the Washington-imposed embargo would ruin American farmers. So he had defied the President of the United States and shipped the forbidden grain by diverting it to other foreign companies, which relayed it to Russia. He had brought down the wrath of the American executive branch on his head. Laws had been presented to Congress to curtail the power of his family-held company, to make it public, to put it under some sort of regulatory control. But the Greenwell money contributed to congressmen and senators soon put a stop to that nonsense.

Greenwell loved the Socrates Club because it was luxurious but not so luxurious as to invite the envy of the less fortunate. Also, because it was not known to the media—its members owned most of the TV stations, newspapers and magazines. And also it made him feel young, enabled him to participate socially in the lives of younger men who were equal in power.

He had made a good deal of extra money during that grain embargo, buying wheat and corn from embattled American farmers and selling it dear to a desperate Russia. But he had made sure that the extra money benefited the people of the United States. What he had done had been a matter of principle, the principle being that his intelligence was greater than that of government functionaries. The extra money, hundreds of millions of dollars, had been funneled into museums, educational foundations, cultural programs on TV, especially music, which was Greenwell's passion.

Greenwell prided himself on being civilized, based on his having been sent to the best schools, where he was taught the social behavior of the responsible rich and a civilized feeling of affection for his fellowman. That he was strict in the dealings of his business was his form of art; the mathematics of millions of tons of grain sounded in his brain as clearly and sweetly as chamber music.

One of his few moments of ignoble rage had occurred when a very young professor of music in a university chair established by one of his foundations published an essay that elevated jazz and rock 'n' roll music above Brahms and Schubert and dared to call classical music "funereal." Greenwell had vowed to have the professor removed from his chair, but his inbred courtesy prevailed. Then the young professor had published another essay in which the unfortunate phrase was "Who gives a shit for Beethoven?" And that was the end of that. The young professor never really knew what happened, but a year later he was giving piano lessons in San Francisco.

The Socrates Club had one extravagance, an elaborate communications system. On the morning that President Kennedy announced to the secret meeting of advisers the ultimatum he would give the Sultan of Sherhaben, all twenty men in the Socrates Club had the information within the hour. Only Greenwell knew that this information had been supplied by Oliver Oliphant, the Oracle.

It was a matter of doctrine that these yearly retreats of great men were in no way used to lay plans or organize conspiracies; they were merely a means for communicating general aims, to inform a general interest, to clear away confusion in the operation of a complicated society. In that spirit George Greenwell on Tuesday invited three other great men to one of the cheerful pavilions just outside the tennis courts to have lunch.

The youngest of these men, Lawrence Salentine, owned a major TV network and some cable companies, newspapers in three major cities, five magazines and one of the biggest movie studios. He owned, through subsidiaries, a major book-publishing house. He also owned twelve local TV stations in major cities. That was in the United States alone. He was also a powerful presence in the media of foreign countries. Salentine was only forty-five years old, a lean and handsome man with a full head of silvery hair, a crown of curls in the style of the Roman emperors but now much in fashion with intellectuals and people in the arts and in Hollywood. He was impressive in appearance and in intelligence, and was one of the most powerful men in American politics. There was not a congressman or senator or a member of the Cabinet who did not return his calls. He had not, however, been able to become friendly with President Kennedy, who seemed to take personally the hostile attitude the media had shown the new social programs proposed by the Kennedy administration.

The second man was Louis Inch, who owned more important real estate in the great cities of America than any other individual or company. As a very young man—he was now only forty—he had first grasped the true importance of building straight up into the air to a seemingly impossible degree. He had bought airspace rights over many existing buildings and then built the enormous skyscrapers that increased the value of buildings tenfold. He more than anyone else had changed the very light of the cities, had made endless dark canyons between commercial buildings that proved to be more needed than anyone had supposed. He had made rents so impossibly high in New York, Chicago and Los Angeles for ordinary families that only the rich or very well off could live comfortably in those cities. He had cajoled and bribed municipal officials to give him tax abatements, and to do away with rent controls to such a degree that he boasted that his rental charge per square foot would someday equal Tokyo's.

His political influence, despite his ambitions, was less than that of the others meeting in the pavilion. He had a personal fortune of over five billion dollars, but his wealth had the inertness of land. His real strength was more sinister. His aims were the amassing of wealth and power without real responsibility to the civilization he lived in. He had extensively bribed public officials and construction unions. He owned casino hotels in Atlantic City and Las Vegas, shutting out the mobster overlords in those cities. But in doing so, he had, in the curious way of the democratic process, acquired the support of the secondary figures in criminal empires. All the service departments of his numerous hotels had contracts with firms that supplied tableware, laundry services, service help, liquor and food. He was linked through subordinates to this criminal underworld. He was, of course, not so foolish as to allow that link to be more than a microscopic thread. The name of Louis Inch had never been touched by any hint of scandal—thanks not only to his sense of prudence, but to the absence of any personal charisma.

For all these reasons he was actually despised on a personal level by nearly all the members of the Socrates Club. He was tolerated because one of his companies owned the land surrounding the club and there was always the fear that he might put up cheap housing for fifty thousand families and drown the club area with Hispanics and blacks.

The third man, Martin Mutford, dressed in slacks, a blue blazer, and a white shirt open at the collar, was a man of sixty, and was perhaps the most powerful of the four because he had control of money in so many different areas. As a young man he had been one of the Oracle's protégés and had learned his lessons well. He would tell admiring stories about the Oracle to the delight of the audiences in the Socrates Club.

Mutford had based his career on investment banking, and at the very start, because of the influence of the Oracle, or so he claimed, he had gotten off to a shaky start. As a young man he had been sexually vigorous, as he put it. Much to his surprise, the husbands of some of the young wives he seduced came looking for him not for revenge but for a bank loan. They had little smiles on their faces and were very good-humored. By instinct he granted the personal loans, which he knew they would never pay back. At the time he did not know that loan officials at banks took gifts and bribes to give unsafe loans to small businesses. The paperwork was easy to get around, the people who ran banks wanted to loan money—that was their business, that was their profit, and so their regulations were purposely written in such a way as to make it easy for loan officers. Of course there had to be a parade of paperwork, memos of interviews, etc. But Mutford cost the bank a few hundred thousand dollars before he was transferred to another branch and another city by what he thought was a fortunate circumstance but what he later realized was simply a tolerant shrug of his superiors.

The errors of youth behind him, forgiven, forgotten, valuable lessons learned, Mutford rose in his world. Thirty years later Mutford sat in the pavilion of the Socrates Club and was the most powerful financial figure in the United States. He was chairman of a great bank and owned substantial stock in the TV networks; he and his friends had control of the giant automobile industry and had linked up with the air travel industry. He had used money as a spiderweb to snare a large share of electronics. He also sat on the boards of Wall Street investment firms that put together deals to buy out huge conglomerates to add to another huge conglomerate. When these battles were at their most fierce, Mutford would send out a wave of money as drenching as the sea to settle the issue. Like the other three, he "owned" certain members of the Congress and the Senate.

The four men sat at the round table in the pavilion outside the tennis courts. California flowers and New England–like greenery surrounded them. George Greenwell said, "What do you fellows think of the President's decision?"

Mutford said, "It's a damn shame what they did to his daughter. But destroying fifty billion dollars' worth of property is way out of proportion."

A waiter, a Hispanic wearing white slacks and a short-sleeved shirt with the club logo, took their drink orders.

Salentine said thoughtfully, "The American people will think of Kennedy as a real hero if he pulls it off. He will be reelected in a landslide."

Greenwell said, "But it is far too drastic a response, we all know that. Foreign relations will be damaged for years to come."

Mutford said, "The country is running wonderfully well. The legislative branch finally has the executive branch under some sort of control. Will the country benefit from a swing of power the opposite way?"

Inch said, "What the hell can Kennedy do even if he gets reelected? The Congress controls and we have a big say with them. There are not more than fifty members of the House who are elected without our money. And in the Senate, there's not a man among them that is not a millionaire. We don't have to worry about the President."

Greenwell had been looking beyond the tennis courts to the marvelous blue Pacific Ocean that was so quiet yet majestic. The ocean that at this very moment was cradling billions of dollars' worth of ships carrying his grain all over the world. It gave him a slightly guilty feeling that he could starve or feed almost the entire world.

He started to speak, but was interrupted by the waiter, who came with their drinks. Greenwell was prudent at his age and had asked for mineral water. He sipped at his glass, and after the waiter left he spoke in carefully modulated tones. His exquisite courtesy was the sort that comes to a man who has regretfully made brutal decisions in his life. "We must never forget," he said, "that the office of the President of the United States can be a very great danger to the democratic process."

Salentine said, "That's nonsense. The other officials in the government prevent him from making a personal decision. The military, benighted as they are, would not permit it unless it was reasonable, you know that, George."

Greenwell said, "That's true, of course. In normal times. But look at Lincoln, he actually suspended habeas corpus and civil liberties during the Civil War; look at Franklin Roosevelt, he got us into World War Two. Look at the personal powers of the President. He has the power to absolutely pardon any crime. That is the power of a king. Do you know what can be done with such power? What allegiance that can create? He has almost infinite powers if there is not a strong Congress to check him. Luckily we have such a Congress. But we must look ahead, we must make sure that the executive arm remains subordinate to the duly elected representatives of the people."

Salentine said, "With TV and other media Kennedy wouldn't last a day if he tried anything dictatorial. He simply hasn't got that option. The strongest belief in America today is the creed of individual freedom." He paused for a moment and said, "As you know well, George. You defied that infamous embargo."

Greenwell said, "You're missing the point. A bold President can surmount those obstacles. And Kennedy is being very bold in this crisis."

Inch said impatiently, "Are you arguing that we should present a united front against Kennedy's ultimatum to Sherhaben? Personally, I think it's great that he's being tough. Force works, pressure works, on governments as well as people."

Early in his career Inch had used pressure tactics on tenants in housing developments under rent control when he wanted to empty the buildings. He had withheld heat and water and prohibited maintenance; he had made the lives of thousands of people extremely uncomfortable. He had "tipped" certain sections of suburbia, flooding them with blacks to drive out white residents; he had bribed city and state governments, and made the Federal regulators rich. He knew what he was talking about. Success was built on applying pressure.

Greenwell said, "Again, you're missing the point. In an hour we have a screen conference call with Bert Audick. Please forgive me that I promised this without consulting you—I thought it too urgent to wait, events are moving so quickly. But it's Bert Audick whose fifty billion dollars will be destroyed, and he is terribly concerned. And it is important to look into the future. If the President can do this to Audick, he can do it to us."

"Kennedy is unsound," Mutford said thoughtfully.

Salentine said, "I think we should have some sort of consensus before the conference call with Audick."

"He's really perverted in his obsession with oil preservation," Inch said. Inch had always felt that oil in some way conflicted with the interests of real estate.

"We owe it to Bert to give him our fullest consideration," Greenwell said.

The four men were gathered in the communications center of the Socrates Club when the image of Bert Audick flashed on the TV screen. He greeted them with a smile, but the face on the screen was an unnatural red, which could be the color tuning or the effect of some sort of rage. Audick's voice was calm.

"I'm going to Sherhaben," he said. "It may be a last look at my fifty billion bucks."

The men in the room could speak to the image as if the man himself were present at the club. They could see their own images on their monitor, the image that Audick could see in his office. They had to guard their faces as well as their voices.

"You're actually going?" Inch said.

"Yes," Audick said. "The Sultan is a friend of mine and this is a very touchy situation. I can do a lot of good for our country if I'm there personally."

Salentine said, "According to the correspondents on my media payroll, Congress and the Senate are trying to veto the President's decision. Is that possible?"

The image of Audick smiled at them. "Not only possible but almost certain. I've talked to Cabinet members. They are proposing that the President be removed temporarily from office by reason of his personal vendetta, which shows an imbalance of the mind. Under an amendment of the Constitution, that is legal. We need only get the signatures of the Cabinet and the Vice President on a petition that Congress will ratify. Even if the suspension is for only thirty days, we can halt the destruction of Dak. And I guarantee that the hostages will be released while I am in Sherhaben. But I think all of you should offer support to Congress to remove the President. You owe that to American democracy, as I owe it to my stockholders. We all know damn well that if anybody but his daughter had been killed, he would never have chosen this course of action."

Greenwell said, "Bert, the four of us have talked this over and we have agreed to support you and the Congress—that's our duty. We will make the necessary phone calls, our efforts will be coordinated. But Lawrence Salentine has a few pertinent observations he'd like to present."

Audick's face on the screen showed anger and disgust. He said, "Larry, this is no time for your media to sit on the fence, believe me. If Kennedy can cost me fifty billion dollars, there may come a time when all your TV stations could be without a Federal license and then you can go fuck yourself. I won't lift a finger to help you."

Greenwell winced at the vulgarity and directness of the response. Inch and Mutford smiled. Salentine showed no emotion. He answered in a calm soothing voice.

"Bert," he said. "I'm with you all the way, never doubt that. I think a man who arbitrarily decides to destroy fifty billion dollars to reinforce a threat is undoubtedly unbalanced and not fit to head the government of the United States. I'm with you, I assure you. The television media will be breaking into their scheduled programs with bulletins that President Kennedy is being psychiatrically evaluated, that the trauma of his daughter's death may have temporarily disordered his reason. That should prepare the groundwork for Congress. But this touches an area where I have a little more expertise than most. The President's decision will be embraced by the American people—the natural mob reaction to all acts of national power plays. If the President succeeds in his action and he gets the hostages back, he will command untold allegiance and votes. Kennedy has intelligence and energy, if he gets one foot in the door he can sweep Congress away." Salentine paused for a moment, trying to choose his words very carefully. "But if his threats fail—hostages killed, problem not solved—then Kennedy is finished as a political power."

On the console the image of Bert Audick flinched. He said in a very quiet serious tone, "That is not an alternative. If it goes that far, then the hostages must be saved, our country must win. Besides, the fifty billion dollars will already be lost. No true American wants the Kennedy mission to fail. They may not want a mission with such drastic action, but once it has been started we must see that it succeeds."

"I agree," Salentine said, though he did not. "I absolutely agree. I have another point. Once the President sees the danger from Congress, the first thing he will want to do is address the nation on television. Whatever Kennedy's faults, he is a magician on the tube. Once he presents his case on that TV screen the Congress will be in a great deal of trouble in this country. What if Congress does depose Kennedy for thirty days? Then there is the possibility that the President is right in his diagnosis, that the kidnapers make this a long-drawn-out affair with Kennedy on the sidelines, out of all the heat." Again Salantine paused, trying to be careful. He said, "Then Kennedy becomes an even greater hero. Our best scenario is to just let him alone, win or lose. That way there is no long-term danger to the political structure of this country. That may be best."

"I lose fifty billion dollars that way, right?" Bert Audick said. The face on the huge TV screen was clearly reddening with anger. There had never been anything wrong with the color control.

Mutford said, "It is a considerable sum of money, but it's not the end of the world."

Bert Audick's face on the screen was an astonishing blood-red. Salentine thought again that it might be the controls—no man could stay alive and turn such vivid hues. Audick's voice reverberated through the room: "Fuck you, Martin, fuck you. And it's more than fifty billion. What about the loss of revenue while we rebuild Dak? Will your banks loan me the money then without interest? You've got more cash up your asshole than the U.S. Treasury, but would you give me the fifty billion? Like shit you would."

Greenwell said hastily, "Bert, Bert, we are with you. Salentine was just pointing out a few options you may not have thought of under the pressure of events. In any event we could not stop Congress's action even if we tried. Congress will not permit the executive to dominate on such an issue. Now, we all have work to do, so I suggest this conference come to an end."

Salentine smiled and said, "Bert, those bulletins about the President's mental condition will be on television in three hours. The other networks will follow our lead. Call me and tell me what you think, you may have some ideas. And one other thing, if Congress votes to depose the President before he requests time on TV, the networks can refuse him the time on the basis that he has been certified as mentally incompetent and is no longer President."

"You do that," Audick said, his face fading now to a natural color. And the conference call ended with courteous good-byes.

Salentine said, "Gentlemen, I suggest we all fly to Washington in my plane. I think we should all pay a visit to our old friend Oliver Oliphant."

Mutford smiled. "The Oracle, my old mentor. He'll give us some answers."

Within the hour they were all on their way to Washington.

Summoned to meet with President Kennedy, the ambassador of Sherhaben, Sharif Waleeb, was shown secret CIA videotapes of Yabril having dinner with the Sultan in the Sultan's palace. The Sherhaben ambassador was genuinely shocked. How could his Sultan be involved in such a dangerous endeavor? Sherhaben was a tiny country, a gentle country, peace-loving, as was wise for a militarily weak power.

The meeting was in the Oval Office with Bert Audick present. The President was accompanied by two staff members, Arthur Wix, the national security adviser, and Eugene Dazzy, the chief of staff.

After he was formally presented, the Sherhaben ambassador said to Kennedy, "My dear Mr. President, you must believe I had no knowledge of this. You have my personal, my most abject, my most heartfelt apologies." He was close to tears. "But I must say one thing I truly believe. The Sultan could never have agreed to harm your poor daughter."

Francis Kennedy said gravely, "I hope that is true because then he will agree to my proposal."

The ambassador listened with an apprehension that was more personal than political. He had been educated at an American university and was an admirer of the American way of life. He loved American food, American alcoholic drinks, American women and their rebelliousness under the male yoke. He loved American music and films. He had donated money to all the necessary politicos and made bureaucrats in the American State Department rich. He was an expert on oil and a friend of Bert Audick.

Now he was in despair over his personal misfortune, but he was not really worried about Sherhaben and its Sultan. The worst that could happen would be economic sanctions. The American CIA would mount covert operations to displace the Sultan, but this might be to his advantage.

So he was profoundly shocked by Kennedy's carefully articulated speech. "You must listen closely," Francis Kennedy said. "In three hours you will be on a plane to Sherhaben to bring my message to your Sultan personally. Mr. Bert Audick, whom you know, and my national security adviser, Arthur Wix, will accompany you. And the message is this. In twenty-four hours your city of Dak will be destroyed."

Horrified, his throat constricted, the ambassador could not speak.

Kennedy continued: "The hostages must be released and

the terrorist Yabril must be turned over to us. Alive. If the Sultan does not do this, the state of Sherhaben itself will cease to exist."

The ambassador looked so stricken that Kennedy thought he might have trouble comprehending. Kennedy paused for a moment and then went on reassuringly. "All this will be in the documents I will send with you to present to your Sultan."

Ambassador Waleeb said dazedly, "Mr. President, forgive me, you said something about destroying Dak?"

Kennedy said, "That is correct. Your Sultan will not believe my threats until he sees the city of Dak in ruins. Let me repeat: the hostages must be released, Yabril must be surrendered and secured so that he cannot take his own life. There will be no more negotiations."

The ambassador said incredulously, "You cannot threaten to destroy a free country, tiny as it is. And if you destroy Dak, you destroy billions of dollars' worth of American investment."

"That may be true," Kennedy said. "We will see. Make sure your Sultan understands that I am immovable in this matter—that is your function. You, Mr. Audick and Mr. Wix will go in one of my personal planes. Two other aircraft will accompany you. One to bring back the hostages and the body of my daughter. The other to bring back Yabril."

The ambassador could not speak, he could scarcely think. This was surely a nightmare. The President had gone mad.

When he was alone with Bert Audick, Audick said to him grimly, "That bastard meant what he said, but we have a card to play. I'll talk to you on the plane."

In the Oval Office Eugene Dazzy took notes.

Francis Kennedy said, "Have you arranged for all the

documents to be delivered to the ambassador's office and to the plane?"

Dazzy said, "We dressed it up a little. Wiping out Dak is bad enough, but we can't say in print that we will destroy the whole country of Sherhaben. But your message is clear. Why send Wix?"

Kennedy smiled and said, "The Sultan will know that when I send him my national security adviser I'm very serious. And Arthur will repeat my verbal message."

"Do you think it will work?" Dazzy said.

"He'll wait for Dak to go down," Kennedy said. "Then it sure as hell will work unless he's crazy."

CHAPTER
11

TO IMPEACH THE President of the United States in twenty-four hours seemed almost impossible. But four hours after Kennedy's ultimatum to Sherhaben, Congress and the Socrates Club had this victory well within their grasp.

After Christian Klee had left the meeting, the computer surveillance section of his FBI special division gave him a complete report on the activities of the leaders of Congress and the members of the Socrates Club. Three thousand calls were listed. Charts and records of all the meetings held were also part of the report. The evidence was clear and overwhelming. Within the next twenty-four hours the House and Senate of the United States would try to impeach the President.

Christian, furious, put the reports in his briefcase and rushed over to the White House. But before he left, he told

Peter Cloot to move ten thousand agents from their normal-duty posts and send them to Washington.

At this same time late Wednesday Senator Thomas Lambertino, the strongman of the Senate, with his aide Elizabeth Stone and Congressman Alfred Jintz, the Democratic Speaker of the House, were meeting in Lambertino's office. Sal Troyca, chief aide to Congressman Jintz, was there to cover up, as he often said, the asshole of his boss, who was an idiot manqué. About Sal Troyca's cunning there was no doubt, not only in his own mind but on Capitol Hill.

In that warren of rabbity legislators, Sal Troyca was also a champion womanizer and genteel promoter of relationships between the sexes. Troyca had already noted that the senator's chief aide, Elizabeth Stone, was a beauty, but he had to find out how devoted she was. And right now he had to concentrate on the business at hand.

Troyca read aloud the pertinent sentences of the Twenty-fifth Amendment to the United States Constitution, editing out sentences and words here and there. He read slowly and carefully in a beautifully controlled tenor voice: " 'Whenever the Vice President and a majority of either the principal officers of the executive departments' "—in an aside to Jintz he whispered, "That's the Cabinet"; then his voice grew more emphatic—" 'or of *such other body as Congress may by law provide,* transmit to . . . the Senate and . . . House of Representatives their written declaration that the President is unable to discharge the powers and duties of his office, the Vice President shall immediately assume the powers and duties of the office as Acting President.' "

"Bullshit," Congressman Jintz yelled. "It can't be that easy to impeach a President."

"It's not," said Senator Lambertino in a soothing voice. "Read on, Sal."

Sal Troyca thought bitterly that it was typical that his boss did not know the Constitution, holy as it was. He gave up. Fuck the Constitution, Jintz would never understand. He would have to put it in plain language. He said, "Essentially the Vice President and the Cabinet must sign a declaration of incompetence to impeach Kennedy. Then the Vice President becomes President. One second later Kennedy enters his counterdeclaration and says he's OK. He's President again. Then Congress decides. During that delay Kennedy can do what he wants."

Congressman Jintz said, "And there goes Dak."

Senator Lambertino said, "Most of the Cabinet members will sign the declaration. We'll have to wait for the Vice President—we can't proceed without her signature. Congress will have to meet no later than ten P.M. Thursday to decide the issue in time to prevent the destruction of Dak. And to win we must have a two-thirds vote of the House and Senate. Now, can the House do the job? I guarantee the Senate."

"Sure," Congressman Jintz said. "I got a call from the Socrates Club, they are going to lean on every member of the House."

Troyca said respectfully, "The Constitution says, any other body the Congress may provide by law. Why not bypass all that Cabinet and vice-presidential signing and make Congress that body? Then they can decide forthwith."

Congressman Jintz said patiently, "Sal, it won't work. It can't look like a vendetta. The voting public would be on his side and we'd have to pay for it later. Remember Kennedy is popular with the people—a demagogue has that advantage over responsible legislators."

Senator Lambertino said, "We should have no trouble following procedure. The President's ultimatum to Sherhaben is far too extreme and shows a mind temporarily unbalanced by his personal tragedy. For which I have the utmost sympathy and sorrow. As indeed we all do."

Congressman Jintz said, "My people in the House come up for reelection every two years. Kennedy could knock a bunch of them out if he's declared competent after the thirty-day period. We have to *keep* him out."

Senator Lambertino nodded. He knew that the senatorial six-year term always grated on House members. "That's true," he said, "but remember, it will be established that he has serious psychological problems, and that can be used to keep him out of office simply by the Democratic party refusing him the nomination."

Troyca had noted one thing. Elizabeth Stone had not uttered a word during the meeting. But she had a brain for a boss; she didn't have to protect Lambertino from his own stupidity.

So Troyca said, "If I may summarize, if the Vice President and the majority of the Cabinet vote to impeach the President, they will sign the declaration this afternoon. The President's personal staff will still refuse to sign. It would be a great help if they did, but they won't. According to the Constitutional procedure, the one essential signature is that of the Vice President. A Vice President, by tradition, endorses all of the President's policies. Are we absolutely positive she will sign? Or that she won't delay? Time is of the essence."

Jintz laughed and said, "What Vice President doesn't want to be President? She's been hoping for the last three years that he'd have a heart attack."

For the first time Elizabeth Stone spoke. "The Vice President does not think in that fashion. She is absolutely loyal to the President," she said coolly. "It is true that she is almost certain to sign the declaration. But for all the right reasons."

Congressman Jintz looked at her with patient resignation and made a pacifying gesture. Lambertino frowned. Troyca kept his face impassive, but inwardly he was delighted.

Troyca said, "I still say bypass everybody. Let Congress go right to the bottom line."

Congressman Jintz rose from his comfortable armchair. "Don't worry, Sal, the Vice President can't seem to be too much in a hurry to push Kennedy out. She will sign. She just doesn't want to look like a usurper." "Usurper" was a word often used in the House of Representatives in reference to President Kennedy.

Senator Lambertino regarded Troyca with distaste. He disliked a certain familiarity in the man's manner, the questioning of the plans of his betters. "This action to impeach the President is certainly legal, if unprecedented," he said. "The Twenty-fifth Amendment to the Constitution doesn't specify medical evidence. But his decision to destroy Dak is evidence."

Troyca couldn't resist. "Once you do this there will certainly be a precedent. A two-thirds vote of Congress can impeach any President. In theory anyway." He noted with satisfaction that he had won Elizabeth Stone's attention at least. So he went on. "We'd be another banana republic— only in reverse, the legislature being the dictator."

Senator Lambertino said curtly, "By definition that cannot be true. The legislature is elected by the people directly, it cannot dictate as one man can."

Troyca thought with contempt, Not unless the Socrates Club gets on your ass. Then he realized what had made the senator angry. The senator thought of himself as presidential timber and didn't like someone saying that the Congress could get rid of the President whenever it liked.

Jintz said, "Let's wind this up—we all have a hell of a lot of work to do. This is really a move to a more genuine democracy."

Troyca was still not used to the direct simplicity of great men like the senator and the Speaker, how with such sincerity they went to the very heart of their own self-interest. He saw a certain look on the face of Elizabeth Stone and realized she was thinking exactly what he was thinking. Oh, he was going to take his shot at her no matter what the cost. But he said with his patented sincerity and humility, "Is it at all possible that the President may declare that Congress is overruling an executive order that they disagree with and then defy the vote of the Congress? May he not go to the nation on television tonight before the Congress meets? And won't it seem plausible to the public that since Kennedy's staff refuses to sign the declaration, Kennedy is OK? There could be a great deal of trouble. Especially if the hostages are killed after Kennedy has been impeached. There could be tremendous repercussions on the Congress."

Neither the senator nor the congressman seemed impressed by this analysis. Jintz patted him on the shoulder and said, "Sal, we've got it all covered, you just make sure the paperwork gets done."

At that moment the phone rang and Elizabeth Stone picked it up. She listened for a moment and then said, "Senator, it's the Vice President."

Before making her decision, Vice President Helen Du Pray decided to take her daily run.

The first woman Vice President of the United States, she was fifty-five years of age and by any standard an extraordinarily intelligent woman. She was still beautiful, possibly because in her twenties, then a pregnant wife and assistant district attorney, she became a health-food nut. She had also become a runner in her teens before she married. An early lover had taken her on his runs, five miles a day and not jogging. He had quoted Latin, *"Mens sana in corpore sano,"* and translated for her, "If the body is healthy, the mind is healthy." For his condescension in translating and his taking literally the truth of the quotation—how many healthy minds have been brought to dust by a too healthy body—she had discharged him as a lover.

But just as important were her dietary disciplines, which dissolved the poisons in her system and generated a high energy level with the extra bonus of a magnificent figure. Her political opponents would joke that she had no taste buds, but this was not true. She could enjoy a rosy peach, a mellow pear, the tangy taste of fresh vegetables, and in the dark days of the soul that no one can escape she could also eat a jarful of chocolate cookies.

She had become a health-food nut by chance. In her early days as a district attorney she had prosecuted a diet-book author for making fraudulent and injurious claims. To prepare for the case she had researched the subject, read everything in the field of nutrition, on the premise that to detect the false you must know what is true. She had convicted the author, made him pay an enormous fine but always felt she owed him a debt.

And even as Vice President of the United States, Helen Du Pray ate sparingly and always ran at least five miles a day— on weekends, she did ten miles. Now on what could be the most important day of her life, with the declaration to impeach the President waiting for her signature, she decided to take a mind-clearing run.

Her Secret Service guard had to pay the price. Originally the chief of her security detail thought her morning run would be no problem. After all, his men were good physical specimens. But Vice President Du Pray not only took her runs early in the morning through woods where guards could not follow, but her once-a-week ten-mile run left her security men straggling far to her rear. The chief was amazed that this woman, in her fifties, could run so fast. And so long.

The Vice President did not want her run disturbed; it was, after all, a sacred thing in her life. It had replaced "fun," meaning it had replaced the enjoyment of food, liquor and sex, the warmth and tenderness that had gone out of her life when her husband had died six years before.

She had lengthened her runs and put aside all thoughts of remarrying; she was too far up the political ladder to risk allying herself to a man who might be a booby trap, with secret skeletons in his closet to drag her down. Her two daughters and an active social life were enough, and she had many friends, male and female.

She had won the support of the feminist groups of the country not with the usual empty political blandishments but with a cool intelligence and a steadfast integrity. She had mounted an unrelenting attack on the antiabortionists and had crucified in debate those male chauvinists who without personal risk tried to legislate what women might do with their bodies. She had won that fight and in the process climbed high up the political ladder.

From a lifetime of experience she disdained the theories that men and women should be more alike; she celebrated their differences. The difference was valuable in a moral sense, as a variation in music is valuable, as a variation in gods is valuable. Oh, yes, there was a difference. She had learned from her political life, from her years as a district attorney, that women were better than men in the most important things in life. And she had the statistics to prove it. Men committed far more murders, robbed more banks, perjured themselves more, betrayed their friends and loved ones more. As public officials they were far more corrupt, as believers in God they were far more cruel, as lovers they were far more selfish, in all fields they exercised power far more ruthlessly. Men were far more likely to destroy the world with war because they feared death so much more than women. But all this aside, she had no quarrel with men.

On this Wednesday, Helen Du Pray started running from her chauffeured car parked in the woods of a Washington suburb. Running from the fateful document waiting on her desk. The Secret Service men spread out, one ahead, another behind, two on the flanks, all at least twenty paces from her. There had been a time when she had delighted in making them sweat to keep up. After all, they were fully clothed while she was in running gear, and they were loaded with guns, ammo and communications equipment. They had a rough time until the chief of security detail, losing patience, recruited champion runners from small colleges, and that had chastened Du Pray a bit.

The higher she rose on the political ladder, the earlier in the morning she got up to run. Her greatest pleasure was when one of her daughters ran with her. It also made for great photos in the media. Everything counted.

Vice President Helen Du Pray had overcome many handicaps to achieve such high office. Obviously, the first was being a woman, and then, not so obviously, being beautiful. Beauty often aroused hostility in both sexes. She overcame this hostility with her intelligence, her modesty and an ingrained sense of morality. She also had her fair share of cunning. It was a commonplace in American politics that the electorate preferred handsome males and ugly females as candidates for office. So Helen Du Pray had transformed a seductive beauty into the stern handsomeness of a Joan of Arc. She wore her silver-blond hair close cropped, she kept her body lean and boyish, she camouflaged her breasts with tailored suits. For armor she wore a string of pearls and on her fingers only her gold wedding ring. A scarf, a frilly blouse, sometimes gloves, were her badges of womanhood. She projected an image of stern femininity until she smiled or laughed and then her sexuality flashed out brilliant as lightning. She was feminine without being flirtatious; she was strong without a hint of masculinity. She was, in short, the very model for the first woman President of the United States. Which she must become if she signed the declaration on her desk.

Now she was in the final stage of her run, emerging from the woods and onto a road where another car was waiting. Her detail of Secret Service men closed in and she was on her way to the Vice President's mansion. After showering she dressed in her "working" clothes, a severely cut skirt and jacket, and left for her office—and the waiting declaration.

It was strange, she thought. She had fought all her life to escape the trap of a single-funneled life. She had been a brilliant lawyer while rearing two children; she had pursued a political career while happily and faithfully married. She had been a partner in a powerful law firm, then a congresswoman, then a senator and all the time a devoted and caring mother. She had managed her life impeccably only to wind up as another kind of housewife, namely, the Vice President of the United States.

As Vice President she had to tidy up after her political 'husband,' the President, and perform his menial tasks. She received leaders of small nations, served on powerless committees with high-sounding titles, accepted condescending briefings, gave advice that was accepted with courtesy but not given truly respectful consideration. She had to parrot the opinions and support the policies of her political husband.

She admired President Francis Xavier Kennedy and was grateful that he had selected her to be on the ticket with him as Vice President, but she differed with him on many things. She was sometimes amused that as a married woman she had escaped being trapped as an unequal partner, yet now in the highest political office ever achieved by an American woman, political laws made her subservient to a political husband.

But today she could become a political widow and she certainly could not complain about her insurance policy, the presidency of the United States of America. After all, this had become an unhappy "marriage." Francis Kennedy had moved too quickly, too aggressively. Helen Du Pray had begun fantasizing about his "death," as many unhappy wives do.

By signing this declaration she could get all the loot. She could take his place. For a lesser woman this would have been a miraculous delight.

She knew it was impossible to control the exercises of the brain, so she did not really feel guilty about her fantasies, but she might feel guilty about a reality she had helped to bring about. When rumors floated that Kennedy would not run for a second term, she had alerted her political network. Kennedy had then given his blessing. This was all changed. Now she had to clear her mind. The declaration, the petition, had already been signed by most of the Cabinet, the Secretaries of State, Defense, Treasury and others. CIA was missing, that clever, unscrupulous bastard Tappey. And of course, Christian Klee, a man she detested. But she had to make up her mind according to her judgment and her conscience. She had to act for the public good, not out of her own ambition.

Could she sign, commit an act of personal betrayal and keep her self-respect? But what was personal was extraneous. Consider only the facts.

Like Christian Klee and many others, she had noted the change in Kennedy after his wife died just before his election to the presidency. The loss of energy. Helen Du Pray knew, as everyone knew, that to make the presidency work you could lead only by building a consensus with the legislative branch. You had to court and cajole and maybe give a few kicks. You had to outflank, infiltrate and seduce the bureaucracy. You had to have the Cabinet under your thumb, and your personal senior staff had to be a band of Attilas and a gaggle of Solomons. You had to haggle, you had to reward and you had to throw a few thunderbolts. In some way you had to make everyone say, "Yes, for the good of the country and the good of me."

Not doing these things had been a fault in Kennedy as President; also he was too far ahead of his time. His staff should have known better. A man as intelligent as Kennedy should have known better. And yet she sensed in Kennedy's moves a kind of moral desperation, an all-out gamble on good against evil.

She believed, and hoped, she was not regressing into an outmoded female sentimentality, that the death of Kennedy's wife was the root of the drift of his administration. But did extraordinary men like Kennedy fall apart merely because of some personal tragedy? The answer to that was yes.

She herself had been born to politics but she had always thought that Kennedy himself had not the temperament. He was more a scholar, scientist, teacher. He had too much idealism; he was, in the best sense of the word, naïve. That is, he was trusting.

The Congress, both houses, had waged brutal war against the executive branch, and usually won the war. Well, it would not happen to her.

Now she picked up the declaration from her desk and analyzed it. The case presented was that Francis Xavier Kennedy was no longer capable of exercising the duties of President because of a temporary mental breakdown. Caused by the murder of his daughter. Which now affected his judgment, so that his decision to destroy the city of Dak and threaten to destroy a sovereign nation became an irrational act, far out of proportion to the degree of provocation, a dangerous precedent that must turn world opinion against the United States.

But then there was Kennedy's argument, which he had presented at the staff and Cabinet conference: This was an international conspiracy in which the Pope of the Catholic Church had been assassinated and the daughter of the President of the United States murdered. A number of hostages were still being held and the conspiracy could spin out the situation for weeks or even months. And the United States would have to set the killer of the Pope free. What an enormous loss of authority to the most powerful nation on earth, the leader of democracy and, of course, democratic capitalism.

So who was to say that the Draconian answer proposed by the President was not the correct answer? Certainly, if

Kennedy was not bluffing, his measures would succeed. The
Sultan of Sherhaben must go down on his knees. What were
the real values here?

Point: Kennedy had made his decision without proper
discussion with his Cabinet, his staff, the leaders of Congress.
That was very grave. That indicated danger. A gang leader
ordering a vendetta.

He had known they would all be against him. He was
convinced he was right. Time was short. This was the deci-
siveness Francis Kennedy had shown even in the years
before he became President.

Point: He had acted within the powers of the chief executive. His decision was legal. The declaration to impeach
Kennedy had not been signed by any member of his personal
staff, those people closest to him. Therefore the charge of
unfitness and mental instability was a matter of opinion that
rested on the decision he had made. Therefore, this declaration to impeach was an illegal attempt to circumvent the
power resting in the executive branch of the government.
The Congress disagreed with the presidential decision and
therefore was attempting to reverse his decision by removing
him. Clearly in violation of the Constitution.

Those were the moral and legal issues. Now she had to
decide what was in her own best interests. That was not
unreasonable in a politician.

She knew the mechanics. The Cabinet had signed, so now
if she signed this declaration she would be the President of
the United States. Then Kennedy would sign his declaration
and she would be Vice President again. Then Congress
would meet and in a two-thirds vote impeach Kennedy and
she would be the President for at least thirty days, until the
crisis was over.

The plus factor: She would be the first woman President

of the United States for a few moments, at the very least. Maybe for the rest of Kennedy's term, which would end the following January. But she should have no illusions. She would never get the nomination after the term ran out.

She would achieve the presidency by what some would see as an act of betrayal—by a woman. It was enough that the literature of civilization had always portrayed women as causing the downfall of great men, that there was the ever-present myth that men could never trust women. She would be regarded as "unfaithful": that great sin of womankind which men never forgave. And she would be betraying the great national myth of the Kennedys. She would be another Modred.

Then it struck her. She smiled as she realized that she was in a "no lose" situation. Just by refusing to sign the declaration.

Congress would not be denied.

Congress, possibly acting illegally without her signature, would impeach Kennedy, and the Constitution decreed that she would succeed to the presidency. But she would have proved her "faithfulness," and if and when Francis Kennedy was restored after thirty days, she would still have his support. She would still have the Kennedy power group behind her nomination. As for the Congress, they were her enemies no matter what she did. So why be their political Jezebel? Their Delilah?

It became clearer and clearer to her. If she signed the declaration, the voting public would never forgive her and the politicians would hold her in contempt. And then, when and if she became President, they would most likely try to demean her also. They would, she thought, probably blame her deficiencies on her menstrual flow, the cruel male expression would be the inspiration for comics all over the country.

She made her decision. She would *not* sign the declaration. That would show she was not greedily ambitious, that she was loyal.

She started writing the statement she would give to her administrative aide to prepare. In it she simply wrote that she could not sign, with a clear conscience, a document that would elevate her to such high power. That she would remain neutral in this struggle. But even this could be dangerous. She crumpled up the paper. She would just refuse to sign; Congress would carry it forward from there. She placed a call to Senator Lambertino. After that she would call other legislators and explain her position. But nothing in writing.

Two days after David Jatney assassinated the cardboard effigy of Kennedy, he was kicked out of Brigham Young University. Jatney did not go back to his home, to his strict Mormon parents, who owned a string of dry-cleaning stores. He knew his fate there, he had suffered it before. His father believed in starting his son at the bottom, handling bundles of sweaty clothes, trousers, dresses, male suit jackets that seemed to weigh a ton. All that woolen cloth and cotton soaked with the warmth of human flesh was agonizing for him to touch.

And like many of the young, he'd had quite enough of his parents. They were good, hardworking people who enjoyed their friends, the business they had built up, and the comradeship of the Mormon Church. They were to him the two most boring people in the world.

And then too they lived a happy life, which irritated David. His parents had loved him when he was little, but grown he was so difficult that they joked that they had been given the wrong child in the hospital. They had home movies of David at every stage: the small baby crawling on the floor, the toddler tottering around the room on holidays, the small boy left at school for the first time, his graduation from grammar school, his receiving a prize for English composition in high school, fishing with his father, hunting with his uncle.

After his fifteenth birthday he refused to let himself be photographed. He was horrified by the banalities of his life recorded on film; he felt like an insect programmed to live a life in an eternity of sameness. He was determined he would never be like his parents, never realizing that this too was another banality.

Physically he was at the opposite pole. Where they were tall and blond, and then massive by middle age, David was dark-skinned, thin and wiry. His parents joked about the difference, but predicted that with age he would grow to be more like them, which filled him with horror. By his fifteenth year he showed a coldness toward them that was impossible to ignore. Their own affection in no way lessened, but they were relieved when he went off to Brigham Young.

He grew handsome, with dark hair that glowed in its blackness. His features were all-American: the nose without a bump, the mouth strong but not too generous, the chin protruding but not intimidatingly so. In the beginning, if you knew him for only a short time, he seemed merely vivacious. His hands were busy when he spoke. Then at other times he would sink into a lassitude that froze him into a sort of sullenness.

In college, his vivaciousness and intelligence made him attractive to the other students. But he was just a little too bizarre in his reactions and was almost always condescending, and sometimes brutally insulting.

The truth was that David was in an agony of impatience to be famous, to be a hero, to have the world know he was special.

With women he had a shy confidence that won them over initially. They found him interesting and so he had his little love affairs. But they never lasted. He was off-putting, he was distant; after the first few weeks of vivacity and good humor he would sink into himself. Even in sex he seemed detached, as if he did not want to lose control of his body. His greatest failing in the area of love was that he refused to worship the beloved, even in the courtship phase, and when he did his best to fall deeply in love it had the aura of a valet exerting himself for a generous tip.

He had always been interested in politics and the social order. Like most young men, he had contempt for authority in any form; the study of history revealed to him that the story of humanity was simply endless warfare between the powerful elite and the helpless multitude. He desired fame to join the powerful.

It was natural that he was voted Chief Hunter in the assassination game played every year at Brigham Young. And it was his clever planning that resulted in victory. He had also supervised the making of the effigy that so resembled Kennedy.

With the shooting of that effigy and the victory banquet afterward, David Jatney experienced a revulsion for his student life. It was time to make a career. He had always written poetry, kept a diary in which he felt he could show his wit and intelligence. Since he was so sure he would be famous, this keeping of a diary with an eye on posterity was not necessarily immodest. And so he recorded, "I am leaving college, I have learned all that they can teach me. Tomorrow

I drive to California to see if I can make it in the movie world."

When David Jatney arrived in Los Angeles, he did not know a single soul. That suited him, he liked the feeling. With no responsibilities, he could concentrate on his thoughts, he could figure out the world. The first night he slept in a small motel room and then found a one-room apartment in Santa Monica that was cheaper than he had expected. He found the apartment through the kindness of a matronly woman who was a waitress in a coffee shop where he took his first breakfast in California. David had eaten frugally—a glass of orange juice, toast and coffee—and the waitress had noticed him studying the rental section of the *Los Angeles Times.* She asked him if he was looking for a place to live and he said yes. She wrote down a phone number on a piece of paper and said it was just a one-room apartment but the rent was reasonable, because the people in Santa Monica had fought a long battle with the real estate interests and there was a tough rent control law. And Santa Monica was beautiful and he would be only a few minutes away from the Venice beach and its boardwalk and it was a lot of fun.

David at first had been suspicious. Why would this stranger be interested in his welfare? She looked motherly, but she had a sexy air about her. Of course she was very old—she must be forty at least. But she didn't seem to be coming on to him. And she gave him a cheery good-bye when he left. He was to learn that people in California did things like this. The constant sunshine seemed to mellow them. Mellowing. That's what it was. It cost her nothing to do him the favor.

David had driven from Utah in the car that his parents had given him for college. In it was his every worldly possession, except for a guitar that he had once tried to learn to play and which was back in Utah. Most important was a portable typewriter, which he used to write his diary, poetry, short stories and novels. Now that he was in California he would try his first screenplay.

Everything fell into place easily. He got the apartment, a little place with a shower but no bath. It looked like a dollhouse with frilly curtains over its one window and prints of famous paintings on the wall. The apartment was in a row of two-story houses behind Montana Avenue, and he could even park his car in the alley. He had been very lucky.

He spent the next fourteen days hanging around the Venice beach and boardwalk, and taking rides up to Malibu to see how the rich and famous lived. He leaned against the steel link fence that cut off the Malibu colony from the public beach and peered through. There was this long row of beach houses that stretched far to the north. Each worth three million dollars and more, and yet they looked like ordinary countrified shacks. They wouldn't cost more than twenty thousand in Utah. But they had the sand, the purple ocean, the brilliant sky, the mountains behind them across the Pacific Coast Highway. Someday he would sit on the balcony of one of those houses and gaze over the Pacific.

At night in his dollhouse he sank into long dreams of what he would do when he too was rich and famous. He would lie awake until the early hours of the morning weaving his fantasies. It was a lonely and curiously happy time.

He called his parents to give them his new address, and his father gave him the number of a producer to call at one of the movie studios, a childhood friend named Dean Hocken. David waited a week. Finally he made the call and got through to Hocken's secretary. She asked him to hold. In a few moments she came back on the phone and told him that Mr. Hocken was not in. He knew it was a con, that he was being sloughed off, and he felt a surge of anger at his father for being so dumb. But he gave the secretary his phone number when she asked. He was still on his daybed brooding angrily an hour later when the phone rang. It was Dean Hocken's secretary, and she asked him if he was free at eleven the next morning to see Mr. Hocken in his office. He said he was, and she told him that she would leave a pass at the gate so that he could drive onto the studio lot.

When he hung up the phone, David was surprised at the gladness welling up in him. A man he had never seen had honored a schoolboy friendship. And then he was ashamed of his own debasing gratitude. Sure, the guy was a big wheel; sure, his time was valuable—but eleven in the morning? That meant he would not be asked to lunch. It would be one of those quick courtesy interviews so the guy wouldn't feel guilty. So that his relatives back in Utah could point out that he didn't have a big head. A mean politeness basically without value.

But the next day turned out differently from what he had expected. Dean Hocken's office was in a long low building on the movie lot, and impressive. There was a receptionist in a big waiting room whose walls were covered with posters of bygone movies. Two other offices behind the reception room held two more secretaries, and then a larger, grander office. This office was furnished beautifully with deep armchairs and sofas and rugs; the walls were hung with original paintings, and there was a bar with a large refrigerator. In a corner was a working desk topped with leather. On the wall above the desk was a huge photograph of Dean Hocker shaking hands with President Francis Xavier Kennedy. There was a coffee table littered with magazines and bound scripts. The office was empty.

The secretary who had brought him in said, "Mr. Hocken will be with you in ten minutes. Can I get you a drink or some coffee?"

David was polite in his refusal. He could see that the young secretary was giving him an appraising glance, so he used his real shit-kicker's voice. He knew he made a good impression. Women always liked him at first; it was only when they got to know him better that they didn't like him, he thought. But maybe that was because he didn't like them when he got to know them better.

He had to wait for fifteen minutes before Dean Hocken came into the office through a back door that was almost invisible. For the first time in his life David was really impressed. This was a man who truly looked successful and powerful; he radiated confidence and friendliness as he grabbed David's hand.

Dean Hocken was tall and David cursed his own shortness. Hocken was at least six foot two and he looked amazingly youthful, though he must be the same age as David's father, which was fifty-five. He wore casual clothes, but his white shirt was whiter than any Jatney had ever seen. His jacket was some sort of linen and hung beautifully on his frame. The trousers were linen also, sort of off-white. Hocken's face seemed without a wrinkle and painted over with bronze ink sprayed from the sun.

Hocken was as gracious as he was youthful. He diplomatically revealed a homesickness for the Utah mountains, the Mormon life, the silence and peace of rural existence, the quiet cities with their tabernacles. And he also revealed that he had been a suitor for the hand of David's mother.

"Your mother was my girlfriend," Dean Hocken said. "Your father stole her away from me. But it was for the best, those two really loved each other, made each other happy."

And David thought, yes, it was true, his mother and father really loved each other and with their perfect love they had shut him out. In the long winter evenings they sought their warmth in a conjugal bed while he watched his TV. But that had been a long time ago.

He watched Dean Hocken talk and be charming and he saw the age beneath that carefully preserved outward armor of bronzed skin stretched too tight for nature. The man had no flesh beneath his chin, not a sign of the wattles that had grown on his father. He wondered why the man was being so nice to him.

"I've had four wives since I left Utah," Hocken said, "and I would have been much happier with your mother." David watched for the usual signs of egoism, the hint that his mother too might have been much happier if she had stuck with the successful Dean Hocken. But he saw none. The man was still a country boy beneath that California polish.

Jatney listened politely and laughed at the jokes. He called Dean Hocken "sir" until the man told him to please just call him "Hock," and then he didn't call the man anything. Hocken talked an hour and then looked at his watch and said abruptly, "It was good seeing somebody from down home, but I guess you didn't come to hear about Utah. What do you do?"

"I'm a writer," David said. "The usual stuff, a novel that I threw away and some screenplays, I'm still learning." He had never written a novel.

Hocken nodded approval of his modesty. "You have to earn your dues. Here's what I can do for you right now. I can get you a spot in the reader's department on the studio payroll. You read scripts and write a summary and your opinion. Just a half page on each script you read. That's how I started. You get to meet people and learn the basics. Truth is, nobody pays much attention to the reports, but do your best. It's just a starting point. Now I'll arrange all this and one of my secretaries will get in touch with you in a few days. And soon we'll have dinner together. Give my best to your mother and father." And then Hock escorted David to the door. They were not going to have lunch, David thought, and the promise of dinner would stretch out forever. But at least he would get a job, he would get one foot in the door, and then when he wrote his screenplays, everything would change.

Vice President Helen Du Pray's refusal to sign was a shocking blow to Congressman Jintz and Senator Lambertino. Only a female could be so contrary, so blind to political necessity, so dull of wit as to not grab this chance to be President of the United States. But they would have to do without her. They went over their options—the deed must be done. Sal Troyca had been on the right track; all the preliminary steps must be eliminated. The Congress must designate itself the body to decide from the very beginning. But Lambertino and Jintz were still trying for some way to make Congress seem impartial. They never noticed that in that moment Sal Troyca had fallen in love with Elizabeth Stone.

"Never fuck a woman over thirty" had always been Sal Troyca's creed. But for the first time he was thinking an exception might be made for the aide to Senator Lambertino. She was tall and willowy with wide gray eyes and a face that was sweet in repose. She was obviously intelligent yet knew how to keep her mouth shut. But what made him fall in love was that when they learned Vice President Helen Du Pray was refusing to sign the declaration, she gave Sal a smile that acknowledged him as a prophet—only he had proposed the correct solution.

For Troyca there were many good reasons for his stance. One, women didn't really like to fuck as much as men, they were more at risk in many different ways. But before thirty, they had more juice and less brains. Over thirty their eyes got squinty, they got too crafty, they started to think that men had it too good, were getting the better of nature and society's bargain. You never knew whether you were getting a casual piece of ass or signing some sort of promissory note. But Elizabeth Stone looked demurely horny in that slender virginal way some women have, and besides she had more power than he did. He would not have to worry that she was hustling. It didn't matter that she must be close to forty.

Planning strategy with Congressman Jintz, Senator Lambertino noted that Troyca had an interest in his female aide. That didn't bother him. Lambertino was one of the personally virtuous men in the Congress. He was sexually clean, with a wife of thirty years and four grown children. He was financially clean, wealthy in his own right. He was as politically clean as any political man in America can be, but in addition he genuinely had the interests of the people and country at heart. True, he was ambitious, but that was the very essence of political life. His virtue did not make him oblivious of the machinations of the world. The refusal of the Vice President to sign the declaration had astonished Congressman Jintz, but the senator was not so easily surprised. He had always thought the Vice President a very clever woman. Lambertino wished her well, especially since he believed that no woman had the enduring political connections, or money patrons, to win the presidency. She would be a very vulnerable opponent in a fight for the coming nomination.

"We have to move fast," Senator Lambertino said. "The Congress must designate a body or itself to declare the President unfit."

"How about ten senators on a blue-ribbon panel?" Congressman Jintz said with a sly grin.

Senator Lambertino said with a burst of irritation, "How about a fifty-member House of Representatives committee with their heads up their asses?"

Jintz said placatingly, "I have a helpful surprise for you, Senator. I think I can get one of the President's staff to sign the declaration to impeach him."

That would do the trick, Troyca thought. But which one could it be? Never Klee, not Dazzy. It had to be either Oddblood Gray or the NSA guy, Wix. He thought, no, Wix was in Sherhaben.

Lambertino said briskly, "We have a very painful duty today. A historical duty. We better get started."

Troyca was surprised that Lambertino did not ask for the name of the staff member, then realized that the senator did not want to know.

"You have my hand on that," Jintz said and extended his arm to give that handshake that was famous as an unbreakable pledge.

Albert Jintz had achieved his eminence as a great Speaker of the House by being a man of his word. The newspapers often carried articles to this effect. A Jintz handshake was better than any handcuffing legal document. Though he looked like an alcoholic bank embezzler cartoon character, short and round, with a cherry-red nose and head dripping with white hair like a Christmas tree in a snowstorm, he was considered the most honorable man in Congress, politically.

When he promised a chunk of pork from the bottomless barrel of the budget, that pork was delivered. When a fellow congressman wanted a bill blocked, and Jintz owed him a political debt, that bill was blocked. When a congressman who wanted a personal bill came through with his quid pro quo, it was a done deal. True, he often leaked secret matters to the press, but that was why so many articles on his impeccable handshake were printed.

And now this afternoon Jintz had to do the scut work of making sure the House would vote for the impeachment of President Kennedy. Hundreds of phone calls and dozens of promises had to be made to ensure that two-thirds vote. It was not that Congress wouldn't do it, but a price had to be paid. And it all had to be done in less than twenty-four hours.

Sal Troyca walked through his congressman's suite of offices, his brain marshaling all the phone calls he had to make, all the documents he had to prepare. He knew he was involved in a great moment of history, and he also knew that his career could be washed away if there was some terrible reversal. He was amazed that men like Jintz and Lambertino, whom he held in a kind of contempt, could be so courageous as to put themselves in the front line of battle. This was a very dangerous step they were taking. Under a very shady interpretation of the Constitution they were prepared to make the Congress a body that could impeach the President of the United States.

He moved through the spooky green light of a dozen computers being worked by office staff. Thank God for computers, how the hell did things ever get done before? Passing one computer operator, he touched her shoulder in a com-

radely gesture that could not be taken for sexual harassment
and said, "Don't make any dates—we'll be here until morning."

The New York Times Magazine had recently published an
article on the sexual mores of Capitol Hill, where both the
Senate and the House and their staffs were housed. The
article noted that of the elected 100 senators and 435 congressmen and their huge staffs, the population was in the
many thousands, of which more than half were females.

The article had suggested that there was a great deal of
sexual activity among these citizens. The article had said
that because of long hours and the tension of working under
political deadlines the staff had little social life and perforce
had to seek a little recreation on the job. It was noted that
congressional offices and senatorial suites were furnished
with couches. The article explained that in government bu-
reaus there were special medical clinics and doctors whose
duties were the discreet treatment of venereal infection. The
records were, of course, confidential, but the writer claimed
he had been given a peek and the percentage of infection was
higher than the national average. The writer attributed this
not so much to promiscuity as to the incestuous social envi-
ronment. The writer then wondered if all this fornication
was affecting the quality of lawmaking on Capitol Hill,
which he referred to as the Rabbit Warren.

Sal Troyca had taken the article personally. He averaged
a sixteen-hour working day six days a week and was on call
Sundays. Was he not entitled to a normal sex life like any
other citizen? Damn it, he didn't have time to go to parties,
to romance women, to commit himself to a relationship. It
all had to happen here, in the countless suites and corridors,
in the smoky green light of computers and military ringing
of telephones. You had to fit it into a few minutes of banter,

a meaningful smile, the involved strategies of work. That fucking *Times* writer went to all the publishers' parties, took out people for long lunches, chatted leisurely with journalist colleagues, could go to hookers without a newspaper reporting the seamy details.

Troyca went into his private office, then into the bathroom, and gave a sigh of relief as he sat on the toilet, pen in hand. He scribbled notes on all the things he had to do. He washed his hands, juggling pad and pen, with the congressional logo etched in gold computer lines, and, feeling much better (the tension of impeaching a President had knotted his stomach), went to the small mobile liquor cart and took ice from the tiny refrigerator to fix himself a gin and tonic. He thought about Elizabeth Stone. He was sure there was nothing between her and her senator boss. And she was smart, smarter than him, she had kept her mouth shut.

The door of his office opened and the girl he had patted on the shoulder came in. She had an armful of computer printout sheets and Sal sat at his desk to go over them. She stood beside him. He could feel the heat of her body, a heat generated by the long hours she had put in on the computer that day.

Troyca had interviewed this girl when she had applied for the job. He often said that if only the girls who worked in the office kept looking as good as on their interview day, he could put them all in *Playboy*. And if they remained as demure and sweet, he would marry them. The girl's name was Janet Wyngale, and she was really beautiful. The first day he saw her, a line from Dante had flashed through Troyca's mind, "Here is the goddess that will subjugate me." Of course he would not allow such a misfortune to happen. But she was that beautiful that first day. She was never as beautiful again. Her hair was still blond, but not gold; her

eyes were still that amazing blue, but she wore glasses and
was a little ugly without the first perfect makeup. Nor were
her lips as cherry-red. Her body was not as voluptuous as on
the first day, which was natural since she was a hard worker
and dressed comfortably now to increase her efficiency. He
had, all in all, made a good decision; she was not yet squinty-
eyed.

Janet Wyngale, what a great name. She was leaning over
his shoulder to point out things on the computer sheets. He
was conscious she had switched her feet so that she was
standing more beside him than behind him. Her golden hair
brushed his cheek, silky, warm and smelling of crushed
flowers.

"Your perfume is great," Sal Troyca said, and he was
almost shivering when the heat of her body gusted over him.
She didn't move or say anything. But her hair was like a
Geiger counter over his cheek picking up the radiating lust
in his body. It was a friendly lust, two buddies in a jam
together. They would be going over computer sheets all
through the night, answering a witch's brew of telephone
calls, calling emergency meetings. They would fight side by
side.

Holding the computer sheets in his left hand, Troyca let
his right hand touch the back of her thigh under her skirt.
She didn't move. They were both staring intently at the
computer sheets. He let his hand stay perfectly still, let it
burn on satiny skin that electrified his scrotum. He was not
conscious that the computer sheets had fallen to the desk.
Her flowered hair drowned his face and he swiveled and both
his hands were under her skirt, both his hands like little feet
running over that field so satiny under the nylon of her
panties. Underneath to the pubic hair and the wet agonizing
sweetness of the flesh beneath. Troyca levitated from his

seat, it seemed to him he was motionless in the air, his body forming a supernatural eagle's nest into which Janet Wyngale, with a fluttering of wings, came to rest on his lap. Miraculously she was sitting right on his cock, which had mysteriously emerged and they were face-to-face kissing; he drowning in crushed flowers, groaning with passion, and Janet Wyngale kept repeating a passionate endearment, which he finally understood. "Lock the door," she was saying, and Troyca freed his wet left hand and flipped the electronic button that enclosed them in that perfect brief moment of ecstasy. Both tumbled to the floor in a graceful dive and she had her long legs wrapped around his neck, and he could see the long milk-white thighs and they climaxed together in perfect unison, Troyca whispering ecstatically, "Ah, heaven, heaven."

Then miraculously they were both standing, rosy-cheeked, their eyes flashing with delight, renewed, jubilant, ready to face the grueling long hours of work together. Gallantly Troyca passed her the gin and tonic with its joyful tinkling of ice cubes. Graciously and thankfully she wet her parched mouth. Sincerely and gratefully Troyca said, "That was wonderful." Lovingly she patted his neck and kissed him—"It was great."

Moments later they were back at the desk studying the computer sheets in earnest, concentrating on the language and the figures. Janet was a wonderful editor. Sal felt an enormous gratitude, and murmured with genuine courtesy, "Janet, I'm really crazy about you. As soon as this crisis is over we got to have a date, OK?"

"Umm," Janet said. She gave him a warm smile. A friendly smile. "I love working with you," she said.

CHAPTER
12

TELEVISION NEVER HAD such a glorious week. On Sunday the assassination of the Pope had been repeated scores of times on the networks, on the cable channels, on PBS special reports. On Tuesday the murder of Theresa Kennedy had been even more continuously repeated, her murder floated through the airways of the universe endlessly and endlessly.

The face of Yabril, hawklike in the desert, hovering over the hostages, flew through every home in America. He became the mythical monster goblin on the late evening news, an ever-recurring nightmare to haunt the dreams of America. Messages of sympathy by the millions poured into the White House. In all of the great cities the citizens of America appeared on the streets wearing black arm bands. And so when the television stations climaxed late Wednesday with the leaked news of President Francis Kennedy's ultimatum to the Sultan of Sherhaben, great mobs congregated all through the United States in a wild frenzy of jubilation. There was no question they supported the President's decision. Indeed the TV correspondents who interviewed citizens on the street were appalled at the ferocity of the comments. The common cry was "Nuke the bastards." Finally orders came from the top TV network news chiefs to stop covering the street scenes and to halt the interviews. The orders originated from Lawrence Salentine, who had formed a council with the other owners of the media.

In the White House President Francis Kennedy didn't have time to grieve for his daughter. He was on the hot line to other heads of state to reassure them there was to be no territorial grabbing in the Middle East and to plead for cooperation and make them understand his own stance was irrevocable: that the President of the United States was not bluffing, that the city of Dak would be destroyed, and that if the ultimatum was not obeyed the Sultanate of Sherhaben too would be destroyed.

Arthur Wix and Bert Audick, together with Ambassador Waleeb, were already on their way to Sherhaben in a fast jet passenger plane not yet available to the civilian aircraft industry. Oddblood Gray was frantically trying to rally Congress behind the President and by the end of the day knew he had failed. Eugene Dazzy calmly dealt with all the memoranda from Cabinet members and the Defense establishment, his Walkman firmly set over his ears to discourage unnecessary conversation from his staff. Christian Klee was appearing and disappearing on mysterious errands.

Senator Thomas Lambertino and Congressman Alfred Jintz held constant meetings through Wednesday with colleagues in the House and Senate on the action to impeach Kennedy. The Socrates Club called in all their markers. True, it had to be admitted that the interpretation of the

Constitution was a little murky in the assertion that Congress could designate itself as the deciding body, but the situation warranted such a drastic action—Kennedy's ultimatum to Sherhaben was so obviously based on personal emotions and not on reasons of state.

By late Wednesday the coalition was set. Both houses, with barely two thirds of the vote assured, would convene on Thursday night, just hours before Kennedy's deadline to destroy the city of Dak.

Lambertino and Jintz kept Oddblood Gray fully informed, hoping he could persuade Francis Kennedy to rescind his ultimatum to Sherhaben. Oddblood Gray told them that the President would not do so. He then briefed Francis Kennedy.

Francis Kennedy said, "Otto, I think you and Chris and Dazzy should have a late dinner with me tonight. Make it about eleven. And don't plan to get home right away."

The President and his staff dined in the Yellow Room, which was Kennedy's favorite, though this made for a lot of extra work for the kitchen and waiters. As usual the meal was very simple for Kennedy, a small grilled steak, a dish of thinly sliced tomatoes and then coffee with a variety of cream and fruit tarts. Christian and the others were offered the option of fish. None of them ate more than a few bites.

Kennedy seemed to be perfectly at ease, the others were awkward. They all wore black arm bands on their sleeves, as did Kennedy. Everyone in the White House, including the servants, wore identical black bands, which seemed archaic to Christian. He knew that Eugene Dazzy had sent out the memorandum ordering this to be done.

"Christian," Kennedy said, "I think it's time we share our problem. But it goes no further. No memorandum."

"It's serious," Christian said. And he outlined what had

happened in the atom bomb scare. He informed them that on the advice of their lawyer the two young men had refused to talk.

Oddblood Gray said incredulously, "There's a nuclear device planted in New York City? I don't believe it. All this shit can't be happening at once."

Dazzy said, "Are you sure they really did plant a nuclear device?"

Christian said, "I think there is only a ten percent chance." He believed that there was more than a ninety percent chance but he was not willing to tell them that.

"What are you going to do about it?" Dazzy said.

"We've got the nuclear search teams out," Christian said. "But there's a time element." He spoke directly to Kennedy. "I still need your signature to activate the medical interrogation team for the PVT test." He explained Section IX of the Atomic Weapons Control Act.

"No," Francis Kennedy said.

They were all astonished by the President's refusal.

"We can't take a chance," Dazzy said. "Sign the order."

Kennedy smiled and said, "The invading of an individual's brain by government officials is a dangerous action." He paused for a moment and said, "We can't sacrifice a citizen's individual rights just on suspicion. Especially such potentially valuable citizens as those two young men. Chris, when you have more confirmation, ask again." Then Kennedy said to Oddblood Gray, "Otto, brief Christian and Dazzy on the Congress."

Gray said, "Here is their game plan. They know now that the Vice President will not sign the declaration to impeach you under the Twenty-fifth Amendment. But enough of the Cabinet members have signed so that they can still take action. They will designate Congress as the other body to determine your fitness. They will convene late Thursday and then vote to impeach. Just to cancel you from the negotiations for the release of the hostages. Their argument is that you are under too much stress because of the death of your daughter.

"When you're removed, the Secretary of Defense will countermand your orders to bomb Dak. They are counting on Bert Audick to convince the Sultan to release the hostages during that thirty-day period. The Sultan will almost certainly comply."

Kennedy turned to Dazzy. "Put out a directive. No member of this government will contact Sherhaben. Doing so will be regarded as treason."

Dazzy said softly, "With most of your Cabinet against you, there is no possibility your orders will be carried out. At this moment you have no power."

Kennedy turned to Christian Klee. "Chris," he said, "they need a two-thirds vote to remove me from office, right?"

"Yes," Christian said. "But without the Vice President's signature, it's basically illegal."

Kennedy looked into his eyes. "Isn't there anything you can do?"

In that moment Christian Klee's mind made another leap. Francis thought he could do something, but what was it? Christian said tentatively, "We can call on the Supreme Court and say that the Congress is acting against the Constitution. The language is vague in the Twenty-fifth Amendment. Or we can argue that Congress is acting contrary to the spirit of the amendment by substituting itself as the instigating party after the Vice President has refused to sign. I can contact the Court so they can rule right after the Congress votes."

He saw the look of disappointment in Kennedy's eyes and he racked his brain furiously. He was missing something.

Oddblood Gray said worriedly, "The Congress is going to attack your mental capacity. They keep bringing up the week you disappeared. Just before your inauguration."

Kennedy said, "That's nobody's business."

Christian became aware that the others were waiting for him to speak. They knew he had been with the President that mysterious week. He said, "What happened in that week won't damage us."

Francis Kennedy said, "Euge, prepare the papers for firing the whole Cabinet except for Theodore Tappey. Prepare them as soon as possible and I'll sign right away. Have the press secretary give it to the media before Congress meets."

Eugene Dazzy made notes, then asked, "What about the chairman of the Joint Chiefs of Staff? Fire him too?"

"No," Francis Kennedy said. "Basically he's with us, the others ruled against him. Congress couldn't do this if it weren't for those bastards in the Socrates Club."

Christian said, "I've been handling the interrogation of the two young kids. They choose to remain silent. And if their lawyer has it his way, they will be released on bail tomorrow."

Dazzy said sharply, "There's a section in the Atomic Security Act that enables you to hold them. It suspends the right of habeas corpus, civil liberties. You must know that, Christian."

"Number one," Christian said, "what's the point of holding them if Francis refuses to sign the medical interrogation order? Their lawyer applies for bail, and if we refuse them we still must have the President's signature to suspend habeas corpus in this case. Francis, are you willing to sign an order for a suspension of habeas corpus?"

Kennedy smiled at him. "No, Congress will use that against me."

Christian was confident now. Still, for a moment, he felt a little sick and bile rose in his mouth. Then it passed and he knew what Kennedy wanted, he knew what he had to do.

Kennedy sipped his coffee; they had finished their meal, but none of them had taken more than a few bites. Kennedy said, "Let's discuss the real crisis. Am I still going to be President in forty-eight hours?"

Oddblood Gray said, "Rescind the order to bomb Dak, turn over the negotiations to a special team, and no action to remove you will be taken by the Congress."

"Who gave you that deal?" Kennedy asked.

"Senator Lambertino and Congressman Jintz," Otto Gray said. "Lambertino is a genuine good guy and Jintz is responsible in a political affair like this. They wouldn't double-cross us."

"OK, that's another option," Kennedy said. "That and going to the Supreme Court. What else?"

Dazzy said, "Go on TV tomorrow before Congress convenes and appeal to the nation. The people will be for you, and that may give Congress pause."

"OK," Kennedy said. "Euge, clear it with the TV people for me to go on over all the networks. Just fifteen minutes is what we need."

Dazzy said softly, "Francis, it's an awful big step we're taking. The President and the Congress in such a direct confrontation and then calling upon the masses to take action. It could get very messy."

Gray said, "That guy Yabril will string us out for weeks and make this country look like a big lump of shit."

Christian said, "There's a rumor that one of the staff in this room or Arthur Wix is going to sign that declaration to remove the President. Whoever it is should speak now."

Kennedy said impatiently, "That rumor is nonsense. If one of you were going to do that, you would have resigned beforehand. I know all of you too well—none of you would betray me."

After dinner they went from the Yellow Room to the little movie theater on the other side of the White House. Kennedy had told Dazzy that he wanted all of them to see the TV footage of the murder of his daughter.

In the darkness the nervous voice of Eugene Dazzy said, "The TV coverage starts now." For a few seconds the movie screen was streaked with black lines that seemed to scramble from top to bottom.

Then the screen lit up with brilliant colors, the TV cameras focusing on the huge aircraft squatting on the desert sand. Next the cameras zoomed to the figure of Yabril presenting Theresa Kennedy in the doorway. Kennedy watched again how his daughter smiled slightly and waved to the camera. It was an odd wave, a wave of reassurance yet of subjugation. Yabril was beside her, then slightly behind her. And then there was the movement of the right arm, the gun not visible, and the flat report of the shot and then the billowing ghostly pink mist and the body of Theresa Kennedy falling. Kennedy heard the wail of the crowd and recognized it as grief and not triumph. Then the figure of Yabril appeared in the doorway. He held his gun aloft, an oily gleaming tube of black metal. He held it as a gladiator holds a sword, but there were no cheers. The film came to an end. Eugene Dazzy had edited it severely.

The lights came on, but Kennedy remained still. He felt

a familiar weakening of his body. He couldn't move his legs
or his torso. But his mind was clear, there was no shock or
disorder in his brain. He did not feel the helplessness of
tragedy's victim. He would not have to struggle against fate
or God. He only had to struggle against his enemies in this
world and he would conquer them.

He would not let mortal man defeat him. When his wife
died, he'd had no recourse against the hand of God, the
faults of nature. He had bowed his entire being in accept-
ance. But his daughter's man-made death, engineered by
malice—*that* he could punish, and redress. This time he
would not bow his head. Woe to that world, to his enemies,
woe to the wicked in this world.

When he was finally able to lift his body from the chair,
he smiled reassuringly to the men around him. He had accomplished his purpose. He had made his closest and most
powerful friends suffer with him. They would not now so
easily oppose the actions he must take.

Kennedy left the room and his staff sat in silence. It almost
seemed as if the air of power, burnt with misuse, had spread
a sulfurous odor through the room. The terror that had
sprung from the desert of Sherhaben had even more frighteningly invaded this room.

What remained unsaid was that now they were perhaps
more worried about Francis Kennedy than about Yabril.

Oddblood Gray finally broke the silence. "Do you think
the President has gone a little crazy?" he said.

Eugene Dazzy shook his head. "It doesn't matter. Maybe
we're all a little crazy. We have to support him now. We have
to win."

Dr. Zed Annaccone was one of those short thin men with a
big chest. He looked extraordinarily alert and what seemed

like superciliousness in his facial expression was actually just the confidence of a man who believed he knew more about the important things on this earth than anyone else. Which was quite true.

Dr. Annaccone was the medical science adviser to the President of the United States. He was also the director of the National Brain Research Institute and the administrative head of the Medical Advisory Board of the Atomic Security Commission. Once at a White House dinner party, Klee had heard him say that the brain was such a sophisticated organ that it could produce whatever chemicals the body needed. And Klee had simply thought, So what?

The doctor, reading his mind, patted him on the shoulder and said, "That fact is more important to civilization than anything you guys can do here in the White House. And all we need is a billion dollars to prove it. What the hell is that, one aircraft carrier?" Then he had smiled at Klee to show that he meant no offense.

And now he was smiling when Klee walked into his office.

"So," Dr. Annaccone said, "finally even the lawyers come to me. You realize our philosophies are directly opposed?"

Klee knew that Dr. Annaccone was about to make a joke about the legal profession and was slightly irritated. Why did people always make wise-ass remarks about lawyers?

"Truth," Dr. Annaccone said. "Lawyers always seek to obscure it, we scientists try to reveal it." He smiled again.

"No, no," Klee said and smiled to show he had a sense of humor. "I'm here for information. We have a situation that calls for that special PET study under the Atomic Weapons Control Act."

"You know you have to get the President's signature on that," Dr. Annaccone said. "Personally I'd do the procedure for many other situations, but the civil libertarians would kick my ass."

"I know," Christian said. Then he explained the situation of the atom bomb and capture of Gresse and Tibbot. "Nobody thinks there is really a bomb, but if there is, then the time factor is crucially important. And the President refuses to sign the order."

"Why?" Dr. Annaccone asked.

"Because of the possible brain damage that could occur during the procedure," Klee said.

This seemed to surprise Annaccone. He thought for a moment. "The possibility of significant brain damage is very small," he said. "Maybe ten percent. The greater danger is the rare incidence of cardiac arrest and the even rarer side effect of complete and total memory loss. Complete amnesia. But even that shouldn't dissuade him in this case. I've sent the President papers on it, I hope he reads them."

"He reads everything," Christian said. "But I'm afraid it won't change his mind."

"Too bad we don't have more time," Dr. Annaccone said. "We are just completing tests that will result in an infallible lie detector based on computer measurement of the chemical changes in the brain. The new test is much like the PET but without the ten percent damage risk. It will be completely safe. But we can't use that now; there would be too many elements of doubt until further data are compiled to satisfy the legal requirements."

Christian felt a tinge of excitement. "A safe, infallible lie detector whose findings would be admitted into court?" he said.

"As to being admitted into a court of law, I don't know," Dr. Annaccone said. "Scientifically, when our tests have been thoroughly analyzed and compiled by the computers, the new brain lie-detector test will be as infallible as DNA and fingerprinting. That's one thing. But to get it enacted into law is another. The civil liberties groups will fight it to the death. They're convinced that a man should not be used to testify against himself. And how would people in Congress like the idea that they could be made to take such a test under criminal law?"

Klee said, "I wouldn't like to take it."

Annaccone laughed. "Congress would be signing its own political death warrant. And yet where's the true logic? Our laws were made to prevent confessions obtained by foul means. However, this is science." He paused for a moment. "How about business leaders or even errant husbands and wives?"

"That's a little creepy," Klee admitted.

Dr. Annaccone said, "But what about all those old sayings, like, 'The truth shall make you free'? Like, 'Truth is the greatest of virtues.' Like, 'Truth is the very essence of life.' That man's struggle to discover truth is his greatest ideal?" Dr. Annaccone laughed. "When our tests are verified, I'll bet my institute budget will get chopped."

Christian said, "That's my area of competence. We dress up the law. We specify that your test can be used only in important criminal cases. We restrict its use to the government. Make it like a strictly controlled narcotics substance or arms manufacturing. So if you can get the test proven scientifically, I can get the legislation." Then he asked, "Exactly how the hell does that work anyway?"

"The new PET?" Dr. Annaccone said. "It's very simple. Physically not invasive. No surgeon with a blade in his hand. No obvious scars. Just a small injection of a chemical substance into the brain through the blood vessels. Chemical self-sabotage with psychopharmaceuticals."

"It's voodoo to me," Christian said. "You should be in jail with those two physics guys."

Dr. Annaccone laughed. "No connection," he said. "Those guys work to blow up the world. I work to get at the inner truths—how man really thinks, what he really feels."

But even Dr. Annaccone knew that a brain lie-detector test meant legal trouble. "This will be perhaps the most important discovery in the medical history of our time," Dr. Annaccone said. "Imagine if we could read the brain. All you lawyers would be out of a job."

Christian said, "Do you think it's possible to figure out how the brain works, really?"

Dr. Annaccone shrugged. "No," he said. "If the brain were that simple, we would be too simple to figure it out." He gave Christian another grin. "Catch-22. Our brain will never catch up with the brain. Because of that, no matter what happens, mankind can never be more than a higher form of animal." He seemed overjoyed by this fact.

He became abstracted for a moment. "You know there's a 'ghost in the machine,' Koestler's phrase. Man has two brains really, the primitive brain and the overlying civilized brain. Have you noticed there is a certain unexplainable malice in human beings. A useless malice?"

Christian said, "Call the President about the PET. Try to persuade him."

Dr. Annaccone said, "I will. He is really being too chicken. The procedure won't damage those kids a bit."

The rumor that one of the White House personal staff would sign the petition to remove Kennedy from the presidency had set off warning signals in Christian Klee's head.

Eugene Dazzy was at his desk surrounded by three secretaries taking notes for actions to be taken by his own personal staff. He wore his Walkman over his ears but the sound was turned off. And his usual good-humored face was grim. He looked up at his uninvited visitor and said, "Chris, this is the worst possible time for you to come snooping around."

Christian said, "Eugene, don't bullshit me. How come nobody's curious about who the rumored traitor on the staff is. That means everybody knows, except me. And I'm the guy who should know."

Dazzy dismissed his secretaries. They were alone in the office. Dazzy smiled at Christian. "It never occurred to me you didn't know. You keep track of everything with your FBI and Secret Service, your stealth intelligence and listening devices. Those thousands of agents the Congress doesn't know you have on the payroll. How come you're so ignorant?"

Christian said coldly, "I know you're fucking some dancer twice a week in one of those apartments that belong to Jeralyn's restaurant."

Dazzy sighed. "That's it. This lobbyist who loans me the apartment came to see me. He asked me to sign the removal-of-the-President document. He wasn't crude about it, there were no direct threats, but the implication was clear. Sign it or my little sins would be all over the papers and television." Dazzy laughed. "I couldn't believe it. How could they be so dumb?"

Christian said, "So what answer did you give?"

Dazzy smiled. "I crossed his name off my 'friends' list. I barred his access. And I told him I would give my old buddy Christian Klee his name as a potential threat to the security of the President. Then I told Francis. He told me to forget the whole thing."

Christian said, "Who sent the guy?"

Dazzy said, "The only guy who would dare is a member

of the Socrates Club. And that would be our old friend Martin 'Take It Private' Mutford."

Christian said, "He's smarter than that."

"Sure, he is," Dazzy said grimly. "Everybody is smarter than that until they get desperate. When the VP refused to sign the impeachment memorandum, they became desperate. Besides, you never know when somebody will cave in."

Christian still didn't like it. "But they know you. They know that under all that flab you're a tough guy. I've seen you in action. You ran one of the biggest companies in the United States, you cut IBM a new asshole just five years ago. How could they think you'd cave in?"

Dazzy shrugged. "Everybody always thinks he's tougher than anybody else." He paused. "You think so yourself, though you don't advertise it. I do. So does Wix and so does Gray. Francis doesn't think it. He just can be. And we have to be careful for Francis. We have to be careful he doesn't get too tough."

Christian Klee paid a call on Jeralyn Albanese, who owned the most famous restaurant in Washington, D.C., naturally named Jera's. It had three huge dining rooms separated by a very lush lounge bar. The Republicans gravitated to one dining room, the Democrats to another, and members of the executive branch and the White House ate in the third room. The one thing on which all parties agreed was that the food was delicious, the service superb, and the hostess one of the most charming women in the world.

Twenty years before, Jeralyn, then a woman of thirty, had been employed by a lobbyist for the banking industry. He had introduced her to Martin Mutford, who had not yet earned the nickname "Take It Private" but was already on the rise. Martin Mutford had been charmed by her wit, her brashness and her sense of adventure. For five years they had an affair that did not interfere with their public lives. Jeralyn Albanese continued her career as a lobbyist, a career much more complicated and refined than generally supposed, requiring a great deal of research skill and administrative genius. Oddly enough, one of her most valuable assets was having been a tennis champion in college.

As an assistant to the chief lobbyist for the banking industry, she spent a good part of her week amassing financial data to persuade experts on the congressional finance committees to pass legislation favorable to banking. Then she was hostess at conference dinners with congressmen and senators. She was astonished by the horniness of these calm judicial legislators. In private, they were like rioting gold miners, they drank to excess, they sang lustily, they grabbed her ass in a spirit of old-time American folksiness. She was amazed and delighted by their lust. It developed naturally that she went to the Bahamas and to Las Vegas with the younger and more personable congressmen, always under the guise of conferences, and even once to London to a convention of economic advisers from all over the world. Not to influence the vote on a bill, not to perpetrate a swindle, but if the vote on a bill was borderline, when a girl as pretty as Jeralyn Albanese presented the customary foot-high stack of opinion papers written by eminent economists, you had a very good chance of getting that teetering vote. As Martin Mutford said, "On the close ones it's very hard for a man to vote against a girl who sucked his cock the night before."

It was Mutford who had taught her to appreciate the finer things in life. He had taken her to the museums in New York; he had taken her to the Hamptons to mingle with the rich and the artists, the old money and the new money, the famous journalists and the TV anchors, the writers who did serious novels and the important screenplays of big movies. Another pretty face didn't make much of a splash there, but being a good tennis player gave her an edge.

Jeralyn had more men fall in love with her because of her tennis playing than because of her beauty. And it was a sport that men who were mere hackers, as politicians and artists usually were, loved to play with good-looking women. In mixed doubles, Jeralyn could establish a sporting rapport with partners, flashing her lovely limbs in their struggle for victory.

But there came a time when Jeralyn had to think of her future. At forty years of age she was not married, and the congressmen she would have to lobby were in their unappealing sixties and seventies.

Martin Mutford was eager to promote her in the high realms of banking, but after the excitement of Washington, banking seemed dull. American lawmakers were so fascinating with their outrageous mendacity in public affairs, their charming innocence in sexual relationships. It was Mutford who came up with the solution. He, too, did not want to lose Jeralyn in a maze of computer reports. In Washington her beautifully furnished apartment was a refuge from his heavy responsibilities. It was Mutford who came up with the idea that she could own and run a restaurant that would be a political hub.

The funds were supplied by American Sterling Trustees, a lobbyist group that represented banking interests, in the form of a five-million-dollar loan. Jeralyn had the restaurant built to her specifications. It would be an exclusive club, an auxiliary home for the politicos of Washington. Many congressmen were separated from their families while Congress was in session, and the Jera restaurant was a place where they could spend lonely nights. In addition to the three dining rooms and lounge and bar, there was a room with TV and a reading room that had a copy of all the major magazines published in the United States and England. There was another room for chess or checkers or cards. But the ultimate attraction was the residential area built on top of the restaurant. It was three stories high and held twenty apartments, which were rented by the lobbyists, who loaned them out to congressmen and important bureaucrats for secretive liaisons. Jera was known to be the very soul of discretion in these matters. Jeralyn kept the keys.

It amazed Jeralyn that these hardworking men had the time for so much dalliance. They were indefatigable. And it was the older ones with established families, some with grandchildren, who were the most active. Jeralyn loved to see these same congressmen and senators on television, so sedate and distinguished-looking, lecturing on morals, decrying drugs and loose living and emphasizing the importance of old-fashioned values. She never felt they were hypocrites really. After all, men who had spent so much of their lives and time and energy for their country deserved extra consideration.

She didn't like the arrogance, the smarmy self-assured smugness of the younger congressmen, but she loved the old guys, such as the stern-faced wrathful senator who never smiled in public but cavorted at least twice a week bare-assed with young "models"—and old Congressman Jintz, with his body like a scarred zeppelin and a face so ugly that the whole country believed he was honest. All of them looked absolutely awful in private, shedding their clothes. But they charmed her.

Rarely did the women members of Congress come to the restaurant and never did they make use of the apartments. Feminism had not yet advanced so far. To make up for this,

Jeralyn gave little lunches in the restaurant for some of her girlfriends in the arts, pretty actresses, singers and dancers.

It was none of her business if these young pretty women struck up friendships with the highly placed servants of the people of the United States. But she was surprised when Eugene Dazzy, the huge slobby chief of staff to the President of the United States, took up with a promising young dancer and arranged for Jeralyn to slip him a key to one of the apartments above the restaurant. She was even more astonished when the liaison grew to the status of a "relationship." Not that Dazzy had that much time at his disposal—the most he spent in the apartment was a few hours after lunch. And Jeralyn was under no illusion as to what the rent-paying lobbyist could get out of it. Dazzy's decisions would not be influenced, but at least he would, on rare occasions, take the lobbyist's calls to the White House so that the lobbyist's clients would be impressed by such access.

Jeralyn gave all this information to Martin Mutford when they gossiped together. It was understood that the information between the two of them was not to be used in any way and certainly not in any form of blackmail. That could be disastrous and destroy the main purpose of the restaurant, which was to further the atmosphere of good fellowship and earn a sympathetic ear for the lobbyists who were footing the bill. Plus the fact that the restaurant was Jeralyn's main source of livelihood and she would not allow it to be jeopardized.

So Jeralyn was very much surprised when Christian Klee dropped in on her when the restaurant was almost empty between lunch and dinner. She received him in her office. She liked Klee, though he ate at Jera's infrequently and had never tried to make use of the apartments above. But she had no feeling of apprehension; she knew that there was nothing he could reproach her for. If some scandal was brewing, no matter what newspaper reporters were up to, or what one of the young girls would say, she was in the clear.

She murmured some words of commiseration about the terrible times he must be going through, what with the murder and the hijacking, but was careful not to sound as if she were fishing for inside information. Klee thanked her.

Then he said, "Jeralyn, we've known each other a long time and I want to alert you, for your protection. I know what I'm about to say will shock you as much as it does me."

Oh, shit, Jeralyn thought. Somebody is making trouble for me.

Christian Klee went on. "A lobbyist for financial interests is a good friend of Eugene Dazzy and he tried to lay some bullshit on him. He urged Dazzy to sign a paper that would do President Kennedy a great deal of harm. He warned Dazzy that his using one of your apartments could be made public and ruin his career and his marriage." Klee laughed. "Jesus, who would ever have thought Eugene was capable of a thing like that. What the hell, I guess we're all human."

Jeralyn was not fooled by Christian's good humor. She knew she had to be very careful or her whole life might go down the drain. Klee was Attorney General of the United States, and had acquired the reputation of being a very dangerous man. He could give her more trouble than she could handle, even though her ace in the hole was Martin Mutford. She said, "I didn't have anything to do with all that. Sure, I gave Dazzy the key to one of the apartments upstairs. But hell, that was just a courtesy of the house. There are no records of any kind. Nobody could pin anything on me or Dazzy."

"Sure, I know that," Christian said. "But don't you see, that lobbyist would never dare pull that shit on his own? Somebody higher up told him what to do."

Jeralyn said uneasily, "Christian, I swear I never blabbed to anyone. I would never put my restaurant in jeopardy. I'm not that dumb."

"I know, I know," Christian said reassuringly. "But you and Martin have been very good friends for a very long time. You may have told him, just as a piece of gossip."

Now Jeralyn was really horrified. Suddenly she was between two powerful men who were about to do battle. More than anything else in the world she wanted to step outside the arena. She also knew that the worst thing to do was lie.

"Martin would never try such a dumb thing," she said. "Not that kind of stupid blackmail." By saying this, she admitted she had told Martin and yet could deny that she had explicitly confessed.

Christian was still reassuring. He saw that she had not guessed the real purpose of his visit. He said, "Eugene Dazzy told the lobbyist to go fuck himself. Then he told me the story and I said I would take care of it. Now, of course, I know they can't expose Dazzy. For one thing, I'd come down on you and this place so hard you'd think a tank hit you. You'd have to identify all the people in Congress who used those apartments. There would be one hell of a scandal. Your friend was just hoping Dazzy would lose his nerve. But Eugene figured that one out."

Jeralyn was still unbelieving. "Martin would never instigate something so dangerous. He's a banker." She smiled at Christian, who sighed and decided it was time to get tough.

"Listen, Jeralyn," he said. "Do I have to remind you that old 'Take It Private' Martin is not your usual nice stolid conservative banker. He's had a few trouble spots in his life.

And he didn't make his billions by playing it safe. He's cut things a bit close before." He paused for a moment. "Now he's meddling in something very dangerous for you and for him."

Jeralyn gave a contemptuous wave of her hand. "You said yourself you knew I had nothing to do with whatever the hell he is doing."

"True," Christian said. "I know that. But now Martin is a man I have to watch. And I want you to help me watch him."

Jeralyn was adamant. "Like hell," she said. "Martin has always treated me decently. He's a real friend."

Christian said, "I don't want you to be a spy. I don't want any information about his business dealings or about his personal life. All I'm asking is that if you know anything or find out any moves he's going to make against the President, you give me fair warning."

"Oh, fuck you," Jeralyn said. "Get the hell out of here, I have to get ready for the supper crowd."

"Sure," Christian said amiably. "I'm leaving. But remember this, I *am* the Attorney General of the United States. We're in tough times and it doesn't hurt to have me as a friend. So use your own judgment when the time comes. If you slip me just a little warning, no one will ever know. Use your own good sense."

He left. He had accomplished his purpose. Jeralyn might tell Martin Mutford about their interview, which was fine, for that would make Mutford more cautious. Or she would not tell Martin and when the time came she'd snitch. Either way he couldn't lose.

The driver cut off the siren and they were gliding through the gates of the Oracle's estate. Christian noted that there were three limousines waiting in the circular driveway. And it was curious that the drivers were in their seats behind the wheel and not outside smoking cigarettes. Beside each car lounged a tall well-dressed man. Christian nailed them at once. Bodyguards. So the Oracle had important visitors. And this must be why the old man had summoned him so urgently.

Christian was greeted by the butler, who led him to a living room furnished for a conference. The Oracle was in his wheelchair waiting. Around the table were four members of the Socrates Club. Christian was surprised to see them. His latest report had been that all four were in California.

The Oracle motored his wheelchair to the head of the table. "You must forgive me, Christian, for this slight deception," he said. "I felt that it was important that you meet with my friends at this critical time. They are anxious to talk to you."

Servants had set the conference table with coffee and sandwiches. There were also drinks being served, the servers summoned by a buzzer the Oracle could reach beneath the table. The four members of the Socrates Club had already refreshed themselves. Martin Mutford had lit a huge cigar and unbuttoned his collar, loosened his tie. He looked a little grim, but Christian knew that this grimness was often a tightening of the muscles to conceal fear.

He said, "Martin, Eugene Dazzy told me one of your lobbyists gave him some bad advice today. I hope you had nothing to do with that."

"Dazzy can weed out good from bad," Mutford said. "Otherwise he wouldn't be the President's chief of staff."

"Sure, he can," Christian said. "And he doesn't need advice from me on how to break balls. But I can give him a hand."

Christian could see that the Oracle and George Greenwell did not know what he was talking about. But Lawrence Salentine and Louis Inch were smiling slightly.

Inch said impatiently, "That's unimportant, not relevant to our meeting here tonight."

"What the hell is the purpose?" Christian said.

It was Salentine who answered him in a smooth calming voice—he was used to handling confrontations. "This is a very difficult time," he said. "I think even a dangerous time. All responsible people must work together for a solution. All the people here favor the deposing of President Kennedy for a period of thirty days. Congress will vote tomorrow night in special session. Vice President Du Pray's refusal to sign makes things difficult, but not impossible. It would be very helpful if you as a member of the President's personal staff would sign. That is what we are asking you to do."

Christian was so astonished he could not answer. The Oracle broke in. "I agree. It will be better for Kennedy not to handle this particular issue. His action today was completely irrational and springs from a desire for vengeance. It could lead to terrible events. Christian, I implore you to listen to these men."

Christian said very deliberately, "There is not one chance in hell." He spoke directly to the Oracle. "How could you be party to this? How can you, of all people, be against me?"

The Oracle shook his head. "I'm not against you," he said.

Salentine said, "He can't just destroy fifty billion dollars because he suffered a personal tragedy. That's not what democracy is about."

Christian had regained his composure. He said in a reasonable tone of voice, "That is not the truth. Francis Kennedy has thought this out. He doesn't want the hijackers to string us along for weeks, milking TV time on your net-

works, Mr. Salentine, with the United States being held up
to ridicule. For Christ's sake, they killed the Pope of the
Catholic Church, they murdered the daughter of the President of the United States. You want to negotiate with them
now? You want to set the killer of the Pope free? You call
yourself patriots? You say you worry about this country?
You are a bunch of hypocrites."

For the first time, George Greenwell spoke. "What about
the other hostages? Are you willing to sacrifice them?"

And Christian shot back without thinking, "Yes." He
paused and then said, "I think the President's way is the best
possible chance to get them out alive."

Greenwell said, "Bert Audick is in Sherhaben now, as you
know. He has assured us that he can persuade the hijackers
and the Sultan to release the remaining hostages."

Christian said contemptuously, "I heard him assure the
President of the United States that no harm would come to
Theresa Kennedy. And now she's dead."

Salentine said, "Mr. Klee, we can argue all these minor
points till doomsday. We haven't got the time. We were
hoping you would join us and make it easier. What must be
done will be done whether you agree to it or not. I assure you
of that. But why make this struggle more divisive? Why not
serve the President by working with us?"

Christian looked at him coldly. "Don't bullshit me. Let
me tell you this, I know you men carry a lot of weight in this
country, weight that is unconstitutional. My office will inves-
tigate all of you as soon as this crisis is over."

Greenwell gave a sigh. The violent and senseless ire of
young men was boring to a man of his experience and age.
He said to Christian, "Mr. Klee, we all thank you for coming. And I hope there will be no personal animosity. We are
acting to help our country."

Christian said, "You are acting to save Audick his fifty billion dollars." He had a flash of insight. These men did not have a real hope of recruiting him. This was simply an intimidation. That he would possibly remain neutral. Then he got their sense of fear. They feared him. That he had the power and, more important, he had the will. And the only one who could have warned them about him was the Oracle.

They were all silent. Then the Oracle said, "You can go, I know you have to get back. Call me and let me know what's happening. Keep me abreast."

Hurt by the Oracle's betrayal, Christian said, "You could have warned me."

The Oracle shook his head. "You wouldn't have come. And I couldn't convince my friends that you wouldn't sign. I had to give them their shot." He paused for a moment. "I'll see you out," he said to Christian. And he rolled his wheelchair out of the room. Christian followed him.

Before Christian left the room, he turned to the Socrates Club and said, "Gentlemen, I beg of you, don't let the Congress do this." He gave off such a grave menace that nobody spoke.

When the Oracle and Klee were alone on the top of the ramp leading to the entrance foyer, the Oracle braced his wheelchair. He lifted his head, so freckled with the brown of aging skin, and said to Christian, "You are my godson, and you are my heir. All this doesn't change my affection for you. But be warned. I love my country and I perceive your Francis Kennedy as a great danger."

For the first time Christian Klee felt a bitterness against this old man he had always loved. "You and your Socrates Club have Francis by the balls," he said. "You people are the danger."

The Oracle was studying him. "But you don't seem too

worried. Christian, I beg of you, don't be rash. Don't do something irrevocable. I know you have a great deal of power and, more important, a great deal of cunning. You are gifted, I know. But don't try to overpower history."

"I don't know what you are talking about," Christian said. He was in a hurry now. He had his last stop to make before going back to the White House.

The Oracle sighed. "Remember, no matter what happens you still have my affection. You are the only living person I love. And if it is within my power I will never let anything happen to you. Call me, keep me abreast."

Even in his anger Christian felt again his old affection for the Oracle. He squeezed his shoulder and said, "What the hell, it's only a political difference, we've had them before. Don't worry—I'll call you."

The Oracle gave him a crooked smile. "And don't forget my birthday party. When this is all over. If we are both alive."

And Christian to his astonishment saw tears dropping onto the withered aged cheeks. He leaned over to kiss that face, parched, cool as glass.

Christian Klee was late getting back to the White House. His last stop had been to secretly interrogate Gresse and Tibbot.

He went directly to Oddblood Gray's office, but the secretary told him that Gray was having a conference with Congressman Jintz and Senator Lambertino. The secretary looked frightened. She had heard rumors that Congress was trying to remove President Kennedy from office.

Christian said, "Buzz him, tell him it's important and let me use your desk and phone. You go to the ladies' room."

Gray answered the phone thinking he was talking to his secretary. "It'd better be important," he said.

Christian said, "Otto, it's Chris. Listen, I've just been asked by some guys in the Socrates Club to sign the removal memo. Dazzy was asked to sign, they tried to blackmail him over that affair with the dancer. I know Wix is on his way to Sherhaben, so he's not signing the petition. Are you signing?"

Oddblood Gray's voice was very silky. "It's funny, I've just been asked to sign by two gentlemen in my office. I already told them I would not. And I told them nobody else on the personal staff would sign. I didn't have to ask *you*." There was sarcasm in his voice.

Christian said impatiently, "I knew you wouldn't sign, Otto. But I had to ask. But look, put out some lightning bolts. Tell those guys that as the Attorney General I'm launching an investigation into the blackmail threat on Dazzy. Also, that I have a lot of stuff on some of those congressmen and senators that won't look too good in the papers and I'll leak it. Especially their business links with members of the Socrates Club. This is no time for your Oxonian bullshit."

Gray said smoothly, "Thanks for the advice, old buddy. But why don't you take care of your stuff and I'll take care of mine. And don't ask other people to wave your sword around, wave it yourself."

There had always been a subtle antagonism between Oddblood Gray and Christian Klee. Personally they liked and respected each other. Both were physically impressive. Gray had a social bravery, and he had achieved everything on his own. Christian Klee had been born to wealth but had refused to live the life of a rich man. They were both respected by the world. They were both devoted to Francis Kennedy. They were both skilled lawyers.

And yet they were both wary of each other. Gray had the

utmost faith in the progress of society through law, which was why he was so valuable as the President's liaison man with Congress. And he had always distrusted the consolidation of power that Klee had put together. It was too much that in a country like the United States any man should be director of the FBI, chief of the Secret Service and also Attorney General. True, Francis Kennedy had explained the reason for this concentration of power—that it was to help protect the President himself against the threat of assassination. But Gray still didn't like it.

Klee had always been a little impatient with Gray's scrupulous attention to every legality. Gray could afford to be the punctilious statesman; he dealt with politicians and political problems. But Christian Klee felt he had to shovel away the murderous shit of everyday life. The election of Francis Kennedy had brought out all the vermin from the woodwork of America. Only Klee knew about the thousands of murder threats the President had received. Only Klee could stamp out the vermin. And he couldn't always observe the finer points of the law to do his job. Or so Klee believed.

Now was a case in point. Klee wanted to use power, Gray the velvet glove.

"OK," said Christian. "I'll do what I have to do."

"Fine," Gray said. "Now me and you can go together to see the President. He wants us in the Cabinet Room as soon as I'm through here."

Gray had been deliberately indiscreet while on the phone with Klee. Now he faced Congressman Jintz and Senator Lambertino and gave them a rueful smile. "I'm sorry you had to hear that," he said to them. "Christian doesn't like this impeachment business, but he makes it a personal thing when it's a matter of the country's welfare."

Senator Lambertino said, "I advised against approaching

Klee. But I thought we had a chance with you, Otto. When the President appointed you as liaison with Congress, I thought it a foolhardy thing to do, what with all our Southern colleagues who are not fully reconstructed. But I must say you have won them over in these past three years. If the President listened to you, so many of his programs would not have gone down in Congress."

Gray kept his face impassive. He said in his silky voice, "I'm glad you came to me. But I think Congress is making a big mistake with this impeachment proceeding. The Vice President hasn't signed up. Sure, you've got nearly all of the Cabinet, but none of the staff. So Congress will have to vote to make itself the impeachment body. That is one hell of a big step. That will mean that the Congress can override the express vote of the people of this country."

Gray got up and started pacing the room. Usually he never did this when he was negotiating because he knew the impression he made. He was too overpowering physically, and it would seem like an offensive gesture of domination. He was nearly six feet four, and his physique was that of an Olympic athlete. His clothes were beautifully tailored and he had just a touch of an English accent. He looked exactly like those powerful executives shown in TV ads except that his skin was the color of coffee rather than white. But this once he wanted to use a whiff of intimidation.

"You are both men I have admired in Congress," he said. "We have always understood each other. You know I advised Kennedy not to go forward with his social programs until he had laid a better groundwork. All three of us understand one important thing. There is no greater opening for tragedy than a stupid exercise of power. It is one of the most common mistakes in politics. But that is exactly what Congress is going to do when they impeach the President. If you succeed, you start a very dangerous precedent in our government that can lead to fatal repercussions when some President acquires excess power in the future. He may then make his first aim the emasculation of Congress. And what you gain here is short-term. You prevent the destruction of Dak and its fifty-billion-dollar investment by Bert Audick. And the people of this country will despise you, for make no mistake, the people support Kennedy's action. Maybe for the wrong reasons—we all know that the electorate is too easily swayed by obvious emotions, emotions we as governors have to control and redirect. Kennedy right now can order atom bombs dropped on Sherhaben and the people of this country would approve. Stupid, OK? But that's how the masses feel. You know that. So the smart thing is for the Congress to lie back, to see if Kennedy's actions get the hostages back and the hijackers in our prisons. Then everybody's happy. If the policy fails, if the hijackers slaughter the hostages, then you can remove the President and look like heroes."

Gray had tried his best pitch, but he knew it was hopeless. From long experience, he had learned that once they wished to do something, even the wisest men or women would do it. No manner of persuasion could change their minds.

Congressman Jintz did not disappoint him. "You are arguing against the will of the Congress, Otto."

Senator Lambertino said, "Really, Otto, you're fighting a lost cause. I know your loyalty to the President. I know that if everything had gone well the President would have made you a Cabinet member. And let me tell you, the Senate would have approved. That still can happen, but not under Kennedy."

Gray nodded his thanks. "I appreciate that, Senator. But I can't comply with your request. I think the President is justified in the action he's taken. I think that action will be effective. I think the hostages will be released and the criminals given into custody."

Jintz said abruptly and crudely, "This is all beside the point. We can't let him destroy the city of Dak."

Senator Lambertino said softly, "It's not just the money. Such a savage act would hurt our relationships with every country in the world. You see that, Otto."

Gray said, "Let me tell you this. Unless Congress cancels its special session tomorrow, unless it withdraws the motion to impeach, the President will appeal directly to the people of the United States on television. Please present this to your fellow members." He resisted saying, "And to the Socrates Club."

They parted company with those protestations of goodwill and affection that were political good manners long before the murder of Julius Caesar. Then Gray went out to pick up Klee for the meeting with the President.

But his last speech had shaken Congressman Jintz. Jintz had accrued a great deal of wealth during his many years in Congress. His wife was a partner or stockholder in cable television companies in his home state; his son's law firm was one of the biggest in the South. He had no material worries. But he loved his life as a congressman; it brought him pleasures that could not be bought with mere money. The marvelous thing about being a successful politician was that old age could be as happy as your youth. Even when you became a doddering old man, your brain floating away in a flood of senile cells, everyone still respected you, listened to you, kissed your ass. You had the congressional committees and subcommittees, you could wallow in the pork barrels. You could still help steer the course of the greatest country in the world. Though your body was old and feeble, young virile men trembled before you. At some time, Jintz knew, his appetite for food and drink and women would fade, but if there was still one last living cell in his brain he could enjoy power. And how can you really fear the nearness of death when your fellowman still obeys you?

And so Jintz was worried. Was it possible that by some catastrophe his seat in Congress could be lost? There was no way out. His very life depended on the removal of Francis Kennedy from office. He said to Senator Lambertino, "We can't let the President go on TV tomorrow."

CHAPTER
13

DAVID JATNEY SPENT a month reading scripts that seemed to him utterly worthless. He wrote the less than half page of summary, then wrote his opinion on the same page. His opinion was supposed to be only a few sentences but he usually finished using the rest of the space on the page.

At the end of the month the office supervisor came to his desk and said, "David, we don't have to know how witty you are. Just two sentences of opinion will be fine. And don't be so contemptuous of these people, they didn't piss on your desk, they just try to write movies."

"But they are terrible," Jatney said.

The supervisor said, "Sure, they are, do you think we'd let you read the good ones? We have more experienced people for that. And, besides, this stuff you call dreadful, every one of them has been submitted by an agent. An agent hopes to make money from them. So they have passed a very stringent test. We don't accept scripts over the transom because of lawsuits, we're not like book publishers. So no matter how lousy they are, when agents submit, we have to read them. If we don't read the agents' bad scripts, they don't send us the good ones."

David said, "I could write better screenplays,"

The supervisor laughed. "So can we all." He paused for a moment and then said, "When you've written one, let me read it."

A month later David did just that. The supervisor read it in his private office. He was very kind. He said gently, "David, it doesn't work. That doesn't mean you can't write. But you don't really understand how movies work. It shows in your summaries and critiques but your screenplay shows it too. Listen, I'm trying to be helpful. Really. So starting next week you'll be reading the novels that have been published and have been considered possible for movies."

David thanked him politely but felt the familiar rage. Again it was the voice of the elder, the supposedly wiser, the ones who had the power.

It was just a few days later that Dean Hocken's secretary called and asked if he was free for dinner that night with Mr. Hocken. He was so surprised it took him a moment to say yes. She told him it would be at Michael's restaurant in Santa Monica at 8:00 P.M. She started to give him directions to the restaurant, but he told her he lived in Santa Monica and knew where it was, which was not strictly true.

But he had heard of Michael's restaurant. David Jatney read all the newspapers and magazines and he listened to the gossip in the office. Michael's was the restaurant of choice for the movie and music people who lived in the Malibu colony. When he hung up the phone, he asked the manager if he knew exactly where Michael's was located, mentioning casually that he was having dinner there that night. He saw that the manager was impressed. He realized that he should have waited until after this dinner before submitting his screenplay. It would then have been read in a different context.

That evening when David walked into Michael's restaurant he was surprised that only the front part was under a roof—the rest of the restaurant was in a garden made beautiful with flowers and large white umbrellas that formed a secure canopy against rain. The whole area was glowing with lights. It was just beautiful, the balmy open air of April, the flowers gushing their perfume and even a gold moon overhead. What a difference from a Utah winter. It was at this moment that David Jatney decided never to go home again.

He gave his name to the receptionist and was surprised when he was led directly to one of the tables in the garden. He had planned on arriving ahead of Hocken; he knew his role and intended to play it well. He would be absolutely respectful, he would be waiting at the restaurant for good old Hock to arrive and that would be acknowledging his power. He still wondered about Hocken. Was the man genuinely kind or just a Hollywood phony being condescending to the son of a woman who once rejected him and now must, of course, be regretting it?

He saw Dean Hocken at the table he was being led to, and with Hocken were a man and a woman. The first thing that registered on David was that Hocken had deliberately given him a later time so that he would not have to wait—an extraordinary kindness that almost moved him to tears. For in addition to being paranoid and ascribing mysterious evil motives to other people's behavior, David could also ascribe wildly benevolent reasons.

Hocken got up from the table to give him a down-home

hug and then introduced him to the man and woman. David recognized the man at once. His name was Gibson Grange, and he was one of the most famous actors in Hollywood. The woman's name was Rosemary Belair, a name that David was surprised he didn't recognize because she was beautiful enough to be a movie star. She had glossy black hair worn long and her face was perfect in its symmetry. Her makeup was professional and she was dressed elegantly in a dinner dress over which was some sort of little jacket.

They were drinking wine; the bottle rested in a silver bucket. Hocken poured David a glass.

The food was delicious, the air balmy, the garden serene, none of the cares of the world could enter here, David felt. The men and women at the tables around them exuded confidence; these were the people who controlled life. Someday he would be like them.

He listened through the dinner, saying very little. He studied the people at his table. Dean Hocken, he decided was legitimate and as nice as he appeared to be. Which did not necessarily mean that he was a good person, David thought. He became conscious that though this was ostensibly a social occasion, Rosemary and Hock were trying to talk Gibson Grange into doing a picture with them.

It seemed that Rosemary Belair was also a producer—in fact, the most important female producer in Hollywood.

David listened and watched. He took no part in the conversation, and when he was immobile his face was as handsome as in his photographs. The other people at the table registered it but he did not interest them and David was aware of this.

And it suited him right now. Invisible, he could study this powerful world he hoped to conquer. Hocken had arranged this dinner to give his friend Rosemary a chance to talk

Gibson Grange into doing a picture with her. But why? There was a certain easiness between Hocken and Rosemary that could not be there unless they had been through a sexual period. It was the way Hocken soothed Rosemary when she became too excited in her pursuit of Gibson Grange. At one time she said to Gibson, "I'm a lot more fun to do a picture with than Hock."

And Hocken laughed and said, "We had some pretty good times, didn't we, Gib?"

And the actor said, "Hah, we were all business." He said this without cracking a smile.

Gibson Grange was a "bankable" star in the movie business. That is, if he agreed to do a movie, that movie was financed immediately by any studio. Which was why Rosemary was so anxiously pursuing him. He also looked exactly right. He was in the old American Gary Cooper style, lanky, with open features; he looked as Lincoln would have looked if Lincoln had been handsome. His smile was friendly, and he listened to everyone intently when he or she spoke. He told a few good-humored anecdotes about himself that were funny. This was especially endearing. Also, he dressed in a style that was more homespun than Hollywood, baggy trousers and a ratty yet obviously expensive sweater with an old suit jacket over a plain woolen shirt. And yet he magnetized everyone in the garden. Was it because his face had been seen by so many millions and shown so intimately by the camera? Were there mysterious ozone layers where his face remained forever? Was it some physical manifestation not yet solved by science? The man was intelligent, David could see that. His eyes as he listened to Rosemary were amused but not condescending, and though he seemed to always agree with what she was saying, he never committed himself to anything. He was the man David dreamed of being.

They lingered over their wine. Hocken ordered dessert—wonderful French pastries—David had never tasted anything so good. Both Gibson Grange and Rosemary Belair refused to touch the desserts, Rosemary with a shudder of horror and Gibson Grange with a slight smile. But it was Rosemary who would surely let herself be tempted in the future; Grange was secure, David thought. Grange would never touch dessert again in his life, but Rosemary's fall was inevitable.

At Hocken's urging, David ate the other desserts, and then they still lingered and talked. Hocken ordered another bottle of wine, but only he and Rosemary drank from it and then David noticed another undercurrent in the conversation—Rosemary was putting the make on Gibson Grange.

Rosemary had barely talked to David at all during the evening, and now she ignored him so completely that he was forced to chat with Hocken about the old days in Utah. But both of them finally became so entranced by the contest between Rosemary and Gibson that they fell silent.

For as the evening wore on and more wine was drunk Rosemary mounted a full seduction. It was of alarming intensity, an awesome display of sheer will. She presented her virtues. First were the movements of her face and body—somehow the front of her dress had slipped down to show more of her breasts. There were the movements of her legs, which crossed and recrossed, then hiked the gown higher to show a glint of thigh. Her hands moved about, touching Gibson on his face when she was carried away by what she was saying. She showed her wit, told funny anecdotes, and revealed her sensitivity. Her beautiful face was alive to show each emotion, her affection for the people she worked with, her worries about members of her immediate family, her concern about the success of her friends. She avowed her deep affection for Dean Hocken himself, how good old Hock had helped her in her career, rewarded her with advice and influence. Here good old Hock interrupted to say how much she deserved such help because of her hard work on his pictures and her loyalty to him, and as he said this, Rosemary gave him a long look of grateful acknowledgment. At this moment, David, completely enchanted, said that it must have been a great experience for both of them. But Rosemary, eager to renew her pursuit of Gibson, cut David off in midsentence.

David felt a tiny shock at her rudeness but surprisingly no resentment. She was so beautiful, so intent on gaining what she desired, and what she desired was becoming clearer and clearer. She must have Gibson Grange in her bed that night. Her desire had the purity and directness of a child, which made her rudeness almost endearing.

But what David admired above all was the behavior of Gibson Grange. The actor was completely aware of what was happening. He noticed the rudeness to David and tried to make up for it by saying, "David, you'll get a chance to talk someday," as if apologizing for the self-centeredness of the famous, who have no interest in those who have not yet acquired their fame. But Rosemary cut him off too. And Gibson politely listened to her. But it was more than politeness. He had an innate charm that was part of his being. He regarded Rosemary with genuine interest. His eyes sparkled and never wandered from her eyes. When she touched him with her hands he patted her back. He made no bones about it, he liked her. His mouth, too, always parted in a smile that displayed a natural sweetness that softened his craggy face into a humorous mask.

But he was obviously not responding in the proper fashion for Rosemary. She was pounding on an anvil that gave off no sparks. She drank more wine and then played her final card. She revealed her innermost feelings.

She talked directly to Gibson, ignoring the other two men at the table. Indeed she had maneuvered her body so that it was very close to Gibson, isolating them from David and Hocken.

No one could doubt the passionate sincerity in her voice. There were even tears in her eyes. She was baring her soul to Gibson. "I want to be a real person," she said. "I would like to give up all this shit of make-believe, this business of movies. It doesn't satisfy me. I want to go out to make the world a better place. Like Mother Teresa, or Martin Luther King. I'm not doing anything to help make the world grow. I could be a nurse or a doctor, I could be a social worker. I hate this life, these parties, this always being on a plane for meetings with important people. Making decisions about some damned movie that won't help humanity. I want to do something real." And then she reached out and clutched Gibson Grange's hand.

It was marvelous for David to see why Grange had become such a powerful star in the movie business, why he controlled the movies he appeared in. For Gibson Grange somehow had his hand in Rosemary's, somehow he had slid his chair away from her, somehow he had captured his central position in the tableau. Rosemary was still staring at him with an impassioned look on her face, waiting for his response. He smiled at her warmly, then tilted his head downward and to the side so that he addressed David and Hocken.

Gibson Grange said with affectionate approval, "She's slick."

Dean Hocken burst into laughter, David could not repress a smile. Rosemary looked stunned, but then said in a tone of jesting reproof, "Gib, you never take anything seriously except your lousy movies." And to show she was not offended she held out a hand, which Gibson Grange gently kissed.

David wondered at all of them. They were so sophisticated, they were so subtle. He admired Gibson Grange most of all. That he would spurn a woman as beautiful as Rosemary Belair was awe-inspiring, that he could outwit her so easily was godlike.

David had been ignored by Rosemary all evening, but he acknowledged her right to do so. She was the most powerful woman in the most glamorous business in the country. She had access to men far worthier than he. She had every right to be rude to him. David recognized that she did not do so out of malice. She simply found him nonexistent.

They were all astonished that it was nearly midnight; they were the last ones in the restaurant. Hocken stood up and Gibson Grange helped Rosemary put on her jacket again, which she had taken off in the middle of her passionate discourse. When Rosemary stood up she was a little off balance, a little drunk.

"Oh, God," she said. "I don't dare drive myself, the police in this town are so awful. Gib, will you take me back to my hotel?"

Gibson smiled at her. "That's in Beverly Hills. Me and Hock are going out to my house in Malibu. David will give you a ride, won't you, David?"

"Sure," Dean Hocken said. "You don't mind, do you, David?"

"Of course not," David Jatney said. But his mind was spinning. How the hell was this coming about? Good old Hock was looking embarrassed. Obviously Gibson Grange had lied, didn't want to take Rosemary home because he didn't want to have to keep fending the woman off. And

Hock was embarrassed because he had to go along with the lie or else he would get on the wrong side of a big star, something a movie producer avoided at all costs. Then he saw Gibson give him a little smile and he could read the man's mind. And of course that was it, that was why he was such a great actor. He could make audiences read his mind by just wrinkling his eyebrows, tilting his head, a dazzling smile. With just that look, without malice but celestial good humor, he was saying to David Jatney, "The bitch ignored you all evening, she was rude as hell to you, now I have put her in your debt." David looked at Hocken and saw that he was now smiling, not embarrassed. In fact, he looked pleased as if he too had read the actor's look.

Rosemary said abruptly, "I'll drive myself." She did not look at David when she said it.

Hocken said smoothly, "I can't allow that, Rosemary, you are my guest and I did give you too much wine. If you hate the idea of David driving you, then of course I'll take you back to your hotel. Then I'll order a limo to Malibu."

It was, David realized, superbly done. For the first time he detected insincerity in Hocken's voice. Of course Rosemary could not accept Hocken's offer. If she did so, she would be offering a grievous insult to the young friend of her mentor. She would be putting both Hocken and Gibson Grange to a great deal of inconvenience. And her primary purpose in getting Gibson to take her home would not be accomplished anyway. She was caught in an impossible situation.

Then Gibson Grange delivered the final blow. He said, "Hell, I'll ride with you, Hock. I'll just take a nap in the backseat to keep you company to Malibu."

Rosemary gave David a bright smile. She said, "I hope it won't be too much trouble for you."

"No, it won't," David said. Hocken clapped him on the shoulder, Gibson Grange gave him a brilliant smile and a wink. And that smile and wink gave David another message. These two men were standing by him as males. A lone powerful female had shamed one of their fellow males and they were punishing her. Also, she had come on too strong to Gibson, it was not a woman's place to do so with a male more than equal in power. They had just administered a masterful blow to her ego, to keep her in her place. And it was all done with such marvelous good humor and politeness. And there was another factor. These men remembered when they had been young and powerless as David was now; they had invited him to dinner to show that their success did not leave them faithless to their fellow males, a time-hallowed practice perfected over centuries to forestall any envious revenge. Rosemary had not honored this practice, had not remembered her time of powerlessness, and tonight they had reminded her. And yet David was on Rosemary's side; she was too beautiful to be hurt.

They walked out into the parking lot together, and then when the other two men roared away in Hocken's Porsche, David led Rosemary to his old Toyota.

Rosemary said, "Shit, I can't get out at the Beverly Hills Hotel from a car like that." She looked around and said, "Now I have to find my car. Look, David, do you mind driving me back in my Mercedes, it's somewhere around here, and I'll have a hotel limo bring you back. That way I won't have to have my car picked up in the morning. Could we do that?" She smiled at him sweetly, then reached into her pocketbook and put on spectacles. She pointed to one of the few remaining cars in the lot and said, "There it is." David, who had spotted her car as soon as they were outside, was puzzled. Then he realized she must be extremely near-sighted. Maybe it was nearsightedness that made her ignore him at dinner.

She gave him the key to her Mercedes, and he unlocked the door on her side and helped her in. He could smell the wine and perfume composted on her body and felt the heat of her bones like burning coal. Then he went to the other side of the car to get in the driver's seat, and before he could use the key the door swung open—Rosemary had unlocked it from the inside to open it for him. He was surprised by this, he would have judged it not in her character.

It took him a few minutes to figure out how the Mercedes worked. But he loved the feel of the seat, the smell of the reddish leather—was it a natural smell or did she spray the car with some sort of special leather perfume? And the car handled beautifully; for the first time he understood the acute pleasure some people took from driving.

The Mercedes seemed to just flow through the dark streets. He enjoyed driving so much that the half hour to the Beverly Hills Hotel seemed to pass in an instant. In all that time Rosemary did not speak to him. She took off her spectacles and put them back into her purse and then sat silent. Once she glanced at his profile as if appraising him. Then she just stared straight ahead. David never once turned to her or spoke. He was enjoying the dream of driving a beautiful woman in a beautiful car, in the heart of the most glamorous town in the world.

When he stopped at the canopied entrance to the Beverly Hills Hotel, he took the keys out of the ignition and handed them to Rosemary. Then he got out and went around to open her door. At the same moment one of the valet parking men came down the red-carpeted runway and Rosemary handed him the keys to her car, and David realized he should have left them in the ignition.

Rosemary started up the red-carpeted runway to the entrance of the hotel, and David knew she had completely forgotten about him. He was too proud to remind her about offering a limo to take him back. He watched her. Under the green canopy, the balmy air, the golden lights, she seemed like a lost princess. Then she stopped and turned; he could see her face, and she looked so beautiful that David Jatney's heart stopped.

He thought she had remembered him, that she expected him to follow her. But she turned again and tried to go up the three steps that would bring her to the doors. At that moment she tripped, her purse went flying out of her hands and everything in that purse scattered on the ground. By that time David had dashed up the red carpet runway to help her.

The contents of the purse seemed endless—it was magical in the way it continued to spill out its contents. There were solitary lipsticks, a makeup case that burst open and poured mysteries of its own, there was a ring of keys that immediately broke and scattered at least twenty keys around the carpet. There was a bottle of aspirin and prescription vials of different drugs. And a huge pink toothbrush. There was a cigarette lighter and no cigarettes, there was a tube of Binaca and a little plastic bag that held blue panties and some sort of device that looked sinister. There were innumerable coins, some paper money and a soiled white linen handkerchief. There were spectacles, gold-rimmed, spinsterish without the adornment of Rosemary's classically sculptured face.

Rosemary looked at all this with horror, then burst into tears. David knelt on the red-carpeted runway and started to sweep everything into the purse. Rosemary didn't help him. When one of the bellmen came out of the hotel, David had him hold the purse with its mouth open while he shoveled the stuff into it.

Finally he had gotten everything, and he took the now full purse from the bellman and gave it to Rosemary. He could see her humiliation and wondered at it. She dried her tears and said to him, "Come up to my suite for a drink until your limo comes, I haven't had a chance to speak to you all evening."

David smiled. He was remembering Gibson Grange saying, "She's slick." But he was curious about the famous Beverly Hills Hotel and he wanted to stay around Rosemary.

He thought the green-painted walls were weird for a high-class hotel—dingy, in fact. But when they entered the huge suite he was impressed. It was beautifully decorated and had a large terrace—a balcony. There was also a bar in one corner. Rosemary went to it and mixed herself a drink, then after asking him what he wanted, mixed him one. He had asked for just a plain scotch; though he rarely drank, he was feeling a little nervous. She unlocked the glass sliding doors to the terrace and led him outside. There was a white glass-topped table and four white chairs. "Sit here while I go to the bathroom," Rosemary said. "Then we'll have a little chat." She disappeared back into the suite.

David sat in one of the chairs and sipped his scotch. Below him were the interior gardens of the Beverly Hills Hotel. He could see the swimming pool and the tennis courts, the walks that led to the bungalows. There were trees and individual lawns, the grass greener under moonlight, and the lighting glancing off the pink-painted walls of the hotel gave everything a surrealistic glow.

It was no more than ten minutes later when Rosemary reappeared. She sat in one of the chairs and sipped her drink. Now she was wearing loose white slacks and a white pullover cashmere sweater. She had pushed the sleeves of her sweater up above her elbows. She smiled at him, it was a dazzling smile. She had washed her face clean of makeup and he liked her better this way. Her lips were now not voluptuous, her eyes not so commanding. She looked younger and more vulnerable. Her voice when she spoke seemed easier, softer, less commanding.

"Hock tells me you're a screenwriter," she said. "Do you have anything you'd like to show me? You can send it to my office."

"Not really," David said. He smiled back at her. He would never let himself be rejected by her.

"But Hock said you had one finished," Rosemary said. "I'm always looking for new writers. It's so hard to find something decent."

"No," David said. "I wrote four or five but they were so terrible I tore them up."

They were silent for a time, it was easy for David to be silent; it was more comfortable for him than speech. Finally Rosemary said, "How old are you?"

David lied and said, "Twenty-six."

Rosemary smiled at him. "God, I wish I were that young again. You know, when I came here I was eighteen. I wanted to be an actress, and I was a half-assed one. You know those one-line parts on TV, the salesgirl the heroine buys something from? Then I met Hock and he made me his executive assistant and taught me everything I know. He helped me set up my first picture and he helped all through the years. I love Hock, I always will. But he's so tough, like tonight. He stuck with Gibson against me." Rosemary shook her head. "I always wanted to be as tough as Hock," she said. "I modeled myself after him."

David said, "I think he's a very nice gentle guy."

"But he's fond of you," Rosemary said. "Really, he told me so. He said you look so much like your mother and you act just like her. He says you're a really sincere person, not a hustler." She paused for a moment and then said, "I can see that too. You can't imagine how humiliated I felt when all that stuff spilled out of my purse. And then I saw you picking everything up and never looking at me. You were really very sweet." She leaned over and kissed him on the cheek. He could smell a different sweeter fragrance coming from her body now.

Abruptly she stood up and went back into the suite; he followed her. She closed the glass door of the terrace and locked it and then she said, "I'll call for your limo." She picked up the phone. But instead of pressing the buttons she held it in her hand and looked at David. He was standing very still, standing far enough away not to be in her space. She said to him, "David, I'm going to ask you something that might sound odd. Would you stay with me tonight? I feel lousy and I need company, but I want you to promise you won't try to do anything. Could we just sleep together like friends?"

David was stunned. He had never dreamed this beautiful woman would want someone like him. He was dazzled by his good fortune. But then Rosemary said sharply, "I mean it, I just want someone nice like you to be with me tonight. You have to promise you won't do anything. If you try, I'll be very angry."

This was so confusing to David that he smiled, and as if not understanding, he said, "I'll sit on the terrace or sleep on the couch here in the living room."

"No," Rosemary said. "I just want somebody to hug me and go to sleep with. I just don't want to be alone. Can you promise?"

David heard himself say, "I don't have anything to wear. In bed, I mean."

Rosemary said briskly, "Just take a shower and sleep naked, it won't bother me."

There was a foyer from the living room of the suite that led to the bedroom. In this foyer was an extra bathroom, in which Rosemary told David to take his shower. She did not want him to use her bathroom. David showered and brushed his teeth using soap and tissues. There was a bathrobe hanging from the back of the door with blue-stitching script that said elegantly "Beverly Hills Hotel." He went into the bedroom and found Rosemary was still in her bathroom. He stood there awkwardly, not wanting to get into the bed that had already been turned down by the night maid. Finally Rosemary came out of the bathroom wearing a flannel nightgown that was so elegantly cut and printed that she looked like a doll in a toy store. "Come on, get in," she said. "Do you need a Valium or a sleeping pill?" And he knew she had already taken one. She sat at the edge of the bed and then got in and finally David got into the bed but kept his bathrobe on. They were lying side by side when she turned the light out on her night table. They were in darkness. "Give me a hug," she said, and they embraced for a long moment and then she rolled away to her side of the bed and said briskly, "Pleasant dreams."

David lay on his back staring up at the ceiling. He didn't dare take off the bathrobe, he didn't want her to think that he wanted to be naked in her bed. He wondered if he should tell Hock about this the next time they met, but he understood that it would become a joke that he had slept with such a beautiful woman and nothing had happened. And maybe Hock would think he was lying. He wished he had taken the sleeping pill Rosemary had offered him. She was already asleep—she had a tiny snore just barely audible.

David decided to go back to the living room and got out

of bed. Rosemary came awake and said sleepily, "Could you get me a drink of Evian water." David went into the living room and fixed two Evian waters with a little ice. He drank from his glass and refilled it. Then he went back into the bedroom. By the light in the foyer he could see Rosemary sitting up, the bed sheets tight around her. He offered a glass and she reached out a bare arm for it. In the dark room he touched her upper body before finding her hand to give her the glass, and realized she was naked. As she was drinking he slipped into the bed but he let his bathrobe fall to the floor.

He heard her put the glass on the night table and then he put out his hand and touched her flesh. He felt the bare back and the softness of her buttocks. She rolled over and into his arms and his chest was against her bare breasts. Her arms were around him and the hotness of their bodies made them kick off the covers as they kissed. They kissed for a long time, her tongue in his mouth, and then he couldn't wait any longer and he was on top of her, and her hand as smooth as satin, a permission, guided him into her. They made love almost silently as if they were being spied upon until both their bodies together arched in the flight toward climax and they lay back separate again.

Finally she whispered, "Now go to sleep." She kissed him gently on the side of the mouth.

He said, "I want to see you."

"No," she whispered.

David reached over and turned on her table light. Rosemary closed her eyes. She was still beautiful. Even with desire sated, even though she was stripped of all the arts of beauty, the enhancements of coquetry, the artifices of special light. But it was a different beauty.

He had made love out of animal need and proximity, a

natural physical expression of his body. She had made love out of a need in her heart, or some spinning need in her brain. And now in the glow of the single light, her naked body was no longer formidable. Her breasts were small with tiny nipples, her body smaller, her legs not so long, her hips not so wide, her thighs a little slender. She opened her eyes, looking directly into his, and he said, "You're so beautiful." He kissed her breasts and as he did so she reached up and turned out the light. They made love again and then fell asleep.

When David woke and reached out, she was gone. He threw on his clothes and put on his watch. It was seven in the morning. He found her out on the terrace in a red jogging suit against which her black hair seemed even darker. A table had been wheeled in by room service, and on it were a silver coffee pitcher and a silver milk jug and an array of plates with metal covers over them to keep the food warm.

Rosemary smiled at him and said, "I ordered for you. I was just going to wake you up. I have to get my run in before I start work."

He sat down at the table, and she poured him coffee and uncovered a dish that held eggs and sliced-up bits of fruit. Then she drank her orange juice and got up. "Take your time," she said. "Thanks for staying last night."

David wanted her to have breakfast with him, he wanted her to show that she really liked him, he wanted to have a chance to talk, to tell her about his life, to say something that would make her interested in him. But now she was putting a white headband over her hair and lacing up her jogging shoes. She stood up. David said, not knowing his face was twitching with emotion, "When will I see you again?" And as soon as he said it he knew he had made a terrible mistake.

Rosemary was on her way to the door but she stopped.

"I'm going to be awfully busy the next few weeks. I have to go to New York. When I come back I'll give you a call." She didn't ask for his number.

Then another thought seemed to strike her. She picked up the phone and called for a limo to bring David back to Santa Monica. She said to him, "It will be put on my bill—do you need any cash to tip the driver?"

David just looked at her for a long moment. She picked up her purse and opened it and said, "How much will you need for the tip?"

David couldn't help himself. He didn't know his face was twitching with a malice and a hatred that were frightening. He said insultingly, "You'd know that better than me." Rosemary snapped her purse shut and went out of the suite.

He never heard from her. He waited for two months, and then one day on the movie studio lot he saw her come out of Hocken's office with Gibson Grange and Dean. He waited near Hocken's parking space so that they would have to greet him. Hocken gave him a little hug and said they had to have dinner and asked how the job was going. Gibson Grange shook his hand and gave him a sly but friendly smile, the handsome face radiating its easy good humor. Rosemary looked at him without smiling. And what really hurt was that for a moment it seemed to David that she had really forgotten him.

CHAPTER
14

MATTHEW GLADYCE, the press secretary to the President, knew that in the next twenty-four hours he would make the most important decision of his professional life. It was his job to control the responses of the media to the tragic and world-shocking events of the last three days. It would be his job to inform the people of the United States just exactly what their President was doing to cope with these events, and to justify his actions. Gladyce had to be very careful.

Now on this Thursday morning after Easter, in the middle of the crisis fireball, Matthew Gladyce cut himself off from direct contact with the media. His junior assistants held the meetings in the White House Press Conference Room but were limited to handing out carefully composed press releases and ducking shouted questions.

Matthew did not answer the phones constantly ringing in his office; his secretaries screened all his calls and brushed off

insistent reporters and high-powered TV commentators trying to call in markers he owed them. It was his job to protect
the President of the United States.

Matthew Gladyce knew from his long experience as a
journalist that there was no ritual more revered in America
than the traditional insolence of the print and TV media
toward important members of the establishment. Imperious
TV anchor stars shouted down affable Cabinet members,
knocked chips off the shoulders of the President himself,
grilled candidates for high office with the ferocity of prose-
cuting attorneys. The newspapers printed libelous articles in
the name of free speech. At one time he had been a part of
all this and even admired it. He had enjoyed the inevitable
hatred that every public official has for representatives of the
media. But three years as press secretary had changed this.
Like the rest of the administration—indeed, like all government figures throughout history—he had come to distrust
and devalue that great institution of democracy called free
speech. Like all authority figures, he had come to regard it
as assault and battery. The media were sanctified criminals
who robbed institutions and private citizens of their good
name. Just to sell their newspapers and commercials to three
hundred million people.

And today he would not give those bastards an inch. He
was going to throw his fastball by them.

He thought back on the last four days and all the questions
he had fielded from the media. The President had cut himself
off from all direct communication and Matthew Gladyce
had carried the ball. On Monday it had been: "Why haven't
the hijackers made any demands? Is the kidnaping of the
President's daughter linked to the killing of the Pope?"
Those questions eventually answered themselves, thank

God. Now it was established. They were linked. The hijackers had made their demands.

Gladyce had issued the press release under the direct supervision of the President himself. These events were a concerted attack on the prestige and worldwide authority of the United States. Then the murder of the President's daughter and the stupid fucking questions: "How did the President react when he heard of the murder?" Here Gladyce had lost his temper. "What the fuck do you think he felt, you stupid bastard?" he told the anchor person. Then there had been another stupid question: "Does this bring back memories of when the President's uncles were murdered?" At that moment Gladyce decided he would leave these press conferences to his juniors.

But now he had to take the stage. He would have to defend the President's ultimatum to the Sultan of Sherhaben. He would leave out the threat to destroy the Sultanate of Sherhaben. He would say that if the hostages were released and Yabril imprisoned, the city of Dak would not be destroyed—in language to leave him an out when Dak was destroyed. But most important of all was that the President of the United States would go on television in the afternoon with a major address to the nation.

He glanced out of the window of his office. The White House was surrounded by TV trucks and media correspondents from all over the world. Well, fuck them, Gladyce thought. They would only know what he wanted them to know.

Thursday
Sherhaben

THE ENVOYS OF the United States arrived in Sherhaben. Their plane set down on a runway far from the hostage lane commanded by Yabril and still surrounded by Sherhaben troops. Behind those troops were the hordes of TV trucks, media correspondents from all over the world and a vast crowd of onlookers who had traveled from the city of Dak.

The ambassador of Sherhaben, Sharif Waleeb, had taken pills to sleep through most of the voyage. Bert Audick and Arthur Wix had talked, Audick trying to persuade Wix to modify the President's demands so that they could get the release of the hostages without any drastic action.

Finally Wix told Audick, "I have no leeway to negotiate. I have a very strict brief from the President—they've had their fun and now they are going to pay."

Audick said grimly, "You're the national security adviser—for God's sake, advise."

Wix said stonily, "There is nothing to advise. The President has made his decision."

Upon arrival at the Sultan's palace, Wix and Audick were escorted to their palatial suites by armed guards. Indeed the palace seemed to be overrun with military formations. Ambassador Waleeb was ushered into the presence of the Sultan, where he formally presented the ultimatum documents.

The Sultan did not believe in the threat, thinking that anybody could terrify this little man. He said, "And when Kennedy told you this, how did he appear? Is he a man who utters such wild threats merely to frighten? Would his gov-

ernment even support such an action? He would be gambling
his whole political career on this one throw of the dice. Is
it not merely a negotiating ploy?"

Waleeb rose from the gold brocade chair in which he had
been sitting. Suddenly his tiny puppetlike figure became impressive. He had a good voice, the Sultan noted. "Your
Highness," Waleeb said. "Kennedy knew exactly what you
would say, word for word. Within twenty-four hours after
the destruction of Dak, if you do not comply with his demands, all Sherhaben will be destroyed. And that is why Dak
cannot be saved. That is the only way he can convince you
of his most serious intent. He also said that after Dak is
destroyed you will agree to his demands but not before. He
was calm, he smiled. He is no longer the man he was. He is
Azazel."

Later the two envoys of the President of the United States
were brought to a beautiful reception room that included
air-conditioned terraces and a swimming pool. They were
attended by male servants in Arab dress who brought them
food and drinks that were not alcoholic. Surrounded by
counselors and bodyguards, the Sultan greeted them.

Ambassador Waleeb made the introductions. Bert Audick
the Sultan knew. They had been closely locked on past oil
deals. And Audick had been his host the several times he had
visited America, a discreet and obliging host. The Sultan
greeted Audick warmly.

The second man was the surprise, and in the lurch of his
heartbeat the Sultan recognized the presence of danger and
began to believe the reality of Kennedy's threat. For the
second of the tribunes, as the Sultan thought of them, was
none other than Arthur Wix, the President's national security adviser, and a Jew. He was by reputation the most

powerful military figure in the United States and the ultimate enemy of the Arab states in their fight against Israel. The Sultan noted that Arthur Wix did not offer his hand, but only bowed with cold courtesy.

The next thought in the Sultan's mind was that if the President's threat was real, why would he send such a high official into such danger? What if he took these tribunes as hostages, would they not perish in any attack on Sherhaben? And indeed would Bert Audick come and risk a possible death? From what he knew of Audick, certainly not. So that meant there was room for negotiation and that the Kennedy threat was a bluff. Or, Kennedy was simply a madman and did not care what happened to his envoys and would carry out his threat anyway. He looked around at his reception room that served as his chamber of state. It was far more luxurious than anything in the White House. The walls were painted gold, the carpets were the most expensive in the world with exquisite patterns that could never be duplicated, the marble the purest and most intricately carved. How could all this be destroyed?

The Sultan said with quiet dignity, "My ambassador has given me the message from your President. I find it very hard to believe that the leader of the free world would dare to utter such a threat, much less implement it. And I am at a loss. What influence can I have over this bandit Yabril? Is your President another Attila the Hun? Does he imagine he rules ancient Rome rather than America?"

It was Audick who spoke first. He said, "Sultan Maurobi, I came here as your friend, to help you and your country. The President means to do as he threatens. It seems you have no alternative, you must give up this man Yabril."

The Sultan was quiet for a long moment, then turned to Arthur Wix. He said ironically, "And what are you doing here? Can America spare an important man like yourself if I refuse to comply with your President's demands?"

"The fact that you would hold us as hostages if you refused those demands was carefully discussed," Arthur Wix said. He was absolutely impassive. He did not show the anger and hatred he was feeling for the Sultan. "As the head of an independent country you are quite justified in your anger and in your counterthreat. But that is the very reason I am here. To assure you that the necessary military orders have been given. As the commander in chief of American military forces the President has that power. The city of Dak will shortly be no more. Twenty-four hours after that, if you do not comply, the country of Sherhaben will also be destroyed. All this will be no more"—he made a sweeping gesture around the room—"and you will be living on the charity of the rulers of your neighboring countries. You will be a Sultan still, but you will be a Sultan of nothing."

The Sultan did not show his rage. He turned to the other American and said, "Do you have anything to add?"

Bert Audick said almost slyly, "There is no question that Kennedy means to carry out his threat. But there are other people in our government who disagree. This action may doom his presidency." He said almost apologetically to Arthur Wix, "I think we have to bring this out in the open."

Wix looked at him grimly. He had feared this possibility. Strategically it was always possible that Audick might try to make an end run. The bastard was going to try to undermine the whole deal. Just to save his fucking fifty billion.

Arthur Wix looked venomously at Audick and said to the Sultan, "There is no room for negotiation."

Audick gave Wix a defiant glance and then addressed the Sultan again, "I think it fair, based on our long relationship, to tell you there is one hope. And I feel I must do it now in front of my countryman, rather than in a private audience with you as I could easily do. The Congress of the United States is holding a special session to impeach President Kennedy. If we can announce the news that you are releasing the hostages, I guarantee Dak will not be destroyed."

The Sultan said, "And I will not have to give up Yabril?"

"No," Audick said. "But you must not insist on the release of the Pope's killer."

The Sultan, for all his good manners, could not completely disguise the note of glee when he said, "Mr. Wix, is this not a more reasonable solution?"

"My President impeached because a terrorist murdered his daughter? And then the murderer goes free?" Wix said. "No, it is not."

Audick said, "We can always get that guy later."

Wix gave him a look of such contempt and hatred that Audick knew that this man would be his enemy for life.

The Sultan said, "In two hours we will all meet with my friend Yabril. We will dine together, and come to an agreement. I will persuade him with sweet words or force. But the hostages will go free as soon as we learn that the city of Dak is safe. Gentlemen, you have my promise as a Muslim and as the ruler of Sherhaben."

Then the Sultan gave orders for his communications center to notify him of the congressional vote as soon as it was known. He had the American envoys escorted to their rooms to bathe and change their clothing.

The Sultan had ordered Yabril to be smuggled off the plane and brought to the palace. Yabril was made to wait in the huge reception hall, and he noted that it was filled with the Sultan's uniformed security guards. There had been other signs that the palace was on an alert status. Yabril sensed immediately that he was in danger, but there was nothing to be done.

When Yabril was ushered into the Sultan's reception room, he was relieved that the Sultan embraced him. Then the Sultan briefed him on what happened with the American tribunes. The Sultan said, "I promised them you would release the hostages without further negotiations. Now we await the decision of the American Congress."

Yabril said, "But that means that my friend Romeo has been deserted by me. It is a blow to my reputation."

The Sultan smiled and said, "When they try him for murder of the Pope, your cause will gain that much more publicity. And the fact that you go free after that coup and murdering the daughter of the President of the United States, *that* is glory. But what a nasty little surprise you gave me at the end. To kill a young girl in cold blood. That was not to my liking and really not clever."

"It made a certain point," Yabril said. "I never intended for her to get off that plane alive."

"And now you must be satisfied," the Sultan said. "In effect you have unseated the President of the United States. Which was beyond your wildest dreams."

The Sultan gave a command to one of his retinue. "Go to the quarters of the American, Mr. Audick, and bring him here to us."

When Bert Audick came into the room, he did not offer to shake hands with Yabril or make any gesture of friendliness. He simply stared. Yabril bowed his head and smiled. He was familiar with these types, these bloodsuckers of Arabian lifeblood, who made contracts with Sultans and kings to enrich America and other foreign states.

The Sultan said, "Mr. Audick, please explain to my friend the mechanics of how your Congress will dispose of your President."

Audick did so. He was convincing, Yabril believed him. But he asked, "What if something goes wrong and you do not get your two-thirds vote?"

Audick said grimly, "Then you, me and the Sultan here are shit out of luck."

President Francis Xavier Kennedy looked over the papers that Matthew Gladyce gave him and then initialed them. He saw the look of satisfaction on Gladyce's face and knew exactly what it meant. That together they were putting one over on the American public. At another time, in other circumstances, he would have squelched that smug look, but Francis Kennedy realized that this was the most dangerous single moment in his political career and he must use every weapon available.

This evening the Congress would try to impeach him; they would use the vague wording of the Twenty-fifth Amendment to the Constitution in the attempt to do so. Maybe he could win the battle in the long run, but by then it would be too late. Bert Audick would arrange the release of the hostages, the escape of Yabril in return for the remaining hostages. The death of his daughter would go unavenged; the murderer of the Pope would go free. But Kennedy counted on his appeal to the nation over TV to launch such a wave of protesting telegrams as to make Congress waver. He knew the people would support his action; they were outraged at the murder of the Pope and of his daughter. They felt his heartbreak. And at that moment he felt a fierce communion with the people. They were his allies against the corrupt

Congress, the pragmatic and merciless businessmen like Bert Audick.

All through his life he had felt for the tragedies of the unfortunate, the mass of people struggling through life. Early in his career he had sworn to himself that he would never be corrupted by that love for money that seemed to generate the accomplishments of gifted men. He grew to despise the power of the rich, money used as a sword. But he had always felt, he realized now, that he was some sort of champion who was invulnerable and above the woes of his fellowman. He had never before grasped the hatred that the underclass must feel. But he felt it now. Now the rich, the powerful, would bring him down, now he must win for his own sake.

But he refused to be distracted by hatred. His mind must be clear in the coming crisis. Even if he should be impeached, he must make sure he would return to power. And then his plans would be far-reaching. The Congress and the rich might win this battle, but he saw clearly that they must lose the war. The people of the United States would not suffer humiliation gladly, there would be another election in November. This whole crisis could result in his favor even if he lost; his personal tragedy would be one of his weapons. But he had to be careful to hide his long-range plans even from his staff.

Kennedy understood he was preparing himself for ultimate power. There was no other course except to submit to defeat and all its anguish, and that he could never survive.

On Thursday afternoon, nine hours before the special session of Congress that would impeach the President of the United States, Francis Kennedy met with his advisers, his staff and Vice President Helen Du Pray.

It was to be their last strategy session before the congressional vote, and they all knew the enemy had the necessary two thirds. Kennedy saw immediately that the mood in the room was one of depression and defeat.

He gave them all a cheerful smile and opened the meeting by thanking the CIA chief, Theodore Tappey, for not having signed the impeachment proposal. Then he turned to Vice President Du Pray and laughed, a genuine good-humored laugh.

"Helen," he said, "I wouldn't be in your shoes for anything in the world. Do you realize how many enemies you made when you refused to sign the impeachment papers? You could have been the first woman President of the United States. Congress hates you because without your signature they can't get away with it. Men will hate you for being so magnanimous. Feminists will consider you a traitor. God, how did an old pro like you get in such a fix? By the way, I want to thank you for your loyalty."

"They are wrong, Mr. President," Du Pray said. "And they are wrong now to pursue it. Is there a chance for any negotiation with Congress?"

"I can't negotiate," Kennedy said. "And they won't." Then he said to Dazzy, "Have my orders been followed—is the naval air fleet on its way to Dak?"

"Yes, sir," Dazzy said, then shifted uncomfortably in his chair. "But the chiefs of staff have not given the final 'go.' They will hold back until Congress votes tonight. If the impeachment succeeds, they will send the planes home." He paused for a moment. "They haven't disobeyed you. They have followed your orders. They just figure they can countermand everything if you lose tonight."

Kennedy turned to Du Pray. His face was grave. "If the impeachment succeeds, you will be the President," he said.

"You can order the chiefs of staff to proceed with the destruction of the city of Dak. Will you give that order?"

"No," she said. There was a long, uncomfortable silence in the room. She kept her face composed and spoke directly to Kennedy. "I have proved my loyalty to you," she said. "As your Vice President, I supported your decision on Dak, as it was my duty to do. I resisted the demand to sign the impeachment papers. But if I become President, and I hope with all my heart I will not, then I must follow my own conscience and make my own decision."

Kennedy nodded. He smiled at her and it was a gentle smile that broke her heart. "You are perfectly right," he said. "I asked the question merely as a point of information, not to persuade." He addressed the others in the room. "Now the most important thing is to get a bare-bones script ready for my television speech. Eugene, have you cleared networks? Have they broadcast bulletins that I will speak tonight?"

Eugene Dazzy said cautiously, "Lawrence Salentine is here to see you about that. It looks fishy. Shall I have him sent here? He's in my office."

Kennedy said softly, "They wouldn't dare. They wouldn't dare to show their muscle so out in the open." He was thoughtful for a long moment. "Send him in."

While they waited they discussed how long the speech would be. "Not more than a half hour," Kennedy said. "I should get the job done by then."

And they all knew what he meant. Francis Kennedy on television could overpower any audience. It was the magical speaking voice with the music of the great Irish poets. It didn't hurt that his thinking, the progress of his logic, was always absolutely clear.

When Lawrence Salentine was ushered in, Kennedy spoke

to him directly and without a greeting. "I hope you're not going to say what I think you're going to say."

Salentine said coolly, "I have no way of knowing what you're thinking. I've been chosen by the other networks to give you our decision not to give you airtime tonight. For us to do so would be to interfere in the impeachment process."

Kennedy smiled and said to him, "Mr. Salentine, the impeachment, even if it's successful, will last for only thirty days. And then what?"

It was not Francis Kennedy's style to be threatening. It occurred to Salentine that he and the heads of the other networks had embarked on a very dangerous game. The legal justification of the federal government to issue and review licenses for TV stations had become archaic in practical terms, but a strong President could put new teeth in it. Salentine knew he had to go very carefully.

"Mr. President," he said, "it is because we feel our responsibility is so important that we must refuse you the airtime. You are in the process of impeachment, much to my regret, and to the sorrow of all Americans. It is a very great tragedy, and you have all my sympathy. But the networks agree that letting you speak will not be in the best interests of the nation or our democratic process." He paused for a moment. "But after the Congress votes, win or lose, we will give you airtime."

Francis Kennedy laughed angrily and said, "You can go."

Lawrence Salentine was escorted out by one of the Secret Service guards.

Then Kennedy said to his staff, "Gentlemen, believe me when I tell you this." Kennedy's face was unsmiling, the blue of his eyes seemed to have gone from a light to heavier slate-blue, "They have overplayed their hand. They have violated the spirit of the Constitution."

For miles around the White House, traffic had become congested with only thin corridors to pass through official vehicles. TV cameras and their backup trucks commanded the whole area. Congressmen on their way to Capitol Hill were unceremoniously grabbed by TV journalists and questioned on this special meeting of the Congress. Finally, an official bulletin appeared on TV networks that the Congress was convening at 11:00 P.M. to vote on a motion to remove President Kennedy from office.

In the White House itself, Kennedy and his staff had already done everything they could to ward off the attack. Oddblood Gray had called senators and congressmen, pleading with them. Eugene Dazzy had made countless calls to different members of the Socrates Club, trying to enlist the support of some segments of big business. Christian Klee had sent legal briefs to the leaders of the Congress stressing that without the signature of the Vice President the removal was illegal.

Just before eleven, Kennedy and his staff met in the Yellow Room to watch the big television screen that was wheeled in. Although the session of Congress would not be broadcast over commercial networks, it was being photographed for later use, and a special cable brought it to the White House.

Congressman Jintz and Senator Lambertino had done their work well. Everything had been synchronized perfectly. Sal Troyca and Elizabeth Stone had worked closely together to iron out administrative details. All the necessary documents had been prepared for the turnover of government.

In the Yellow Room, Francis Kennedy and his personal staff watched the proceedings on their television. It would take Congress time to go through all the formalities of speeches and roll calls to vote. But they knew what the outcome would be. The Congress and the Socrates Club had built a steamroller for this occasion. Kennedy said to Odd-blood Gray, "Otto, you did your best."

At that moment, one of the White House duty officers came in and handed Dazzy a memo sheet. Dazzy looked at it, then studied it. The shock on his face was evident. He handed the memorandum to Kennedy.

On the TV screen, by a margin far exceeding the necessary two thirds, the Congress had just voted to impeach President Francis Xavier Kennedy.

Friday 6 A.M.

Sherhaben

IT WAS 11:00 P.M., Thursday, Washington time, but six in the morning in Sherhaben, when the Sultan had everyone summoned to the terraced reception room for an early breakfast. The Americans—Bert Audick and Arthur Wix—arrived shortly. Yabril was escorted in by the Sultan. A huge table was laden with countless fruits and beverages, both hot and cold.

Sultan Maurobi was smiling broadly. He did not introduce Yabril to the Americans and there was no pretense of any courtesy.

The Sultan said, "I am happy to announce—more than

that, my heart overflows with joy—that my friend Yabril has agreed to the release of your hostages. There will be no further demands from him and I hope no further demands from your country."

Arthur Wix, his face beaded with sweat, said, "I cannot negotiate or change in any way the demands of my President. You must give up this murderer."

The Sultan smiled and said, "He is no longer your President. The American Congress has voted to impeach him. I am informed that the orders to bomb the city of Dak have already been canceled. The hostages will be freed, you have your victory. There is nothing else you can ask."

Yabril felt a great rush of energy go through his body—he had brought about the impeachment the President of the United States. He stared into Wix's eyes and saw the hatred there. This was the highest man in the mightiest army on the face of the globe, and he, Yabril, had defeated him. For a moment his mind held the image of himself pressing the gun against the silky hair of Theresa Kennedy. He remembered again that sense of loss, of regret, when he pulled the trigger, the little burn of anguish as her body tumbled away in the desert air. He bowed his head to Wix and the other men in the room.

The Sultan Maurobi motioned for the servants to bring platters of fruit and drink to his guests. Arthur Wix put down his glass and said, "Are you sure that your information that the President has been impeached is absolutely correct?"

The Sultan said, "I will arrange for you to speak directly to your office in the United States." He paused. "But first, I have my duty as a host."

The Sultan commanded they must have one last full meal together, and insisted that the final arrangements for the release of the hostages be made over this meal. Yabril took his place at the right hand of the Sultan, Arthur Wix on the left.

They were resting on the divans along the low table when the Sultan's prime minister came hurrying in and begged the Sultan to come into the other room for a few moments. The Sultan was impatient, until finally the prime minister whispered something into his ear. The Sultan raised his eyebrows in surprise and then said to his guests, "Something has happened quite unforeseen. All communication to the United States has been cut off, not just to us, but all over the world. Please continue your breakfast while I confer with my staff."

But after the Sultan left, the men around the table did not speak. Only Yabril helped himself to the food.

The Americans moved away from the table to go to the terrace. The servants brought them cool drinks. Yabril continued to eat.

Bert Audick said to Wix, "I hope Kennedy hasn't done something foolish. I hope he hasn't tried to buck the Constitution."

Wix said, "God, first his daughter, now he's lost his country. All because of that little prick in there eating like a fucking beggar."

Audick said, "It is terrible, all of it." Then he went inside and said to Yabril, "Eat well, I hope you have a good place to hide in the years to come. There will be a lot of people looking for you."

Yabril laughed. He had finished eating and was lighting a cigarette. "Oh, yes," he said. "I will be a beggar in Jerusalem."

At that moment the Sultan Maurobi came into the room. He was followed by at least fifty armed men, who stationed themselves to command the room. Four of them stood behind Yabril. Four others stood behind the Americans on the terrace. There was surprise and shock on the Sultan's face. His skin seemed yellow, his eyes were wide open, the eyelids seemed to fold back. "Gentlemen," he said haltingly, "my dear sirs, this will be as incredible to you as it is to me. The Congress has annulled their vote impeaching Kennedy and he has declared martial law." He paused and let his hand rest on Yabril's shoulder. "And, gentlemen, at this moment planes from the American Sixth Fleet are destroying my city of Dak."

Arthur Wix asked almost jubilantly, "The city of Dak is being bombed?"

"Yes," the Sultan said. "A barbaric act but a convincing one."

They were all looking at Yabril, who now had four armed men very closely surrounding him. Yabril said thoughtfully, "Finally I will see America, it has always been my dream." He looked at the Americans but spoke to the Sultan. "I think I would have been a great success in America."

"Without a doubt," the Sultan said. "Part of the demand is that I deliver you alive. I'm afraid I must give the necessary orders so that you do not harm yourself."

Yabril said, "America is a civilized country. I will go through a legal process that will be long and drawn out, since I will have the best lawyers. Why should I harm myself? It will be a new experience, and who knows what can happen? The world always changes. America is too civilized for torture, and besides I have endured torture under the Israelis, so nothing will surprise me." He smiled at Wix.

Wix said quietly, "As you once observed, the world changes. You haven't succeeded. You won't be such a hero."

Yabril laughed delightedly. His arms went up in an exuberant gesture. "I have succeeded," he almost shouted. "I've

torn your world off its axis. Do you think your mealy-
mouthed idealism will be listened to after your planes have
destroyed the city of Dak? When will the world forget my
name? And do you think I will step off the stage now when
the best is yet to come?"

The Sultan clapped his hands and shouted an order to the
soldiers. They grabbed Yabril and put handcuffs on his
wrists and rope around his neck. "Gently, gently," the Sultan said. When Yabril was secure he touched him gently on
the forehead. He said, "I beg your forgiveness, I have no
choice. I have oil to sell and a city to rebuild. I wish you well,
old friend. Good luck in America."

Thursday Night
New York City

AS CONGRESS IMPEACHED President Francis Xavier
Kennedy, as the world awaited the resolution of the terrorist
crisis, there were many hundreds of thousands of people in
New York who didn't give a flying fuck. They had their own
lives to lead and their own problems. This mild spring night
many of these thousands converged in the Times Square area
of New York City, a place that had once been the very heart
of the greatest city in the world, where once The Great
White Way, Broadway itself, ran down from Central Park
to Times Square.

These people had varied interests. Horny suburban

middle-class men haunted the adult pornographic book-shops. Cineasts surveyed miles of film of naked men and naked women indulging themselves in the most intimate sexual acts with varied animals in best-friend character roles. Teenaged gangs with lethal but legal screwdrivers in their pockets sallied forth as gallantly as the knights of old to slay the dragons of the well-to-do, and with the irrepressible high spirits of the young, to have some laughs. Pimps, prostitutes, muggers, murderers, set up shop after dark without having to pay overhead for the bright neon light of what was left of the Great White Way. Tourists came to see Times Square, where the ball fell on New Year's Eve and proclaimed the coming of another joyous New Year. On most of the build-ings in the area and the slum streets leading into it were posters with a huge red heart and inside that red heart the inscription I LOVE NEW YORK. Courtesy of Louis Inch.

On that Thursday near midnight, Blade Booker was hanging out in the Times Square Bar and Cinema Club looking for a client. Booker was a young black man noted for his ability to hustle. He could get you coke, he could get you H, he could get you a wide assortment of pills. He could also get you a gun but nothing big. Pistols, revolvers, little .22's, but after he got himself one he didn't really get into that any-more. He wasn't a pimp, but he was very good with the ladies. He could really talk to their shit, and he was a great listener. Many a night he spent with a girl and listened to her dreams. Even the lowest-down hooker who would do things with men that took his breath away had dreams to tell. Booker listened, he enjoyed listening, it made him feel good when ladies told him their dreams. He loved their shit. Oh, they would hit the numbers, their astrological chart showed that in the coming year a man would love them, they would have a baby, or have kids grow up to be doctors, lawyers, college professors, be on TV; their kids could sing or dance or act or do comedy as good as Richard Pryor, maybe even become another Eddie Murphy.

Blade Booker was waiting for the Swedish Cinema Palace to empty out after the completion of its X-rated film. Many of the cinema lovers would stop here for a drink and a hamburger and in hopes of seeing some pussy. They would straggle in singly, but you could spot them by the abstracted look in their eyes, as if they were pondering an insoluble scientific problem. Also most of them had a melancholy look on their faces. They were lonely people.

There were hookers all over the place, but Booker had his very own placed in a strategic corner. Men at the bar could see her at a little table that her huge red purse almost covered. She was a blond girl from Duluth, Minnesota, big-boned, her blue eyes iced with heroin. Booker had rescued her from a fate worse than death, namely, a life on a farm where the cold winter would chill her tits as hard as boulders. But he was always careful with her. She had a reputation, and he was one of the few who would work with her.

Her name was Kimberly Ansley, and just six years ago she had chopped up her pimp with an ax while he was sleeping. Watch out for girls named Kimberly and Tiffany, Booker always said. She had been arrested and prosecuted, tried and convicted, but convicted only of manslaughter with the defense proving she had numerous bruises and had been "not responsible" because of her heroin habit. She had been sentenced to a correctional facility, cured, declared sane and released to the streets of New York. There she had taken up residence in the slums around Greenwich Village, supplied with an apartment in one of the housing projects built by the city that even the poor were fleeing.

Blade Booker and Kimberly were partners. He was half pimp, half roller; he took pride in that distinction. Kimberly would pick up a cineast in the Times Square Bar, and then lead her customer to a tenement hallway near Ninth Avenue for quick sexual acts. Then Blade would step from the shadows and clunk the man on the head with a New York Police Department blackjack. They would split the money in the man's wallet, but Blade got the credit cards and jewelry. Not out of greed but because he didn't trust Kimberly's judgment.

The beauty of this was that the man was usually an errant husband reluctant to report the incident to the police and have to answer questions about just what he was doing in a dark hall on Ninth Avenue when his wife was waiting for him in Merrick, Long Island, or Trenton, New Jersey. For safety's sake, both Blade and Kim would simply avoid the Times Square Bar for a week. And Ninth Avenue. They would move to Second Avenue. In a city like New York that was like going to another black hole in the galaxy. That was why Blade Booker loved New York. He was invisible, like The Shadow, The Man with a Thousand Faces. And he was like those insects and birds he saw on the TV public broadcasting channels who changed color to blend with the terrain, the insects who could burrow into the earth to escape predators. In short, unlike most citizens, Blade Booker felt safe in New York.

On Thursday night the pickings were slim. But Kimberly was beautiful in this light, her blond hair glowing like a halo, her white powdered breasts, moonlike, rising none too shyly out of her green low-cut dress. A gentleman with sly good-humored charm, only faintly overladen with lust, brought his drink to her table and politely asked her if he could sit down. Blade watched them and wondered at the ironies of the world. Here was this well-dressed man, undoubtedly some kind of hotshot like a lawyer or professor or, who knows, some low-grade politician like a city councillor or state senator, sitting down with an ax murderer, and for dessert would get a bop on the head. And just because of his cock. That was the trouble. A man walked through life with only half a brain because of his cock. It was really too bad. Maybe before he bopped the guy he would let him stick it into Kimberly and get his nuts off and then bop him. He looked like a nice guy, he was really being a gentleman, lighting Kimberly's cigarette, ordering her a drink, not rushing her, though he was obviously dying to get off.

Blade finished his drink when Kim gave him the signal. He saw Kim start to get up, fussing with her red purse, rummaging in it for God knows what. Blade left the bar and went out into the street. It was a clear night in early spring and the smell of hot dogs and hamburgers and onions frying on the grills of open-air food stands made him hungry, but he could wait until the work was done. He walked up Forty-second Street. There were still crowds although it was midnight, and people's faces were colored by the countless neon lights of the rows of cinemas, the giant billboards, the cone-shaped glare of hotel searchlights. He loved the walk from Seventh Avenue to Ninth. He entered the hallway and positioned himself in the well. He could step out when Kim embraced her client. He lit a cigarette and took the blackjack out of its holster beneath the jacket.

He could hear them coming into the hall, the door clicking shut, Kim's purse clattering. And then he heard Kim's voice giving the code phrase: "It's just one flight." He waited for a couple of minutes before he stepped out of the well and hesitated because he saw such a pretty picture. There was Kim on the first step, legs apart, lovely massive white thighs uncovered and the nice man so well dressed, with his dick out and shoving it into her. Kim seemed to rise for a moment into the air, and then Blade saw with horror that she was still rising, and the steps were rising with her and then he saw above her head the clear sky as if the whole top of the building had been sheared off. He lifted the blackjack to beg, to pray, to give witness, that his life could not be over. All this happened in a fraction of a second.

Cecil Clarkson and Isabel Domaine had come out of a Broadway theater after seeing a charming musical and strolled down to Forty-second Street and Times Square. They were both black, as indeed were a majority of the people to be seen on the streets here, but they were in no way similar to Blade Booker. Cecil Clarkson was nineteen years of age and took writing courses at the New School for Social Research. Isabel was eighteen and went to every Broadway and off-Broadway play because she loved the theater and hoped to be an actress. They were in love as only teenagers can be, absolutely convinced that they were the only two people in the world. And as they walked up from Seventh Avenue to Eighth the blinding neon signs bathed them in benevolent light; their beauty created a magic around them which shielded them from the wino beggars, the half-crazed drug addicts, the hustlers, the pimps and the would-be muggers. And Cecil was big, obviously a strong young man who looked as if he would kill anybody who even touched Isabel's body.

They stopped at a huge frankfurter and hamburger open-air grill and ate alongside the counter; they did not venture inside, where the floor was filthy with discarded paper napkins and paper plates. Cecil drank a beer and Isabel a Pepsi with their hot dogs and hamburgers. They watched the surging humanity that filled the sidewalks even at this late hour. They looked with perfect equanimity at the wave of human flotsam, the dregs of the city, rolling past them, and it never entered their minds that there was any danger. They felt pity for these people who did not have their promise, their future, their present and everlasting bliss. When the wave receded they went back into the street and started the walk from Seventh to Eighth. Isabel felt the spring air on her face and buried her face in Cecil's shoulder, one hand on his chest, the other caressing his neck. Cecil felt a vaulting tenderness. They were both supremely happy, the young in love as billions and billions of human beings had been before them, living one of the few perfect moments in life. Then suddenly to Cecil's astonishment all the garish red and green lights blotted out and all he could see was the vault of the sky, and then both of them in their perfect bliss dissolved into nothing.

A group of eight tourists visiting New York City for an Easter-week vacation walked down from St. Patrick's Cathedral on Fifth Avenue, turned on Forty-second Street and sauntered toward where a forest of neon light beckoned. When they reached Times Square they were disappointed. They had seen it on TV on New Year's Eve, when hundreds of thousands gathered to appear on television and greet the coming New Year.

It was so dirty, there was a carpet of garbage that covered the streets. The crowd seemed menacing, drunk, drugged, or driven insane by being enclosed by the great towers of steel through which they had to move. The women were garishly dressed, like the women in the stills outside the porno cinemas. They seemed to move through different levels of hell, the void of a sky with no stars, the streetlamps a puslike spurt of yellow.

The tourists, four married couples from a small town in Ohio, their children grown, had decided to take a trip to New York as a sort of celebration. They had completed a certain stage in their lives, fulfilled a necessary destiny. They had married, they had brought up children, they had been able to have moderately successful careers. Now there would be a new beginning for them, the start of a new kind of life. The main battle had been won.

The triple-X cinemas didn't interest them, there were plenty in Ohio. What did interest and frighten them about Times Square was that it was so ugly and the people filling the streets seemed so evil. The tourists all wore great big red *I Love New York* buttons that they had purchased on their first day. Now one of the women took off her button and threw it into the gutter.

"Let's get out of here," she said.

The group turned and walked back toward Sixth Avenue, away from the great corridor of neon. They had almost turned the corner when they heard a distant *boom* and then a faint rustle of wind, and then down the long avenues from Ninth to Sixth came rushing a tornado of air filled with soda cans, garbage baskets and a few cars that seemed to be flying. With an animal instinct the group turned the corner of Sixth Avenue out of the path of the rushing wind, but were swept off their feet by a tumult of air. From far away they heard the crashing of buildings falling to the ground, the screams of thousands of dying people. They stood crouched low in the shelter of the corner, not knowing what had happened.

They had walked just outside the radius of destruction caused by the explosion of the nuclear bomb. They were eight survivors of the greatest calamity that had befallen a peacetime United States.

One of the men struggled to his feet and helped the others. "Fucking New York," he said. "I hope all the cabdrivers got killed."

The police patrol car that moved slowly through traffic between Seventh and Eighth avenues held two young cops, one Italian and one black. They didn't mind being stuck in traffic, it was the safest place in the precinct. They knew that down the darker side streets they could flush thieves stealing radios out of cars, low-grade pimps and muggers making menacing moves toward the peaceful pedestrians of New York, but they didn't want to get involved in those crimes. Also, it was now a policy of the New York Police Department to allow petty crimes. There had spread in New York a sort of license for the underprivileged to prey on the successful law-abiding citizens of the city. After all, was it right that there were men and women who could afford fifty-thousand-dollar cars with radios and music systems worth a thousand dollars, while there were thousands of homeless who didn't have the price of a meal or who could not afford a sterile healthy needle for a fix? Was it right that these well-to-do, mentally fat, placid citizens, who had the effrontery to walk the streets of New York without a gun or even a lethal screwdriver in their pockets, felt they could enjoy the fabulous sights of the greatest city on earth and not pay a certain price? After all there still was a spark in America of that ancient revolutionary spirit that could not resist certain temptations. And the courts of law, the higher echelons of the police, the editorials of the most respectable newspapers slyly endorsed the republican spirit of thievery, mugging, burglaries, rapes and even murders on the streets of New

York. The poor of the city had no other recourse; their lives had been blighted by poverty, by a stultified family life, the very architecture of the city. Indeed one columnist made a case that all these crimes could be laid at the door of Louis Inch, the real estate lord who was restructuring the city of New York with mile-high condos that shut off the sun with slats of steel.

The two police officers watched Blade Booker leave the Times Square Bar. They knew him well. One officer said to the other, "Should we follow him?" and the other said, "A waste of time, we could catch him in the act and he'd get off." They saw the big blonde and her john come out and take the same route up toward Ninth Avenue. "Poor guy," one of the cops said, "he thinks he's going to get laid and he's gonna get rolled." The other cop said, "He'll have a lump on his head as big as his hard-on." They both laughed.

Their car still moving slowly by inches, both policemen watched the action on the street. It was midnight, their shift would soon be over, and they didn't want to get into anything that would keep them out on the street. They watched the innumerable prostitutes stand in the way of pedestrians, the black drug dealers hawking their wares as boldly as a TV pitchman, the muggers and pickpockets jostling prospective victims and trying to engage tourists in conversation. Sitting in the darkness of the patrol car and gazing out on the streets bright with neon lights, they saw all the dregs of New York slouching toward their particular hells.

The two cops were constantly alert, afraid that some maniac would shove a gun through the window and start shooting. They saw two drug hustlers fall into step beside a well-dressed man, who tried to hurry away but was restrained by four hands. The driver of the patrol car pressed the gas pedal and drew up alongside. The drug hustlers dropped their hands; the well-dressed man smiled with relief. At that moment both sides of the street caved in and buried Forty-second Street from Ninth to Seventh avenues.

All the neon lights of the Great White Way, fabulous Broadway, were blotted out. The darkness was lit by fires, buildings burning, bodies on fire. Flaming cars moved like torches in the night. And there was a great clanging of bells and sustained shrieking of sirens as fire engines, ambulances and police vehicles moved into the stricken heart of New York.

Ten thousand people were killed and twenty thousand were injured when the nuclear bomb planted by Gresse and Tibbot exploded in the Port Authority Building on Eighth Avenue and Forty-second Street.

The explosion was a great boom of sound followed by a howling wind and then the screaming of cement and steel torn asunder. The blast did its damage with mathematical precision. The area from Seventh Avenue to the Hudson River and from Forty-second to Forty-fifth streets was completely flattened. Outside that area, the damage was comparatively minimal. It was the mercy and the genius of Gresse and Tibbot that radiation was lethal only within that area.

All through the borough of Manhattan, glass windows shattered and cars in the streets were smashed by falling debris. And within an hour after the explosion the bridges of Manhattan were clogged with vehicles fleeing the city to New Jersey and Long Island.

Of the dead more than 70 percent were black or Hispanic; the other 30 percent were white New Yorkers and foreign tourists. On Ninth and Tenth avenues, which had become a camping ground for the homeless, and in the Port Authority Building itself, in which many transients were sleeping, the bodies were charred into small logs.

CHAPTER
15

THE WHITE HOUSE Communications Center received news of the atom bomb explosion in New York City exactly six minutes after midnight, and the duty officer immediately informed the President. Twenty minutes later President Francis Kennedy addressed the Congress. He was attended by Vice President Du Pray, Oddblood Gray and Christian Klee.

Kennedy was very grave. In the most crucial moment of his life, there was no time for anything but the most straightforward dialogue. Officially he was no longer President of the United States. But he spoke as if he still had full authority as chief of state.

"I come to you tonight without rancor," he said. "This great tragedy, this great blow to our nation must unite us. You must now know that I took the right course. This is the latest blow in the terrorist Yabril's plan, the one he thinks will make the United States of America sink to its knees, capitulate to his demands. We must now come to the conclusion that there is a far-reaching conspiracy against the United States. We are compelled now to gather our strength and act together. Surely now we must be in agreement.

"I therefore ask you to nullify your impeachment of me. But let me be honest, if you do not, I must still try to save this country. I will reject your act of impeachment, declare it unlawful and declare martial law to prevent any further damaging acts of terror. Let me inform you that this Congress, this glorious body that has protected the freedom of America throughout its lifetime, is now protected by six divisions of the Secret Service and an Army Special Forces regiment. When this crisis is over, you may again vote to impeach me, but not until then. This is the greatest danger that this country has ever faced, I cannot let it go unchallenged. I beg of you, do not let our great country be divided because of political differences. Do not let our country descend into civil war deliberately provoked by our enemies. Let us unite against them. Nullify your vote of impeachment."

There rose a great murmur in the hall. The Congress realized that what Kennedy had told them was not only that they were safe, but that they were also at his mercy.

Senator Lambertino was the first to speak after Kennedy. He proposed that the vote be nullified and that both houses of Congress give their full support to the President of the United States, Francis Xavier Kennedy.

Congressman Jintz rose to second the motion. He declared that events had proven Kennedy to be in the right, that it had been an honest disagreement. He affirmed that the President and the Congress would go forward hand in hand to preserve America against its enemies. He gave his word on that.

The vote was taken. The previous vote to impeach the President was nullified.

Unanimously.

Christian Klee marveled at Francis Kennedy's brilliant performance. There was no questioning his sincerity. But for the first time in all these years, Christian had caught Kennedy in an outright and conscious lie. He had told the Congress of the United States that Yabril was implicated in the atom bomb explosion. And Christian Klee knew that there was no such evidence. And Kennedy knew it was not true.

So he had been right, Christian Klee thought, he had divined what Francis had wanted him to do.

BOOK
IV

BOOK

VI

CHAPTER 16

PRESIDENT FRANCIS KENNEDY, secure in power and office, his enemies defeated, contemplated his destiny. There was a final step to be taken, the final decision to be made. He had lost his wife and child, his personal life had lost all meaning. What he did have was a life entwined with the people of America. How far did he want to go with that commitment?

He announced that he would run for reelection in November, and organized his campaign. Christian Klee was ordered to put legal pressure on all the big businesses, especially the media companies, to keep them from interfering with the election process. Vice President Helen Du Pray was mobilizing the women of America. Arthur Wix, who was a power in Eastern liberal circles, and Eugene Dazzy, who monitored the enlightened business leaders of the country, mobilized money. But Francis Kennedy knew that in the last analysis all this was peripheral. Everything would rest on himself, on how far the people of America would be willing to go with him personally.

There was one crucial point: this time the people must elect a Congress solidly behind the President of the United States. What he wanted was a Congress that would do exactly what he wanted them to do.

So now Francis Kennedy had to perceive the innermost feelings of America. It was a nation in shock.

At Oddblood Gray's suggestion, they traveled to New York together. They walked down Fifth Avenue to lead a memorial parade to the great crater made by the atom bomb explosion. They did this to show the nation that there was no longer any danger of radiation, that there was no danger of another hidden bomb. Kennedy performed his part of the memorial ceremony for the dead and the dedication of the land to build a park for all the people to remember. Part of his speech was devoted to the dangers of unrestricted freedom for the individual in this dangerous technocratic age. And his belief that individual freedom must be subordinated to further the social contract, that the individual must give up something to improve the life of the social mass. He said this in passing, but it was much noted by the media.

Oddblood Gray was overcome by a sense of repulsive irony when he heard the deafening cheers of the crowd. Could such a terrible act of destruction be so lucky for one man?

In the smaller cities and rural areas, after the shock and horror had worn off, there was a grim satisfaction. New York had gotten what it deserved. It was too bad that the bomb had not been bigger and blown up the whole city with its hedonistic rich, its conniving Semites, criminal blacks. There was, after all, a just God in heaven. He had picked the right place for this great punishment. But through the country there was also fear—that their fate, their lives, their very world and their posterity were in hostage to fellowmen who were aberrant. All this Kennedy sensed.

Every Friday night Francis Kennedy made a TV report to the people. These were really thinly disguised campaign speeches, but now he had no trouble getting airtime.

He used certain catchphrases and little speeches that went straight to the heart.

"We will declare war on the everyday tragedies of human existence," he said. "Not on other nations."

He repeated the famous question used in his first campaign: "How is it that following the end of every great war, when trillions of dollars have been spent and thrown away on death, there is prosperity in the world? What if those trillions had been spent for the betterment of mankind?"

He joked that for the cost of one nuclear submarine the government could finance a thousand homes for the poor. For the cost of a fleet of Stealth bombers it could finance a million homes. "We'll just make believe they got lost on maneuvers," he said. "Hell, it's happened before, and with valuable lives lost besides. We'll just make believe it happened." And when critics pointed out that the defense of the United States would suffer, he said that statistical reports from the Defense Department were classified and that nobody would know about the decrease in defense spending.

He announced that in his second term he would be even tougher on crime. He would again fight to give all Americans the opportunity to buy a new home, cover their health care costs, and make certain they were able to get a higher education. He emphasized that this was not socialism. The costs of these programs would be paid for simply by taking a little bite out of the rich corporations of America. He declared that he did not advocate socialism, that he just wanted to protect the people of America from the "royal" rich. And he said this over and over again.

For the Congress and members of the Socrates Club, the President of the United States had declared war upon them.

The Socrates Club decided to hold a seminar in California on how to defeat Kennedy in the November election. Lawrence Salentine was very worried. He knew that the Attorney General was preparing serious indictments resulting from the activities of Bert Audick and was mounting investigations of Martin Mutford's financial dealings. Greenwell was too clean to be in trouble, Salentine didn't worry about him. But Salentine knew that his own media empire was very vulnerable. They had gotten away with murder for so many years that they had gotten careless. His publishing company, books and magazines were OK. Nobody could harm print media, the Constitutional protection was too strong. Except of course that a prick like Klee might get the postal charges raised.

But Salentine really worried about his TV empire. The airwaves, after all, belonged to the government and were doled out by them. The TV stations were only licensed. And it had always been a source of bewilderment to Salentine that the government allowed private enterprise to make so much money out of these airwaves without levying the proper tax. He shuddered at the thought of a strong federal communication commissioner under Kennedy's direction. It could mean the end of the TV and cable companies as now constituted.

Louis Inch, ever the patriot, harbored a somewhat disloyal admiration for President Kennedy. Still hailed as the most hated man in New York, he volunteered to restore the bomb-blighted area in that city. The damaged blocks were to be purified with marble monuments enclosed in a green woodland. He would do it at cost, take no profit and have it up in six months. Thank God the radiation had been minimal.

Everybody knew that Inch got things done much better than any government agency. Of course he knew he would still make a great deal of money through his subsidiary companies in construction, planning commissions and advisory committees. And the publicity would be invaluable.

Inch was one of the richest men in America. His father had been the usual hard-nosed big-city landlord, failing to maintain heat in apartment buildings, skimping on services, forcing out tenants in order to build more expensive apartments. Bribery of building inspectors was a skill Louis Inch learned at his father's knee. Later, armed with a university degree in business management and law, he bribed city councilmen, borough presidents and their staffs, even mayors.

It was Louis Inch who fought the rent control laws in New York, it was Louis Inch who put together the real estate deals that built skyscrapers alongside Central Park. A park that now had an awning of monstrous steel edifices to house Wall Street brokers, professors at powerhouse universities, famous writers, chic artists, the chefs of expensive restaurants.

Community activists charged that Inch was responsible for the horrible slums on the Upper West Side and in the Bronx, in Harlem and in Coney Island simply by the amount of reasonable housing he had destroyed in his rebuilding of New York. Also that he was blocking the rehabilitation of the Times Square district, while secretly buying up buildings and blocks. To this Inch retorted that these troublemakers were people who, if you had a bagful of shit, would demand half of it.

Another Inch strategy was his support of city laws that required landlords to rent housing space to anyone regardless of race, color or creed. He had given speeches supporting those laws because they helped to drive the small landlord out of the market. A landlord who had only the upstairs and/or the basement of his house to rent had to take in drunks, schizophrenics, drug hustlers, rapists, stickup artists. Eventually these small landlords would become discouraged, sell their houses and move to the suburbs.

But Inch was beyond all that now—he was stepping up in class. Millionaires were a dime a dozen; Louis Inch was one of the hundred or so billionaires in America. He owned bus systems, he owned hotels and he owned an airline. He owned one of the great hotel casinos in Atlantic City and he owned apartment buildings in Santa Monica, California. It was the Santa Monica properties that gave him the most trouble.

Louis Inch had joined the Socrates Club because he believed that its powerful members could help solve his Santa Monica real estate problems. Golf was a perfect sport for hatching conspiracies. There were the jokes, the good exercise and the agreements struck. And what could be more innocent? The most rabid investigator from congressional committees or the hanging judges of the press could not accuse golfers of criminal intent.

The Socrates Club turned out to be better than Inch expected. He became friendly with the hundred or so men who controlled the country's economic apparatus and political machinery. It was in the Socrates Club that Louis Inch became a member of the Money Guild that could buy the entire congressional delegation of a state in one deal. Of course you couldn't buy them body and soul—you were not talking abstractions here, like the Devil and God, good and evil, virtue and sin. No, you were talking politics. You were talking of what was possible. There were times when a congressman had to oppose you to win reelection. It was true that 98 percent of the congressmen were always reelected, but there were always the 2 percent that had to listen to their constituents.

Louis Inch dreamed the impossible dream. No, not to be President of the United States, he knew his landlord imprint could never be erased. His smudging the very face of New York was an architectural murder. There were a million slum dwellers in New York, Chicago and especially Santa Monica who would fill the streets ready to put his head on a pike. No, his dream was to be the first trillionaire in the modern civilized world. A plebeian trillionaire, his fortune won with the callused hands of a workingman.

Inch lived for the day when he could say to Bert Audick, "I have a thousand units." It had always irritated him that Texan oil men talked in units—a "unit" in Texas was one hundred million dollars. Audick had said about the destruction of the city of Dak, "God, I lost five hundred units there." And Inch vowed someday to say to Audick, "Hell, I got about a thousand units tied up in real estate," and Audick would whistle and say, "A hundred billion dollars." And then Inch would say to him, "Oh, no, a trillion dollars. Up in New York a unit is a billion dollars." That would settle that Texas bullshit once and for all.

To make that dream come true, Louis Inch capitalized on the concept of airspace. That is, he would buy the airspace above existent buildings in major cities and build on top of them. Airspace could be bought for peanuts; it was a new concept, as marshlands had been when his grandfather bought them, knowing that technology would solve the problem of draining the swamps and turn them into profitable building acres. The problem was to prevent the people and their legislators from stopping him. That would take time and an enormous investment, but he was confident it could be done. True, cities like Chicago, New York, Dallas and Miami would be gigantic steel-and-concrete prisons, but people didn't have to live there, except for the elite who loved the museums, the cinemas, the theater, the music. There would of course be little boutique neighborhoods for the artists.

And of course the thing was that when Louis Inch finally succeeded, there would no longer be any slums in New York City. There would simply be no affordable rents for the petty criminal and working classes. They would come in from the suburbs, on special trains, on special buses, and they would be gone by nightfall. The renters and buyers of the Inch Corporation condos and apartments could go to the theater, the discos and the expensive restaurants and not worry about the dark streets outside. They could stroll along the avenues, even venture into the side streets, and could walk the parks, in comparative safety. And what would they pay for such a paradise? Fortunes.

Summoned to the meeting of the Socrates Club in California, Louis Inch began a trip across the United States to confer with the great real estate corporations of the big cities. From them he exacted their promise to contribute money to defeat Kennedy. Arriving in Los Angeles a few days later, he decided to make a side trip to Santa Monica before going to the seminar.

Santa Monica is one of the most beautiful towns in America, mainly because its citizens have successfully resisted the efforts of real estate interests to build skyscrapers, voted laws to keep rents stable and control construction. A fine apartment on Ocean Avenue, overlooking the Pacific, cost only one sixth of the average citizen's income. This was a situation that had driven Inch crazy for twenty years.

Inch thought Santa Monica an outrage, an insult to the American spirit of free enterprise; these units under today's conditions could be rented for ten times the going rate. He had bought up many of the apartment buildings. These were charming Spanish-style complexes wasteful in their use of valuable real estate, with their inner courtyards and gardens, and their scandalously low two-story heights. And he could not, by law, raise the rents in this paradise. Oh, the airspace above Santa Monica was worth billions, the view of the Pacific Ocean worth more billions. Sometimes Inch had crazy ideas about building vertically on the ocean itself. This made him dizzy.

He did not of course try to directly bribe the three city councillors he invited to Michael's but he told them his plans, he showed how everybody could become multimillionaires if certain laws were changed. He was dismayed when they showed no interest. But that was not the worst part. When Inch got into his limousine, there was a shattering explosion. Glass flew all around the interior of the limo, the back window disintegrated, the windshield suddenly sprouted a large hole and spiderwebs appeared in the rest of the glass.

When the police arrived, they told Inch that a rifle bullet had done the damage. When they asked him if he had any enemies, Louis Inch assured them with all sincerity that he did not.

The Socrates Club's special seminar on "Demagoguery in Democracy" commenced the next day.

Those present were Bert Audick, now under a RICO indictment; George Greenwell, who looked like the old wheat stored in his gigantic Midwest silos; Louis Inch, his hand-some pouting face pale from his near death the day before; Martin "Take It Private" Mutford, wearing an Armani suit that could not hide his going to fat; and Lawrence Salentine.

Bert Audick took the floor first. "Would somebody explain to me how Kennedy is not a communist?" he said. "Kennedy wants to socialize medicine and home building. He has me indicted under the RICO laws and I'm not even Italian." Nobody laughed at his little joke, so he went on. "We can dick around all we want but we have to face one central fact. He is an immense danger to everything we in this room stand for. We have to take drastic action."

George Greenwell said quietly, "He can get you indicted but he can't get you convicted—we still have due process in this country. Now, I know you have endured great provoca-tion. But if I hear any dangerous talk in this room I walk out. I will listen to nothing treasonous or seditious."

Audick took offense. "I love my country better than any-one in this room," he said. "That's what gripes me. The indictment says I was acting in a treasonable way. Me! My ancestors were in this country when the fucking Kennedys were eating potatoes in Ireland. I was rich when they were bootleggers in Boston. Those gunners fired at American planes over Dak but not by my orders. Sure, I gave the Sultan of Sherhaben a deal, but I was acting in the interest of the United States."

Salentine said dryly, "We know Kennedy is the problem. We're here to discuss a solution. Which is our right and our duty."

Mutford said, "What Kennedy's telling the country is bullshit. Where is the capital mass going to come from to support all these programs? He is talking a modified form of communism. If we can hammer that home in the media, the people will turn away from him. Every man and woman in this country thinks they'll be a millionaire someday and they're already worrying about the tax bite."

"Then how come all the polls show Francis Kennedy will win in November?" Salentine asked irritably. As so many times before, he was a little astonished by the obtuseness of powerful men. They seemed to have no awareness of Kennedy's enormous personal charm, his appeal to the mass of people, simply because they themselves were impervious to that charm.

There was a silence and then Martin Mutford spoke. "I had a look at some of the legislation being prepared to regulate the stock market and banks. If Kennedy gets in, there will be mighty slim pickings. And if he gets his regulatory-agency people in, the jails will be filled with very rich people."

"I'll be there waiting for them," Audick said, grinning. For some reason he seemed to be in a very good humor despite his indictment. "I should be a trusty by then, I'll make sure you all have flowers in your cells."

Inch said impatiently, "You'll be in one of those country-club jails playing with computers that keep track of your oil tankers."

Audick had never liked Louis Inch. He didn't like a man who piled up human beings from underground to the stars, and charged a million dollars for apartments no bigger than a spittoon. Audick said, "I'm sure my cell will have more room than one of your fancy apartments. And once I'm in, don't be too fucking sure you can get oil to heat those sky-scrapers. And another thing, I'll get a better break gambling in jail than in your Atlantic City casinos."

Greenwell, as the oldest and most experienced in dealing with the government, felt he had to take charge of the conversation. "I think we should, through our companies and other representatives, pour a great deal of money into the campaign of Kennedy's opponent. Martin, I think you should volunteer to be the campaign manager."

Martin Mutford said, "First let's decide what kind of money we are talking about and how it's to be contributed."

Greenwell said, "How about a round sum of five hundred million dollars."

Audick said, "Wait a minute, I've just lost fifty billion and you want me to go for another unit?"

Inch said maliciously, "What's one unit, Bert. Is the oil industry going chickenshit on us? You Texans can't spare a lousy one hundred million?"

Salentine said, "TV time costs a lot of money. If we are going to saturate the airwaves from now until November that's five whole months. That's going to be expensive."

"And your TV network gets a big chunk of that," Inch said aggressively. He was proud of his reputation as a fierce negotiator. "You TV guys put in your share out of one pocket and it appears like magic in your other pockets. I think that should be a factor when we contribute."

Mutford said, "Look, we're talking peanuts here," which outraged the others. "Take It Private" Mutford was famous for his cavalier treatment of money. To him it was only a telex transporting some sort of spiritual substance from one ethereal body to another. It had no reality. He gave casual girlfriends a brand-new Mercedes, a bit of eccentricity he had learned from rich Texans. If he had a mistress for a year he bought her an apartment house to make her old age secure. Another mistress had a house in Malibu, another a castle in Italy and an apartment in Rome. He had bought an illegitimate son a piece of a casino in England. It had cost him nothing, merely slips of paper signed. And he always had a place to stay whenever he traveled. The Albanese girl owned her famous restaurant and building the same way. And there were many others. Money meant nothing to "Private" Mutford.

Audick said aggressively, "I paid my share with Dak."

Mutford said, "Bert, you're not in front of congressional committees arguing oil depletion allowances."

"You have no choice," Inch told Audick. "If Kennedy gets elected and he gets his Congress, you go to jail."

George Greenwell was wondering again whether he should dissociate himself officially from these men. After all, he was too old for these adventures. His grain empire stood in less danger than the fields of these other men. The oil industry too obviously blackmailed the government to make scandalous profits. His own grain business was low-key; people in general did not know that only five or six privately held companies controlled the bread of the world. Greenwell feared that a rash, belligerent man like Bert Audick could get them all in really serious trouble. Yet he enjoyed the life of the Socrates Club, the week-long seminars filled with interesting discussions on the affairs of the world, the sessions of backgammon, the rubbers of bridge. But he had lost that hard desire to get the best of his fellowmen.

Inch said, "Come on, Bert, what the hell is a lousy unit to the oil industry? You guys have been sucking the public tit-dry with your oil depletion allowance for the last hundred years."

Martin Mutford laughed. "Stop the bullshit," he said. "We are all in this together. And we will all hang together if Kennedy wins. Forget about the money and let's get down to business. Let's figure out how to attack Kennedy in this campaign. How about his failure to act on that atom bomb threat in time to stop the explosion? How about the fact that he has never had a woman in his life since his wife died? How about that maybe he's secretly screwing broads in the White House like his uncle Jack did? How about a million things? How about his personal staff? We have a lot of work to do."

This distracted them. Audick said thoughtfully, "He doesn't have any woman. I've already had that checked out. Maybe he's a fag."

"So what?" Salentine said. Some of the top stars on his network were gay and he was sensitive on the subject. Audick's language offended him.

But Louis Inch unexpectedly took Audick's point. "Come on," he said to Salentine, "the public doesn't mind if one of your goofy comedians is gay, but the President of the United States?"

"The time will come," Salentine said.

"We can't wait," Mutford said. "And besides, the President is not gay. He's in some sort of sexual hibernation. I think our best shot is to attack him through his staff," Mutford added thoughtfully. He considered for a moment and then said, "The Attorney General, Christian Klee, I've had some people check into him. You know he's a somewhat mysterious guy for a public figure. Very rich, much richer than people think, I've taken a sort of unofficial peek at his banking records. Doesn't spend much, he's not keeping women or into drugs, that would have showed up in his cash flow. A brilliant lawyer who doesn't really care that much for law. Not into good works. We know he is devoted to Kennedy, and his protection of the President is a marvel of efficiency. But that efficiency hampers Kennedy's campaign because Klee won't let him press the flesh. All in all I'd concentrate on Klee."

Audick said, "Klee was CIA, high up in operations. I've heard some weird stories about him."

"Maybe those stories could be our ammunition," Mutford said.

"Only stories," Audick said. "And you'll never get anything out of the CIA files, not with that guy Tappey running the show."

Greenwell said casually, "I happen to have some information that the President's chief of staff, that man Dazzy, has a somewhat messy personal life. His wife and he quarrel and he sees a young girl."

Oh shit, Mutford thought, I have to get them off this. Jeralyn Albanese had told him all about Christian Klee's threat.

"That's too minor," he said. "What do we gain even if we force Dazzy out? The public will never turn against the President for a staff member screwing a young girl, not unless it's rape or harassment."

Audick said, "So we approach the girl and give her a million bucks and have her yell rape."

Mutford said, "Yeah, but she has to holler rape for three years of screwing and having her bills paid. It won't wash."

It was George Greenwell who made the most valuable contribution. "We should concentrate on the atom bomb explosion in New York. I think Congressman Jintz and Senator Lambertino should create investigating committees in the House and in the Senate, subpoena all the government officials. Even if they come up with nothing concrete, there will be enough coincidences so that the news media can have a field day. That's where you have to use all your influence," he said to Salentine. "That is our best hope. And now I suggest we all get to work." Then he said to Mutford, "Set up your campaign committees. I guarantee you'll get my hundred million. It is a very prudent investment."

When the meeting broke up, it was only Bert Audick who considered more radical measures.

Right after the meeting Lawrence Salentine was summoned by President Francis Kennedy. When Salentine appeared in the Oval Office, he saw that Attorney General Christian Klee was also present, which made him even more wary. There were no civilities; this was not the charming Kennedy but, Salentine felt, a man seeking some sort of vengeance.

Kennedy said, "Mr. Salentine, I don't want to mince words. I want to be absolutely frank. My Attorney General, Mr. Klee, and I have discussed filing RICO criminal charges against your TV network and the other networks. He has persuaded me that it may be too harsh a punishment. Specifically you and the other media giants were in a conspiracy to remove me from the presidency. You supported Congress in their impeachment of me."

Salentine said, "It was in our function as a media company to report on a political development."

Klee said coldly, "Cut the bullshit, Lawrence, you guys ganged up on us."

Kennedy said, "That's past history. Let's go on. You media companies have been having a picnic for years, decades. I am not going to allow a corporate umbrella to dominate the communications media of this country. Ownership of TV stations will be limited to TV. They cannot own book companies. They cannot own magazines. They cannot own newspapers. They cannot own movie studios. They cannot own cable companies. That is too much power. You run too much advertising. That is going to be limited. I want you to take that message back to your friends. During the impeachment process you unlawfully barred the President of the United States from the airwaves. That will never happen again."

Salentine told the President that he didn't believe Congress would allow him to do what he planned. Kennedy grinned at him, and said, "Not this Congress, but we have an election in November. And I'm going to run for reelection. And I'm going to campaign for people in Congress who will support my views."

Lawrence Salentine went back to his fellow TV station owners and gave them the bad news. "We have two courses of action," he said. "We can start helping the President out by supporting him when we cover his actions and his policies. Or we can remain free and independent and oppose him when we feel it necessary." He paused for a moment and said, "This may be a very perilous time for us. Not just loss of revenue, not just regulatory restrictions, but if Kennedy goes far enough it may even be our losing our licenses."

This was too much. It was inconceivable that the network licenses could be lost. It would be like the homesteaders in early frontier days seeing their land go back to the government. The granting of TV station licenses, the free access to the airwaves had always belonged to people like Salentine. It seemed to them now a natural right. And so the owners made the decision that they would not truckle to the President of the United States, that they would remain free and independent. And that they would expose Kennedy as the dangerous menace to American democratic capitalism that he surely was. Salentine would relay this decision to the important members of the Socrates Club.

Salentine brooded for days on how to mount a TV campaign against the President on his TV network without making it seem too obvious. After all, the American public believed in fair play; they would resent a blatant hatchet job. The American public believed in the due process of law though they were the most criminal populace in the world.

He moved carefully. First step, he had to enlist Cassandra Chutt, who had the highest-rated national news program. Of course, he couldn't be too direct; anchor people jealously guarded against overt interference. But they had not achieved their eminence without playing ball with top management. And Cassandra Chutt knew how to play ball.

Salentine had nurtured her career over the last twenty years. He had known her when she was on the early-morning programs and then when she had switched to evening news. She had always been shameless in her pursuit of advancement. She had been known to collar a Secretary of State and burst into tears, shouting that if he did not give a two-minute interview she would lose her job. She had cajoled and flattered and blackmailed the celebrated into appearing on her prime-time interview program and then savaged them with personal and vulgar questions. Salentine thought Cassandra Chutt the rudest person he had ever known in the broadcasting business.

Salentine invited her to dinner in his apartment. He enjoyed the company of rude people.

When Cassandra arrived the next evening, Salentine was editing a videotape. He brought her to his workroom, which had the latest equipment in videos and TV and monitoring and cutting machines, all accompanied by small computers.

Cassandra sat on a stool and said, "Oh shit, Lawrence, do I have to watch you make your cut of *Gone with the Wind* again?" By way of answer he brought her a drink from the small bar in a corner of the room.

Salentine had a hobby. He would take a videotape of a movie (he had a collection of what he thought were the one hundred best movies ever made) and recut it to make it better. Even in his most favorite movies there would be a scene or dialogue that he thought not well done or unnecessary, and he would remove it with editing machines. Now arrayed in the bookcase of his living room were one hundred videotapes of the best motion pictures, somewhat shorter, but perfect. There were even some movies that had their unsatisfactory endings chopped off.

While he and Cassandra Chutt ate the dinner served by a butler, they talked about her future programs. This always put Cassandra Chutt in a good mood. She told Salentine of her plans to visit the heads of the Arab states and bring them together on one program, with the president of Israel. Then a program with three European prime ministers chatting with her. And then she was exuberant about going to Japan to interview the Emperor. Salentine listened patiently. Cassandra Chutt had delusions of grandeur but every once in a while she came up with a stunning coup.

Finally he interrupted her and said jokingly, "Why don't you get President Kennedy on your program?"

Cassandra Chutt lost her good humor. "He'll never give me a break after what we did to him."

"It didn't turn out so well," Salentine said. "But if you can't get Kennedy, then why not go to the other side of the fence? Why not get Congressman Jintz and Senator Lambertino to give their side of the story?"

Cassandra Chutt was smiling at him. "You sneaky bastard," she said. "They lost. They are losers and Kennedy is going to slaughter them in the elections. Why should I have losers on my program. Who the hell wants to watch losers on TV?"

Salentine said, "Jintz tells me they have very important information on the atom bomb explosion, that maybe the administration dragged its heels. That they didn't utilize properly the nuclear search teams, which might have located the bomb before it exploded. And they will say that on your program. You'll make headlines all over the world."

Cassandra Chutt was stunned. Then she started to laugh. "Oh, Christ," she said. "This is terrible, but right after you said that, the question, the very next question I thought to ask those two losers, was this: 'Do you honestly think the President of the United States is responsible for the ten thousand deaths in the explosion of the nuclear bomb in New York?' "

"That's a very good question," Salentine said.

In the month of June, Bert Audick traveled on his private plane to Sherhaben to discuss with the Sultan the rebuilding of Dak. The Sultan entertained him royally. There were dancing girls, fine food, and a consortium of international financiers the Sultan had assembled who would be willing to invest their money in a new Dak. Audick spent a wonderful week of hard work picking their pockets for a hundred-million-dollar "unit" here and a "unit" there, but the real money would have to come from his own oil firm and the Sultan of Sherhaben.

On the final night of his stay he and the Sultan were alone together in the Sultan's palace. At the end of the meal the Sultan banished the servants and bodyguards from the room.

He smiled at Audick and said, "I think now we should get down to our real business." He paused for a moment. "Did you bring what I requested?"

Bert Audick said, "I want you to understand one thing. I am not acting against my country. I just have to get rid of that Kennedy bastard or I'll wind up in jail. And he's going to track down all the ins and outs of our dealings over the past ten years. So what I am doing is very much in your interest."

"I understand," the Sultan said gently. "And we are far removed from the events that will happen. Have you made sure the documents cannot be traced to you in any way?"

Bert Audick said, "Of course." He then handed over the leather briefcase beside him. The Sultan took it and drew out a file that contained photographs and diagrams.

The Sultan looked at them. They were photos of the White House interiors, and the diagrams showed the control posts in different parts of the building. "Are these up to date?" the Sultan asked.

"No," Bert Audick said. "After Kennedy took office three years ago, Christian Klee, who's head of the FBI and the Secret Service, changed a lot of it around. He added another floor to the White House for the presidential residence. I know that the fourth floor is like a steel box. Nobody knows what the setup is. Nothing is ever published, and they sure as hell don't let people know. It's all secret except to the President's closest advisers and friends."

"This can help," the Sultan said.

Audick shrugged. "I can help with money. We need fast action, preferably before Kennedy gets reelected."

"The Hundred can always use the money," the Sultan said. "I'll see that it gets to them. But you must understand that these people act out of their own true faith. They are not hired assassins. So they will have to believe the money comes from me as head of an oppressed small country." He smiled. "After the destruction of Dak, I believe Sherhaben quali-fies."

Audick said, "That's another matter I've come to discuss.

My company lost fifty billion dollars when Dak was destroyed. I think we should restructure the deal we have on your oil. You were pretty rough last time."

The Sultan laughed but in a friendly way. "Mr. Audick," he said, "for over fifty years the American and British oil companies raped the Arab lands of their oil. You gave ignorant nomad sheiks pennies while you made billions. Really it was shameful. And now your countrymen get indignant when we want to charge what the oil is worth. As if we had anything to say about the price of your heavy equipment and your technological skills for which you charge so dearly. But now it is your turn to pay properly, it is your turn even to be exploited if you care to make such a claim. Please don't be offended, but I was even thinking of asking you to sweeten our deal."

They recognized in each other a kindred soul who never missed the chance to pursue a negotiation. They smiled at each other in a friendly fashion.

"I guess the American consumer will have to pick up the bill for the crazy President they voted into office," Audick said. "I sure hate to do it to them."

"But you will," the Sultan said. "You are a businessman, after all, not a politician."

"On my way to being a jailbird," Audick said with a laugh. "Unless I get lucky and Kennedy disappears. I don't want you to misunderstand me. I would do anything for my country, but I sure as hell won't let the politicians push me around."

The Sultan smiled in agreement. "No more than I would let my parliament." He clapped his hands for servants and then he said to Audick, "Now I think it is time for us to enjoy ourselves. Enough of this dirty business of rule and power. Let us live life while we still have it."

Soon they were sitting down to an elaborate dinner. Audick enjoyed Arab food, he was not squeamish like other Americans; the heads and eyeballs of sheep were mother's milk to him.

As they were eating, Audick said to the Sultan, "If you need money for some worthy cause, I can arrange for its transfer from an untraceable source on my end. It is very important to me that we do something about Kennedy."

"I understand completely," the Sultan said. "And now, no more talk of business. I have a duty as your host."

Annee, who had been hiding out with her family in Sicily, was surprised when she was summoned to a meeting with fellow members of the Hundred.

She met with them in Palermo. They were two young men she had known when they were all university students in Rome. The oldest, now about thirty years of age, she had always liked very much. He was tall, but stooped, and wore gold-rimmed glasses. He had been a brilliant scholar, destined for a distinguished career as a professor of Etruscan studies. In personal relationships he was gentle and kind. His political violence sprang from a mind that detested the cruel illogic of a capitalistic society. His name was Giancarlo.

The other member of the First Hundred she knew as the firebrand of leftist parties at the university. A loudmouth, but a brilliant orator who enjoyed spurring crowds to violence though he himself was essentially inept in action. His character changed after he was picked up by the antiterrorist special police and severely interrogated. In other words, Annee thought, they had kicked the shit out of him and put him in the hospital for a month. Sallu, for that was his name, then talked less and acted more. Finally he was recognized as one of the Christs of Violence, one of the First Hundred.

Both of these men, Giancarlo and Sallu, now lived underground to elude the antiterrorist police. And they had arranged this meeting with care. Annee had been summoned to the town of Palermo and instructed to wander and sightsee until she was contacted. On the second day she had encountered a woman named Livia in a boutique who had taken her to a meeting in a small restaurant where they were the only customers. The restaurant had then closed its doors to the public; the proprietors and the single waiter were obviously members of the cadre. Then Giancarlo and Sallu had emerged from the kitchen. Giancarlo was in chef's regalia and his eyes were twinkling with amusement. In his hands was a huge bowl of spaghetti dyed black with the ink of chopped squid. Sallu, behind him, carried a wooden basket filled with sesame-seeded golden bread and a bottle of wine.

The four of them—Annee, Livia, Giancarlo and Sallu—sat down to lunch. Giancarlo served them portions of spaghetti from the bowl, and the waiter brought them salad, a dish of pink ham and a black-and-white grainy cheese.

"Just because we fight for a better world, we shouldn't starve," Giancarlo said. He was smiling and seemed completely at ease.

"Nor die of thirst," Sallu said as he poured the wine. But he was nervous.

The women let themselves be served; as a matter of revolutionary protocol, they did not assume the stereotypical feminine role. But they were amused: they were here to take orders from men.

As they were eating, Giancarlo opened the conference. "You two have been very clever," he said. "It seems you are not under suspicion for the Easter operation. So it has been decided that we can use you for our new task. You are both extremely qualified. You have the experience, but more important, you have the will. So you are being called. But I must warn you. This is more dangerous than Easter."

Livia asked, "Do we have to volunteer before we hear the details?"

It was Sallu who answered, and abruptly, "Yes."

Annee said impatiently, "You always go through this routine and ask, 'Do you volunteer?' Do we come here for this lousy spaghetti? When we come we volunteer. So get on with it."

Giancarlo nodded; he found her entertaining. "Of course. Of course," he said.

Giancarlo took his time. He ate and said contemplatively, "The spaghetti is not so bad." They all laughed and right off that laugh he said, "The operation is directed against the President of the United States. He must be liquidated. Mr. Kennedy is linking our organization with the atom bomb explosion in his country. His government is planning special operations teams to target us on a global basis. I have come from a meeting where our friends from all over the world have decided to cooperate on this operation."

Livia said, "In America, that's impossible for us. Where would we get the money, the lines of communication, how can we set up safe houses and recruit personnel? And above all, the necessary intelligence. We have no base in America."

Sallu said, "Money is no problem. We are being funded. Personnel will be infiltrated and have only limited knowledge."

Giancarlo said, "Livia, you will go first. We have secret support in America. Very powerful people. They will help you set up safe houses and lines of communication. You will have funds available in certain banks. And you, Annee, will go in later as chief of operations. So you will have the tricky part."

Annee felt a thrill of delight. Finally she would be an operational chief. Finally she would be the equal of Romeo and Yabril.

Livia's voice broke into her thoughts. "What are our chances?" Livia asked.

Sallu said reassuringly, "Yours are very good, Livia. If they get onto us, they'll let you ride free so they can scoop up the whole operation. By the time Annee goes operational, you will be back in Italy."

Giancarlo said to Annee, "That's true. Annee, you will be at the greater risk."

"I understand that," Annee said.

"So do I," Livia said. "I meant, what are our chances for success?"

"Very small," Giancarlo said. "But even if we fail, we gain. We state our innocence."

They spent the rest of the afternoon going over the operational plans, the codes to be used, the plans for the development of the special networks.

It was dusk when they were finished and Annee asked the question that had been unasked the whole afternoon. "Tell me, then, is the worst scenario that this could be a suicide mission?"

Sallu bowed his head. Giancarlo's gentle eyes rested on Annee and he nodded. "It could be," he said. "But that would be your decision, not ours. Romeo and Yabril are still alive, and we hope to free them. And I promise the same if you are captured."

CHAPTER
17

CHRISTIAN KLEE'S SPECIAL division of the FBI ran computer surveillance on the Socrates Club and members of Congress. Klee always started his morning going through their reports. He personally operated his desktop computer, which held personal dossiers under his own secret codes.

This particular morning he called up the file of David Jatney and Cryder Cole. Klee had a fondness for his hunches and his hunch was that Jatney could be trouble. He no longer had to worry about Cole; that young man had become an enthusiastic motorcyclist and bashed his head against a stone cliff in Provo, Utah. He studied the video image that appeared on his monitor, the sensitive face, the dark recessed eyes. How the face changed from handsomeness in repose to one of frightening intensity when he became emotional. Were the emotions ugly or just the structure of the face? Jatney was under a loose surveillance, it was just a hunch.

But when Klee read the written reports on the computer, he felt a sense of satisfaction. The terrible insect buried in the egg that was David Jatney was breaking out of its shell.

David Jatney had fired his rifle at Louis Inch because of a young woman named Irene Fletcher. Irene was delighted that someone had tried to kill Inch but never knew it was her lover who had fired the shot. This despite the fact that every day she beseeched him to tell her his innermost thoughts.

They had met on Montana Avenue, where she was one of the salesgirls in the famous Fioma Bake Shop, which sold the best breads in America. David went there to buy biscuits and rolls and chatted with Irene when she served him. One day she said to him, "Would you like to go out with me tonight? We can eat Dutch."

David smiled at her. She was not one of the typical blond California girls. She had a pretty round face with a determined look, her figure was just a little buxom, and she looked as if she might be just a little too old for him. She was about twenty-five. But her gray eyes had a lively sparkle and she always sounded intelligent in their conversations, so he said yes. And truth to tell, he was lonely.

They started a casual, friendly love affair; Irene Fletcher did not have the time for something more serious, nor the inclination. She had a five-year-old son, and she lived in her mother's house. She was very active in local politics and was intensely involved in Eastern religions, which was not at all unusual for a young person in Southern California. For Jatney it was a refreshing experience. Irene often brought her young son, Campbell, to meetings that sometimes lasted far into the night, and she simply wrapped her little boy in an Indian blanket and put him to sleep on the floor as she vigorously pointed out the merits of a candidate for political office or the latest seer from the Far East. Sometimes David went to sleep on the floor with the young boy.

To Jatney, it was a perfect match—they had nothing in common. He hated religion and despised politics. Irene detested the movies and was interested only in books on exotic religions and left-wing social studies. But they kept each other company, each filled a hole in the other's existence. When they had sex they were both a little offhand, but were always friendly. Sometimes Irene succumbed to a tenderness during sex that she immediately minimized afterward.

It was helpful that Irene loved to talk and David loved to be silent. They would lie in bed and Irene would talk for hours and David would listen. Sometimes she was interesting and sometimes she was not. It was interesting that there was a continuous struggle between the real estate interests and the small homeowners and renters in Santa Monica. Jatney could sympathize with this. He loved Santa Monica; he loved the low skyline of two-story houses and one-story shops, the Spanish-looking villas, the general air of serenity, the total absence of chilling religious edifices like the Mormon tabernacles in his home state of Utah. He loved the great expanse of the Pacific, lying unobscured by glass and stone skyscrapers. He thought Irene a heroine for fighting to preserve all this against the ogres of the real estate interests.

She talked about her current Indian gurus and played their lectures on her tapes. These gurus were far more pleasant and humorous than the stern elders of the Mormon Church he had listened to while growing up, and their beliefs seemed more poetic, their miracles purer, more spiritual, more ethereal than the famous Mormon tablets of gold and the angel Moroni. But finally, they were just as boring with their rejection of the pleasures of this world and the fruits of success on earth, all of which Jatney so desperately desired.

And Irene would never stop talking, she achieved a kind of ecstasy when she talked even of the most ordinary things. Unlike Jatney, she found her life, ordinary as it was, altogether meaningful.

Sometimes when she was carried away and dissected her emotions for a full hour without interruption, he would feel that she was a star in the heavens growing larger and brighter and that he himself was falling into a bottomless black hole that was the universe, falling and falling while she never noticed.

He liked too that she was generous in material things but thrifty with her personal emotions. She would never really come to grief, she would never fall into that universal darkness. Her star would always expand, never lose its light. And he was grateful that this should be so. He did not want her company in the darkness.

One night they went for a walk on the beach just outside Malibu. It seemed weird to David Jatney that here was this great ocean on one side, then a row of houses and then mountains on the other side. It didn't seem natural to have mountains almost bordering an ocean. Irene had brought along blankets and a pillow and her child. They lay on the beach and the little boy, wrapped in blankets, fell asleep.

Irene and David sat on their blanket and were overcome by the beauty of the night. For that little moment they were in love with each other. They watched the ocean, which was blue-black in the moonlight, and the little thin birds hopping ahead of the incoming waves. "David," Irene said, "you have never told me anything really about yourself. I want to love you. You won't let me know you."

David was touched. He laughed a little nervously and then said, "The first thing you should know about me is that I'm a Ten-Mile Mormon."

"I didn't even know you were a Mormon," Irene said.

"If you are brought up a Mormon, you are taught that you must not booze or smoke or commit adultery," David said. "So when you do it you make sure you are at least ten miles from where anybody knows you." And then he told her about his childhood. And how he hated the Mormon Church.

"They teach you that it's OK to lie if it helps the Church," David said. "And then the hypocritical bastards give you all this shit about the angel Moroni and some gold bible. And they wear angel pants, which I have to admit my mother and father never believed in, but you could see those fucking angel pants hanging on their clotheslines. The most ridiculous thing you ever saw."

"What're angel pants?" Irene asked. She was holding his hand to encourage him to keep speaking.

"It's sort of a robe they wear so they won't enjoy screwing," David said. "And they are so ignorant they don't know that Catholics in the sixteenth century had the same kind of garment, a robe that covers your whole body except for a single hole in it so you can screw, supposedly without enjoying it. When I was a kid I could see angel pants hanging from the laundry lines. I'll say this for my parents, they didn't buy that shit, but because he was an elder in the church they had to fly the angel pants." David laughed and then said, "God, what a religion."

"It's fascinating, but it sounds so primitive," Irene said.

David thought, And what the hell is so civilized about all those fucking gurus who tell you that cows are sacred, that you are reincarnated, that this life means nothing, all that voodoo karma bullshit. But Irene felt his tensing and wanted to keep him talking. She slid her hands inside his shirt and felt his heart beating furiously.

"Did you hate them?" she asked.

"I never hated my parents," he said. "They were always good to me."

"I meant the Mormon Church," Irene said.

David said, "I hated the Church ever since I can remember. I hated it as a little kid. I hated the faces of the elders, I hated the way my mother and father kissed their asses. I hated their hypocrisies. If you disagree with the rulings of the Church, they could even have you murdered. It's a business religion, they all stick together. That's how my father got rich. But I'll tell you the thing that disgusted me the most. They have special anointments and the top elders get secretly anointed and so they get to go to heaven ahead of other people. Like somebody slipping you to the head of the line while you're waiting for a taxi or a table in a popular restaurant."

Irene said, "Most religions are like that except the Indian religions. You just have to watch out for karma." She paused a moment. "That is why I try to keep myself pure of greed for money, why I can't fight my fellow human being for the possessions of this earth. I have to keep my spirit pure. We're having special meetings, there is a terrible crisis in Santa Monica right now. If we're not on the alert, the real estate interests will destroy everything we've fought for and this town will be full of skyscrapers. And they'll raise the rents and you and I will be forced out of our apartments."

She went on and on, and David Jatney listened with a feeling of peace. He could lie on this beach forever, lost in time, lost in beauty, lost in the innocence of this girl, who was so unafraid of what would happen to her in this world.

She was telling him about a man named Louis Inch, who was trying to bribe the city council so that they would change the building and rental laws. She seemed to know a lot about this man Inch, she had researched him. The man could be an elder in the Mormon Church. Finally Irene said, "If it wasn't so bad for my karma, I'd kill the bastard."

David laughed. "I shot the President once." And he told her about the assassination game, the Hunt, when he had been a one-day hero at Brigham Young University. "And the Mormon elders who run the place had me thrown out," he said.

But Irene was now busy with her small son, who'd had a bad dream and waked up screaming. She soothed him and said to David, "This guy Inch is having dinner with some of the town council tomorrow night. He's taking them to Michael's and you know what that means. He'll try to bribe them. I really would like to shoot the bastard."

David said, "I'm not worried about my karma, I'll shoot him for you." They both laughed.

The next night David cleaned the hunting rifle he had brought from Utah and fired the shot that broke the glass in Louis Inch's limousine. He had not really aimed to hit anyone; in fact the shot had come much closer to the victim than he had intended. He was just curious to see if he could bring himself to do it.

CHAPTER
18

IT WAS SAL TROYCA who decided to nail Christian Klee. Going over testimonies to the congressional committees of inquiry into the atom bomb explosion, he noted Klee's testimony that the great international crisis of the hijacking took precedence. But then there were glitches; Troyca noticed that there was a time gap. Christian Klee had disappeared from the White House scene. Where had he gone?

They wouldn't find out from Klee, that was certain. But the only thing that could have made Klee disappear during that crisis was something terribly important. What if Klee had gone to interrogate Gresse and Tibbot?

Troyca did not consult with his boss, Congressman Jintz; he called Elizabeth Stone, the administrative aide to Senator Lambertino, and arranged to meet her at an obscure restaurant for dinner. In the month since the atom bomb crisis the two of them had formed a partnership, in both public and private life.

On their first date, initiated by Troyca, they had come to an understanding. Elizabeth Stone beneath her cool, impersonal beauty had a fiery sexual temperament, but her mind was cold steel. The first thing she said was "Our bosses are going to be out of their jobs in November. I think you and I should make plans for our future."

Sal Troyca was astonished. Elizabeth Stone was famous for being one of those aides who are the loyal right arms for their congressional chiefs.

"The fight isn't over yet," he said.

"Of course it is," Elizabeth Stone said. "Our bosses tried to impeach the President. Now Kennedy is the biggest hero this country has known since Washington. And he will kick their asses."

Troyca was instinctively a more loyal person to his chief. Not out of a sense of honor, but because he was competitive, he didn't want to think of himself as being on a losing side.

"Oh, we can stretch it out," Elizabeth Stone said. "We don't want to look like the kind of people who desert a sinking ship. We'll make it look good. But I can get us both a better job." She smiled at him mischievously and Troyca fell in love with that smile. It was a smile of gleeful temptation, a smile full of guile and yet an admission of that guile, a smile that said that if he wasn't delighted with her, he was a jerk. He smiled back.

Sal Troyca had, even to his own way of thinking, a sort of greasy, piglike charm that worked only on certain women, and that always surprised other men and himself. Men respected Troyca because of his cunning, his high level of energy, his ability to execute. But the fact that he could charm women so mysteriously aroused their admiration.

Now he said to Elizabeth Stone, "If we become partners, does that mean I get to fuck you?"

"Only if you make a commitment," Elizabeth Stone said.

There were two words Sal Troyca hated more than any of the others in the English language. One was "commitment" and the other was "relationship."

"You mean like we should have a real relationship, a commitment to each other, like love?" he said. "Like the house niggers used to make to their masters down in your dear old South?"

She sighed. "Your macho bullshit could be a problem," she said. Then she went on: "I can make a deal for us. I've been a big help to the Vice President in her political career. She owes me. Now you have to see reality. Jintz and Lambertino are going to be slaughtered in the November election. Helen Du Pray is reorganizing her staff and I'm going to be one of her top advisers. I have a spot for you as my aide."

Sal said smilingly, "That's a demotion for me. But if you're as good in the sack as I think you are, I'll consider it."

Elizabeth Stone said impatiently, "It won't be a demotion, since you won't have a job. And then when I go up the ladder, so do you. You'll wind up with your own staff section as an aide to the Vice President."

She paused for a moment. "Listen," she said, "we were attracted to each other in the senator's office, not love maybe, but certainly lust at first sight. And I've heard about you screwing your aides. But I understand it. We both work so hard, we don't have time for a real social life or a real love life. And I'm tired of screwing guys just because I'm lonely a couple of times a month. I want a real relationship."

"You're going too fast," Troyca said. "Now, if it was on the staff of the President . . ." He shrugged and grinned to show that he was kidding.

Elizabeth Stone gave him her smile again. It was really a hardboiled sort of grin but Troyca found it charming. "The Kennedys have always been unlucky," she said. "The Vice President could be the President. But please be serious. Why can't we have a partnership, if that's what you prefer to call it? Neither one of us wants to get married. Neither of us wants children. Why can't we sort of half live with each other, keep our own places, of course, but sort of live together? We can have companionship and sex and we can work together as a team. We can satisfy our human needs and operate at the highest point of efficiency. If it works, it could be a great arrangement. If it doesn't, we can just call it quits. We have until November."

They went to bed that night and Elizabeth Stone was a revelation to Troyca. Like many shy, reserved people, man or woman, she was genuinely ardent and tender in bed. And it helped that the act of consummation took place in Elizabeth Stone's town house. Troyca had not known that she was independently wealthy. Like a true Wasp, he thought, she had concealed that fact, where he would have flaunted it. Troyca immediately saw that the town house would be a perfect place for both of them to live, much better than his just adequate flat. Here with Elizabeth Stone he could set up an office. The town house had three servants and he would be relieved of time-consuming and worrying details like sending clothes out for cleaning, shopping for food and drink.

And Elizabeth Stone, ardent feminist though she was, performed like some legendary courtesan in bed. She was a slave to his pleasure. Well, it was only the first time women were like that, Troyca thought. Like when they first came to be interviewed for a job, they never looked as good after that. But in the month that followed, she proved him wrong.

They built up an almost perfect relationship. It was wonderful for both of them after their long hours with Jintz and Lambertino to come home, go out for a late supper and then sleep together and make love. And in the morning they would go to work together. He thought for the first time in his life about marriage. But he knew instinctively that this was something Elizabeth would not want.

They lived contained lives, a cocoon of work, companionship and love, for they did come to love each other. But the best and most delicious part of their times together was their scheming on how to change the events of their world. They both agreed that Kennedy would be reelected to the presidency in November. Elizabeth was sure that the campaign being mounted against the President by Congress and the Socrates Club was doomed to failure. Troyca was not so sure. There were many cards to play.

Elizabeth hated Kennedy. It was not a personal hatred; it was that steely opposition to someone she thought of as a tyrant. "The important thing," she said, "is that Kennedy not be allowed to have his own Congress in the next election. That should be the battleground. It's clear from Kennedy's statements in the campaign that he will change the structure of American democracy. And that would create a very dangerous historical situation."

"If you are so opposed to him now, how can you accept a position on the Vice President's staff after the election?" Sal asked her.

"We're not policymakers," Elizabeth said. "We're administrators. We can work for anybody."

• • •

So after a month of intimacy, Elizabeth was surprised when Sal asked that they meet in a restaurant rather than in the comfort of the town house they now shared. But he had insisted.

In the restaurant over their first drinks, Elizabeth said, "Why couldn't we talk at home?"

Sal said thoughtfully, "You know, I've been studying a lot of documents going a long way back. Our Attorney General, Christian Klee, is a very dangerous man."

"So?" Elizabeth said.

"He may have your house bugged," Sal said.

Elizabeth laughed, "You are paranoid," she said.

"Yeah," Sal said. "Well, how about this. Christian Klee had those two kids, Gresse and Tibbot, in custody and didn't interrogate them right away. But there's a time gap. And the kids were tipped off and told to keep their mouths shut until their families supplied lawyers. And what about Yabril? Klee has him stashed, nobody can get to see or talk to him. Klee stonewalls and Kennedy backs him up. I think Klee is capable of anything."

Elizabeth Stone said thoughtfully, "You can get Jintz to subpoena Klee to appear before a congressional committee. I can ask Senator Lambertino to do the same thing. We can smoke Klee out."

"Kennedy will exercise executive privilege and forbid him to testify," Sal said. "We can wipe our asses with those subpoenas."

Elizabeth was usually amused by his vulgarities, especially in bed, but she was not amused now. "His exercising executive privilege will damage him," she said. "The papers and TV will crucify him."

"OK, we can do that," Sal said. "But how about if just you and me go to see Oddblood Gray and try to pin him down?

We can't make him talk but maybe he will. He's an idealist at heart, and maybe psychologically he's horrified at the way Klee botched the atom bomb incident. Maybe he even knows something concrete."

It was unfortunate that they picked Oddblood Gray to question. Gray was reluctant to see them, but Elizabeth's friendship with Vice President Helen Du Pray was the deciding factor in their favor. Gray had a tremendous respect for Du Pray.

Sal Troyca opened the discussion by asking, "Isn't it odd that the Attorney General, Christian Klee, had those two young men in custody before the explosion and never got any information out of them?"

"They stood on their Constitutional rights," Gray said cautiously.

Troyca said dryly, "Klee has the reputation of being a rather forceful and resourceful man. Could two kids like Gresse and Tibbot stand up against him?"

Gray shrugged. "You never know about Klee," he said.

It was Elizabeth Stone who put the question directly. "Mr. Gray," she said, "do you have any knowledge or even have any reason to believe that the Attorney General secretly interrogated those two young men?"

Gray felt a sudden rush of anger at this question. But wait, why the hell should he protect Klee? he thought. After all, most of the people killed in New York had been black. "This is off the record," he said, "and I will deny it under oath. Klee did conduct a secret interrogation with all the listening devices turned off. There is no record. It is possible to believe the worst. But if you do, you must believe the President had no part in it."

CHAPTER
19

ON THIS EARLY MAY MORNING before meeting with the President, Helen Du Pray went on a five-mile run to clear her head. She knew that not only the administration but she herself was at a very dangerous crossroad.

It was pleasant to know that at this point in time she was a hero to Kennedy and the senior staff because she had refused to sign the petition to remove Kennedy—even though that feeling sprang from a concept of male honor that she held in contempt.

There were many dangerous problems. What had Klee really done? Was it possible he could have prevented the atom bomb explosion? And had he let it explode because he knew it would save the President? She could believe that of Klee but not of Francis Kennedy. And surely that could only have been done with Kennedy's consent?

And yet. And yet. There was in the persona of Kennedy

now an aura of danger. It was clear that he would try to get a subservient Congress to do his will. And what would he make that Congress do? It was clear that Kennedy was going to press for RICO indictments against all the important members of the Socrates Club. That was an extremely dangerous use of power. Would he discard all democratic and ethical principles to further his vision of a better America? Kennedy was trying to protect Klee, and Oddblood Gray was rebelling against this. Helen Du Pray feared this dissension. A President's staff existed to serve the President. The Vice President must follow the President. Must. Unless she resigned. And what a terrible blow that would be to Kennedy. And the end of her political career. She would be the ultimate betrayer. And poor Francis, what would he do about Yabril?

For she recognized that Kennedy could become as ruthless as his opponents: the Congress, the Socrates Club, Yabril. Oh, Francis could destroy them all—the tragedies of his life had warped his brain irreversibly.

She felt the sweat on her back, her thigh muscles ached, she dreamed of running forever and ever and never going back to the White House.

Dr. Zed Annaccone dreaded his meeting with President Kennedy and his staff. It made him slightly ill to talk science and mix it in with political and sociological targets. He would never have accepted being the President's medical science adviser if it hadn't been for the fact that it was the only way to ensure the proper funding of his beloved National Brain Research Institute.

It wasn't so bad when he dealt with Francis Kennedy directly. The man was brilliant and had a flair for science, though the newspaper stories that claimed the President would have made a great scientist were simply absurd. But Kennedy certainly understood the subtle value of research and how even the most farfetched of scientific theories could have almost miraculous results. Kennedy was not the problem. It was the staff and the Congress and all the bureaucratic dragons. Plus the CIA and the FBI, who kept looking over his shoulder.

Until he began serving in Washington, Dr. Annaccone had not truly realized the awful gap between science and society in general. It was scandalous that while the human brain had made such a great leap forward in the sciences, the political and sociological disciplines had remained almost stationary.

He found it incredible that mankind still waged war, at enormous cost and to no advantage. That individual men and women still killed each other, when there were treatments that could dissipate the murderous tendencies in human beings. He found it contemptible that the science of genetic splicing was attacked by politicians and the news media as if tampering with biology were a corruption of some holy spirit. Especially when it was obvious that the human race as now genetically constituted was doomed.

Dr. Annaccone had been briefed on what the meeting would be about. There was still some doubt as to whether the exploding of the atom bomb had been part of the terrorist plot to destabilize American influence in the world—that is, whether there was a link between the two young physics professors, Gresse and Tibbot, and the terrorist leader Yabril. He would be asked whether they should use the PET brain scan to question the prisoners and determine the truth.

Which made Dr. Annaccone irritable. Why hadn't they asked him to run the PET before the atom bomb exploded? Christian Klee claimed that he had been tied up in the hijacking crisis and that the bomb threat had not seemed that serious. Typical asshole reasoning. And President Kennedy had refused Klee's request for the PET brain scan for humanitarian reasons. Yes, if the two young men were innocent and damage was done to their brains during the scan it would be an inhuman act. But Annaccone knew that this was a politician covering his ass. He had briefed Kennedy thoroughly on the procedure, and Kennedy understood that the PET scan was almost completely safe, and would make the subject answer truthfully. They could have located the bomb and disarmed it. There would have been time.

It was regrettable, to say the least, that so many people had been killed or injured. But Annaccone felt a sneaking admiration for the two young scientists. He wished he had their balls, for they had made a real point, a lunatic one, true, but a point. That as man in general became more knowledgeable, the probability that individuals would cause an atomic disaster increased. It was also true that the greed of the individual entrepreneur or the megalomania of a political leader could do the same. But these two kids were obviously thinking of sociological controls, not scientific ones. They were thinking of repressing science, halting its march forward. The real answer, of course, was to change the genetic structure of man so that violence would become an impossible act. To put brakes in the genes and in the brain as you put brakes on a locomotive. It was that simple.

While waiting in the Cabinet Room of the White House for the President to arrive, Annaccone dissociated himself from the rest of the people there by reading his stack of memoranda and articles. He always felt himself resistant to the President's staff. Christian Klee kept track of the National Brain Research Institute and sometimes slapped a secrecy order on his research. Annaccone didn't like that and used diversionary tactics when he could. He was often surprised that Klee could outwit him in such matters. The other staff members, Eugene Dazzy, Oddblood Gray and Arthur Wix, were primitives with no understanding of science who immersed themselves in the comparatively unimportant matters of sociology and statecraft.

He noted that Vice President Helen Du Pray was present, as was Theodore Tappey, the CIA chief. He was always surprised that a woman was Vice President of the United States. He felt that science ruled against something like this. In his researches on the brain he always felt he would someday come upon a fundamental difference between the male and female brains and was amused that he did not. Amused because if he found a discrepancy the fur would fly in a delightful way.

Theodore Tappey he always regarded as Neanderthal. Indulging in those futile machinations for a slight degree of advantage in foreign affairs against fellow members of the human race. So futile an endeavor in the long run.

Dr. Annaccone took some papers out of his briefcase. There was an interesting article on the hypothetical particle called the tachyon. Not one person in this room had ever heard of the word, he thought. Though his field of expertise was the brain, Dr. Annaccone had a vast knowledge of all the sciences.

So now he studied the paper on tachyons. Did tachyons really exist? Physicists had been quarreling about that for the last twenty years. Tachyons, if they existed, would fracture Einstein's theories; tachyons would travel faster than the speed of light, which Einstein had said was impossible. Sure, there was the apology that tachyons were already moving faster than light from the beginning, but what the hell was that? Also the mass of a tachyon is a negative number. Which supposedly was impossible. But the impossible in real life could be possible in the spooky world of mathematics. And then what could happen? Who knew? Who cared? Certainly nobody in this room, which held some of the most powerful men on the planet. An irony in itself. Tachyons might change human life more than anything these men could conceive.

Finally the President made his entrance and the people in the room stood up. Dr. Annaccone put away his papers. He might enjoy this meeting if he kept alert and counted the eye blinks in the room. Research showed that eye blinks could reveal whether a person was lying or not. There was going to be a lot of blinking.

Francis Kennedy came to the meeting dressed comfortably in slacks and a white shirt covered by a sleeveless blue cashmere sweater, and with a good humor extraordinary in a man beset by so many difficulties.

After greeting them he said, "We have Dr. Annaccone with us today so that we can settle the problem of whether the terrorist Yabril was in any way connected with the atom bomb explosion. Also to respond to the charges that have been made in the newspapers and on television that we in the administration could have found the bomb before it exploded."

Helen Du Pray felt she must ask the question. "Mr. President, in your speech to Congress you said Yabril was part of the atom bomb conspiracy. You were emphatic. Was that based on hard evidence?"

Kennedy was prepared for this question and answered with calm precision. "I believed it was true then, I believe it is true now."

"But on what hard evidence?" Oddblood Gray pressed.

Kennedy's eyes met Klee's for an instant before he turned to Annaccone and broke into a friendly grin. "That's why we're here. To find out. Dr. Annaccone, what are your thoughts on this subject? Maybe you can help us. And as a favor to me, stop figuring out the secrets of the universe on that pad of yours. You've discovered enough to get us into trouble."

Dr. Annaccone had been scribbling mathematical equations on the memo pad in front of him. He realized that this was a rebuke in the guise of a compliment. He said, "I still don't understand why you didn't sign the order for the PET scan before the nuclear device exploded. You already had the two young men in custody. You had the authority under the Atomic Weapons Control Act."

Christian said quickly, "We were in the middle of what we thought was a far more important crisis, if you remember. I thought it could wait another day. Gresse and Tibbot claimed they were innocent and we had only enough evidence to grab them. We didn't have enough to indict. Then Tibbot's father got tipped off and we had a bunch of very expensive lawyers threatening a lot of trouble. So we figured we'd wait until the other crisis was over and maybe we had a little more evidence."

Vice President Du Pray said, "Christian, do you have any idea how Tibbot Senior was tipped off?"

Christian said, "We are going over all the telephone company records in Boston to check the origin of calls received by Tibbot Senior. So far no luck."

The head of the CIA, Theodore Tappey, said, "With all your high-tech equipment, you should have found out."

"Helen, you've got them off on a tangent," Kennedy said. "Let's stick to the main point. Dr. Annaccone, let me answer your question. Christian is trying to take some heat off me, which is why a President has a staff. But I made the decision not to authorize the brain probe. According to the protocols, there is some danger of damaging the brain and I didn't want to risk it. The two young men denied everything, and there was no evidence that a bomb existed except for the warning letter. What we have here is really a scurrilous attack by the news media supported by the members of Congress. I want to pose a specific question. Do we eliminate any collusion between Yabril and Professors Tibbot and Gresse by having the PET brain scan done on all of them? Would that solve the problem?"

Dr. Annaccone said crisply, "Yes. But now you have a different circumstance. You are using the Atomic Weapons Control Act to gather evidence in a criminal trial, not to discover the whereabouts of a nuclear device. The act does not authorize PET scanning under those circumstances."

"Besides," Dazzy added, "with their legal defense we'll never get anywhere near those kids."

President Kennedy gave Dazzy a cold smile. "Doctor," he said, "we still have Yabril. I want Yabril to undergo the brain probe. The question he will be asked is this: Was there a conspiracy? And was the atom bomb explosion part of his plan? Now, if the answer is yes, the implications are enormous. There may still be a conspiracy going on. And it may involve much more than New York City. Other members of the terrorist First Hundred could plant other nuclear devices. Now do you understand?"

Dr. Annaccone said, "Mr. President, do you think that is really a possibility?"

Kennedy said, "We have to erase any doubt. I will rule that this medical interrogation of the brain is justified under the Atomic Weapons Control Act."

Arthur Wix said, "There will be one hell of an uproar. They'll claim we're performing a lobotomy."

Eugene Dazzy said dryly, "Aren't we?"

Dr. Annaccone was suddenly as angry as anyone was allowed to be in the presence of the President of the United States. "It is not a lobotomy," he said. "It is a brain scan with chemical intervention. The patient is completely the same after the interrogation is completed."

"Unless there's a little slipup," Dazzy said.

The press secretary, Matthew Gladyce, said, "Mr. President, the outcome of the test will dictate what kind of announcement we make. We have to be very careful. If the test proves there was conspiracy linking Yabril, Gresse and Tibbot, we'll be in the clear. If the probe proves there is no collusion, you're going to have a lot of explaining to do."

Kennedy said curtly, "Let's go on to other things."

Eugene Dazzy read from the memo in front of him. "The Congress wants to haul Christian up in front of one of their investigating committees. Senator Lambertino and Congressman Jintz want to take a crack at him. They are claiming, and they planted it all over in the media, that Attorney General Christian Klee is the key to any funny work that went on."

"Invoke executive privilege," Kennedy said. "As President, I order him not to appear before any congressional committee."

Dr. Annaccone, bored with the political discussions, said jokingly, "Christian, why don't you volunteer for our PET scan? You can establish your innocence unequivocally. And endorse the morality of the procedure."

"Doc," Christian said, "I'm not interested in establishing my innocence, as you call it. Innocence is the one fucking thing your science will never be able to establish. And I'm not interested in the morality of a brain probe that will determine the veracity of another human being. We are not discussing innocence or morals here. We are discussing the employment of power to further the functioning of society. Another area in which your science is useless. As you've often said to me, don't dabble in something in which you are not expert. So go fuck yourself."

It was rare at these staff meetings that emotions were allowed to be unrestrained. It was even rarer for vulgar language to be used when Vice President Du Pray was attending staff meetings—not that the Vice President was a prudish woman. Yet the people in the Cabinet Room were surprised at Christian Klee's outburst.

Dr. Annaccone was taken aback. He had just made a little joke. He liked Klee, as most people did. The man was urbane and civilized, and he seemed more intelligent than most lawyers. Dr. Annaccone, as a great scientist, prided himself on his understanding of practically everything in the universe. He now suffered the regrettable petty human vulnerability of having his feelings hurt. So without thinking he said, "You used to be in the CIA, Mr. Klee. The CIA headquarters building has a marble tablet that reads, 'Know the truth and the truth shall set you free.' "

Christian had regained his good humor. "I didn't write it," he said. "And I doubt it."

Dr. Annaccone had also recovered. And he had started analyzing. Why the furious response to his jocular question? Did the Attorney General, the highest law official in the land, really have something to hide? He'd dearly love to have the man on the probe's test table.

Francis Kennedy had been watching this byplay with a grave yet amused eye. Now he said gently, "Zed, when you have the brain lie-detector test perfected, so it can be done without side effects, we may have to bury it. There's not a politician in this country who could live with that."

Dr. Annaccone interrupted. "All these questions are irrelevant. The process has been discovered. Science has begun its exploration of the human brain. You can never halt a process once it has begun. Luddites proved that when they tried to halt the Industrial Revolution. You couldn't outlaw the use of gunpowder, as the Japanese learned when they banned firearms for hundreds of years and were overwhelmed by the Western world. Once the atom was discovered you could no longer stop the bomb. The brain lie-detector test is here to stay, I assure you all."

Klee said, "It violates the Constitution."

President Kennedy said briskly, "We may have to change the Constitution."

Matthew Gladyce said, with a look of horror on his face, "If the news media heard this conversation they could run us right out of town."

Kennedy said, "It's your job to tell the public what we've said in the proper language, and at the proper time. Remember this. The people of America will decide. Under the Constitution. Now, I think the answer to all our problems is to mount a counterattack. Christian, press the prosecution of Bert Audick under the RICO laws. His company will be charged with a criminal conspiracy with the Sultanate of Sherhaben to defraud the American public by illegally creating oil shortages to raise prices. That's number one."

He turned to Oddblood Gray. "Rub the congressional nose in the news that the new Federal Communications Commission will deny the licenses of the major network TV stations when they come up for renewal. And the new laws will control those stacked-deck deals on Wall Street and by the big banks. We'll give them something to worry about, Otto."

Helen Du Pray knew that she had every right to disagree in the private meetings even though as the Vice President it was mandatory to agree with the President publicly. Yet she hesitated before she said cautiously, "Don't you think we're making too many enemies at one time? Wouldn't it be even better to wait until we've been elected for a second term? If we do indeed get a Congress more sympathetic to our policies, why fight the present Congress? Why unnecessarily set all the business interests against us when we are not in a position of prime strength?"

"We can't wait," Kennedy said. "They are going to attack us no matter what we do. They are going to continue to try to prevent my reelection, and my Congress, no matter how conciliatory we are. By attacking them we make them reconsider. We can't let them go ahead as if they didn't have a worry in the world."

They were all silent, and then Kennedy rose and said to his staff, "You can work out the details and draw up the necessary memos."

It was then that Arthur Wix spoke about the Congress-inspired media campaign to attack President Kennedy by highlighting how many men and how much money was spent to guard the President.

Wix said, "The whole thrust of their campaign is to paint you as some kind of Caesar and your Secret Service as some sort of imperial palace guard. To the public, ten thousand men and one hundred million dollars to guard just one man, even the President of the United States, seems excessive. It makes a lousy public relations image."

They were all silent. The memory of the Kennedy assassinations made this a particularly touchy issue. Also, all of them, being so close to Kennedy, were aware that the President went in some sort of physical fear. So they were surprised when Kennedy turned to the Attorney General and said, "In this case I think our critics are right. Christian, I know I gave you the veto on any change in protection, but how about if we make an announcement that we will cut the Secret Service White House Division in half. And the budget in half also. Christian, I'd like you not to use your veto on this."

Christian smiled and said, "Maybe I went a little overboard, Mr. President. I won't use my veto, which you could always veto." Everyone laughed.

But Gladyce was a little worried by this seemingly easy victory. "Mr. Attorney General, you can't just say you'll do it and not do it. The Congress will be all over our budget and appropriations figures," Gladyce said.

"Okay," Christian said. "But when you give out the press release, make sure you emphasize it is over my strong objections and make it seem like the President is bowing to the pressure of the Congress."

Kennedy said, "I thank you all. This meeting is adjourned."

The director of the White House Military Office, Colonel Henry Canoo (USA, Ret.), was the most cheerful and unflappable man in the administration. He was cheerful because he had what he thought was the best job in the country. He was responsible to no one but the President of the United States, and he controlled presidential secret funds credited to the Pentagon that were not subject to audit except by himself and the President. Also he was strictly an administrator; he decided no questions of policy, did not even have to offer advice. He was the one who arranged for all the airplanes and helicopters and limos for the President and his staff. He was the one who disbursed funds for the construction and maintenance of buildings used by the White House that were classified secret. He ran the administration of the "Football," the warrant officer and his briefcase that held atom bomb codes for the President. Whenever the President wanted to do something that cost money that he didn't want the Congress or the news media to know about, Henry Canoo disbursed money from the secret fund and stamped the fiscal sheets with the highest security classification.

So in the late May afternoon when Attorney General Klee came into his office, Henry Canoo greeted him warmly. They had done business together before, and early on in his administration the President had given Canoo instructions that the Attorney General could have anything he wanted from the secret fund. The first few times Canoo had checked it out with the President but not any longer. "Christian," he said jovially, "are you looking for information or cash?"

"Both," Christian said. "First the money. We are going to promise publicly to cut down on the Secret Service Division fifty percent and to cut the security budget. I have to go through the motions. It will be a paper transfer, nothing will change. But I don't want Congress to sniff out a financial trail. So your office of the military adviser will tap the Pentagon budget for the money. Then stamp it with your top-security classification."

"Jesus," Henry Canoo said. "That's a lot of money. I can do it, but not for too long."

"Just until the election in November," Christian said.

"Then we'll either be out on our ass or in too strong for Congress to make any difference. But right now we have to look good."

"OK," Canoo said.

"Now the information," Christian said. "Have any of the congressional committees been sniffing around lately?"

"Oh, sure," Canoo said. "More than usual. They keep trying to find out how many helicopters the President has, how many limos, how many big aircraft, shit like that. They try to find out what the executive branch is doing. If they knew how many we really have, they'd shit."

"What congressman in particular?" Christian asked.

"Jintz," Canoo said. "He has that admin. assistant, Sal Troyca, a clever little bastard. He says he just wants to know how many copters we have, and I tell him three. He says 'I hear you have fifteen' and I say 'What the hell would the White House do with fifteen?' But he was pretty close, we have sixteen."

Klee was surprised. "What the hell do we do with sixteen?"

"Copters always break down," Canoo said. "If the President asks for a chopper, am I going to tell him no because they're in the shop? And, besides, somebody on the staff is always asking for a chopper. You're not so bad, Christian, but Tappey at CIA and Wix sure put in a lot of chopper time. And Dazzy too, for what reason I don't know."

"And you don't want to know," Christian said. "I want reports from you on any Congress snooper who tries to find out what the logistics are in supporting the presidential mission. It has a bearing on security. Reports to me and top classifications."

"OK," Canoo said cheerfully. "And anytime you need

some work done on your personal residence we can tap the fund for that too."

"Thanks," Christian said, "I have my own money."

In the late evening of that day, President Kennedy sat in the Oval Office and smoked his thin Havana cigar. He reviewed the events of the day. Everything had gone exactly as he had planned. He had shown his hand just enough to win the support of his staff.

Klee had reacted in character, as if he read his President's mind. Canoo had checked with him. Annaccone was malleable. Helen Du Pray might be a problem if he wasn't careful, but he needed her intelligence and her political base of the women's organizations.

Francis Kennedy was surprised at how well he felt. There was no longer any depression and his energy level was higher than it had ever been since his wife had died. Was it because he had at last gained control of the huge and complex political machinery of America?

CHAPTER 20

PRESIDENT KENNEDY wanted Christian Klee to come to breakfast in the White House bedroom suite. It was rare that meetings were held in Kennedy's private living quarters.

Jefferson, the President's private butler and Secret Service guard, served the large breakfast and then discreetly withdrew to the pantry room, to appear only when summoned by the buzzer.

Kennedy said casually, "Did you know Jefferson was a great student, a great athlete? Jefferson never took shit from anybody." He paused and said, "How did he become a butler, Christian?"

Christian knew he had to tell the truth. "He is also the best agent in the Secret Service. I recruited him myself and especially for this job."

Kennedy said, "The same question applies—why the hell would he take a Secret Service job? And as a butler?"

Christian said, "He has a very high rank in the Secret Service."

Kennedy said, "Yeah, but still."

"I organized a very elaborate screening procedure for these jobs. Jefferson was the best man, and in fact he is the White House team leader."

"Still," Kennedy said.

"I promised him that before you left the White House I would get him an appointment in Health, Education and Welfare, a job with clout."

"Ah, that's clever," Kennedy said, "but how does his résumé look from butler to clout? How the hell can we do that?"

"His résumé will read executive assistant to me," Christian said.

Kennedy lifted the coffee mug, its white glaze adorned with stenciled eagles. "Now, don't take this wrong, but I've noticed that all my immediate servants in the White House are very good at their jobs. Are they all in the Secret Service? That would be incredible."

"A special school and a special indoctrination appealing to their professional pride," Christian said. "Not all."

Kennedy laughed out loud and said, "Even the chefs?"

"Especially the chefs," Christian said, smiling. "All chefs are crazy." Like many men, Christian always used a gag line to give himself time to think. He knew Kennedy's method for preparing to go on dangerous ground, showing good humor plus a piece of knowledge he wasn't supposed to have.

They ate their breakfast, Kennedy playing what he called "mother," passing plates and pouring. The china except for Kennedy's special coffee mug was beautiful, with the blue presidential seal and as fragile as an eggshell. Kennedy finally said almost casually, "I'd like to spend an hour with

Yabril. I expect you to handle it personally." He saw the anxious look on Christian's face. "Only for an hour and only for this one time."

Christian said, "What's to be gained, Francis? It could be too painful for you to bear." There were lines in Kennedy's face that Christian had never noticed before.

"Oh, I can bear it," Kennedy said.

"If the meeting leaks, there will be a lot of questions," Christian said.

"Then make sure it doesn't leak," Kennedy said. "There will be no written record of the meeting and it won't be entered in the White House log. Now, when?"

"It will take a few days to make the necessary arrangements," Christian said. "And Jefferson has to know."

"Anybody else?" Kennedy asked.

"Maybe six other men from my special division," Christian said. "They will have to know Yabril is in the White House but not necessarily that you're seeing him. They'll guess, but they won't know."

Kennedy said, "If it's necessary I can go to where you're holding him."

"Absolutely not," Christian said. "The White House is the best place. It should be in the early hours after midnight. I suggest 1:00 A.M."

Kennedy said. "The night after tomorrow. OK."

"Yes," Christian said. "You'll have to sign some papers, which will be vague, but will cover me if something goes haywire."

Kennedy sighed as if in relief, then said briskly, "He's not a superman. Don't worry. I want to be able to talk to him freely and for him to answer lucidly and of his own free will. I don't want him drugged or coerced in any way. I want to understand how his mind works and maybe I won't hate him so much. I want to find out how people like him truly feel."

"I must be physically present at this meeting," Christian said awkwardly. "I'm responsible."

"How about you waiting outside the door with Jefferson?" Kennedy asked.

Christian, panicked by the implication of this request, slammed down the fragile coffee cup and said earnestly, "Please, Francis, I can't do that. Naturally he'll be secured, he will be physically helpless, but I still have to be between the two of you. This is one time I have to use the veto you gave me." He tried to hide his fear of what Francis might do.

They both smiled. It had been part of their deal when Christian had guaranteed the safety of the President. That Christian as head of the Secret Service could veto any presidential exposure to the public. "I've never abused that power," Christian said.

Kennedy made a grimace. "But you've exercised it vigorously. OK, you can stay in the room but try to fade into the Colonial woodwork. And Jefferson stays outside the door."

"I'll set everything up," Christian said. "But, Francis, this can't help you."

Christian Klee prepared Yabril for the meeting with President Kennedy. There had, of course, been many interrogations, but Yabril had smilingly refused to answer any questions. He had been very cool, very confident, and was willing to make conversation in a general way—discuss politics, Marxist theory, the Palestinian problem, which he called the Israeli problem—but he refused to talk about his background or his terrorist operations. He refused to talk about Romeo, his partner, or about Theresa Kennedy and her murder or his relationship with the Sultan of Sherhaben.

Yabril's prison was a small ten-bed hospital built by the

FBI for the holding of dangerous prisoners and valuable informers. This hospital was staffed by Secret Service medical personnel and guarded by Klee's Secret Service special division agents. There were five of these detention hospitals in the United States: one in the Washington, D.C., area, another in Chicago, one in Los Angeles, one in Nevada and another on Long Island.

These hospitals were sometimes used for secret medical experiments on volunteer prison inmates. But Klee had cleared out the hospital in Washington, D.C., to hold Yabril in isolation. He had also cleaned out the hospital in Long Island to hold the two young scientists who had planted the atom bomb.

In the Washington hospital, Yabril lived in a medical suite fully equipped to abort any suicide attempt by violence or fasting. There were physical restraints and equipment for intravenous feeding.

Every inch of Yabril's body, including his teeth, had been X-rayed, and he was always restrained by a specially made loose jacket that permitted him only partial use of his arms and legs. He could read and write and walk with little steps, but could not make violent movements. He was also under twenty-four-hour surveillance through a two-way mirror by teams of Secret Service agents from Klee's special division.

After Christian left President Kennedy, he went to visit Yabril knowing that he had a problem. With two of the Secret Service agents he entered Yabril's suite. He sat on one of the comfortable sofas and had Yabril brought in from the bedroom. He pushed Yabril gently into one of the armchairs and then had his agents check the restraints.

Yabril said contemptuously, "You're a very careful man, with all your power."

"I believe in being careful," Christian told him gravely.

"I'm like those engineers who build bridges and buildings to withstand a hundred times more stress than possible. That's how I run my job."

"They are not the same thing," Yabril said. "You cannot foresee the stress of Fate."

"I know," Christian said. "But it relieves my anxieties and it serves well enough. Now the reason for my visit: I've come to ask you a favor." At this Yabril laughed, a fine derisive laugh but a laugh of genuine mirth.

Christian stared at him and smiled. "No, seriously, this is a favor it is in your power to grant or refuse. Now listen carefully. You've been treated well—that is my doing and also the laws of this country. I know it's useless to threaten. I know you have your pride, but it is a small thing I ask, one that will not compromise you in any way. And in return I promise to do everything I can so that nothing unfortunate will happen. I know that you still have hope. You think your comrades of the famous First Hundred will come up with something clever so that we will have to set you free."

Yabril's thin dark face lost its saturnine mirthfulness. He said, "We tried several times to mount an action against your President Kennedy, very complicated and clever operations. They were all suddenly and mysteriously wiped out before we could even get into this country. I personally conducted an investigation into these failures and the destruction of our personnel. And the trail always led to you. And so I know we're in the same line of work. I know that you're not one of those cautious politicians. So just tell me the courtesy you want. Assume I'm intelligent enough to consider it very carefully."

Christian leaned back on the sofa. Part of his brain noted that since Yabril had found his trail he was far too dangerous ever to be let free under any circumstances. Yabril had been foolish to let out that information. Then Christian concentrated on the business at hand. He said, "President Kennedy is a very complicated man, he tries to understand events and people. And so he wants to meet you face-to-face and ask you questions, engage in a dialogue. As one human being to another. He wants to understand what made you kill his daughter; he wants, perhaps, to absolve himself of his own feelings of guilt. Now, all I ask is that you talk to him, answer his questions. I ask you not to reject him totally. Will you do that?"

Yabril, loosely locked in his jacket, tried to raise his arms in a gesture of rejection. He totally lacked physical fear, and yet the idea of meeting the father of the girl he had murdered aroused an agitation that surprised him. After all, it had been a political act, and a President of the United States should understand that better than anyone. Still, it would be interesting to look into the eyes of the most powerful man in the world and say, "I killed your daughter. I injured you more grievously than you can ever injure me, you with your thousand ships of war, your tens of thousands of thunderbolt aircraft."

Yabril said, "Yes, I will do you this little favor. But you may not thank me in the end."

Klee got up from the sofa and lightly put a hand on Yabril's shoulder, but Yabril shrugged him away with contempt. "It doesn't matter," Klee said. "And I will be grateful."

Two days later, an hour after midnight, President Kennedy entered the Yellow Oval Room of the White House to find Yabril already seated in a chair by the fireplace. Christian was standing behind him.

On a small oval table inlaid with a shield of the Stars and

Stripes was a silver platter of tiny sandwiches, a silver coffee-pot and cups and saucers rimmed with gold. Jefferson poured the coffee into the three cups and then retreated to the door of the room and put his wide shoulders back against it. Kennedy could see that Yabril, who bowed his head to him, was immobilized in the chair. "You haven't sedated him?" Kennedy said sharply.

"No, Mr. President," Christian said. "Those are jacket and legging restraints."

"Can't you make him more comfortable?" Kennedy said.

"No, sir," Christian said.

Kennedy spoke directly to Yabril. "I'm sorry, but I don't have the last word in these matters. I won't keep you too long. I would just like to ask you a few questions."

Yabril nodded. Because of the restraints, it was with some difficulty that he helped himself to one of the sandwiches, which were delicious. And it helped his pride in some way that his enemy could see that he was not completely helpless. He studied Kennedy's face, and was struck by the fact that this was a man who in other circumstances he would have instinctively respected and trusted to some degree. The face showed suffering but a powerful restraint of that suffering. It also showed a genuine interest in his discomfort; there was no condescension or false compassion. And yet with all this there was a grave strength.

Yabril said softly and more politely and perhaps more humbly than he intended, "Mr. Kennedy, before we begin you must first answer me one question. Do you really believe that I am responsible for the atom bomb explosion in your country?"

"No," Kennedy said. And Christian was relieved that he did not give any further information.

"Thank you," Yabril said. "How could anyone think me

so stupid? And I would resent it if you tried to use that accusation as a weapon. You may ask me anything you like."

Kennedy motioned to Jefferson to leave the room and watched him do so. Then he spoke softly to Yabril. Christian lowered his head as if not to hear. He really did not want to hear.

Kennedy said, "We know you orchestrated the whole series of events. The murder of the Pope, the hoax of letting your accomplice be captured so that you could demand his release. The hijacking of the plane. And the killing of my daughter, which was planned from the very beginning. Now we know this for certain, but I would like you to tell me if this is true. By the way, I can see the logic of it."

Yabril looked at Kennedy directly. "Yes, that is all true. But I'm amazed that you put it all together so quickly. I thought it clever."

Kennedy said, "I'm afraid it's nothing to be proud of. It means that basically I have the same kind of mind that you do. Or that there is not much difference in the human mind when it comes to deviousness."

"Still, it was maybe too clever," Yabril said. "You broke the rules of the game. But of course it was not chess, the rules were not so strict. You were supposed to be a pawn with only a pawn's moves."

Kennedy sat down and drank a bit of his coffee, a polite social gesture. Christian could see he was very tense, and, of course, to Yabril the seeming casualness of the President was transparent. Yabril wondered what the man's real intentions were. It was obvious that they were not malicious; there was no intent to use power to frighten or harm him.

"I knew from the very beginning," Kennedy said. "With the hijacking of the plane, I knew you would kill my daughter. When your accomplice was captured, I knew it was part of your plan. I was surprised by nothing. My advisers did not agree until later in your scenario. So what concerns me is that my mind must be something like yours. And yet it comes to this. I can't imagine myself doing such an operation. I want to avoid taking that next step and that is why I wanted to talk to you. To learn and foresee, to guard myself against myself."

Yabril was impressed by Kennedy's courteous manner, the evenness of his speech, his seeming desire for some kind of truth.

Kennedy went on. "What was your gain in all this? The Pope will be replaced; my daughter's death will not alter the international power structure. Where was your profit?"

Yabril thought, The old question of capitalism, it comes down to that. Yabril felt Christian's hands rest lightly on his shoulders for a moment. Then he hesitated before he said, "America is the colossus to which the Israeli state owes its existence. This by definition is what oppresses my countrymen. And your capitalistic system oppresses the poor people of the world and even your own country. It is necessary to break down the fear of your strength. The Pope is part of that authority, the Catholic Church has terrorized the poor of the world for countless centuries, with hell and even heaven; how disgraceful. And it went on for two thousand years. To bring about the Pope's death was more than a political satisfaction."

Christian had wandered away from Yabril's chair but was still alert, ready to interpose himself. He opened the door to the Yellow Oval Room to whisper to Jefferson for a moment. Yabril noted all this in silence, then went on: "But all my actions against you failed. I mounted two very elaborate operations to assassinate you and they failed. You may one day ask your Mr. Klee the details, they may astonish you.

The Attorney General, what a benign title, I must confess it misled me at the beginning. He destroyed my operations with a ruthlessness that compelled my admiration. But then, he had so many men, so much technology. I was helpless. But your own invulnerability ensured your daughter's death, and I know how that must trouble you. I speak frankly, since that is your wish."

Christian came back to stand behind the chair and tried to avoid Kennedy's look. Yabril felt a strange tinge of fear, but he went on. "Consider," Yabril said and half raised his arms to make an emphatic gesture, "if I hijack a plane, I am a monster. If the Israelis bomb a helpless Arab town and kill hundreds, they are striking a blow for freedom; more, they are avenging the famous holocaust with which Arabs had nothing to do. But what are our options? We do not have the military power, we do not have the technology. Who is the more heroic? Well, in both cases the innocent die. And what about justice? Israel was put in place by foreign powers, my people were thrown out into the desert. We are the new homeless, the new Jews, what an irony. Does the world expect us not to fight? What can we use except terror? What did the Jews use when they fought for the establishment of their state against the British? We learned everything about terror from the Jews of that time. And those terrorists are now heroes, those slaughterers of the innocent. One even became the prime minister of Israel and was accepted by the heads of state as if they never smelled the blood on his hands. Am I more terrible?"

Yabril paused for a moment and tried to rise, but Christian pushed him back down in his chair. Kennedy made a gesture for him to go on.

Yabril said, "You ask what I accomplished. In one sense I failed, and the proof is that I am here a prisoner. But what a blow I dealt to your authority in the world. America is not so great, after all. It could have ended better for me, but it's still not a total loss. I exposed to the world how ruthless your supposedly humane democracy really is. You destroyed a great city, you mercilessly subdued a foreign nation to your will. I made you peel off your thunderbolts to frighten the whole world and you alienated part of the world. You are not so beloved, your America. And in your own country you have polarized your political factions. Your personal image has changed and you have become the terrible Mr. Hyde instead of the saintly Dr. Jekyll."

Yabril paused for a moment to control the violent energy of the emotions that had passed over his face. He became more respectful, more grave.

"I come now to what you want to hear and what is painful for me to say. Your daughter's death was necessary. She was a symbol of America because she was the daughter of the most powerful man on earth. Do you know what that does to people who fear authority? It gives them hope, never mind that some may love you, that some may see you as benefactor or friend. People hate their benefactors in the long run. They see you are no more powerful than they are, they need not fear you. Of course it would have been more effective if I had gone free. How would that have been? The Pope dead, your daughter killed and then you are forced to set me free. How impotent you and America would have seemed before the world."

Yabril leaned back in the chair to lessen the weight of restraint and smiled at Kennedy. "I made only one mistake. I misjudged you completely. There was nothing in your history that could foreshadow your actions. You, the great liberal, the ethical modern man. I thought you would release my friend. I thought you would not be able to put the pieces together quickly enough and I never dreamed you would commit such a great crime."

Kennedy said, "There were very few casualties when the city of Dak was bombed—we dumped leaflets hours before."

Yabril said, "I understand that. It was a perfect terrorist response. I would have done the same myself. But I would never have done what you did to save yourself. Set off an atom bomb in one of your own cities."

"You are mistaken," Kennedy said. And Christian was relieved again that he did not offer more information. And he was also relieved to see that Kennedy did not take the accusation seriously. In fact Kennedy went on immediately to something else.

"Tell me," Kennedy said, "how can you justify in your own heart the things you have done, your betrayals of human trust? I've read your dossier. How can any human being say to himself, I will better the world by killing innocent men, women and children, I will raise humanity out of its despair by betraying my best friend—all this without any authority given by God or his fellow beings. Compassion aside, how do you even dare to assume such power?"

Yabril waited courteously as if he expected another question. Then he said, "The acts I committed are not so bizarre as the press and moralists claim. What about your bomber pilots who rain down destruction as if the people below them were mere ants? Those good-hearted boys with every manly virtue. But they were taught to do their duty. I think I am no different. Yet I do not have the resources to drop death from thousands of feet in the air. Or naval guns that obliterate from twenty miles away. I must dirty my hands with blood. I must have moral strength, the mental purity to shed blood directly for the cause I believe in. Well, that is all terribly obvious, an old argument, and it seems cowardly to even make it. But you say how do I have the courage to assume that authority without being approved by some higher source? That is more complicated. Let me believe that the suffering I have seen in my world has given me that authority. Let me say that the books I have read, the music I have heard, the example of far greater men than myself, have given me the strength to act on my own principles. It is more difficult for me than you who have the support of hundreds of millions and so commit your terror as a duty to them, as their instrument."

Here Yabril paused to sip at his coffee cup. Then he went on with a calm dignity: "I have devoted my life to revolution against the established order, the authority I despise. I will die believing what I have done is right. And as you know, there is no moral law that exists forever."

Finally Yabril was exhausted and stretched back in his chair, arms appearing broken from the restraints. Kennedy had listened without any sign of disapproval. He did not make any counterargument. There was a long silence and finally Kennedy said, "I can't argue morality—basically, I've done what you have done. And as you say, it is easier to do when one does not personally bloody his hands. But again as you say, I act from a core of social authority, not out of my own personal animosity."

Yabril interrupted him. "That is not correct. Congress did not approve your actions; neither did your Cabinet officers. Essentially you acted as I did, on your own personal authority. You are my fellow terrorist."

Kennedy said, "But the people of my country, the electorate, approve."

"The mob," Yabril said. "They always approve. They refuse to foresee the dangers of such actions. What you did was wrong politically and morally. You acted on a desire for personal vengeance." Yabril smiled. "And I thought you would be above such an action. So much for morality."

Kennedy was silent for a time as if giving careful consideration to his answer. Then he said, "I hope you're wrong, time will tell. I want to thank you for speaking to me so frankly, especially since I understand you refused to cooperate in former interrogations. You know, of course, that the best law firm in the United States has been retained for you by the Sultan of Sherhaben and shortly they will be permitted to consult with you on your defense."

Kennedy smiled and rose to leave the room. He was almost at the door when it swung open. Then as he was about to walk through it he heard Yabril's voice. Yabril had struggled to his feet despite his restraints and fought to keep his balance. He was erect when he said, "Mr. President." Kennedy turned to face him.

Yabril lifted his arms slowly, resting them crookedly under the nylon and wire jacket. "Mr. President," he said again, "you do not deceive me. I know I will never see or talk to my lawyers."

Christian had interposed his body between the two men and Jefferson was by Kennedy's side.

Kennedy gave Yabril a cold smile. "You have my personal guarantee that you will see and talk to your lawyers," he said, and walked out of the room.

At that moment Christian Klee felt an anguish close to nausea. He had always believed he knew Francis Kennedy but now he realized he did not. For in one clear moment he had seen a look of pure hatred on Kennedy's face that was alien to everything in his character.

BOOK

V

CHAPTER
21

WHEN FRANCO SEBBEDICCIO was a little boy in Sicily he had chosen the side of law and order not only because it seemed the stronger side but because he loved the sweet consolation of living under strict rules of authority. The Mafia had been too impressionistic, the world of commerce too dicey, and so he had become a policeman and thirty years later was the head of the antiterrorist division of all Italy.

He now had under arrest the assassin of the Pope, a young Italian of good family named Armando Giangi, code-named Romeo. The code name irritated Sebbediccio intensely. Sebbediccio had incarcerated Romeo in the deepest cells of his Roman prison.

Under surveillance was Rita Fallicia, whose code name was Annee. She had been easy to track down because she had been a troublemaker since her teens, a firebrand at the university, a pugnacious leader of demonstrations and linked to the abduction of a leading banker of Milan.

The evidence had come flooding in. The safe houses had been cleaned by the terrorist cadres, but those poor bastards had no way of knowing the scientific resources of a national police organization. There was a towel with traces of semen that identified Romeo. One of the captured men had given evidence under severe interrogation. But Sebbediccio had not arrested Annee. She was to remain free.

Franco Sebbediccio worried that the trial of these guilty parties would glorify the Pope's murder and that they would become heroes and spend their prison sentences without too much discomfort. Italy did not have a death penalty, so they could receive only life imprisonment, which was a joke. With all the reduction of time for good behavior and the different conditions for amnesties they would be set free at a comparatively young age.

It would have been different if Sebbediccio could have conducted the interrogation of Romeo in a more serious fashion. But because this scoundrel had killed a Pope, his rights had become a cause in the Western world. There were protesters and human rights groups from Scandinavia and England and even letters from America. All these proclaimed that the two murderers must be handled humanely, not subjected to torture, not ill treated in any way. And orders had come down from the top: Don't disgrace Italian justice with anything that might offend the left-wing parties in Italy. Kid gloves.

But he, Franco Sebbediccio, would cut through all the nonsense and send a message to the terrorists. Franco Sebbediccio was determined that this Romeo, this Armando Giangi, would commit suicide.

. . .

Romeo had spent his months in prison weaving a romantic dream. Alone in his cell he had chosen to fall in love with the American girl, Dorothea. He remembered her waiting for him at the airport, the tender scar on her chin. In his reveries, she seemed so beautiful, so kind. He tried to remember their conversation that last night he spent with her in the Hamptons. Now in his memory, it seemed to him that she had loved him. That her every gesture had dared him to declare his desire so that she could show her love. He remembered how she sat, so gracefully, so invitingly. How her eyes stared at him, great dark pools of blue, her white skin suffused with blushes. And now he cursed his timidity. He had never touched that skin. He remembered the long slim legs and imposed them around his neck. He imagined the kisses he would rain on her hair, her eyes, the length of her lithe body.

And then Romeo dreamed of how she stood in the sunlight, draped in chains, staring at him in reproach and despair. He weaved fantasies of the future. She would serve only a short term in prison. She would be waiting for him. And he would be freed. By amnesty or by the trading of hostages, perhaps by pure Christian mercy. And then he would find her.

There were nights when he despaired and thought of Yabril's treachery. The murder of Theresa Kennedy had never been in the plan, and he believed in his heart that he would never have consented to such an act. He felt a disgust for Yabril, for his own beliefs, for his own life. Sometimes he would weep quietly in the darkness. Then he would console himself and lose himself in his fantasies of Dorothea. It was false, he knew. It was a weakness, he knew, but he could not help himself.

. . .

Romeo in his bare cell received Franco Sebbediccio with a sardonic grin. He could see the hatred in this old man's peasant eyes, could sense his bewilderment that a person from a good family who enjoyed a pleasant, luxurious life could become a revolutionary. He was also aware that Sebbediccio was frustrated that the international public watch restrained him from treating his prisoner as brutally as he might wish.

Sebbediccio had himself locked in with the prisoner, the two of them alone with two guards and an observer from the governor's office watching but unable to hear from right outside the door. It was almost as if the burly older man were inviting some sort of attack. But Romeo knew that it was simply that the older man had confidence in the authority of his position. Romeo had a contempt for this kind of man, rooted in law and order, handcuffed by his beliefs and bourgeois moral standards. Therefore he was extremely surprised when Sebbediccio said to him casually, but in a very low voice, "Giangi, you are going to make life easier for everyone. You are going to commit suicide."

Romeo laughed. "No, I'm not, I'll be out of jail before you die of high blood pressure and ulcers. I'll walk the streets of Rome when you're lying in your family cemetery. I'll come and sing to the angels on your tombstone. I'll be whistling when I walk away from your grave."

Sebbediccio said patiently, "I just wanted to let you know that you and your cadre are going to commit suicide. Two of my men were killed by your friends to intimidate me and my associates. Your suicides will be my answer."

Romeo said, "I can't please you. I'm enjoying life too much. And with all the world watching, you don't dare to even give me a good kick in the ass."

Sebbediccio gave him a benevolent smile. He had an ace in the hole.

Romeo's father, who all his life had done nothing for humanity, had done something for his son. He had shot himself. A Knight of Malta, father of the murderer of the Pope, a man who had lived his whole life for his own selfish pleasure, he had unfathomably decided to don the mantle of guilt.

When Romeo's newly widowed mother asked to visit her son in his prison cell and was refused, the newspapers took up her cause. The telling blow was struck by Romeo's defense lawyer as he was interviewed on television. "For God's sake, he just wants to see his mother." Which struck a responsive chord not only in Italy but all over the Western world. Many newspapers gave it a front-page headline, quoting verbatim, "For God's sake, he just wants to see his mother!"

Which was not strictly true: Romeo's mother wanted to see him, he did not want to see her.

With pressure so great, the government was forced to allow Mother Giangi to visit her son. Which enraged Franco Sebbediccio, who had opposed this visit; he wanted to keep Romeo in seclusion, to keep him cut off from the outside world. What kind of a world was it that dared grant such kindness to the killer of a Pope? But the governor of the prison overrode him.

The governor had a palatial office and summoned Sebbediccio to it. He said, "My dear sir, I have my instructions, the visit is to be allowed. And not in his cell, where the conversation can be monitored, but in this office itself. With nobody within earshot, but recorded by cameras in the last five minutes of the hour—after all, the media must be allowed to profit."

Sebbediccio said, "And for what reason is this allowed?"

The governor gave him the smile he usually reserved for the prisoners and the members of his staff who had become almost like the prisoners themselves. "For a son to see his widowed mother. What could be more sacred?"

Sebbediccio said harshly, "A man who murders the Pope? He has to see his mother?"

The governor shrugged. "Those far above us have decided. Reconcile yourself. Also, the defense lawyer insists that this office be swept for bugs, so don't think you can plant electronic gear."

"Ah," Sebbediccio said, "and how is the lawyer going to do the debugging?"

"He will hire his own electronic specialists," the governor said. "They will do their job in the lawyer's presence immediately before the meeting."

Sebbediccio said, "It is essential, it is vital that we hear that conversation between them."

"Nonsense," the governor said. "His mother is your typical rich Roman matron. She knows nothing and he would never confide anything of importance to her. This is just another silly episode in the quite ridiculous drama of our times. Don't take it seriously."

But Sebbediccio did take it seriously. He considered it another mockery of justice, another example of scorn for authority. And he hoped Romeo might let something slip when he talked to his mother.

As head of the antiterrorist division for all Italy Sebbediccio had a great deal of power. The defense lawyer was already on the secret list of left-wing radicals who were put under surveillance. His phone was tapped, his mail intercepted and read before it was delivered. And so it was easy to find the electronic company the defense planned to use to sweep the governor's office. Sebbediccio used a friend to set up an "accidental" meeting in a restaurant with the owner of the electronics company.

Even without the help of force, Franco Sebbediccio could be persuasive. It was a small electronics corporation, making a profit but by no means enjoying an overwhelming success. Sebbediccio pointed out that the antiterrorist division had great need of electronic sweeping equipment and personnel, that it could interpose security vetoes on the companies selected. In short that he, Sebbediccio, could make the company rich.

But there must be trust and profit on both sides. In this particular case, why should the electronics company care about the murderers of the Pope, why should it jeopardize its future prosperity over such an inconsequential matter as the recording of a meeting between the mother and son? Why could not the electronics company plant the bug as it was supposedly debugging the governor's office? And who would be the wiser? And Sebbediccio himself would arrange to have the bug removed.

It was done in a very friendly way, but somewhere during the dinner Sebbediccio made it understood that if he was refused, the electronics company would run into a great deal of trouble in the coming years. Although he himself had no personal animosity, how could his government service possibly trust people who protected the murderer of the Pope?

It was all agreed and Sebbediccio let the other man pick up the check. He was certainly not going to pay for it out of his personal funds, and to be reimbursed on his expense voucher might lead to a paper trail years later. Besides, he was going to make the man rich.

The meeting between Armando "Romeo" Giangi and his mother was therefore fully recorded and heard only by Sebbediccio, and he was delighted with it. He took his time in removing the bug simply out of curiosity at what the snotty governor of the prison was really like, but there he got nothing.

Sebbediccio took the precaution of playing the tape in his home while his wife slept. None of his colleagues must know about it. He was not a bad man and he almost wept when Mother Giangi sobbed over her son, implored him to tell the truth that he had not really killed the Pope, that he was shielding a bad companion. Sebbediccio could hear the woman's kisses as they rained down upon the face of her murderous son. Then the kissing and wailing stopped and the conversation became very interesting to Sebbediccio.

He heard Romeo's voice attempting to calm his mother down. "I don't understand why your husband killed himself," Romeo said. He felt such disdain for the man, he could never acknowledge him as his father. "He didn't care about his country or the world, and, forgive me, he didn't even love his family. He lived a completely selfish and egocentric life. Why did he feel it necessary to shoot himself?"

The mother's voice came hissing from the tape. "Out of vanity," she said. "All his life your father was a vain man. Every day to his barber, once a week to his tailor. At the age of forty he took singing lessons. To sing where? And he spent a fortune to become a Knight of Malta and never a man so devoid of the Holy Spirit. On Easter he had a white suit made with the palm cross woven especially into the cloth. Oh, what a grand figure in Roman society. The parties, the balls, his appointment to cultural committees whose meetings he never attended. And the father of a son graduated from the university, he was proud of your brilliance. Oh, how he promenaded on the streets of Rome. I never saw a man so happy and so empty." There was a pause on the tape. "After what you did, your father could never appear in Roman society again. That empty life was finished, and for that loss he killed himself. But he can rest easy. He looked beautiful in his coffin with his new Easter suit."

Then came Romeo's voice on the tape saying what delighted Sebbediccio. "My father never gave me anything in life, and by his suicide he stole my option. And death was my only escape."

Sebbediccio listened to the rest of the tape in which Romeo let his mother persuade him to see a priest, and then when the TV cameras and reporters were let into the room Sebbediccio turned it off. He had seen the rest on TV. But he had what he wanted.

When Sebbediccio paid his next visit to Romeo, he was so delighted that when the jailer unlocked the cell he entered doing a little dance step and greeted Romeo with great joviality.

"Giangi," he said, "you are becoming even more famous. It is rumored that when we have a new Pope he may ask mercy for you. Show your gratitude, give me some of the information I need."

Romeo said, "What an ape you are."

Sebbediccio bowed and said, "That's your last word, then?"

It was perfect. He had a recording that said Romeo was thinking of killing himself.

A week later the news was released to the world that the murderer of the Pope, Armando "Romeo" Giangi, had committed suicide by hanging himself in his cell.

In New York, Annee had mounted the mission. She was very conscious of the fact that she was the first woman chief of a First Hundred operational strike. She was determined she would not fail.

The two safe houses, apartments on New York's East Side, had been stocked with food, weapons and other necessary material. The assault teams would arrive a week before the strike date, and she would order them to stay in their apartments until the final day. The escape routes had been set up for any survivors, through Mexico and Canada. She planned to remain in America for a few months, in still another safe house.

Despite her duties Annee had a lot of time to kill and spent it roaming through the city. She was appalled by the slums, especially Harlem; she thought she had never seen a city so dirty, so ill kept, with whole districts looking as if they had been hit by artillery fire. She was disgusted by the mass of homeless, the snarling rudeness of the service people, the cold hostility of the public servants. She had never been to a place so mean-spirited.

The ever-present danger was another matter. The city was a war zone, more perilous than Sicily, for in Sicily violence had strict laws of self-interest, logically conceived, whereas in New York the violence sprang from the malodorous sickness of some animal herd.

There had come one particularly eventful day that made Annee resolve that she would stay in her apartment as much as possible. She went to a late-afternoon American film, a film that irritated her with its moronic machismo. The muscular hero she would have loved to encounter, just to show him how easy it would be to shoot his balls off.

After the film she had strolled along Lexington Avenue to make calls in public phone booths required by her mission. She went into a famous restaurant to give herself a small treat and was affronted by the rudeness of the staff and enraged by the pale imitation of Roman cuisine offered to her. How dare they. In France the owner of the restaurant would be lynched. In Italy the Mafia would burn the restaurant down as a public service.

So, in truth, it came as a tonic when the city of New York tried to make her submit to the final indignities it visited on thousands of its inhabitants and visitors.

During her late evening stroll, the exercise necessary to enable her to sleep, she suffered two separate attempts to rape or rob her.

The first attack, at the beginning of twilight, truly astonished her. It happened right on Fifth Avenue as she was looking at the display in Tiffany's store window. A man and a woman, very young, not more than twenty, pressed her on either side. The young man had the lynxlike face of the hopeless drug addict. He was extremely ugly, and Annee, who admired physical beauty, immediately disliked him. The young girl was pretty but had the petulance of the spoiled American teenager Annee had observed on the streets. She was dressed in the harlot's mode made fashionable by the latest screen idols. Both were white.

The young man pressed hard against her and Annee felt hard metal through the thin jacket she was wearing. She was not alarmed.

"I've got a gun," the young man whispered. "Give my girl your bag. Nice and friendly. No fuss and you won't get hurt."

"Do you vote?" Annee asked.

The young man, distracted, said, "What?" His girlfriend stretched out her hand for the bag. Annee took the girl's hand, then swung her around as a shield, at the same time using her other hand to hit the girl full in the face with her ringed other hand. An incredible amount of blood splashed

Tiffany's elegantly dressed window, causing passersby to stop in amazement.

Annee said coolly to the young man, "You've got a gun, shoot." By this time he had swung his body around away from where he held the gun in his pocket. The fool had seen that move in gangster movies. He didn't know it was a completely useless stance unless the victim froze. But to be on the safe side she grabbed the man's other arm and pulled it out of its socket. As the young man screamed in agony his hand came out of the pocket and a screwdriver clanged against the pavement. Of course, Annee thought, stupid adolescent cunning. She walked away from them.

At this point it would have been prudent to return to her apartment, but out of some territorial imperative she continued her stroll. But then, right on Central Park South, lined with its expensive luxury hotels, guarded by its uniformed doormen, and limousines parked along the street with burly chauffeurs, she was surrounded by four black youths.

They were handsome high-spirited fellows that she liked on sight. They were very much like the youthful rascals in Rome who felt it their duty to accost women in the streets. One of the youths said to her playfully, "Hey, baby, take a walk in the park with us. You'll have a good time."

They barred her path, she could not move forward. She was amused by them, she did not doubt she would have a good time. It was not they who angered her, it was the doormen and the chauffeurs who deliberately ignored her plight.

"Go away," she said, "or I'll scream and those doormen will call the police." She knew she could not scream, could not afford to do so because of her mission.

One of the youths, grinning, said, "Go ahead and scream, lady." But she could see them poised on their toes ready to flee.

When she did not scream, another of the youths understood immediately that she would not. "Hey, she won't scream," he said. "You hear her accent? I bet she has some drugs. Hey, lady, give us some."

They all laughed with delight. One of them said, "Or else we'll call the police." And they laughed again.

Before leaving Italy, Annee had been briefed on the dangers of New York. But she was a highly trained operational agent and had absolute confidence in that training. So she had refused to carry a gun, fearing that it might compromise the mission. However she wore a specially designed zircon ring that could do a great deal of damage. And in her handbag was a pair of scissors more lethal than a Venetian dagger. So she did not feel herself in any danger. She only worried about the police becoming involved and being questioned by them. She was sure that she could escape without any fuss.

But she had not taken into account her nervousness and natural ferocity. One of the youths reached out a hand to touch her hair and Annee hissed, "Get out of my way, you black bastard, or I'll kill you."

All four went quiet, their good humor gone. She saw the hurt brooding look come into their eyes and she felt a pang of guilt. She realized that she had made a mistake. She had called them black bastards out of no racial prejudice. It was merely a form of Sicilian invective, where when you quarreled with a hunchback you called him a hunchback bastard, if you quarreled with a cripple you called him a cripple bastard. But how could these young men know this? She almost apologized. But it was too late.

One of the youths said, "I'm gonna punch this white cunt in the face." And in that moment Annee went out of control. She flicked her ringed hand into his eye. A hideous slit appeared that seemed to detach the youth's eyelid from his face. The other youths stared in horror as Annee calmly turned a corner and then ran.

That was enough even for Annee. Back in her apartment she was filled with remorse for having been so rough, for endangering the mission with her willfulness. She had actually sought out trouble to relieve her own attack of nerves.

She must take no further risks, she must not leave the apartment except for the duties necessary to complete the mission. She must stop calling up her memories of Romeo, control her rage at his murder. And most important of all she must make a final decision. If all else failed, would she turn this into a suicide mission?

Christian Klee flew to Rome to have dinner with Sebbediccio. He noted that Sebbediccio had almost twenty bodyguards, which did not seem to affect his appetite.

The Italian was in high spirits. "Wasn't it fortunate that our Pope killer took his own life?" he said to Klee. "What a circus the trial would have been with all our left-wingers marching in support. It's too bad that fellow Yabril wouldn't do you the same favor."

Klee laughed. "Different systems of government. I see you're well protected."

Sebbediccio shrugged. "I think they are after bigger game. I have some information for you. That woman, Annee, that we've let run loose. Somehow we lost her. But we suspect that she's now in America."

Klee felt a thrill of excitement. "Do you know what port of embarkation? What name she is using?"

"We don't know," Sebbediccio said. "But we think she is now operational."

"Why didn't you pick her up?" Christian said.

"I have high hopes for her," Sebbediccio said. "She is a very determined young lady and she will go far in the terrorist movement. I want to use a big net when I take her. But you have a problem, my friend. We hear rumors that there is an operation in the United States. It can only be against Kennedy. Annee, as fierce as she may be, cannot do it alone. Therefore, there must be other people involved. Knowing your security for the President, they will have to mount an operation that would require a goodly number with material and safe houses. On that I have no information. You had better set to work."

Klee did not need to ask why the Italian security chief had not sent this information through regular channels to Washington. He knew Sebbediccio did not want his close surveillance of Annee made part of an official record in the United States; he did not trust the Freedom of Information Act in America. Also, he wanted Christian Klee in his personal debt.

In Sherhaben, Sultan Maurobi received Christian Klee with the utmost friendliness, as if there had never been the crisis of a few months before. The Sultan was affable but appeared on guard and a little puzzled. "I hope you bring me good news," he said to Klee. "After all the regrettable unpleasantness, I am very anxious to repair relations with the United States and, of course, your President Kennedy. In fact, I hope your visit is in regard to this matter."

Klee smiled. "I came for that very purpose," he said. "You are in a position, I think, to do us a service that might heal the breach."

"Ah, I am very happy to hear that," the Sultan said. "You know, of course, that I was not privy to Yabril's intentions. I had no foreknowledge of what Yabril would do to the President's daughter. Of course, I have expressed this officially, but would you tell the President personally that I have grieved over this for the past months. I was powerless to avert the tragedy."

Klee believed him, that the murder had not been in the original plans. And he thought how all-powerful men like Sultan Maurobi and Francis Kennedy were helpless in the face of uncontrollable events, the will of other men.

But now he said to the Sultan, "Your giving up Yabril has reassured the President on that point." This they both knew was mere politeness. Klee paused for a moment and then went on. "But I'm here to ask you to do me a personal service. You know I am responsible for the safety of my President. I have information that there is a plot to assassinate him. That terrorists have already infiltrated into the United States. But it would be helpful if I could get information as to their plans and to their identity and location. I thought that with your contacts you might have heard something through your intelligence agencies. That you might give me some scraps of information. Let me emphasize that it will only be between the two of us. You and I. There will be no official connection."

The Sultan seemed astonished. His intelligent face screwed up into an expression of amused disbelief. "How can you think such a thing?" he asked. "After all your destruction, after all our tragedies, would I get involved in such dangerous activities? I am the ruler of a small rich country that is powerless to remain independent without the friendship of great powers. I can do nothing for you or against you."

Klee nodded his head in agreement. "Of course that is true. But Bert Audick came to visit you and I know that had to do with the oil industry. But let me tell you that Mr. Audick is in very serious trouble in the United States. He would be a very bad ally for you to have in the coming years."

"And you would be a very good ally?" the Sultan asked, smiling.

"Yes," Klee said. "I am the ally that could save you. If you cooperate with me now."

"Explain," the Sultan said. He was obviously angered by the implied threat.

Klee spoke very carefully. "Bert Audick is under indictment for conspiracy against the United States government because his mercenaries or those of his company fired on our planes bombing your city of Dak. And there are other charges. His oil empire could be destroyed under certain of our laws. He is not a strong ally at this moment."

The Sultan said slyly, "Indicted but not convicted. I understand that will be more difficult."

"That is true," Klee said. "But in a few months Francis Kennedy will be reelected. His popularity will bring in a Congress that will ratify his programs. He will be the most powerful President in the history of the United States. Then Audick is doomed, I can assure you. And the power structure of which he is a part will be destroyed."

"I still fail to see how I can help you," the Sultan said. And then more imperiously, "Or how you can help me. I understand you are in a delicate position yourself in your own country."

"That may or may not be true," Klee said. "As for my position, which is delicate, as you say, that will be resolved when Kennedy is reelected. I am his closest friend and closest adviser and Kennedy is noted for his loyalty. As to how we can help each other, let me be direct without intending any disrespect. May I do so?"

The Sultan seemed to be impressed and even amused by this courtesy. "By all means," he said.

Klee said, "First, and most important, here is how I can help you. I can be your ally. I have the ear of the President of the United States and I have his trust. We live in difficult times."

The Sultan interrupted smilingly, "I have always lived in difficult times."

"And so you can appreciate what I am saying better than most," Klee retorted sharply.

"And what if your Kennedy does not achieve his aims?" the Sultan said. "Accidents befall, heaven is not always kind."

Christian Klee was cold now as he answered, "What you are saying is, what if the plot to kill Kennedy succeeds? I am here to tell you that it will not. I don't care how clever and daring the assassins may be. And if they try and fail and there is any trace to you, then you will be destroyed. But it doesn't have to come to that. I'm a reasonable man and I understand your position. What I propose is an exchange of information between you and myself on a personal basis. I don't know what Audick proposed to you, but I'm a better bet. If Audick and his crowd wins, you still win. He doesn't know about us. If Kennedy wins, you have me as your ally. I'm your insurance."

The Sultan nodded and then led him to a sumptuous banquet. During the meal the sultan asked Klee innumerable questions about Kennedy. Then finally, almost hesitantly, he asked about Yabril.

Klee looked him directly in the eye. "There is no way that Yabril can escape his fate. If his fellow terrorists think they can get him released by holding even the most important of hostages, tell them to forget about it. Kennedy will never let him go."

The Sultan sighed. "Your Kennedy has changed," he said. "He sounds like a man going berserk." Klee didn't answer. The Sultan went on very slowly. "I think you have convinced me," he said. "I think you and I should become allies."

When Christian Klee returned to the United States, the first person he went to see was the Oracle. The old man received him in his bedroom suite, sitting in his motorized wheelchair, an English tea spread on the table in front of him, a comfortable armchair waiting for Christian opposite.

The Oracle greeted him with a slight wave to indicate that he should sit down. Christian served him tea and a tiny bit of cake and a small finger sandwich, then served himself. The Oracle took a sip of tea and crumbled the bit of cake in his mouth. They sat there for a long moment.

Then the Oracle tried to smile, a slight movement of the lips, the skin so dead it barely moved. "You've got yourself into a fine mess for your fucking friend Kennedy," he said.

The vulgarism, spoken as if from the mouth of an innocent child, made Christian smile. Again he wondered, was it a mark of senility, a decaying of the brain, that the Oracle who had never used profanity was now using it so freely? He waited until he had eaten one of the sandwiches and gulped down some hot tea, then he answered, "Which fix?" he said. "I'm in a lot of them."

"I'm talking about that atom bomb thing," the Oracle

said. "The rest of the shit doesn't matter. But they are accusing you of being responsible for the murder of thousands of citizens of this country. They've got the goods on you, it seems, but I refuse to believe you to be so stupid. Inhuman, yes—after all, you're in politics. Did you really do it?" The old man was not judgmental, just curious.

Who else in the world was there to tell? Who else in the world would understand? "What I'm astonished about," Klee said, "is how quickly they got on to me."

"The human mind *leaps* to an understanding of evil," the Oracle said. "You are surprised because there is a certain innocence in the doer of an evil deed. He thinks the deed so terrible that it is inconceivable to another human being. But that is the first thing they jump at. Evil is no mystery at all, love is the mystery." He paused for a moment, started to speak again and then relaxed back in his chair, his eyes half closed, dozing.

"You have to understand," Christian said, "that letting something happen is so much easier than actually doing something. There was the crisis, Francis Kennedy was going to be impeached by the Congress. And I thought just for a second, if only the atom bomb exploded it would turn things around. It was in that moment that I told Peter Cloot not to interrogate Gresse and Tibbot. I had the time to do it. The whole thing flashed by in that one second and it was done."

The Oracle said, "Give me some more hot tea and another piece of cake." He put the cake in his mouth, tiny crumbs appearing on his scarlike lips. "Yes or no: Did you interrogate Gresse and Tibbot before the bomb exploded? You got the information out of them and then didn't act on it?"

Christian sighed. "They were only kids. I squeezed them dry in five minutes. That's why I couldn't have Cloot at the interrogation. But I didn't want the bomb to explode. It just went so quick."

The Oracle started to laugh. It was a curious laugh even in so old a man. It was a series of grunted heh, heh, heh's. "You've got it ass backwards," the Oracle said. "You had already made up your mind that you would let the bomb explode. Before you told Cloot not to interrogate them. It didn't go by in a second, you planned it all out."

Christian Klee was a little startled. What the Oracle said was true.

"And all this to save your hero, Francis Kennedy," the Oracle said. "The man who can do no wrong except when he sets the whole world on fire." The Oracle had placed a box of thin Havana cigars on the table; Christian took one of them and lit it. "You were lucky," the Oracle said. "Those people that were killed were mostly worthless. The drunken, the homeless, the criminal. And it's not so great a crime. Not in the history of our human race."

"Francis really gave me the go-ahead," Klee said. And that made the Oracle touch a button on his chair so that the back of it straightened to make his body upright and alert.

"Your saintly President?" the Oracle said. "He is far too much a victim of his own hypocrisy, as all the Kennedys were. He could never be party to such an act."

"Maybe I'm just trying to make excuses," Christian said. "It was nothing explicit. But I know Francis so intimately, we're almost like brothers. I asked him for the order so that the medical interrogation team would be able to do a brain probe. That would have settled the whole atom bomb problem immediately. And Francis refused to sign the authorization. Sure, he gave his grounds, good civil libertarian and humanitarian grounds. That was in his character. But that was in his character before his daughter was killed. Not in his character afterwards. And this *was* afterwards. Remember, he had already ordered the destruction of Dak by this time. He gave the threat that he would destroy the whole Sultanate of Sherhaben if the hostages were not released. So his character had changed. His new character would have signed the medical interrogation order. And then when he refused to sign, he gave me a look, I can't describe it, but it was almost as if he were telling me to let it happen."

The Oracle was fully alive now. He spoke sharply. "All that doesn't matter. What matters is that you save your ass. If Kennedy doesn't get reelected, you may spend years in jail. And even if Kennedy gets reelected, there may be some danger."

"Kennedy will win the election," Christian said. "And after that, I'll be OK." He paused for a moment. "I know him."

"You know the old Kennedy," the Oracle said. Then as if he had lost interest he said, "And how about my birthday party? I'm a hundred years old and nobody gives a shit."

Christian laughed. "I do. Don't worry. After the election you'll have a birthday party in the White House Rose Garden. A birthday party for a king."

The Oracle smiled with pleasure, then said slyly, "And your Francis Kennedy will be the king. You do know, don't you, that if he is reelected and carries his congressional candidates with him, he will in effect be a dictator?"

"That's highly unlikely," Christian Klee said. "There has never been a dictator in this country. We have safeguards—too many safeguards, I think sometimes."

"Ah," the Oracle said, "this is a young country yet. We have time. And the Devil takes many seductive forms."

They were silent for a long time, and then Christian rose

to take his leave. They always touched hands when they parted; the Oracle was too fragile for a real handshake.

"Be careful," the Oracle said. "When a man rises to absolute power, he usually gets rid of those closest to him, those who know his secrets."

CHAPTER
22

A FEDERAL JUDGE set Henry Tibbot and Adam Gresse free.

The government did not contest that the arrest had been illegal. The government did not contest that there had been no warrants. Gresse and Tibbot's defense team had exploited every legal loophole.

The people of America were enraged. They blamed the Kennedy administration, they cursed the judicial system. Mobs gathered in the streets of the great cities calling for the death of Gresse and Tibbot. Vigilante groups formed to carry out the justice of the people.

Gresse and Tibbot fled to a hiding place in South America and disappeared into a sanctuary financed by their wealthy parents.

• • •

Two months before the presidential election, polls showed that Francis Kennedy's margin of victory would not be enough to carry his congressional candidates into office.

There were more problems: a scandal involving Eugene Dazzy's mistress; the lingering charges that Attorney General Christian Klee had deliberately permitted the explosion of the atom bomb; the scandal of Canoo and Klee using the funds of the office of the military adviser to beef up the Secret Service.

And perhaps Francis Kennedy himself went too far. America was not ready for his brand of socialism. It was not ready to reject the corporate structure of America. The people of America did not want to be equal, they wanted to be rich. Nearly all the states had their own lottery with prizes running high up into the millions. More people bought lottery tickets than voted in the national elections.

The power of the congressmen and senators already in office was also overwhelming. They had their staffs paid for by the government. They had the vast sums of money contributed by the corporate structure, which they used to dominate TV with brilliantly executed ads. By holding government office they could appear on special political programs on TV and in the newspapers, increasing their name-recognition factor.

With the delicate precision of a Renaissance poisoner, Lawrence Salentine had organized the overall campaign against Kennedy so brilliantly that he was now the leader of the Socrates Club group.

President Kennedy studied his staff report, which predicted that his handpicked candidates for Congress would probably not be elected. The thought that he might again be an impotent leader had a physical effect on him. He felt ill. And beyond that he felt a strange rage that was full of a repugnant malice. He was ashamed of this emotion and concentrated on the classified operational plans from Christian Klee.

He noted that Christian had channeled this report directly to the President. And it was just as well. The information was horrifying, but even more extraordinary was Klee's plan on how to handle the problem.

There would be a sacrifice of moral principle involved, Kennedy thought, and then quite consciously knowing the cost, he scribbled his consent on the memos.

On the third day of September, Christian Klee went to the office of the Vice President unannounced. As an extra precaution, he gave special instructions to Helen Du Pray's Secret Service detail chief before he presented himself to Du Pray's secretary and said his business was urgent.

The Vice President was astonished to see him; it was against all protocol that he should visit her without advance warning or even permission. For a moment he was afraid she might take offense, but she was too intelligent to do so. She knew immediately that Christian Klee would breach protocol only for the most serious problem. In fact, what she felt was apprehension. What new terrible thing could have happened now after the past months?

Klee sensed this uneasiness immediately. "There's nothing to be worried about," he said. "It's just that we have a security problem involving the President. As part of our coverage, we have sealed off your office. It would be best that you not answer the phone but deal with your immediate staff. I will remain with you the entire day, personally."

Du Pray understood immediately that no matter what happened, she was not to take command of the country and that was why Klee was there. "If the President has a security problem, why are you with me?" she said. But without waiting for an answer from Klee, she said, "I will have to check this with the President, personally."

"He is appearing at a political luncheon in New York," Klee said.

"I know that," she said.

Klee looked at his watch. "The President will be calling you in about one half hour," he said.

When the call came, Klee watched Helen Du Pray's face. She seemed to show no astonishment; only twice she asked questions. Good, Klee thought, she would be OK, he didn't have to worry about her. Then she did something that aroused Christian's admiration; he didn't think she had it in her—vice presidents were noted for their timidity. She asked Kennedy if she could speak to Eugene Dazzy, the President's chief of staff. When Dazzy came on the phone, she made a simple query about their work schedule for the next week. Then she hung up. She had been checking to see if the person on the phone had really been Kennedy, despite the fact that she recognized his voice. Of the questions she had asked, only Dazzy would recognize the reference. She was making sure that there was no voice impersonation.

She addressed Klee icily; she knew something was fishy, Klee thought. She said, "The President has informed me that you will be using my office as a command post, that I will be under your instruction. I find this extraordinary. Perhaps you will give me an explanation."

"I apologize for all this," Klee said. "If I could have some coffee, I'll give you a full briefing. You will know as much as the President about this matter." Which was true but a little devious. She would not know as much as Klee.

Helen Du Pray was studying him very intently. She didn't

trust him, Klee knew. But women didn't understand power, they didn't understand the stark efficiency of violence. He gathered up all his energy to convince her of his sincerity. When he was through almost an hour later, she seemed won over. She was a very beautiful woman and intelligent, Christian thought. Too bad that she would never become the President of the United States.

On this glorious summer day, President Francis Kennedy was to speak at a political luncheon held in New York City's Sheraton Hotel Convention Center, which would be followed by a triumphal motorcade down Fifth Avenue. Then he would make a speech near the atom bomb destruction area. The event had been scheduled three months before and had been well publicized. It was the kind of situation that Christian Klee detested, the President was too exposed. There were deranged people, and even the police were a danger in Klee's eyes because they were armed and also because as a police force they were completely demoralized by the uncontrolled crime in the city.

Klee took his own elaborate precautions. Only his operational staff in the Secret Service knew the awesome detail and manpower that was used to protect the President in his rare public appearances.

Special advance teams had been sent ahead. These teams patrolled and searched the area of the visit twenty-four hours a day. Two days before the visit, another thousand men were sent to become part of the crowds that would greet the President. These men formed a line on both sides of the motorcade and in the front of the motorcade and acted as part of the crowd but actually formed a sort of Maginot line. Another five hundred men manned the rooftops, constantly scanning the windows that overlooked the motorcade, and these men were very heavily armed. In addition to this there was the President's own special and personal detail, which numbered a hundred men. And then, of course, there were the Secret Service men under deep cover who were accredited to newspapers and TV stations, who carried newspaper photo cameras and manned mobile TV vehicles.

And Christian Klee had other tricks up his sleeve. In the nearly four years of the Kennedy administration there had been five assassination attempts. None of them had even come close. The would-be killers had been crazies, of course, and were now behind bars in the toughest federal prisons. And Klee made sure that if they got out, he would find a reason to put them back in again. It was impossible to jail all the lunatics in the United States who made threats to kill the President of the United States—by mail, by phone, by conspiring, by shouting it in the streets—but Christian Klee had made their lives miserable for them, so that they would be too busy preserving their own safety to worry about grandiose ideas. He put them under mail surveillance, phone surveillance, personal surveillance, computer surveillance. If they spit on the sidewalk, they were in trouble.

All these precautions, all these arrangements, were in effect this September third when President Francis Xavier Kennedy gave his speech at the political luncheon at the Sheraton Convention Center in New York. Hundreds of Secret Service men were scattered through the audience, and the building was sealed off after his entrance.

On that same September third, Annee went shopping on Fifth Avenue. In her three weeks in the United States, she had helped move everything into place. She had made her phone calls, had her meeting with the two assassination teams that had finally made their way to New York as crewmen on one of Bert Audick's oil tankers. They moved into the two apartments prepared for them. These apartments had already been stocked with weapons procured by a special underground logistics team that had no part of the central plan.

Annee could not know that Christian Klee's FBI was picking up her phone calls in the very air, that every move she made was covered. And that the teams' phone calls to her in the public booths had been intercepted and read by Christian Klee.

What she had not confessed to anyone was her decision to turn this into a suicide mission.

Annee thought how strange it was that she would go shopping just four hours before what would be the end of her life.

Sal Troyca and Elizabeth Stone were working hard at the office, piecing together information that would prove Christian Klee could have prevented the explosion of the atom bomb.

Elizabeth Stone's town house was only a ten-minute ride away. So, at lunchtime, they spent a couple of hours in bed.

Once in bed, they forgot all the stress of the day. After an hour Elizabeth went into the bathroom to take a shower and Sal wandered into the living room, still naked, to turn on the TV. He stood in amazement at what he was seeing. He watched for a few moments longer and then ran into the bathroom and pulled Elizabeth out of the shower. She was a little frightened by his roughness as he dragged her naked and dripping wet into the living room.

There, watching the TV screen, she began to weep. Sal took her in his arms. "Look at it this way," he said, "our troubles are over."

The campaign speech in New York on September third was to be one of the most important stops in President Francis Kennedy's bid for reelection. And it had been planned to have a great psychological effect on the nation.

First, there would be a luncheon at the Sheraton Convention Center on Fifty-eighth Street. There, the President would address the most important and influential men of the city. The luncheon would raise additional funds to rebuild the midtown area in New York that had been leveled by the atom bomb explosion. An architect, without a fee, had designed a great memorial for the devastated area, and the rest of the acreage was to be a small park with a tiny lake. The city was to buy and donate the land.

After the luncheon, the Kennedy party would lead a motorcade that would begin at 125th Street and go down Seventh and Fifth avenues to place the first symbolic wreath of marble on the rubbled heap that remained of Times Square.

As one of the sponsors of the luncheon, Louis Inch was seated on the dais with President Kennedy and expected to accompany him to his waiting car, thus getting some newspaper and TV coverage. But to his surprise, he was cut off by Secret Service men who isolated Kennedy in a human net. The President was escorted through a door at the rear of the platform.

In the streets outside, huge crowds gathered. The Secret Service had cleared the area so that there was a space of at least a hundred feet around the presidential limousine. There were enough Secret Service men to protect the inner hundred feet with a solid phalanx. Outside that, the crowd was controlled by the police. On the edge of this perimeter were photographers and TV camera crews, who immediately surged forward when the advance guard of Secret Service men came out of the hotel. And then, unaccountably, there was a fifteen-minute wait.

The President finally emerged from the hotel shielded from the TV cameras as he rushed toward his waiting car. At that very moment the avenue exploded into a beautifully choreographed bloody ballet.

Six men burst through the police restraining line, mowing down part of the police wall and running toward the President's armored limousine. A second later, another group of six men burst through the opposite perimeter and raked the fifty Secret Service men around the armored limousine with their automatic weapons.

In the very next second eight cars swung into the open area and Secret Service men in combat gear and bulletproof vests that made them seem like gigantic balloons came tumbling out with shotguns and machine pistols and caught the attackers in the rear. They shot with precision and short bursts. In less than thirty seconds, all twelve attackers were lying in the avenue dead, their guns silenced. The presidential limousine roared away from the curb, other Secret Service cars following.

At that moment, Annee, with a supreme effort of will, stepped in the path of the presidential limousine with her two Bloomingdale shopping bags in her hand. The shopping bags were filled with explosive gel, two powerful bombs that she detonated as the car, too late, tried to swerve but hit her. The presidential car flew up into the air at least ten feet off the ground and came down a mass of flames. The force of the explosion blew everyone inside it to bits. And there was absolutely nothing left of Annee except tiny bits of gaily colored paper from the shopping bags.

One TV cameraman had the wit to swing his camera for

a panoramic shot of everything that was visible. Thousands of people had flung themselves to the ground when the firing broke out and were still lying prone as if begging some unforgiving God for mercy. From that prone mass issued streams of blood that came from those who had been hit by the heavy fire from the assassination teams or killed by the explosion of the powerful bombs. Many in the crowd had suffered concussions and, when the terror stopped, rose and staggered in confusion. The camera caught all this for television to horrify the nation.

In the office of Vice President Du Pray, Christian Klee jumped out of his chair and cried out, "What the fuck happened!"

Helen Du Pray stared at the TV screen and then said sharply to Klee, "Who was the poor bastard who took the President's place?"

"One of my Secret Service men," Christian Klee said. "They were *not* supposed to get that close."

Du Pray was looking at Klee very coldly. And then she became angrier than he had ever seen her. "Why the hell didn't you cancel the whole thing?" she shouted. "Why didn't you avert this whole tragedy? There are citizens dead out there in the street who came to see their President. You've wasted the lives of your own men. I promise you, your actions will be questioned by me to the President and to the appropriate congressional committee."

"You don't know what the hell you're talking about," Klee said. "Do you know how many threats are made against the President every day? If we listened to all of them, the President would be a prisoner in the White House."

Helen Du Pray was studying his face while he spoke.

"Why did you use a double *this* time?" she said. "That is an extreme measure. And if it was *that* serious, why did you have the President go there at all?"

"When you are the President, you can ask me those questions," Klee said curtly.

"Where is Francis now?"

Klee stared at her for a moment as if he would not answer. "He's on his way to Washington. We don't know how extensive this plot is, so we want him here. He is very safe."

Du Pray said in a sardonic voice, "OK, now *I* know he's safe. I assume you've briefed the other members of the staff, *they* know he's safe, what about the people of America? When will *they* know he's safe?"

Klee said, "Dazzy has made all the arrangements. The President will go on television and speak to the nation as soon as he sets foot in the White House."

"That's rather a long wait," the Vice President said. "Why can't you notify the media and reassure people now?"

"Because we don't know what's out there," Klee told her smoothly. "And maybe it won't hurt the American public to worry about him a bit."

In that moment, it seemed to Helen Du Pray that she understood everything. She understood that Klee could have cut the whole thing off before it reached the culminating point. She felt an overwhelming contempt for the man, and then, remembering the charges that he could have stopped the atom bomb explosion but didn't, she was convinced that that charge was also true.

But most of all she felt despair: she realized that Klee could never have done this without President Francis Kennedy's consent.

CHAPTER
23

THE ASSASSINATION ATTEMPT rocketed Kennedy to the top of the polls. In November, Francis Xavier Kennedy was reelected to the presidency of the United States. It was a victory so overwhelming that it carried into office nearly all his handpicked candidates for the House and Senate. At long last the President controlled both houses of Congress.

In the period before the inauguration, from November to January, Francis Kennedy set his administration to work drafting new laws for his new and cooperative Congress. In rallying support he was helped by the newspapers and TV, which were weaving fantasies to the effect that Gresse and Tibbot were linked with Yabril and the attempted assassination of the President in one giant conspiracy. The news weeklies had given the issue extensive front-page coverage.

When President Kennedy submitted to his staff his revolutionary plans for transforming the government of the United

States, they were secretly horrified. Big business was to be crippled by strongly chartered regulatory agencies. The corporations would become subject to criminal penalties rather than to civil law intervention. It was clear that the end result would be indictments under the RICO laws. In fact Kennedy had jotted down the names of Inch, Salentine, Audick and Greenwell.

Kennedy emphasized that the surest way to gain public support for his proposal was to eradicate crime in American society. In his plans were proposed amendments to the Constitution that would impose Draconian penalties on criminals. Not only would the rules of evidence be changed, but by law the brain-probe truth test would become mandatory in criminal cases.

But most startling of all was the proposal to establish criminal colonies in the wilds of Alaska for three-time offenders. In effect, life sentences.

Francis Kennedy told his staff: "I want you to study these proposals. If you can't go along with them, even though it will be hurtful to me personally, I am prepared to accept your resignation. I expect your answers within three days."

It was during those three days that Oddblood Gray requested a private meeting with the President. They met in the Yellow Oval Room over lunch.

Gray was extremely formal, deliberately erasing his past relationship with Kennedy. "Mr. President," he said, "I must state to you that I oppose your program to control crime in this country."

Kennedy said gravely, "Those programs are necessary. Finally we have a Congress that will pass the necessary laws."

"I cannot go along with those work camps in Alaska," Gray said.

"Why not?" Kennedy asked. "Only habitual offenders will go. Hundreds of years ago England solved the same problem by sending its criminals to Australia. That worked very well for both sides."

Kennedy had been curt, but Oddblood Gray was in no way intimidated. He said bitterly, "You know that the majority of those criminals will be black."

"Then let them stop committing criminal acts," Kennedy said. "Let them join the political process."

Gray shot back, "Then let your big corporations stop using blacks for slave labor—"

"Get off it, Otto," Kennedy said. "This is not a racial issue. In the years gone by we worked together. I've proved to you many times I'm no racist. Now you can trust me or trust the Socrates Club."

"On this we trust nobody," Oddblood Gray said.

"I'll give you the reality," Kennedy said almost angrily. "Black criminals will be weeded out from the black population. What's wrong with that? Black people are the chief victims. Why should the victims protect their predators? Otto, I have to be frank. White people in this country, rightly or wrongly, are deathly afraid of the black criminal class. What's wrong with most of the black population being integrated into the middle class?"

"What you're proposing is to wipe out a big part of a generation of young blacks," Gray said. "That's the bottom line. I say no." He paused for a moment and then said, "Say I trust you, Francis, what about the next President? He may use that camp to imprison political revolutionaries."

"That's not my intent," Kennedy said. He smiled. "And I may be around longer than you think."

That statement chilled Gray. Was Kennedy thinking of

amending the Constitution so that he could run for a third term? Alarm bells went off in Gray's brain.

"It's not all that simple," he said. And then boldly: "You could change."

And at that moment he could *feel* Kennedy change. Suddenly they had become enemies.

"Either you are with me or you are not," Kennedy said. "You accuse me of wiping out a whole generation of blacks. That is not true. They are going to a work camp where they will be educated and disciplined to support the social contract. I will be far more drastic with the Socrates Club. They don't get that option. I am going to wipe them out."

Gray saw that Kennedy had no doubts. He had never seen the President so resolute or so cold. He felt himself weakening. And then Kennedy put his hand on his shoulder and said, "Otto, don't desert me now. We will build a great America."

"I'll give you my answer after the inaugural," Gray said. "But, Francis, this is agony for me, don't betray me. If my people have to freeze their black asses in Alaska, I want a lot of white asses to freeze with them."

President Kennedy met with his staff in the Cabinet Room. Also present by special invitation were Vice President Du Pray and Dr. Annaccone. Kennedy knew he had to be very careful—these were the people who knew him best, he must not let them divine his actual agenda. He said to them, "Dr. Annaccone has something to say that may astound you."

Kennedy listened abstractedly while Annaccone announced that the PET scan had been perfected so that the 10 percent risk of cardiac arrest and complete memory loss had been reduced to one tenth of 1 percent. He smiled faintly when Helen Du Pray voiced her outrage at any free citizen's being forced by law to take such a test. He had expected that of her. He smiled also when Dr. Annaccone showed his hurt feelings—Zed was too learned a man to be so thin-skinned.

He listened with less amusement when Gray, Wix and Dazzy agreed with the Vice President. He had correctly predicted that Christian Klee would not speak.

They were all watching Kennedy, waiting for him, trying to see which way he would go. He would have to convince them he was right. He began slowly. "I know all the difficulties," he said, "but I am determined to make this test part of our legal system. Not totally—there is still some degree of danger, small as it is. Though Dr. Annaccone has assured me that with further research, even that will be reduced to zero. But this is a scientific test that will revolutionize our society. Never mind the difficulties, we will iron them out."

Annaccone said quietly, "Congress will not pass such a law."

"We'll make them," Kennedy said grimly. "Other countries will use it. Other intelligence agencies will use it. We have to." He laughed and said to Annaccone, "I'll have to cut your budget. Your discoveries cause too much trouble, and put all the lawyers out of work. But with this test no innocent man will ever be found guilty."

Very deliberately he rose and walked to the doors that looked out onto the Rose Garden. Then he said, "I will show how much I believe in this. Our enemies constantly accuse me of being responsible for the atom bomb going off. They say that I could have stopped it. Euge, I want you to help Dr. Annaccone set it up for me. I want to be the first to undergo the PET scan test. Immediately. Arrange for witnessing, the legal formalities."

He smiled at Klee. "They will ask the question 'Are you in any way responsible for the explosion of the atom bomb?'

And I will answer." He paused for a moment and then said, "I will take the test, and so will my Attorney General. Right, Chris?"

"Sure," Klee joked uneasily. "But you first."

At Walter Reed Hospital, the suite reserved for President Kennedy had a special conference room. In it were the President and his personal staff, Wix, Gray, Dazzy and Du Pray, along with Congressman Jintz and Senator Lambertino, and a panel of three qualified physicians who would monitor and verify the results of the brain-scan test. Now they listened to Dr. Annaccone as he explained the procedure.

Dr. Annaccone prepared his slides and turned on the projector. Then he began his lecture. He said, "This test is, as some of you already know, an infallible lie-detector test, the truth assessed by measuring the levels of activity from certain chemicals in the brain. This has been done by the refinement of positron emission tomography (PET) scans. The procedure was first shown to work in a limited way at Washington University School of Medicine in St. Louis. Slides were made of human brains at work."

A large slide showed on the huge white screen in front of them. Then another, and another. Brilliant colors appeared, lighting up the different parts of the brain as patients read, listened or spoke. Or simply just thought about the meaning of a word. Dr. Annaccone used blood and glucose to tag them with radioactive labels.

"In essence, under the PET scan," Dr. Annaccone said, "the brain speaks in living color. A spot in back of the brain lights up during reading. In the middle of the brain against that background of dark blue, you can see an irregular white spot appear with a tiny blotch of pink and a seepage of blue.

That appears during speech. In the front of the brain, a similar spot lights up during the thinking process. Over these images we have laid a magnetic resonance image of the brain's anatomy. The whole brain is now a magic lantern."

Dr. Annaccone looked around the room to see if everyone was following him. Then he went on, "You see that spot in the middle of the brain changing? When a subject lies, there is an increase in the amount of blood flowing through the brain, which then projects another image."

Startlingly, in the center of the white spot there was now a circle of red within a larger yellow irregular field. "The subject is lying," Dr. Annaccone said. "When we test the President, that red spot within the yellow is what we must look for." Dr. Annaccone nodded to the President. "Now we will proceed to the examining room," he said.

Inside the lead-walled room, Francis Kennedy lay on the cold hard table. Behind him a large long metal cylinder loomed. As Dr. Annaccone strapped the plastic mask over Kennedy's forehead and across his chin, Kennedy felt a momentary shiver of fear. He hated anything over his face. His arms were then tied down along his sides. Then he felt Dr. Annaccone slide the table into the cylinder. Inside the cylinder it was narrower than he expected. Blacker. Silent. Now he was surrounded by a ring of radioactive detection crystals.

Then Kennedy heard the echo of Dr. Annaccone's voice instructing him to look at the white cross directly in front of his eyes. The voice sounded hollow. "You must keep your eyes on the cross," the doctor repeated.

In a room five stories below, in the basement of the hospital, a pneumatic tube held a syringe containing radioactive oxygen, a cyclotron of tagged water.

When the order came from the scanning room above, that tube flew, a lead rocket twisting through hidden tunnels behind the walls of the hospital until it reached its target.

Dr. Annaccone opened the pneumatic tube and held the syringe in his hands. He walked over to the foot of the PET scanner and called in to Kennedy. Again the voice was hollow, an echo, when Kennedy heard, "The injection," and then felt the doctor reach into the dark and plunge the needle into his arm.

From the glass-enclosed room at the end of the scanner, the staff could see only the bottom of Kennedy's feet. When Dr. Annaccone joined them again, he turned on the computer high on the wall above, so that they could all watch the workings of Kennedy's brain. They watched as the tracer circulated through Kennedy's blood, emitting positrons, particles of antimatter that collided with electrons and produced explosions of gamma ray energy.

They watched as the radioactive blood rushed to Kennedy's visual cortex creating streams of gamma rays immediately picked up by the ring of radioactive detectors. All the time Kennedy kept staring at the white cross as instructed.

Then, through the microphone piped directly into the scanner, Kennedy heard the questions from Dr. Annaccone.

"What is your full name?"

"Francis Xavier Kennedy."

"What is your occupation?"

"President of the United States."

"Did you in any way conspire to have the atom bomb explode in New York?"

"No, I did not."

"Did you have any knowledge that could have prevented its explosion?"

"No, I did not," Kennedy answered. And inside the black cylinder his words seemed to fall back like the wind on his face.

Dr. Annaccone watched the computer screen above his head.

The computer showed the patterns form in the blue mass of the brain so elegantly formed in Kennedy's curving skull.

The staff watched apprehensively.

But no telltale yellow dot, no red circle appeared.

"The President is telling the truth," Dr. Annaccone said.

Christian Klee felt his knees buckling. He knew he could not pass such a test.

CHAPTER
24

"I DON'T UNDERSTAND how he passed it," Christian Klee said.

The Oracle said with contempt that barely came across because of the frailties of his age, "So now our civilization has an infallible test, a scientific test, mind you, for determining whether a man tells the truth. And the first person who takes it lies and gets away with it. 'We can now solve the darkest riddles of innocence and guilt!' What a laugh. Men and women deceive themselves continually. I'm a hundred years old and I still don't know whether my life was a truth or a lie. I really don't know."

Christian had retrieved his cigar from the Oracle and now he lit it and that small circle of fire made the Oracle's face a mask in a museum.

"I let that atom bomb go off," Christian said. "I'm responsible for that. And when I take that PET scan I will know the truth and so will the scanner. But I thought I understood Kennedy better than anybody. I could always read him. He *wanted* me *not* to interrogate Gresse and Tibbot. He *wanted* that explosion to happen. Then how the hell did he pass that test?"

"If the brain were that simple, we would be too simple to understand it," the Oracle said. "That was the wit of your Dr. Annaccone and I suggest that is your answer. Kennedy's brain refused to acknowledge his guilt. Therefore, the computer in the scanner says he is innocent. You and I know better, for I believe what you say. But he will be forever innocent even in his own heart."

"Unlike Kennedy, I am forever guilty."

"Cheer up," the Oracle said. "You only killed ten or was it twenty thousand people? Your only hope is to refuse to take the test."

"I promised Francis," Christian said. "And the media will crucify me for refusing."

"Then why the hell did you agree to take it?" the Oracle said.

"I thought Francis was bluffing," Christian said. "I thought he couldn't afford to take the test and that he would back down. That's why I insisted he take the test first."

The Oracle showed his impatience by running the motor on his wheelchair. "Climb up on the Statue of Liberty," he said. "Claim your civil rights and your human dignity. You'll get away with it. Nobody wants to see such infernal science become a legal instrument."

"Sure," Christian said. "That's what I have to do. But Francis will know I'm guilty."

The Oracle said, "Christian, if that test asked you whether you were a villain, what would you answer, in all truthfulness?"

Christian laughed, genuinely laughed. "I would answer that no, I wasn't a villain. And I'd pass. That's really funny." Gratefully he pressed the Oracle's shoulder. "I won't forget about your birthday party," he said.

It was Vice President Du Pray who reacted most quickly and most angrily to Klee's statement. She said, "Do you realize that if you refuse you must resign and even then this stance of yours will do great damage to the presidency?"

"I don't see that at all," Klee said. "Do I have to agree to let guys like Annaccone scramble my brain just to keep my job? Or do you think I'm really guilty?" He could see the answer in her eyes and thought he had never seen so handsome a hanging judge. Defensively he added, "There's the Constitution of the United States. I have the individual freedom to refuse such a test."

Otto Gray said sternly, "You're not so keen on the Constitution when it comes to criminals. You're eager to ship them off to Alaska."

Klee said, "Ah, Otto, you don't believe I did it. Do you?" and was relieved when Otto said, "Of course I don't, but you should take the test." He paused for a moment and then said, "Or resign."

Klee turned to Wix and Dazzy. "How about you two?" he asked and smiled at them.

It was Wix who answered first. He said, "I don't have the slightest doubt you're innocent, the charges against you are pure bullshit. But if you refuse to take the brain-scan test you will be guilty in the mind of the public. And then you must leave this administration."

Klee turned to Dazzy. "Eugene?"

Dazzy would not look at him and Dazzy owed him, Klee

thought. Then Dazzy said with a judicious air, "You have to take the test, Christian. Even resigning won't help us much. We've already announced you would take it, as you agreed you would. Why this change of mind? Surely you're not afraid?"

"I promised to show my loyalty to Francis Kennedy," Klee said. "Now I've thought it over and decided the risk is too great."

Dazzy sighed. "I sure as hell wish you had thought it over sooner. As for your resignation, I think that is up to the President."

They all looked at Francis Kennedy. His face was dead white, his eyes, which were usually so pale, seemed to be a darker and deeper blue. But his voice was surprisingly gentle when he spoke to Klee. "Christian," he said, "can I persuade you on the basis of our long and close friendship? I took the test and the risk because I thought it was important for our country and the presidency. And because I was innocent. You've never failed me, Christian. I count on you."

For one moment Klee felt hatred for Francis Kennedy. How could this man conceal his own guilt from himself? And why this best friend of his putting him on the cross of truth? But he said calmly, "I just can't do it, Francis."

Kennedy said soberly, "That's it, then. I don't want you to resign, I won't let you suffer that indignity. Now let's go on."

Dazzy said, "Do we make a statement to the press?"

"No," Kennedy said. "If they ask, say the Attorney General has the flu and will take the test when he is recovered. That will give us a month's time."

"And in a month?" Dazzy said.

"We'll rethink it then," Kennedy said.

President Kennedy summoned Theodore Tappey, the CIA director, to a private meeting in the Yellow Oval Room. He excluded everyone, he wanted no witnesses, no recording.

Kennedy wasted no time on civilities. There was no window dressing of a leisurely tea. He spoke curtly to Tappey. "Theo, we have a big problem that only you and I understand. And only you and I can solve."

"I'll do my best, Mr. President," Tappey said. And Kennedy saw the feral look in his eyes. He scented blood.

"Everything we say here has the highest security classification, it has executive privilege," Kennedy said. "You are not to repeat this to anyone, not even members of my staff." That was when Tappey knew the matter was extremely sensitive because Kennedy cut his staff in on everything.

"It's Yabril," Kennedy said. "I'm sure"—he smiled— "I'm positive, you've thought this all out. Yabril will go on trial. That will rake up all the resentments against America. He will get convicted and sentenced to life imprisonment. But somewhere down the line there will be a terrorist action that takes important hostages. One demand will be to release Yabril. By that time I won't be President and so Yabril will go free. Still a dangerous man."

Kennedy had caught the sight of skepticism in Tappey. The sign was no sign, Tappey was too experienced in deception. His face simply lost all expression, all animation in the eyes, the contour of the lips. He had made himself a blank so as not to be read.

But now Tappey smiled. "You must have read the internal memos my counterintelligence chief has been giving me. That's exactly what he says."

"So how do we prevent all this?" Kennedy asked. But it was a rhetorical question and Tappey did not answer.

Kennedy decided the time had come. "I assure you I can persuade Yabril to take the brain test. I'll take care of him. The public needs to know that the results of the test will link the atom bomb to Yabril and prove once and for all that this was a global conspiracy. We can clear Christian and go after those kids—stage a manhunt and bring them to justice at least."

For the very first time in their relationship, Kennedy saw Tappey looking at him with the shrewd appraising eye of a fellow conspirator. He knew that Tappey thought things out far ahead. "We don't really need Yabril's answers, do we?"

"No," Kennedy said.

Tappey asked, "Is Christian in on this?"

This was difficult for Kennedy. And this was not even the hardest part. He said slowly, "Forget about Christian."

Tappey nodded. Tappey was with him. Tappey understood. Tappey was now looking at Kennedy as a servant might look at a master who was about to ask of him a service that would bind them together forever.

"I guess I don't get anything in writing," Tappey said.

"No," Kennedy said. "I am going to give you specific instructions right now."

"Be very specific," Theodore Tappey said, "if you will, Mr. President."

Kennedy smiled at the coolness of the response. "Dr. Annaccone would never do it," he said. "A year ago I myself would never have dreamed of doing it."

"I understand, Mr. President," Tappey said.

Kennedy knew there could be no further hesitation. "After Yabril agrees to take the test, I switch him to your CIA medical section. Your medical team does the scan. They give the test." He could see the look in Tappey's eyes, the waver of doubt, not of moral outrage, but doubt of feasibility.

"We're not talking murder here," Kennedy said impatiently. "I'm not that stupid or that immoral. And if I wanted that done, I'd be talking to Christian."

Tappey was waiting.

Kennedy knew he had to say the fatal words. "I swear that I ask this for the protection of our country. Whether he's in prison or released, Yabril must no longer be a danger. I want your medical team to go to the extreme limit of the test. According to Dr. Annaccone, it was under that protocol that the side effects occurred. And complete memory was erased. A man without memory, without beliefs and convictions, is harmless. He will live a peaceful life."

Kennedy recognized the look in Tappey's eyes—it was the look of one predator who has discovered another strange species its equal in ferocity.

"Can you assemble a team that will do that?" Kennedy asked.

"When I explain the situation to them," Tappey said. "They would never have been recruited if they were not devoted to their country."

In the dark hours of that night, Theodore Tappey escorted Yabril to Kennedy's quarters. Again the meeting was short and Kennedy was all business. There was no tea, there were no civilities. Kennedy began immediately, he presented his proposal.

Kennedy said to Yabril, "It is very important for America to know whether you were part of the conspiracy of the atom bomb. To erase its fears. It is important to you that your name be cleared in this particular matter. Now, it is true that you will go to trial for your other crimes and you will be sentenced to life imprisonment. But I will promise you that I will allow you to communicate with your friends in the outside world. Let us presume they will be loyal enough to create a hostage situation and demand your release. I would be inclined to agree to such a demand. But I can do that only if you are cleared of guilt in the atom bomb explosion. . . . I see you have some doubts."

Yabril shrugged and said, "I find your offer too generous."

Kennedy summoned all his strength to do what he had to do. He remembered Yabril charming his daughter, Theresa, before putting a gun to her neck. Such charm would not work with Yabril. He could only persuade this man by convincing him of his own strict morality.

"I am doing this to erase fear from the mind of my country," Kennedy said. "That is my greatest concern. My pleasure would be to have you remain in prison forever. So I make this offer out of my sense of duty."

"Then why are you taking such pains to convince me?" Yabril asked.

"It's not in my nature to perform my duty as a matter of form," Kennedy said, and he could see that Yabril was beginning to believe this too, believe that he was a moral man and could be trusted within that morality. Again he summoned the image of Theresa and her belief in Yabril's kindness. Then he said to Yabril, "You were outraged at the suggestion that your people engineered the explosion of an atom bomb. Here is the chance to clear your name and the names of your comrades. Why not take it? Do you fear you will not pass the test? That is always a possibility—it occurs to me now, though I don't really believe it."

Yabril looked directly into Kennedy's eyes. "I don't believe that any man can forgive what I have done to you." He was silent. He looked weary. But he was not deceived. It was the very essence of American corruption to make such a proposition to achieve an immoral political aim.

He knew nothing of what had happened in the last six

months. He had been isolated for deep interrogations. Kennedy pressed on. "Taking this test is your only hope of freedom. Provided you pass it, of course," he said.

Kennedy sighed. "I don't forgive you. But I understand your actions. I understand you feel you did what you did to help our world. As I do what I do now. And it is within my powers. We are different men, I cannot do what you do, and you, I mean you no disrespect, cannot do what I am doing now. To let you go free."

Almost with sorrow, he saw he had convinced Yabril. He continued his persuasion, he used all his wit, all his charm, his appearance of integrity. He projected all the images of what he had once been, of what Yabril had known him to be, before he forfeited the whole of himself to convince Yabril. He knew he was finally successful when he saw the smile on Yabril's face was one of pity and contempt. He knew then that he had won Yabril's trust.

Four days later, after Yabril's PET medical interrogation, after the terrorist had been transferred back to FBI custody, he received two visitors. They were Francis Kennedy and Theodore Tappey.

Yabril was completely unrestrained, unshackled.

The three men spent a quiet hour drinking tea and eating little sandwiches. Kennedy studied Yabril. The man's face seemed to have changed. It was a sensitive face; the eyes were slighly melancholy but good-humored. He spoke little but studied Kennedy and Tappey as though trying to solve some mystery.

He seemed content. He seemed to know who he was. And he seemed to radiate such purity of soul that Kennedy could not bear to look at him and finally took his leave.

. . .

The decision about Christian Klee was even more painful to Francis Kennedy. It had been an unexpected surprise for Christian. Kennedy asked him into the Yellow Room for a private meeting.

But Francis Kennedy opened the meeting quietly by saying, "Christian, I've been closer to you than anybody outside my family. I think we know each other better than anyone else knows us. So you will understand that I have to ask for your resignation to be effective after the inauguration, at a time when I decide to accept it."

Klee looked at that handsome face with its gentle smile. He could not believe that Kennedy was firing him without any explanation. He said quietly, "I know I've cut a few corners here and there. But my ultimate aim was always to keep you from harm."

"You let the nuclear device go off. You could have prevented it."

Christian Klee very coldly considered the situation before him. He would never feel his old affection for Kennedy again. He would never believe in his own humanity, the rightness of what he had done. And suddenly he knew that he could never bear that burden. That Francis Kennedy must share responsibility for what had been done. Even privately.

Klee stared directly into the pale blue eyes he knew so well and searched for mercy there.

"Francis, you wanted me to do what I did. We both knew it was the only thing that could save you—I knew you could not make such a decision. It would have destroyed you, you were so weakened, Francis. Francis, don't condemn me, don't judge me. They would have removed you from power and you could never have borne that. You were very close to despair and I was the only one who could see it. They would have left your daughter unavenged. They would have let Yabril go free, they would have left America disgraced." Klee paused, surprised to see that Francis Kennedy was looking at him so impassively.

Kennedy said, "So you think I was after vengeance."

"Not on Yabril," Klee said. "Maybe on Fate."

"You can stay until after the inauguration," Kennedy said. "You've earned that. But you are a danger spot, a target. I have to make you disappear so I can sweep up the mess."

He paused for a moment. "You were wrong thinking I wanted you to do what you did, Chris. You were wrong to think that I was acting out of a desire for vengeance."

Christian Klee felt a vague dissociation from his world, an anguish he could not even define. He said, "Francis, I know you, I understand you. We were always like brothers. I always felt that, that we really were brothers. And I saved you as a brother should. I made the decision, I took the guilt. I can let the world condemn me, but not you."

He paused for a moment. "You need me, Francis. Even more now, on the course of action you're taking. Let me stay."

Francis Kennedy sighed. Then he said, "I don't question your loyalty, Christian. But after the inauguration you'll have to go. We will never discuss this again."

"I did it to save you," Christian said.

"And you did," Kennedy said.

Christian thought about that day in early December, four years ago, when Francis Kennedy, the President-elect of the United States had waited for him outside the monastery in Vermont. Kennedy had disappeared for a week. Newspapers and his political opponents had speculated that he had been under psychiatric care, that he had broken down, that he was having a secret love affair. But only two people—the abbot of the monastery and Christian Klee—knew the truth: that Francis Kennedy had retreated to deeply and completely mourn the death of his wife.

It was a week after his election that Christian had driven Kennedy to the Catholic monastery just outside White River Junction in Vermont. They were greeted by the abbot, who was the only one who knew Kennedy's identity.

The resident monks lived apart from the world, cut off from all media and even the town itself. These monks communicated only with God and the earth on which they grew their livelihood. They had all taken a vow of silence and did not speak except in prayer or yelps of pain when they were ill or had injured themselves in some domestic accident.

Only the abbot had a television set and access to newspapers. The TV news programs were a constant source of amusement to him. He particularly fancied the concept of the anchor man on the nightly broadcasts and often ironically thought of himself as one of the anchor men of God. He used this idea to remind himself of the necessity for humility.

When the car drove up, the abbot was waiting for them at the monastery gate, flanked by two monks in ragged brown robes and sandaled feet. Christian took Kennedy's bag from the trunk and watched the abbot shake hands with the President-elect. The abbot seemed more like an innkeeper than a holy man. He had a jolly grin to welcome them, and when he was introduced to Christian he said jocularly, "Why don't you stay? A week of silence wouldn't do you any harm. I've seen you on television and you must be tired of talking."

Christian smiled his thanks but did not reply. He was

looking at Francis Kennedy as they shook hands. The handsome face was very composed, the handshake was not emotional—Kennedy was not a demonstrative man. He seemed not to be grieving the death of his wife. He had more the preoccupied look of a man forced to go into the hospital for a minor operation.

"Let's hope we can keep this secret," Christian had said. "People don't like these religious retreats. They might think you've gone nuts."

Francis Kennedy's face twisted into a little smile. A controlled but natural courtesy. "They won't find out," he said. "And I know you'll cover. Pick me up in a week. That should be enough time."

Christian wondered what would happen to Francis in those days. He felt close to tears. He took hold of Francis by the shoulders and said, "Do you want me to stay with you?" Kennedy had shaken his head and walked through the gates of the monastery. On that day Christian thought he had seemed OK.

The day after Christmas was so clear and bright, so cleansed by cold that it seemed as if the whole world were enclosed in glass, the sky a mirror, the earth brown steel. And when Christian drove up to the monastery gate, Francis Kennedy was alone, waiting for him without any luggage, his hands stretched over his head, his body taut and straining upward. He seemed to be exulting in his freedom.

When Christian got out of the car to greet him, Kennedy gave him a quick embrace and a shout of joyous welcome. He seemed to have been rejuvenated by his stay in the monastery. He smiled at Christian, and it was one of his rare brilliant smiles that had enchanted multitudes. The smile that reassured the world that happiness could be won, that man was good, that the world would go on forever to better and better things. It was a smile that made you love him because of its delight in his seeing you. Christian had felt such relief at seeing that smile. Francis would be OK. He would be as strong as he had always been. He would be the hope of the world, the strong guardian of his country and fellowman. Now they would do great deeds together.

And then with that same brilliant smile Kennedy took Christian by the arm, looked into his eyes, and said, simply and yet with amusement, as if it didn't really mean anything, as if he were reporting some minor detail of information, "God didn't help."

And in the cold scrubbed world of a winter morning, Christian saw that finally something had been broken in Kennedy. That he would never be the same man again. That part of his mind had been chopped away. He would be almost the same, but now there was a tiny lump of falseness that had never before existed. He saw that Kennedy himself did not know this and that nobody else would know. And that he, Christian, only knew because he was the one who was here at this point in time, to see the brilliant smile and hear the joking words "God didn't help."

Christian said, "What the hell, you only gave him seven days."

Kennedy laughed. "And he's a busy man," he said.

So they had gotten into the car. They had a wonderful day. Kennedy had never been more witty, had never been in such high spirits. He was full of plans, anxious to get his administration together and make wonderful things happen in the four years to come. He seemed to be a man who had reconciled himself to his misfortune, renewed his energies. And it almost convinced Christian. . . .

• • •

Christian Klee started making arrangements to leave government service. One of the most important things was to erase any traces of his circumventing the law in his protection of the President. He had to remove all the illegal computer surveillances of the members of the Socrates Club.

Sitting at his massive desk in the Attorney General's office, Klee used his personal computer to erase incriminating files. Finally, he called up the file on David Jatney. He had been right on this guy, Klee thought, this guy was the joker in the deck. That darkly handsome face had the lopsided look of a mind unbalanced. Jatney's eyes were bright with the scattered electricity of a neural system at war with itself. And the latest information showed that he was on his way to Washington.

This guy could be trouble. Then he remembered the Oracle's prediction. When a man rises to absolute power, he usually gets rid of those closest to him, those who know his secrets. He had loved Francis for his virtues. Long before the terrible secrets. He thought about it a long time. And then he thought, let fate decide. Whatever happened, he, Christian Klee, could not be blamed.

He pressed the delete key of the computer and David Jatney disappeared without a trace from all government files.

CHAPTER
25

JUST TWO WEEKS before President Francis Kennedy's inauguration, David Jatney had become restless. He wanted to escape the eternal sunshine of California, the richly friendly voices everywhere, the moonlit, balmy beaches. He felt himself drowning in the brown syrupy air of its society, and yet he did not want to go back home to Utah and be the daily witness to his father's and mother's happiness.

Irene had moved in with him. She wanted to save on rent money, to go on a trip to India and study with a guru there. A group of her friends were pooling their resources to charter a plane and she wanted to join them with her little son, Campbell.

David was astonished when she told him her plans. She did not ask him if she could move in with him, she merely asserted her right to do so. That right was based on the fact that they now saw each other three times a week for a movie and to have sex. She had put it to him as one buddy to another, as if he were one of her California friends who routinely moved in with each other for periods of a week or more. It was done not as a cunning preliminary to marriage but as a casual act of comradeship. She had no sense of imposing, that his life would be disrupted by a woman and a child made part of his daily living.

What horrified David most of all was that Irene planned to bring her little boy with her to India. Irene was a woman who had absolute confidence that she could make her way in any world; she was certain that the fates would be good to her. David had visions of the little boy sleeping in the streets of Calcutta with the thousands of the diseased poor of that city. In a moment of anger he once told her he could not understand anyone's believing in a religion that spawned the hundreds of millions who were the most desperately poverty-stricken in the world. She had answered that what happened in this world was unimportant, since what happened in the next life would be so much more rewarding.

Jatney was fascinated by Irene and how she treated her son. She often took little Campbell to her political meetings because she could not always get her mother to baby-sit and was too proud to ask too often. She took him with her sometimes even to work, when the special kindergarten he attended was closed for some reason.

There was no question that she was a devoted mother. But to David her attitude toward motherhood was bewildering. She did not have the usual concern to protect her child or worry about the psychological influences that could harm him. She treated him as one would treat a beloved pet, a dog or a cat. She seemed to care nothing for what the child thought or felt. She was determined that being the mother of a child would not limit her life in any way, that she would not make motherhood a bondage, that she would maintain her freedom. David thought she was a little crazy.

But she was a pretty woman, and when she concentrated on sex, she could be ardent. David enjoyed being with her. She was competent in the everyday details of life and was really no trouble. And so he let her move in.

Two consequences were completely unforeseen by him. He became impotent. And he became fond of Campbell.

He prepared for their moving in by buying a huge trunk to lock up his guns, the cleaning materials and the ammo. He didn't want a five-year-old kid accidentally getting his hands on weapons. And by now, somehow, David Jatney had enough guns to deck out a superhero bandit: two rifles, a machine pistol and a collection of handguns. One was a very small .22-caliber handgun he carried in his jacket pocket in a little leather case that was more like a glove. At night he usually put it beneath his bed. When Irene and Campbell moved in, he locked the .22 in the trunk with the other guns. He put a good padlock on the trunk. Even if the little kid found it open, there was no way he could figure out how to load it. Irene was another story. Not that he didn't trust her, but she was a little weird, and weirdness and guns didn't mix.

On the day they moved in, Jatney bought a few toys for Campbell so he wouldn't be too disoriented. That first night, when Irene was ready to go to bed, she arranged pillows and a blanket on the sofa for the little boy, undressed him in the bathroom and put him into pajamas. Jatney saw the little boy looking at him. There was in that look an old wariness, a glint of fear and very faintly what seemed to be a habitual bewilderment. In a flash Jatney translated that look to himself. As a little boy he knew his father and mother would desert him to make love in their room.

He said to Irene, "Listen, I'll sleep on the sofa and the kid can sleep with you."

"That's silly," Irene said. "He doesn't mind, do you, Campbell?"

The boy shook his head. He rarely spoke.

Irene said proudly, "He's a brave boy, aren't you, Campbell?"

At that moment, David Jatney felt a moment of pure hatred for her. He repressed it and said, "I have to do some writing and I'll be up late. I think he should sleep with you the first few nights."

"If you have to work, OK," Irene said cheerfully.

She held out her hand to Campbell and the little boy jumped off the sofa and ran into her arms. He hid his head in her breasts. She said to him, "Aren't you going to say good night to your uncle Jat?" And she smiled brilliantly at David, a smile that made her beautiful. And he understood it was her own little joke, an honest joke, a way of telling him that this had been the mode of her address and introduction for her child when she lived with other lovers, delicate, fearful moments in her life, and that she was grateful to him for his thoughtfulness, that her faith in the universe was sustained.

The boy kept his head buried in her breasts and David patted him gently and said, "Good night, Campbell." The boy looked up and stared into Jatney's eyes. It was the peculiar questioning look of small children, the regard of an object that is absolutely unknown to their universe.

David was stricken by that look. As if he could be a source of danger. He saw that the boy had an unusually elegant face for one so young. A broad forehead, luminous gray eyes, a firm, almost stern mouth.

Campbell smiled at Jatney and the effect was miraculous.

His whole face beamed with trust. He reached out a hand and touched David's face. And then Irene took him with her into the bedroom.

A few minutes later she came out again and gave him a kiss. "Thanks for being so thoughtful," she said. "We can have a quick screw before I go back in." She made no seductive movement when she said this. It was simply a friendly offer.

David thought of the little boy behind the bedroom door waiting for his mother. "No," he said.

"OK," she said cheerfully and went back into the bedroom.

For the next few weeks Irene was furiously busy. She had taken an additional job for very little pay and long hours at night, to help in the reelection campaign—she was an ardent partisan of Francis Kennedy. She would talk about the social programs he favored, his fight against the rich in America, his struggle to reform the legal system. David thought she was in love with Kennedy's physical appearance, the magic of his voice. He believed that she worked at campaign headquarters because of infatuation rather than political belief.

Three days after she moved in, he dropped by campaign headquarters in Santa Monica and found her working on a computer with little Campbell at her feet. The boy was in a sleeping bag but was wide awake. David could see his open eyes.

"I'll take him home and put him to bed," David said.

"He's OK," Irene said. "I don't want to take advantage of you."

David pulled Campbell out of the sleeping bag; the boy was fully clothed except for his shoes. He took the boy by the hand and he felt warm, soft skin, and for a moment he was happy.

"I'll take him for a pizza and ice cream first, is that OK?" David said to Irene.

She was busy with her computer. "Don't spoil him," she said. "When you're gone, he gets health yogurt out of the fridge." She took a moment to smile at him and then gave Campbell a kiss.

"Should I wait up for you?" he asked.

"What for?" she said quickly, then added, "I'll be late." He went out, leading the little boy by the hand. He drove to Montana Avenue and stopped at a little Italian restaurant that made pizza on the side. He watched Campbell eat. One slice and he mangled that more than he ate it. But he was interested in eating and that made David happy.

In the apartment he put Campbell to bed, letting him wash and change into his pajamas by himself. He made his bed on the sofa, put on the TV very low and watched.

There was a lot of political talk on the air and interviews on the news programs. Francis Kennedy seemed to descend out of all the galaxies of cable. And David had to admit the man was overpowering on TV. He dreamed of being a victorious hero like Kennedy. You could see the Secret Service men with their stone faces hovering in the background. How safe he was, how rich he was, how loved he was. Often David dreamed of being Francis Kennedy. How Rosemary would be in love with him. And he thought about Hock and Gibson Grange. And they would all be eating in the White House and they would all talk to him and Rosemary would talk to him in her excited way, touching his knee, telling him her innermost feelings.

He thought about Irene and what he felt about her. And he realized he was more bewildered than entranced. It seemed to him that with all her openness she was really completely closed to him. He could never really love her. He thought of Campbell, who had been named after the writer Joseph Campbell, famous for his books about myths, the boy so open and guileless with such an elegant innocence of countenance.

Campbell now called him Uncle Jat and always put a little hand in his. Jatney accepted. He loved the innocent touches of affection the boy gave him that Irene never did. And it was during these two weeks that this extension of feeling to another human being sustained him.

When he lost his job at the studio, he would have been in a jam if it had not been for Hock, his "uncle" Hock. When he was fired, there was a message for him to come by Hock's office, and because he thought that Campbell would enjoy visiting a movie studio, he brought the child.

When Hock greeted him, David Jatney felt his overwhelming love for the man, Hock was so warm. Hock sent one of his secretaries immediately to the commissary to get ice cream for the little boy and then showed Campbell some props on his desk that would be used in the movie he was currently producing.

Campbell was enchanted by all this, and Jatney felt a twinge of jealousy. But then he could see it was Hock's way of clearing away an obstacle in their meeting. With Campbell busy playing with the props, Hock shook Jatney's hand and said, "I'm sorry you got fired. They are cutting down the story-reading department and the others had seniority. But stay in touch, I'll get something for you."

"I'll be OK," David Jatney said.

Hock was studying him closely. "You look awfully thin, David. Maybe you should go back home and visit a while. That good Utah air, that relaxing Mormon life. Is this kid your girlfriend's?"

"Yeah," Jatney said. "She's not exactly my girl, she's my

friend. We live together, but she's trying to save money on rent so she can make a trip to India."

Hock frowned for a moment and said, "If you financed every California girl who wanted to go to India, you'd be broke. And they all seem to have kids."

He sat down at his desk, took a huge checkbook out of its drawer and wrote in it. He ripped a piece out of the book, and handed it to Jatney. "This is for all the birthday presents and graduation presents I never had the time to send you." He smiled at Jatney. Jatney looked at the check. He was astonished to see it was for five thousand dollars.

"Ah, c'mon, Hock, I can't take this," he said. He felt tears coming into his eyes, tears of gratitude, humiliation and hatred.

"Sure, you can," Hock said. "Listen, I want you to get some rest and have a good time. Maybe give this girl her airfare to India so she can get what she wants and you'll be free to do what you want." He smiled and then said very emphatically, "The trouble with being friends with a girl is that you get all the troubles of a lover and none of the advantages of a friend. But that's quite a little boy she has. I might have something for him sometime if I ever have the balls to make a kid picture."

Jatney pocketed the check. He understood everything that Hock had said. "Yeah, he's a nice-looking kid."

"It's more than that," Hock said. "Look, he has that elegant face, just made for tragedy. You look at him and you feel like crying."

And Jatney thought how smart his friend Hock was. "Elegant" was just right and yet so odd to describe Campbell's face. Irene was an elemental force—like God, she had constructed a future tragedy.

Hock hugged him and said, "David, stay in touch. I mean

it. Keep yourself together, times always get better when you're young." He gave Campbell one of the props, a beautiful miniature futuristic airplane, and Campbell hugged it to himself and said, "Uncle Jat, can I keep it?" And Jatney saw a smile on Hock's face.

"Say hello to Rosemary for me," David Jatney said. He had been trying to say this all through the meeting.

Hock gave him a startled look. "I will," he said. "We've been invited to Kennedy's inauguration in January, me and Gibson and Rosemary. I'll tell her then."

And suddenly David Jatney felt he had been flung off a spinning world.

Now, lying on the sofa, waiting for Irene to come home, dawn showing its smoky light through the living room window, Jatney thought of Rosemary Belair. How she had turned to him in bed and lost herself in his body. He remembered the smell of her perfume, the curious heaviness, perhaps caused by the sleeping pills traumatizing the muscles in her flesh. He thought of her in the morning in her jogging clothes, her assurance and her assumption of power, how she had dismissed him. He lived over that moment when she had offered to give him cash to tip the limo driver and how he had refused to take the money. But why had he insulted her, why had he said she knew better than he how much was needed, implying that she too had been sent home in such a fashion and in such a circumstance?

He found himself falling asleep in little short gaps of time, listening for Campbell, listening for Irene. He thought of his parents back in Utah; he knew they had forgotten about him, secure in their own happiness, their hypocritical angel pants fluttering outside as they joyfully and unceasingly fornicated in their bare skins. If he called them they would have to part.

David Jatney dreamed of how he would meet Rosemary Belair. How he would tell her he loved her. Listen, he would say, imagine you had cancer. I would take your cancer from you into my own body. Listen, he would say, if some great star fell from the sky I would cover your body. Listen, he would say, if someone tried to kill you I would stop the blade with my heart, the bullet with my body. Listen, he would say, if I had one drop from the fountain of youth that would keep me young forever and you were growing old, I would give you that drop so that you would never grow old.

And he perhaps understood that his memory of Rosemary Belair was haloed by her power. That he was praying to a god to make him something more than a common piece of clay. That he begged for power, unlimited riches, for beauty, for any and all the achievements so that his fellowman would mark his presence on this earth, and so he would not drown silently in the vast ocean of mankind.

When he showed Hock's check to Irene, it was to impress her, to prove to her that someone cared enough about him to give him such a vast amount of money as a casual gift. She was not impressed; in her experience it was a commonplace that friends shared with each other and she even said that a man of Hock's vast wealth could have easily given away a bigger amount. When David offered to give her half the amount of the check so that she could go to India immediately, she refused. "I always use my own money, I work for a living," she said. "If I took money from you, you would feel you have rights over me. Besides, you really want to do it for Campbell, not me."

He was astounded by her refusal and her statement of his interest in Campbell. He had simply wanted to be rid of both of them. He wanted to be alone again to live with his dreams of the future.

Then she asked him what he would do if she took half the money and went to India, what he would do with his half. He noticed she did not suggest he go to India with her. He also noted that she had said "your half of the money," so that in her mind she was accepting his offer.

Then he made the mistake of telling her what he would do with his twenty-five hundred.

"I want to see the country and I want to see Kennedy's inauguration," he said. "I thought it might be fun, something different. You know, take my car and drive through the whole country. See the whole United States. I even want to see the snow and ice and feel real cold."

Irene seemed lost in thought for a moment. Then she went striding briskly through the apartment as if counting her possessions in it. "That's a great idea," she said. "I want to see Kennedy too. I want to see him in person or I'll never really be able to know his karma. I'll put in for my vacation, they owe me tons of days. And it will be good for Campbell to see the country, all the different states. We'll take my van and save on motel bills."

Irene owned a small van, which she had fitted out with shelves to hold books and a small bunk for Campbell. The van was invaluable to her because even when Campbell was a little infant she had taken trips up and down the state of California to attend meetings and seminars on Eastern religions.

David felt trapped as they started off on their trip. Irene was driving—she liked to drive. Campbell was between them, one little hand in David's hand. David had deposited half the check in Irene's bank account for her trip to India, and now his twenty-five hundred would have to be used for three of them instead of only one. The only thing that comforted him was the .22-caliber handgun nestling in its leather glove, the glove in his jacket pocket. The East of America had too many robbers and muggers, and he had Irene and Campbell to protect.

To Jatney's surprise they had a wonderful time the first four days of leisurely driving. Campbell and Irene slept in the van and he slept outside in the open fields until they hit cold weather in Arkansas; they had swung south to avoid the cold as long as possible. Then for a couple of nights they used a motel room, any motel on the route. It was in Kentucky that they first ran into trouble.

The weather had turned cold and they decided to go into a motel for the night. The next morning they drove into town for breakfast in a café/newspaper store.

The counterman was about Jatney's age and very alert. In her egalitarian California way, Irene struck up a conversation with him. She did so because she was impressed by his quickness and efficiency. She often said it was such a pleasure to watch people who were truly expert at the work they did, no matter how menial. She said this was a sign of good karma. Jatney never really understood the word "karma."

But the counterman did. He too was a follower of the Eastern religions, and he and Irene got into a long and involved discussion. Campbell became restless, so Jatney paid the bill and took him outside to wait. It was a good fifteen minutes before Irene came out.

"He's a really sweet guy," Irene said. "His name is Christopher, but he calls himself Krish."

Jatney was annoyed by the wait but said nothing. On the

walk back to the motel Irene said, "I think we should stay here for a day. Campbell needs a rest."

They spent the rest of the morning and afternoon shopping, though Irene bought very little. They had a very early supper in a Chinese restaurant. The plan was to go to bed early so that they could travel east before dark.

But they had been in their motel room for only a few hours when Irene suddenly said she was going to take a little drive through town and maybe pick up a bite to eat. She left, and David played checkers with the little boy, who beat him in every game. The child was an amazing checkers player. Irene had taught him when he was only two years old. At one point Campbell raised his elegant head with the broad brow and said, "Uncle Jat, don't you like to play checkers?"

It was nearly midnight before Irene returned. The motel was on a little high ground, and Jatney and Campbell were looking out the window when the familiar van pulled into the parking lot, followed by another car.

Jatney was surprised to see Irene get out of the passenger side, since she always insisted on driving. From the driver's side the young counterman called Krish emerged and gave her the car keys. She gave a sisterly kiss in return. Two young men got out of the other car, and she gave them sisterly little pecks. Irene started walking toward the motel entrance and the three young men put their arms around one another and serenaded her. "Good night, Irene," they sang, "Good night, Irene." When Irene entered the motel room and still heard them singing, she gave David a brilliant smile.

"They were so interesting to talk to I just forgot the time," Irene said, and she went to the window to wave to them.

"I guess I'll have to go and tell them to stop," David said. Through his mind ran flashes of him firing the handgun in his pocket. He could see the bullets flying through the night into their brains. "Those guys are much less interesting when they sing."

"Oh, you couldn't stop them," Irene said. She picked up Campbell. Holding him in her arms, she bowed to acknowledge their homage and then pointed to the child. The singing stopped immediately. And then David could hear the car moving out of the parking lot.

Irene never drank. But she sometimes took drugs. Jatney could always tell. She had such a lovely brilliant smile on drugs. She had smiled that way one night when he had been waiting up for her in Santa Monica. In that dawn light he had accused her of being in someone else's bed. She had replied calmly, "Somebody had to fuck me, you won't."

Christmas Eve they were still on the road and slept in another motel. It was cold now. They would not celebrate the Christmas season; Irene said that Christmas was false to the true spirit of religion. David did not want to bring back memories of an earlier, more innocent life. But he did buy Campbell a crystal ball with snow flurries, over the objections of Irene. Early Christmas morning he rose and watched the two of them sleep. He always carried the handgun in his jacket now, and he touched the soft leather of its glove. How easy and kind it would be to kill them both, he thought.

Three days later they were in the nation's capital. They had a fair amount of time until the inauguration. David made up the itinerary of all the sights they would see. And then he made a map of the inaugural parade. They would all go see Francis Kennedy take the oath of office as President of the United States.

BOOK

VI

INAUGURATION

DAY

BOOK

VI

INAUGURATION

DAY

CHAPTER

26

ON INAUGURATION DAY, the President of the United States, Francis Xavier Kennedy, was awakened at dawn by Jefferson to be groomed and dressed. The early gray light was actually cheery because a snowstorm had begun. Huge white flakes covered the city of Washington, and in the bulletproof tinted windows of his dressing room Francis Kennedy saw himself imprisoned in those snowflakes, as if he were imprisoned in a glass ball. He said to Jefferson, "Will you be in the parade?"

"No, Mr. President," Jefferson said. "I have to hold the fort here in the White House." He adjusted Kennedy's tie. "Everybody is waiting for you downstairs in the Red Room."

When Kennedy was ready, he shook Jefferson's hand. "Wish me luck," he said. And Jefferson went with him to the elevator. Two Secret Service men took him down to the ground floor.

In the Red Room they were all waiting for him. The Vice President, Helen Du Pray, was stunningly regal in white satin. The President's staff were reflections of the President, all in formal clothes. Arthur Wix, Oddblood Gray, Eugene Dazzy and Christian Klee formed their own little circle, solemn and tense with the importance of the day. Francis Kennedy smiled at them. His Vice President and these four men were his family.

When President Francis Xavier Kennedy stepped out of the White House, he was astonished to see a vast sea of humanity that filled every thoroughfare, that seemed to blot out all the majestic buildings, overflowed all the TV vans and media people behind their special ropes and marked grounds. He had never seen anything like it, and he called to Eugene Dazzy, "How many are out there?"

Dazzy said, "A hell of a lot more than we figured. Maybe we need a battalion of marines from the naval base to help us control traffic."

"No," the President said. He was surprised that Dazzy had responded to his question as if the multitudes were a danger. He thought it a triumph, a vindication of everything he had done since the tragedies of last Easter Sunday.

Francis Kennedy had never felt surer of himself. He had foreseen everything that would happen, the tragedies and the triumphs. He had made the right decisions and won his victory. He had vanquished his enemies. He looked over at the huge crowd and felt an overwhelming love for the people of America. He would deliver them from their suffering, cleanse the earth itself.

Never had Francis Kennedy felt his mind so clear, his

instincts so true. He had conquered his grief over the death of his wife, the murder of his daughter. The sorrow that had fogged his brain had cleared away. He was almost happy now.

It seemed to him that he had conquered fate and by his own perseverance and judgment had made possible this present and glorious future. He stepped out in the snow-filled air to be sworn in and then lead the inaugural parade down Pennsylvania Avenue to start on his road to glory.

David Jatney had registered himself and Irene and Campbell in a motel a little over twenty miles from Washington, D.C., because the capital itself was jammed. The day before the inauguration, they drove into Washington to see the monuments, the White House, the Lincoln Memorial and all the other sights of the capital. David also scouted the route of the inaugural parade to discover the best place to stand.

On the great day they rose at dawn and had breakfast at a roadside diner. Then they went back to the motel to dress in their best clothes. Irene was uncharacteristically careful setting and brushing her hair. She wore her best faded jeans, a red shirt and a green floppy sweater over it that David had never seen before. Had she kept it hidden or had she bought it here in Washington? he wondered. She had gone off by herself for a few hours, leaving Campbell with him.

It had snowed all night and the ground was covered white. Big flakes were lazily drifting through the air. In California there was no need for winter clothing, but on the trip East they had bought windbreakers, a bright red one for Campbell because Irene claimed she could easily find him then if he strayed, Jatney a serviceable bright blue, and Irene a creamy white, which made her look very pretty. She also bought a knitted cap of white wool and a tasseled cap for

Campbell in bright red. Jatney preferred to be bareheaded—he hated any kind of covering.

On this inauguration morning they had time to spare, so they went out into the field behind the motel to build Campbell a snowman. Irene had a spasm of giddy happiness and threw snowballs at Campbell and Jatney. They both very gravely received her missiles but did not throw any back. Jatney wondered at this happiness in her. Could the thought of seeing Kennedy in the coming parade have caused it? Or was it the snow, so strange and magical to her California senses.

Campbell was entranced by the snow. He sifted it through his fingers, watching it disappear and melt in the sunshine. Then he began cautiously destroying the snowman with his fists, punching tiny holes in it, knocking off the head. Jatney and Irene stood a little distance away, watching him. Irene took Jatney's hand in hers, an unusual act of physical intimacy on her part.

"I have to tell you something," she said. "I've visited some people here in Washington—my friends in California told me to look them up. And these people are going to India and I'm going with them, me and Campbell. I've arranged to sell the van, but I'll give you money out of it so you can fly back to Los Angeles."

David let her hand go and put his hands in the pockets of his windbreaker. His right hand touched the leather glove that held the .22 handgun, and for a moment he could see Irene lying on the ground, her blood eating up the snow.

When the anger came he was puzzled by it. After all, he had decided to come to Washington in the pitiful hope that he might see Rosemary, or meet her and Hock and Gibson Grange. He had dreamed these past days that he might even be invited to another dinner with them. That his life might change, that he would get a foot in the door that opened into power and glory. So wasn't it natural for Irene to want to go to India to open the door into a world she yearned for, to make herself something more than an ordinary woman with a small child working at jobs that could never lead to anything? Let her go, he thought.

Irene said, "Don't be mad. You don't even like me anymore. You would have ditched me if it hadn't been for Campbell." She was smiling, a little mockingly but with a touch of sadness.

"That's right," David Jatney said. "You shouldn't take the little kid to wherever the hell you feel like going. You can barely look out for him here."

That made her angry. "Campbell is my child," she said. "I'll bring him up as I please. And I'll take him to the North Pole if I want to."

She paused for a moment and then said, "You don't know anything about it. And I think you're getting a little queer about Campbell."

Again he saw the snow stained with her blood, little flashing rivers, a prickling of red dots. But he said with complete control, "What exactly do you mean?"

"You're a little weird, you know," Irene said. "That's why I liked you in the beginning. But I don't know exactly how weird you are. I worry about leaving Campbell with you sometimes."

"You thought that, and then you left him with me anyway?" Jatney said.

"Oh, I know you wouldn't harm him," Irene said. "But I just thought me and Campbell should split and go on to India."

"It's OK," David said.

They let Campbell completely destroy the snowman, then

they all got into the van and started the twenty-mile drive into Washington. When they pulled into the interstate, they were astonished to see it full of cars and buses as far as the eye could see. They managed to inch into the traffic, but it took four hours before the endless monstrous steel caterpillar spilled them into the capital.

The inaugural parade wound through the broad avenues of Washington, led by the presidential cavalcade of limousines. It progressed slowly, the enormous crowd overflowing the police barricades at spots and impeding progress. The wall of uniformed police began to crumble under the millions of people who pushed against them.

Three cars full of Secret Service men preceded Kennedy's limousine with its bulletproof glass bubble. Kennedy stood inside that glass bubble so that he could acknowledge the cheers of the multitude as he rode through Washington. Little waves of people surged up to the limousine itself, then were driven back by the inner circle of Secret Service men outside the car. But each little wave of frantic worshipers seemed to lap closer and closer. The inner circle of guards were pressed back against the presidential limousine.

The car directly behind Francis Kennedy held more Secret Service men armed with heavy automatic weapons, and other Secret Service men on foot ran alongside it. The next limousine carried Christian Klee, Oddblood Gray, Arthur Wix and Eugene Dazzy. The limousines were barely moving, Pennsylvania Avenue was becoming awash with the crowd, stopping the advance of the cavalcade. Majestically, large flakes of snow descended and formed a white mantle over the crowd.

The car carrying the presidential staff came to a complete

stop, and Oddblood Gray looked out the window. "Oh shit, the President is getting out and walking," he said.

"If *he's* walking we have to walk with him," Eugene Dazzy said.

Gray looked at Christian Klee, and said, "Look—Helen's getting out of her car, too. This is dangerous. Chris, you have to stop him. Use that veto of yours."

"I haven't got it anymore," Klee said.

Arthur Wix said, "I think you'd better call a whole lot more Secret Service men down here."

They all got out of the car and formed a wall to march behind their President.

The large snowflakes were still swirling in the air, but they felt no more substantial on the body of Francis Kennedy than the Communion wafer had felt on his tongue when he was a child. For the first time he wanted to touch physically the people who loved him. He walked up the avenue and shook the hands of those people who pierced the police-manned barriers and then the ring of Secret Service men assembled around him. Every so often a tiny wave of specta-tors managed to wash through, pushed on by the mass of a million spectators behind them. They crested over the Secret Service men who had tried to form a wider circle around their President. Francis Kennedy shook the hands of these men and women and kept his pace. He could feel his hair getting wet from the snow, but the cold air exhilarated him, as did the adulation of the crowd. He was not conscious of any tiredness, or discomfort, though there was an alarming numbness in his right arm and his right hand was swollen from being gripped so often and so harshly; Secret Service men were literally tearing the devoted supporters away from their President. A pretty young woman in a creamy windbreaker had tried to keep holding his hand and he had had to wrench it back to safety.

David Jatney pushed out a space in the crowd that would shelter himself and Irene, who held Campbell in her arms because he would have been trampled otherwise—the crowd kept shifting in waves like an ocean.

They were no more than four hundred yards from the viewing stands when the presidential limousine came into their line of sight. It was followed by official cars holding dignitaries. Behind them was the endless crowd that would pass before the viewing stand in the inaugural parade. David estimated that the presidential limousine was a little more than the length of a football field away from his vantage point. Then he noticed that parts of the crowd lining the avenue had surged out into the avenue itself and forced the cavalcade to halt.

Irene screamed, "He's getting out. He's walking. Oh, my God, I have to touch him." She slung Campbell into Jatney's arms and tried to duck under the barrier, but one of the long line of uniformed police stopped her. She ran along the curb and made it through the initial picket line of policemen only to be stopped by the inner barrier of Secret Service men. Jatney watched her, thinking, If only Irene were smarter, she would have kept Campbell in her arms. The Secret Service men would have recognized that she was not a threat and she might have slipped through while they were thrusting back the others. He could see her being swept back to the curb, and then another wave of people swept her up again and she was one of the few people who managed to slip through and shake the President's hand and then was kissing the President on the cheek before she was roughly pulled away.

David could see that Irene would never make it back to

him and Campbell. She was just a tiny dot in the mass of people that was now threatening to engulf the broad expanse of the avenue. More and more people were pressing against the outer security rim of uniformed police; more and more were hitting against the inner rim of Secret Service men. Both rims were showing cracks. Campbell was beginning to cry, so Jatney reached into the pocket of his windbreaker for one of the candy bars he usually carried for the boy.

And then David Jatney felt a suffusion of warmth through his body. He thought of the past days in Washington, the sight of the many buildings erected to establish the authority of the state: the marble columns of the Supreme Court and the memorials, the stately splendor of the façades—indestructible, irremovable. He thought of Hock's office in its splendor, guarded by his secretaries, he thought of the Mormon Church in Utah with its temples blessed by special and particularly discovered angels. All these to designate certain men as superior to their fellows. To keep ordinary men like himself in their place. And to direct all love on to themselves. Presidents, gurus, Mormon elders built their intimidating edifices to wall themselves away from the rest of humanity, and knowing well the envy of the world, guarded themselves against hate. Jatney remembered his glorious victory in the "hunts" of the university; he had been a hero then, that one time in his life. Now he patted Campbell soothingly to make him stop crying. In his pocket, underneath the cold steel of the .22, his hand found the candy bar and gave it to Campbell. Then, still holding the boy in his arms, he stepped from the curb and ducked under the barriers.

David Jatney was filled with wonder and then a fierce elation. It would be easy. More of the crowd were overflowing the outer rim of uniformed police; more of those were piercing the inner rim of Secret Service agents and getting to shake the President's hand. Those two barriers were crumbling, the invaders marching alongside Kennedy and waving their arms to show their devotion. Jatney ran toward the oncoming President, a wave of spectators piercing the wooden barriers carrying him along. Now he was just outside the ring of Secret Service men who were trying to keep everyone away from the President. But there no longer were enough of them. And with a sort of glee he saw that they had discounted him. Cradling Campbell in his left arm, he put his right hand in the windbreaker and felt the leather glove; his fingers moved onto the trigger. At that moment the ring of Secret Service men crumbled, and he was inside the magic circle. Just ten feet away he saw Francis Kennedy shaking hands with a wild-looking ecstatic teenager. Kennedy seemed very slim, very tall, and older than he appeared on television. Still holding Campbell in his arms, Jatney took a step toward Kennedy.

At that moment a very handsome black man blocked him off. His hand was extended. For a frantic moment Jatney thought he had seen the gun in his pocket and was demanding it. Then he realized that the man looked familiar and that he was just offering a handshake. They stared at each other for a long moment; Jatney looked down at the extended black hand, the black face smiling above it. And then he saw the man's eyes gleam with suspicion, the hand suddenly withdrawn. Jatney with a convulsive wrenching of all his bodily muscles threw Campbell at the black man and drew his gun from the windbreaker.

Oddblood Gray knew, in that moment when Jatney stared into his face, that something terrible was going to happen. He let the boy fall to the ground, and then with a quick shift of his feet put his body in front of the slowly advancing Francis Kennedy. He saw the gun.

Christian Klee, walking to the right and a little behind Francis Kennedy, was using the cellular phone to call for more Secret Service men to help clear the crowd out of the President's path. He saw the man holding the child approach the phalanx guarding Kennedy. And then for just one second he saw the man's face clearly.

It was some vague nightmare coming through—the reality did not sink in. The face he had called up on his computer screen these past nine months, the life he had monitored with computer and surveillance teams had suddenly sprung out of that shadowy mythology into the real world.

He saw the face not in the repose of surveillance photos but in the throes of exalted emotion. And he was struck by how the handsome face had become so ugly, as if seen through some distorted glass.

Klee was already moving quickly toward Jatney, still not believing the image, trying to certify his nightmare, when he saw Gray stretch out his hand. And Christian felt a tremendous feeling of relief. The man could not be Jatney, he was just a guy holding his kid and trying to touch a piece of history.

But then he saw the child in his red windbreaker and little woolen hat being hurled through the air. He saw the gun in Jatney's hand. And he saw Gray fall.

Suddenly Christian Klee, in the sheer terror of his crime, ran toward Jatney and took the second bullet in the face. The bullet traveled through his palate, making him choke on the blood, then there was a blinding pain in his left eye. He was still conscious when he fell. He tried to cry out, but his mouth was full of shattered teeth and crumbled flesh. And he felt a great sense of loss and helplessness. In his shattered brain, his last neurons flashed with thoughts of Francis Kennedy, he wanted to warn him of death, to ask his forgiveness. Christian's brain then flicked out, and his head with its empty eye socket came to rest in a light powdery pillow of snow.

In that same moment Francis Kennedy turned full toward David Jatney. He saw Oddblood fall. Then Christian. And in that moment, all his nightmares, all his memories of other deaths, all his terrors of a malign fate crystallized into paralyzed astonishment and resignation. And in that moment he heard a tremendous vibration in the world, felt for a tiny fraction of a second only the explosion of steel in his brain. He fell.

David Jatney could not believe it had all happened. The black man lay where he had fallen. The white man alongside. The President of the United States was crumpling before his eyes, legs bent outward, arms flying up into the air as his knees finally hit the ground. David Jatney kept firing. Hands were tearing at his gun, at his body. He tried to run, and as he turned he saw the multitude rise and swarm like a great wave toward him and countless hands reach out to him. His face covered with blood, he felt his ear being ripped off the side of his head and saw it in one of the hands. Suddenly something happened to his eyes and he could not see. His body was racked with pain for one single moment and then he felt nothing.

The TV cameraman, his all-seeing eye on his shoulder, had recorded everything for the people of the world. When the gun flashed into sight, he had backed away just enough steps so that everyone would be included in the frame. He caught David Jatney raising the gun, he caught Oddblood Gray making his amazing jump in front of the President and go down, and then Klee receiving a bullet in his face and going down. He caught Francis Kennedy making his turn to face the killer and the killer firing, the bullet twisting Kennedy's head as if he were in a hammerlock. He caught Jatney's look of stern determination as Francis Kennedy fell and the Secret Service men frozen in that terrible moment, all their training for immediate response wiped out in shock. And then he saw Jatney trying to run and being overwhelmed by the multitude. But the cameraman did not get the final shot, which he would regret for the rest of his life. The crowd tearing David Jatney to pieces.

Over the city, washing through the marble buildings and the monuments of power, rose the great wail of millions of worshipers who had lost their dreams.

CHAPTER
27

PRESIDENT HELEN DU PRAY held the Oracle's one-hundredth birthday party in the White House on Palm Sunday, three months after the death of Francis Kennedy.

Dressed to understate her beauty, she stood in the Rose Garden and surveyed her guests. Among them were the former staff members of the Kennedy administration. Eugene Dazzy was chatting with Elizabeth Stone and Sal Troyca.

Eugene Dazzy had already been told his dismissal was to take effect the next month. Helen Du Pray had never really liked the man. And it had nothing to do with the fact that Dazzy had young mistresses and was indeed already being excessively charming to Elizabeth Stone.

President Du Pray had appointed Elizabeth Stone to her staff; Sal Troyca came with the package. But Elizabeth was exactly what she needed. A woman with extraordinary energy, a brilliant administrator, and a feminist who understood political realities. And Sal Troyca was not so bad; indeed he was a fortifying element with his knowledge of the trickeries of the Congress and his low brand of cunning, which could sometimes be so valuable to more sophisticated intelligences, such as Elizabeth Stone's and indeed, thought Du Pray, her own.

After Du Pray assumed the presidency she had been briefed by Kennedy's staff and other insiders of the administration. She had studied all the proposed legislation that the new Congress would consider. She had ordered that all the secret memos be assembled for her, all the detailed plans, including the now infamous Alaska work camps.

After a month of study it became horrifyingly clear to her that Francis Kennedy, with the purest of motives, to better the lot of the people of the United States, would have become the first dictator in American history.

From where she stood in the Rose Garden, the trees not yet in full leaf, President Du Pray could see the faraway Lincoln Memorial and the arching white of the Washington Monument, noble symbols of the city that was the capital of America. Here in the garden were all the representatives of America, at her special invitation. She had made peace with the enemies of the Kennedy administration.

Present were Louis Inch, a man she despised, but whose help she would need. And George Greenwell, Martin Mutford, Bert Audick and Lawrence Salentine. The infamous Socrates Club. She would have to come to terms with all of them, which was why she had invited them to the White House for the Oracle's birthday party. She would at least give them the option of helping build a new America, as Kennedy had not.

But Helen Du Pray knew that America could not be

rebuilt without accommodations on all sides. Also, she knew that in a few years there would be a more conservative Congress elected. She could not hope to persuade the nation as Kennedy, with his charisma and personal romantic history, had done.

She saw Dr. Zed Annaccone seated beside the Oracle's wheelchair. The doctor was probably trying to get the old man to donate his brain to science. And Dr. Annaccone was another problem. His PET brain-scan test was already being discussed in various scientific papers. Du Pray had always seen its virtues and its dangers. She felt it was a problem that should be carefully considered over a long period of time. A government with the capacity to find out the infallible truth could be very dangerous. True, such a test would root out crime and political corruption; it could reform the whole legal structure of society. But there were complicated truths, there were status quo truths, and then was it not true that at certain moments in history, truth could bring a halt to certain evolutionary changes? And what about the psyche of a people who knew the various truths about themselves could be exposed?

She glanced at the corner of the Rose Garden where Oddblood Gray and Arthur Wix were sitting in wicker chairs and talking animatedly. Gray was now seeing a psychiatrist every day for depression. The psychiatrist had told Gray that after the events of the past year it was perfectly normal for him to be suffering from depression. So why the hell was he going to a psychiatrist?

In the Rose Garden the Oracle was now the center of attraction. The birthday cake was being presented to him, a huge cake that covered the entire garden table. On the top, colored in red, white and blue spun sugar, was the Stars and Stripes. The TV cameras moved in; they caught for the nation the sight of the Oracle blowing out the hundred birthday candles. And blowing with him were President Du Pray, Oddblood Gray, Eugene Dazzy, Arthur Wix and the members of the Socrates Club.

The Oracle accepted a piece of cake and then allowed himself to be interviewed by Cassandra Chutt, who had managed this coup with the help of Lawrence Salentine. Cassandra Chutt had already made her introductory remarks while the candles were being blown out. Now she asked, "How does it feel to be one hundred years old?"

The Oracle glared at her malevolently, and at that moment he looked so evil that Cassandra Chutt was glad that this show was being taped for the evening. God, the man was ugly, his head a mass of liver spots, the scaly skin as shiny as scar tissue, the mouth almost nonexistent. For a moment she was afraid that he was deaf, so she repeated herself. She said, "How does it feel to be a century old?"

The Oracle smiled, his facial skin cracking into countless wrinkles. "Are you a fucking idiot?" he said. He caught sight of his face in one of the TV monitors, and it broke his heart. Suddenly he hated his birthday party. He looked directly into the camera and said, "Where's Christian?"

President Helen Du Pray sat by the Oracle's wheelchair and held his hand. The Oracle was sleeping, the very light sleep of old men waiting for death. The party in the Rose Garden went on without him.

Helen remembered herself as a young woman, one of the protégées of the Oracle. She had admired him so much. He had an intellectual grace, a turn of wit, a natural vivacity and joy in life that was everything she herself wanted to have.

Did it matter that he always tried to form a sexual liaison? She remembered the years before and how hurt she had been when his friendship had turned into lechery. She ran her fingers over the scaly skin of his withered hand. She had followed the destiny of power, while most women followed the destiny of love. Were the victories of love sweeter?

Helen Du Pray thought of her own destiny and that of America. She was still astonished that after all the terrible events of the past year the country had settled down so peacefully. True, she had been partly responsible for that; her skill and intelligence had extinguished the fire in the country. But still . . .

She had wept at the death of Kennedy; in a small way she had loved him. She had loved the tragedy written into the bones of his beautifully planed face. She had loved his idealism, his vision of what America could be. She had loved his personal integrity, his purity and selflessness, his lack of interest in material things. And yet despite all this she had come to know that he was a dangerous man.

Helen Du Pray realized that now she had to guard against the belief in her own righteousness. She believed that in a world of such peril, humankind could not solve its problems with strife but only with a never-ending patience. She would do the best she could, and in her heart try not to feel hatred for her enemies.

At that moment the Oracle opened his eyes and smiled. He pressed her hand and began to speak. His voice was very low, and she bent her head close to his wrinkled mouth. "Don't worry," the Oracle said. "You will be a great President."

Helen Du Pray for a moment felt a desire to weep as a child might when praised, for fear of failure. She looked about her in the Rose Garden filled with the most powerful men and women of America. She would have their help, most of them; some she would have to guard against. But most of all she would have to guard against herself.

She thought again of Francis Kennedy. He lay now with his two famous uncles, loved as they had been. And his daughter. Well, Helen Du Pray thought, I will be the best of what Francis was, I will do the best of what he hoped to do. And then, holding tightly to the Oracle's hand, she pondered on the simplicities of evil and the dangerous deviousness of good.

In 1969
The Godfather arrived.

Now, *The Godfather Returns*.

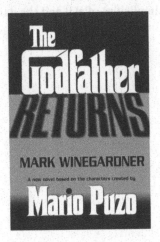

A new novel based on the characters created
by Mario Puzo

Available wherever books are sold

Mario Puzo on
The Godfather

I was ready to forget novels except maybe as a puttering hobby for my old age. But one day a writer friend dropped into my magazine office. As a natural courtesy, I gave him a copy of *The Fortunate Pilgrim*. A week later he came back. He thought I was a great writer. I bought him a magnificent lunch. During lunch, I told him some funny Mafia stories and my ten-page outline. He was enthusiastic. He arranged a meeting for me with the editor of G. P. Putnam's Sons. The editors just sat around for an hour listening to my Mafia tales and said go ahead. They also gave me a $5,000 advance and I was on my way, just like that. Almost—almost, I believed that publishers were human.

It took me three years to finish.…And it was mostly all fun. I remember it as the happiest time of my life. (Family and friends disagree.) I'm ashamed to admit I wrote *The Godfather* entirely from research. I never met a real honest-to-God gangster. I knew the gambling world pretty good, but that's all. After the book became "famous," I was introduced to a few gentlemen related to the material. They were flattering. They refused to believe that I had never been in the rackets. They refused to believe that I had never had the confidence of a Don. But all of them loved the book.

In different parts of the country I heard a nice story: that the Mafia had paid me a million dollars to write *The Godfather* as a public relations con. I'm not in the literary world much, but I hear some writers claim I must have been a Mafia man, that the book could not have been written purely out of research. I treasure the compliment.

—Mario Puzo, *The Godfather Papers,* 1972

The Story Behind the Sequel

By Jonathan Karp

Throughout the decade I was Mario Puzo's editor, I would periodically beg him to write a sequel to *The Godfather.* "Bring back the Corleones!" I would plead. "Whatever happened to Johnny Fontane? Can't you do something with Tom Hagen? Don't you think Michael has some unfinished business?"

Mario was always polite in the face of my wheedling and his response was always the same: No.

I understood why Mario never wanted to continue the story. He was a gambler at heart, and resurrecting *The Godfather* would have been a bad percentage move for him. It was bound to pale in comparison to the original. How do you improve on a legend?

But one day on the phone, Mario did give me his blessing to revisit the Corleones. He told me his family could do whatever they wanted with the rights to *The Godfather* after he died. (His exact phrase was "after I croak," which I remember precisely because it was the first time an author had ever discussed his posthumous career with me in such direct terms.)

Mario left behind two novels, *Omerta* and his partially completed tale of the Borgias, *The Family,* so it was a while before I approached his estate about the prospect of reviving *The Godfather.* After conversations with Mario's eldest son, Anthony Puzo, and his literary agent, Neil Olson, we agreed on a strategy.

We would discreetly search for a writer at roughly the same stage of his or her career as Mario was when he wrote *The Godfather*—mid-forties, with two acclaimed literary novels to his credit, and a yearning to write a larger, more ambitious novel for a broader readership than his previous books had reached. We didn't want a by-the-numbers hired gun. We wanted an original voice, someone who would bring artistry and vision to the Corleone saga, just as director Francis Ford Coppola had done so brilliantly in his film adaptations.

I outlined what we were looking for in a one-page query, which I sent confidentially via e-mail to about a dozen respected literary agents. Within twenty-four hours of sending my confidential email, I received a phone call from *New Yorker* staff writer Nick Paumgarten. He'd heard all about our search and wanted to write about it. At first I was reluctant to cooperate, due to my concern that every would-be goomba in the country would send me a manuscript. Upon further consideration, I realized that there probably weren't a lot of goombas reading *The New Yorker,* and that a story might be a good way to get out the word and attract a broader range of authors.

The day the story was published, *The Godfather Returns* became headline news. I was deluged with calls from almost every major media organization in the United States, as well as many abroad, from CNN to the BBC in New Zealand. The *New York Times Magazine* published a cautionary essay about the dangers of sequels. I appeared on a Detroit radio morning "zoo" show with a Vito Corleone impersonator who warned me that my career might come to an untimely end if I didn't hire him to write the book.

We had set a deadline for the delivery of outlines from potential writers. We stuck to our guidelines—only published authors of acclaimed fiction would be considered. By the day of the deadline, we had been swamped with submissions from well-regarded authors (plus countless more from unpublished ones). As I sorted through the outlines, I was taped by a TV cameraman and interviewed by NBC News correspondent Jamie Gangel, who was covering our search, and who ultimately revealed the winner live on the *Today* show.

I quickly narrowed down the field to about a dozen serious contenders. Some were dismissed on account of inadvisable plot lines. (Michael Corleone falls in love with a Native American activist. Or, the Corleone women take over the family business. Or, Sonny Corleone didn't really die.) Others were rejected because the writers didn't seem to have the right feel for the material.. One literary critic described Mario Puzo's style as "somewhere between pulp and Proust." That's part of the reason for his success—he was an original writer who loved to entertain his readers. He could turn a phrase, and there was a sly ironic undertone to almost everything he wrote, but Mario's greatest talent was for telling a story that stayed with you because the details were so captivating. Our ideal writer would have similar gifts.

From the dozen contenders, we arrived at four finalists. We would have been happy to publish any of them. After consultation with Tony Puzo and Neil Olson, we unanimously agreed that the best candidate was Mark Winegardner. Like Mario, he was an author of two acclaimed literary novels, *The Veracruz Blues* and *Crooked River Burning,* and to our delight, both books had organized crime plot threads. I read *Crooked River Burning* and loved it, not only for its ambition (it's the story of the rise and fall of a great American city over a period of decades), but also because the author shows such compassion for his characters. Mario Puzo's greatest literary inspiration was Dostoevsky, who taught him to see the humanity within the villainous. Winegardner has an equally big heart when writing about his characters. That can be very interesting when you're going to have to kill a lot of them. He was our first choice to write *The Godfather Returns* and we were elated when he accepted. Our selection was international news. When Mark visited Sicily for some background research, it was a front page story there.

Neither Mark nor I have ever worked on a more highly anticipated book. We know the risks of following in the tradition of a pop classic. I'm not worried. Having edited the novel, I'm certain of its quality and its power. The Corleones have become an American myth, and like all great myths, each retelling brings new meaning and new rewards.

Jonathan Karp is editor in chief of Random House.

Q&A with Mark Winegardner

Q. When did you first read *The Godfather*?
A. When I was about twelve. Like a lot of kids who grow up to be writers, I started reading books meant for adults, looking for the dirty parts. I had good reason to believe there might be worthwhile moments there. When I heard Random House was looking for an author, I read it again with new appreciation.

Q. Why did you want to write it?
A. I feel like my entire body of work has been about the mythology of America, and this book fits squarely within that. It's a magnificent opportunity to write about characters that people already know and are invested in, and in some ways, it's as big a thrill as if I were writing about Jesse James or Abraham Lincoln. Particularly when I saw how much more story there was to be told, and how little *The Godfather* had touched on the glory years of the mob in the late 1950s, I was thrilled to have the chance to take a whack at all of that.

Q. Are you nervous about what the reaction will be?
A. I've been writing almost every day of my life for the past twenty years, and it's a wonderful thing to be the author of a book people are waiting for, whether they're sharpening their knives for it or drooling for it. A lot of writers are working away, saying, "Who will ever read this? Who will ever publish this?" The book will come out and either people will like it or not, but it's going to be read, and I'll move on and write other books after this one. There's no downside.

Q. Is this a sequel to the novel or the movies?
A. The novel, definitely. Mario Puzo's book ends in 1955. *The Godfather Returns* will cover the period from 1955 to 1965.

Q. But what about *The Godfather II*? Isn't there some overlap?
A. The parts that weren't in Mario Puzo's novel covered only one year, 1958–1959. A lot of other wicked things were going on that can be revealed only now. I don't address events in the films that aren't in the novel, but I don't contradict them,

either. Everything fits together, and I hope readers will be surprised to discover some of these unexplored avenues. It turns out there's a lot we didn't know about the Corleone family.

Q. Like what?
A. Sorry. I must obey the laws of *omerta*.

Q. You're a creative writing professor and you're not Italian. Are you qualified to be writing about the Mafia?
A. I'm not Sicilian, it's true. Not even Italian American. I'm just a novelist with a vision of how to continue this American saga. I understand I am, however, German Irish, same as Tom Hagen. And he did just fine in this world.

Q. What would you like the book to accomplish?
A. I want it to be a good book, first and foremost. I was always impressed with the way Random House approached this book—that they always seemed quite interested in this not being any kind of publishing gimmick, but a good, literary, page-turner, and I want it to be that. All things being equal, an author shouldn't think too deeply about the thematics of his own book. I'm out to write the best book humanly possible.

Q. Why has *The Godfather* become an American myth?
A. A lot of people have pointed out the story of this family in particular and the mob in general has superseded the western as the core American mythological story. It's something that I was circling around in my last two novels, and I'm glad to have a chance to come in this time for the kill.

P.O. 0004985572 20201218